Midsummer's Secret

L C Bygrave

First Edition

If you are a children's hospice, trust or charity, then please contact me directly for free copies of this novel.

Legal Stuff

Laurence Charles Bigrave under the name of L C Bygrave is the author of this work. The work remains copyright of the author. (Bigrave sounds like Bye-grave)

Midsummer's Secret is a work of fiction. The characters, images, places and events contained therein are the product of the authors imagination or entirely fictitious. Any resemblance to actual persons, living or dead, places and place names, and events past and present is purely coincidental.

The condition of sale of this work is that it shall not be reproduced, re-badged, re-sold, be lent or hired out.

You can contact the author using the following channels:

Twitter: @LozBigrave   Email: lozbigrave@hotmail.com

LinkedIn: https://uk.linkedin.com/in/charles-loz-bigrave-6b937561

ISBN: 978-1533231420

Number of pages: 325; Number of words: 98057

Writing begun: March 2014; Writing complete: May 2016

© 2016 L C BYGRAVE. All rights reserved.

Acknowledgements

Thanks to the Oxford University Museum of Natural History for their kind permission to use some photos, for providing me with inspiration, and for a great day out with my kids. Oh, and you can see a real life flee dressed in miniature clothing there, if you can find it of course.

http://www.oum.ox.ac.uk/

Thanks to Mark Robson, a successful author who took some time to advise a naïve newbie.

http://www.swordpublishing.co.uk/

Thanks to my niece, Bethany Birch, for clueing me in on the lingo of the modern teenager. Boy was it hard work getting anything out of her.

Thanks to The Admiral Nelson pub and restaurant for their kind permission to include them in the book.

http://www.theadmiralnelson.co.uk/

Topsham pool – the community run Lido that inspired me.

https://twitter.com/TopshamPool

Thanks to all these great sources too…

http://www.northamptonshire.gov.uk/en/councilservices/Leisure/libraries/visit-your-library/ListLibraries/Pages/Daventry-Library.aspx

https://en.wikipedia.org/wiki/Main_Page

https://pixabay.com/

https://www.gimp.org/

Thanks to my friends and family who gave their advice, opinion and time proof reading; you know who you are. And thanks to Arthur Guinness for helping me relax.

Finally, thanks to my wife, for making me sandwiches while I typed away for hours on end each weekend… and for putting up with me.

Photo: *'Daventry Lido - the larger pool shortly before being filled in. 2007'*
kindly provided by the Daventry Express

Photo: *'The larger pool showing just how popular the site was'*
Kindly provided to the Daventry in History Facebook page by John R Collins.

For my daughters. You rose tint my world

And for my Dad

Prelude to Adventure

June 7th

Donald opened his eyes and attempted to focus. He saw the black, heavy sky looming above the tree tops. He felt rain drops on his face. He saw lightning race across the heavens and felt the thunder, but he heard no sound, not until the ringing in his ears receded. He realised it was no dream and a rush of dread awoke him.

He sat up nursing his aching head and looked back along the woodland path. He wiped the muddy water from his face and focused as well as he could against the blackness. He thought he may break the terror that froze him and risk moving, until he caught a glimpse of the beast. Another rush – this time of fear. How is this possible he thought? Surely this cursed folklore monster is nothing more than a fairy tale. This fabled wolf-like creature that prey and feed on human flesh. Nevertheless, there it was; its burning eyes looking back at him. This monster was real.

"STAY BACK!" warned Donald. "I'VE GOT A GUN!" but his warning was weak and unfounded and he knew it. The beast wasn't deterred and resumed its pursuit.

Donald scrambled backward before rising to his feet and fleeing once again. He called for help. He screamed for his very life, but the storm raging around him cruelly masked his cries. A side-stitch began to burn below his ribcage like a knife wound as oxygen-rich blood pumped like it had not pumped for years. When his lungs came near bursting he dared to glance behind. He saw the beast gaining ground. It was no use; he simply could not maintain this pace much longer. Poor Donald was done for.

But wait, mercifully ahead was the log cabin he called home; its dim outside light was just visible. If he could make it he may have a chance. He reached the wooden steps and slipped on contact, twisting his ankle. He regained his balance and reached for the door, threw it open and slammed it shut behind. He grasped the key to turn it, but his hands shook so much the simple task seemed impossible. He yelled and cursed a hundred times before he managed it; only then could he peer through the little window into the forest. His breath fogged the glass so he used his sleeve to wipe it, which only resulted in adding a muddy smear to further impede his view. He could make out the silhouette of the beast which had maintained its course to the cabin.

Donald closed the thin curtain and retreated until he bumped the kitchen table. He heard footsteps on the decking outside. A moment later the door knob rattled turning once, then once again in an attempt to enter. There followed a thud and the whole door shook as it was tested for strength. He stood petrified. Quite literally his legs would no longer respond to instruction. He fumbled behind on the table without taking his eyes from the door, feeling for something to use as a weapon. Anything would be better than nothing. His hand knocked over a mug and felt its way through the remains of last night's dinner. Then - a knife: a blunt butter knife but a knife all the same. He held it up and prepared to defend himself.

A moment passed without event, before the lights in the cabin went out. Silence followed, until suddenly and without warning the door flew open. Not just on its hinges, but completely flew into the room as if a tornado had touched down. It struck Donald knocking him backward onto the table, forcing him to drop his meagre weapon. Standing in the doorway was the creature: a humanoid in stature, only this was no human. It seemed to have grown, because now it stood seven feet tall and was so wide it could barely pass through the entrance. Flashes of light burned its monstrous outline against the black canvas, emphasizing its terrible presence. It wore a long black coat down to its ankles; its face and head were covered in hair. It had empty black pools for eyes and fangs protruding from its elongated mouth. It was unmistakable.

"It... it can't be!" stuttered Donald. "What are you? What do you want? STAY BACK! NO!"

Less than a mile away the grand hall stood firm against the weather as it had done for decades. Its vast rooms were devoid of life, until a lone member of staff exited the kitchen on route to the first floor. The storm outside was of no concern to Barker, the long-standing butler to the Midsummer family. He had served his mistress for so many years he had become almost blind to anything else. Despite the late hour he was immaculately presented, wearing shoes that were so shiny you could actually see your face in them. He was tactful, dutiful, mannerly and gracious - all the traits that made a truly great butler.

He traversed the grand staircase and with every step the objects on the tray he bore rattled noisily. The adjoining corridor creaked under foot as he continued towards the last bedroom and the eyes within the many portraits aligning the walls seemed to follow his progress until he arrived. He knocked, waited and entered once the voice inside instructed him to do so.

"Your tea, madam," he announced as he crossed the room. He lay the tray down on a corner of the writing desk and began pouring from the tall silver tea pot.

"Thank you, Barker," replied Lady Midsummer without looking up.

He noticed that she was uneasy and had been crying, so promptly handed her the pristine silk hanky from his breast pocket, into which she blew her nose loudly before handing it back. "Thank *you*, madam." He continued to place a silver platter containing two biscuits beside her tea. "Is it Master Charles again, madam?" he enquired softly.

The old lady raised her cup which shook so much it almost spilled its contents. She took a sip before replying. "What? Oh yes, Barker. I am afraid he's having those nightmares again. He's quite determined to scare me half to death."

"Should I bring something to help you sleep, madam? Hot chocolate, or something stronger - brandy perhaps?"

She looked up and managed a pained smile. "No, thank you, Barker. I think it best I maintain a clear head until this business blows over, but thank you for your concern, as always."

"Of course, madam. Now, if that will be all?"

"Just this letter for posting tomorrow if you will. That horrid person has contacted me again demanding the return of the family treasure, insisting it rightfully belongs to them. It really is quite absurd!"

"One assumes, madam, that he or indeed she, is referring to the infamous ruby – the Sunrise."

Lady Midsummer looked dismayed and pretended not to have heard his comment. She finished writing using ink and a feathered quill that was at least as old as her, before placing the letter into an envelope. Barker handed her a stick of wax which she held in a long candle flame until it began to melt, at which point she withdrew it and applied it to the back. She then pressed the face of a large, golden signet ring into the wax before it had the chance to cool, sealing it, took off her reading glasses and sat back in her chair.

"It's been a long time since I have heard that name old friend. I just hope it is not the beginning of another black chapter for us. This family has seen tenfold its share of tragedy and sadness because of that cursed ruby. Too much blood has been spilt. Anyway, I'm rabbiting on aren't I? That will be all, Barker. Thank you and goodnight."

Barker bowed his head and clicked his heals acknowledging the end of his duties. He collected the letter and tray before returning to the kitchen, where he poured himself a glass of warm milk heated in a saucepan. The rain pitter-pattered against the windows and he watched drops join together and run down the panes. He picked up the letter he had brought from upstairs and felt the wax seal with his thumb. It showed the Midsummer family crest of two deer stags with huge antlers, locked together in ferocious battle. After a moment of rest and reflection he emptied his glass, raised and placed the letter in the 'out' pigeonhole. He then turned off the kitchen lights, followed by those in the dining room and hall before retiring to his room.

At this point the entire ground floor of the house should have been free from its residents yet somebody remained. Somebody who moved almost silently in the darkness. Somebody who didn't belong. Their black, leather-gloved hand reached into the pigeonhole and retrieved the letter deposited by the butler just moments before. The person then immediately exited the house through the door at the rear of the kitchen and headed into the gardens.

From a bedroom window on the first floor a young boy stood looking out over the grounds. He observed the silhouette moving from black shadow to black shadow, but it was only when it stepped into the light could he confirm its presence. Whoever or whatever *it* was, it also saw the boy in the window. The young observer quickly pulled the curtains closed and turned out the light. Below, the mysterious figure turned and disappeared into the darkness.

Part One

1

June 19th

"Wake up, Charlie," said Jess giving him a nudge. He swiftly raised his head from his desk and wiped the drool from his mouth.

"Coming, Auntie!" he exclaimed loudly, to the amusement of his classmates. Charlie had been fast asleep for several minutes and neither the bell indicating schools end or the rest of the class making an exit had awoken him.

"Charlie, it's me, Jess. You were sleeping. Better get yourself together or you'll miss the bus." Jessica Louise Birchwood, known to her friends as Jess, was one of the oldest in her year and popular among her peers. She stood smiling down at Charlie while she tied back her hair. She seemed full of life as usual, for she was naturally energetic and athletic. Charles W Midsummer, on the other hand, sat much lower on the popularity level. Actually, he barely registered at all. He was more than a little overweight and in no way at all was he an athlete, besides holding the school record for the shortest javelin throw. He was, however, outstanding in all other academic fields the mediocre school had to offer.

Their teacher arrived to collect test papers. He quickly scanned through Charlie's efforts and grinned widely. "Outstanding as usual, Charles," he announced cheerfully, before walking away.

"I don't know how you manage it, Charlie," grumbled Jess.

"Manage what, Jess?"

"To get better grades *asleep*, than everyone else manages awake!"

Without waiting for Charlie, she grabbed her backpack and joined the exodus in the corridor, loosening her tie and going with the flow toward the glowing exit. She had just endured back-to-back maths (a subject she found impossibly difficult no matter how hard she tried) with a test on algebraic fractions to boot. She preferred English any day, as it was something that she seemed instinctively good at. Outside the sun was blazing once again. It was late spring and term was approaching its end with an off-the-scale heat wave in the form of piping hot days, muggy nights and regular thundery downpours. It would in fact, go on to be recorded as the hottest June since records began.

Jess placed on a pair of sunglasses and headed toward her bus, finding to her dismay it was once again the defiant, clapped out double-decker that should have been scrapped years ago. She reluctantly climbed the steps and, after acknowledging the driver with a nod, saw the bottom deck already full, meaning she would have to sit in the oven.

There were plenty of seats to choose from up top, where the temperature was already liquefying any discarded chewing gum. She sat at the front where at least the view was decent and opened the narrow window in an attempt to gain some fresh air. She placed on her headphones, put her feet up and hit play. The swing door downstairs slammed shut sealing everyone in and the bus jerked into life.

Thankfully, the journey was a mere fifteen minutes; any longer and Jess would get the urge to vomit. She didn't have a problem travelling, not like that sickly kid downstairs, she just had a problem travelling on *this* particular bus. Her destination and home was Daventry, a village and parish located deep in the rolling countryside of Northrumptonshire. Like many residents of her village, Jess was born in nearby Northrumpton General Hospital and had lived in Daventry her entire life. She therefore knew that the sight of the church spire over the fields indicated she was almost home.

"You awake, Jess?" a voice hollered from behind her. "You don't want to doze off and miss the stop." This was followed by a scrunched up piece of paper bouncing off her head. It was thrown by Zac - one half of the blond-haired, blue-eyed Hewes twins and friend, by proxy, of Jess.

"Dude, leave her alone," scowled Meg, Zac's sister and best friend of Jess.

The twins were incredibly similar in appearance, right down to the same number of freckles on their cheeks and slightly gappy front teeth. Zac had a decent head of hair that came down to his earlobes and was forever pushing his fringe to one side. He was skinny, but somehow still managed to maintain a near insatiable appetite.

Meg's hair reached below her shoulders (she was still trying to catch up with Jess) and today wore it in a side plait. She was skinny like her brother and wore blue-framed glasses, yet despite their physical similarities, they were a world apart in personalities. The one thing they did have in common was their noticeable dislike of one another. Jess saw them and removed her headphones, "Hey guys."

"Are we there yet?" asked Meg, fanning her face with a book.

"Nearly, thank God."

"Not gonna spew are you, Jess?" teased Zac puffing up his cheeks.

"I might, now I've seen your stupid face."

"How did your test go?" asked Meg.

"Less said the better I think."

"That bad, huh?"

The upper deck was suddenly struck by overhanging tree branches, as it always was when they passed by Everdon woods, indicating the journey was almost over. They gathered their bags and waited for the bus to arrive at their stop - one stop earlier today than the usual one just down the road. They were getting off outside the convenience shop in the middle of the village which happened to be the most popular point of departure, as it offered children the chance to top up on sugary confectionary after a long, hard day at school. It also meant an early escape from the sweltering heat on the top deck, if only by a few merciful minutes.

As Jess descended the stairs a sudden stream of bodies rushed by and the books she was holding were knocked from her hands. It was the group of boys who always sat at the back - the furthest point away from the driver. On exiting the bus, it appeared the boys had set upon a luckless individual - one Charles Midsummer - and were throwing his belongings to one another in a piggy-in-the-middle fashion. Some other year seven and eight kids, who were regularly forced to hand over spare change at this point, had made a break for it, relieved that some other unfortunate had taken the flak.

"I say..." whimpered Charlie. "I say, pardon me, but would you mind returning those?" Unsurprisingly, this did little to persuade the bullies to stop. In fact, it had quite the opposite effect and fuelled their goading. As soon as Jess and the twins saw what was going on they marched into the circle and put a stop to it.

"Fun's over, boys!" Jess announced sternly. The gang of nine immediately halted their game as if their mothers themselves had issued the instruction. Being co-residents of a moderately sized village, they all knew Jess, Meg and Zac well, and that they were not such easy targets.

"Alright Jess," said Jake Jenkins, the slick leader of the boy's gang. He smugly stepped forward, removed his oversize sun glasses and handled the discourse on behalf of his underlings. "It's just a bit of fun, didn't mean nothing by it. Besides, Prince Charles here started it. Didn't you, butt-munch?"

"I most certainly did not!" objected Charlie fiercely.

Jess removed her sunglasses and placed them in her top pocket. "I can tell you're lying, Jake, your lips are moving. Anyway, shouldn't you be in detention or something?"

"Nar, they let me out for good behaviour."

"That's funny, they don't usually let monkeys out of the zoo."

Jake hated being opposed more than anything, especially in front of his minions. "What are you laughing at, Hewes?" he snarled. He was addressing Zac, who appeared not to hear him.

"Sorry, but are you addressing me or my sister?"

"You, you gorm! Mind you, it's hard to tell as you look like a girl."

"You know, Jake," Zac casually replied, "talk is cheap - but then again so are you."

"What did you say, *punk?!*" Jake's temper was already reaching boiling point, which was not unusual as violence was his answer to pretty much everything.

"You heard me. Now if you don't mind you're ruining a pleasant sunny afternoon."

"I got your weather forecast right here, *Zachary* - cloudy with a chance of pain!" With fist clenched he lunged toward Zac, who ditched his bag and prepared to defend himself. They both immediately stood down though on the arrival of several pensioners on route to the shop, who seemed to take an age to pass by.

"We'll catch up another time, freckle-face," said Jake backing away. "You going to the park later, girls? I can show you how to skate properly."

"Drop dead, loser," they replied.

"Great, about six then."

Giving Jake the finger, Jess and Meg took Charlie by his arms and led him away. They stood outside the shop entrance watching the gang disperse. "I wonder," pondered Jess, "what makes a bully want to bully? Is it because they're trying to fill a gap in their lives or something?"

"Perhaps they can't help themselves," replied Meg. "You know, like a kleptomaniac can't help stealing."

Always wanting to keep up with his sister's intelligent remarks and especially so in front of Charlie, Zac added his thoughts on the subject. "Sorry, Meg, but I fail to see what a fear of spiders has to do with it. By definition your opinion blows."

Looking pleased with himself, he put his arm around Charlie's shoulder and led him into the shop. The girls linked arms and followed them in. "By definition, Meg," said Jess smiling, "your brother is an idiot."

"I hear that!"

After picking up some refreshments the foursome took the shortcut through the bushes which led them into the playing fields beyond. The wide open space offered a welcome relief from the stuffy bus trip and sultry day at school, even though the afternoon sun was still strong and high in the sky. A number of other school children arrived and, after organising their belongings into makeshift goalposts, started playing football. They burst onto the pitch with gusto as if they had never been allowed outdoors and energetically began a game of shirts versus skins. They were joined by several groups of older pupils who chose to simply sit and do nothing, some in the full sun, others below the sheltering canopies of trees, all relishing being free from grown-ups telling them what to do for an hour or two.

Jess, Charlie and the twins left them all behind and continued to the south of the playing field. They were heading toward an area surrounded by a tall, spiked metal fence, which encircled a patch of land itself large enough to house three football pitches. The area within was wild, unkempt and left to nature. Grass that was once soft and green had given way to dense nettles and brambles. Paved pathways were being forced upward by the roots of trees and several remaining flat-roofed structures had all fallen into decay. To peer through the fence left those who did not know of its past wondering as to why this wasteland was even here. However, for the generation who had visited and loved this place, who had spent every glorious summer day they could within its boundary and for those whose very childhood had been defined by it, it remained a poignant reminder to a wonderful memory.

The children crossed onto the blistering tarmac car park that was so cracked, bumpy and full of broken glass and protruding shrubs that no driver would ever take a vehicle there. They arrived at what used to be the entrance which had been blockaded by several large concrete blocks. One-by-one they took their bags from their shoulders and squeezed between the gates. The wooden sign that hung above them was rotten, but the words on it were still legible.

Welcome to Daventry Open Air Swimming Pool

2

Their den was in the girls changing rooms which only leaked a little when it rained. It used to be in the boys changing room, but the roof of that fell in two winters ago when Daventry saw heavy snow fall. And besides, the girls often remarked that there was a funny smell in that section. There were benches for sitting on and old lockers they used to store stuff in. This included water guns at this time of year as there existed a handy tap just around the corner, which the council had forgotten to turn off when they tomb-stoned the place. It also meant an unlimited supply of precious liquid ammo for seeing off rival gangs, who would have to return home or bring a barrel of water with them to refill their weapons.

They dropped their bags down and sat on the benches, cracked open their cold cans and drank a few large gulps straight down. Despite the heat outside, the lack of glass in the windows of their den meant the temperature inside was refreshingly cool, even on protractor-melting days like today. After a burping contest that Charlie won as a result of downing his entire can in one go, Jess was about to speak but was interrupted.

"AAAAAA-CHOO!" blasted Zac.

"Bless you!" said the others.

"Thank you," sniffed Zac.

"Phew, I sure wish this place was open today," sighed Jess, placing a cold can on her forehead. "Can you imagine an open air pool right here in the village? Totally lush."

"Totally epic," agreed Zac.

"You should come over to mine sometime," said Charlie between burping. "We have a pool you know."

"You have a pool and you didn't tell us?!" replied Meg crossly.

"Sure, I just never thought to mention it I guess."

"You know what…" griped Zac as he crumpled his empty can. "That Jake Jenkins is such a major dork! And to think he has a crush on you, Jess."

"Eww gross!" she replied. "Can you imagine him trying to be romantic? You know, I once saw him take a pack of love hearts from some year-seven kid - and eat the lot without reading a single one. That's how romantic he is! And besides, it would never work, what with me being a Libra and him being, well, a loser!"

"He really is a first-class smeg-head," said Charlie.

"I'll drink to that," agreed Zac, clunking cans together.

"He is kinda cute though," said Meg dreamily, which disgusted the others and earnt her a bombardment of penny sweets and litter.

"You need to get your eyes tested, sis!"

"Well they can't be that bad, *bruv*, you still look dorky to me."

"*Sooo* anyway…" said Jess changing the subject, "what was all that about back at the shop, Charlie? That's the third time in a fortnight." She handed out some sweets to everyone while she waited for an explanation.

"Oh, nothing," Charlie replied. "It's just the usual school idiots, you know how they are."

Meg knew just by looking that he was lying. "Do me a favour, Charlie. It's not like you to be targeted so often, and even I've noticed you've been acting a little detached lately."

Charlie had undergone a tough time making friends at school owing largely to his pedigree roots, so for a while being picked on was a regular event for him. Despite his near-flawless educational record he was the one chosen last in every PE team selection (his one failing subject) and the one who sat closest to the bus driver for protection - before Jess and the twins befriended him that is. They had helped him to 'fit in' better with his peers, giving him basic but vital advice such as: don't wear school uniform to the school disco, and to wear his shorts no higher than waist level. Charlie was also an orphan. The only grand-nephew of Lady Josephine Midsummer, who had raised him as if he were her own. He was a model student benefiting from additional, private home schooling. Add to this the fact he lived in a fifteen-bedroom house in the middle of the country, it was little wonder he was a target for bullies.

"It's *nothing*," Charlie insisted. "Just exam pressure, you know."

"Charlie," pressed Jess.

"Really, it is utterly ridiculous."

"Charlie..."

"Honestly, it's completely absurd. Besides, my lift will be here soon so I had better be heading off..."

"CHARLIE!" shouted Jess and the twins, their patience running thin.

Their friend was clearly reluctant to speak up at first, but after some poking and prodding he finally opened up - and dropped a bombshell. "There's..." he paused and gulped before continuing. "There is a werewolf, at the house."

Stunned silence which seemed to last forever was followed by loud laughter from Meg, Zac and subsequently, Jess, who looked back in complete astonishment.

"A werewolf, are you insane?!" coughed Meg, almost choking on her confectionary.

"The sun must be getting to you," said Zac as he tapped Charlie's head.

"No wonder they're teasing you!" the twins cried in tandem.

"Here, let me help cool your brain," offered Meg, raising a loaded pistol and preparing to fire.

"WAIT!" said Jess, noticing Charlie's pained expression. "Look at him... He's serious!"

Realising this was the case they all quietened down and respectfully shut up for the sake of their troubled friend. "Go on, Charlie," said Jess.

He began explaining himself, stuttering as he went. "I've s-seen him. I've really s-seen it, w-whatever it is... outside the house at night. Come and see for yourselves if you don't believe me."

Jess and the twins looked at one another and immediately tried to find a rational explanation. "It's probably a wolf," said Meg. "Or wild dog, or... something."

"No, it walks upright like a human," replied Charlie.

"A bear?" proposed Jess.

"Um, not in this country."

"What about your gamekeeper then?" asked Zac. "Perhaps he's patrolling the grounds rocking a massive beard. You have a gamekeeper, right?"

"Well, no actually, but..."

"BIGFOOT!" yelled Meg.

"NO, NO," dismissed Charlie. "Listen, it's really tall; it has hairy face and hands and won't come into the light. It only comes out at night and I've seen it three, no four nights in a row now, skulking around in the shadows."

"Still sounds like Bigfoot," replied Meg.

"Four nights, Charlie!" said Jess amazed. "Why didn't you tell us after the first night?"

"Well, I, err, didn't want to seem, you know, foolish or anything. After all I have my reputation to protect."

"You don't have a reputation, Charlie," said Zac bluntly. The girls showed their collective agreement by nodding.

"OK, Charlie," said Jess after some thought. "How about we investigate this curious story of yours? Look, tomorrow is Friday. We'll stay over with you at your house - we'll take Meg's dog, Cookie. He'll let us know if there are any werewolves or anything roaming around the place. How's that sound?"

"I'm in," said Meg excitedly.

"Sounds sur-weet to me," agreed Zac. "With our collective intelligence, we're sure to solve the mystery in no time."

"Collective intelligence?" questioned Jess.

"Word-of-the-day calendar," he replied. "Thought it sounded good. I know, how about we just wing-it and hope for the best?"

"That sounds more like it!"

Meg then realised she wouldn't be able to make Friday night, as she had agreed to help collect glasses at the pub for her parents. It was boat-show weekend, the pub's busiest few days of the year. Jess therefore re-evaluated. "OK, well, how about Saturday for everyone? It's a full moon also so we should get lucky." She joked but Charlie failed to see the funny side.

"Hey, hold on," said Meg, "but didn't Zac have a date on Saturday, you know - with Crazy Maisy Ainsworth? I know cos he's been banging on about it for ages. Haven't you, Romeo?"

"Yeah... well, no actually," replied Zac gloomily.

"Why what happened, bruv? You said you were *in there!*"

"Would you date a scruffy loser?"

"Probably not."

"Well neither would she apparently. Said I'm bottom drawer, whatever that means."

"Aww, it means she's out of your league, bruv. Never mind though, you'll find someone nice one day - someone who smells of armpits just like you..." Zac squirted water in Meg's face before she had the chance to finish insulting him.

"Right then," chuckled Jess, "so if we're all in agreement, then Saturday it is."

"Shall we tell our parents we're staying at each other's houses or something?" Zac asked.

"No need," Jess replied. "I'm sure none of our parents will object to us staying in Midsummer Hall. I mean, it's not like we're going camping in the park. Charlie, can you clear it with your aunt?"

He nodded and looked relieved he had found someone to confide in. "Should be fine by Auntie, oh... and thanks everyone."

They all agreed on the plan and put in hands on top of one another, "One team, one dream."

Jess then looked at Zac and they both unleashed their water guns at the others declaring, "WATER FIGHT!"

Outside the den there was a rustling in one of the bushes and from it emerged two giggling boys - Jake Jenkins and his partner in crime, Bashir, the very same boys that were involved in teasing Charlie earlier. They had been listening to Jess and the others for some time and made their way back to the gate, trying not to laugh too much until they got there.

"Did you hear that, Bash? Werewolves they say! What's up with that?!"

On face-value, Jake was a handsome and well-presented teenager. His hair was short at the sides and rear, but left long enough on top to brush over on one side, or straight up if desired. He also had the initials of his current girlfriend shaved into the back of his head, which was subject to regular change when the relationship inevitably turned sour. The thing was, he was not generally a nice person and took great enjoyment from picking on others, particularly those unwilling to stand up for themselves. He was a spoilt, only child and, as a result, wore only designer clothes and trainers. He always had the latest and most expensive smartphone, yet treated his parents with little more respect than he did his victims.

His number-two and fellow tormenter was Bashir Balakrishna Yoga, aptly known as Basher to his peers. A brutish lump completely devoid of any brain between the ears, his face was rough with acne and he sported a self-pierced eyebrow and lip - the latter of which was currently the cause of a nasty infected oozing. He was feared throughout the playground, not just because of his horrendous laugh, but because he couldn't be reasoned with. The more some poor kid cried, the more he enjoyed it. Like Jake, he was always looking for trouble and the pair were personally responsible for more dead-arms, atomic wedgies, crow-pecks, purple-nurples, knotted-ties, nipple-cripples, wet-willies, flat-tyres, arm-burns, eggings and dinner money snatching than one can count. Their net income of pilfered small change alone in a school term warranted an offshore bank account.

Once out front, Jake sat upon one of the concrete blocks for a moment thinking as he cycled a black flip-top lighter.

"Wot you doing, Jake?" asked Bashir.

"Thinking," Jake replied. "You should try it for once."

"OK... but err, what should I fink about?"

Jake rolled his eyes at his simple-minded friend. "You know, Basher, we could have some fun here. How about we give those brown-nosed teacher's pets a scare they won't forget. The question is though, how do we go about it."

"I dunno," shrugged Bashir looking blank.

"That was a rhetorical question, dumb-ass."

"Oh right, wots that mean?"

"It means... oh forget it. I think I know what to do anyway."

"Wot?"

"Well, if it's a werewolf they want then it's a werewolf we should give them. Don't you think?"

Jake jumped down chuckling to himself and Bashir joined in with his horrid laugh. He soon stopped though and looked confused. "But, Jake - where will we get one from?"

3

June 20th

The following day passed slowly for the children who only had their minds on Charlie's fantastical story he had told the day before. Each of them had lay in bed last night pondering the facts, one minute dismissing it as nonsense, the next imagining if it could be reality. They met as a foursome in afternoon double science, where they shared notes and doodles they had come up with instead of paying attention in earlier classes. Talking quietly between Bunsen burners and tripods, Zac informed the others that during info-tech, he discovered the entire Midsummer estate didn't appear on any internet geographical mapping service. There was simply nothing there, just a blur of undisclosed space like a shrouded video game landscape yet to be explored. Jess reported a similar story, after finding an old ordnance survey map in the school library, which showed the land marked as *Military*.

"Think that's interesting?" whispered Meg across the table. "Then you'll love what I found out. You see I... Zac, give Charlie a nudge – he's dozing again!"

Charlie's face was indeed firmly planted against his palm and he appeared like a dog about to nod off. "Huh! What?" he murmured, after a sharp slap from Zac's ruler.

"As I was saying," continued Meg, "I was speaking with Mr Harris in the art block and..."

"What, Hippy Harris?" asked Jess.

"Yes, Hippy Harris, about the feasibility of *real life* werewolves!"

"And?" asked the others intrigued.

"*And...* he reckons they might just exist!"

"You mean werewolves are *real!*" blurted out Zac, loud enough for the entire class to hear.

"SSHHH," shushed Mr Hopkins, the teacher, glancing up above his spectacles.

"That's what he said!" continued Meg. "Although he had no hard evidence to back it up. He also said that Zombies are real and that a real life Zombie girl actually exists in the Philippines. Apparently she woke up at her own funeral!"

"Zombies are real too?!" bleated Zac, again too loudly.

"HEWES!" boomed Mr Hopkins. "SHUT IT OR YOU'RE OUT!"

"That's very interesting, Meg," replied Jess, "...and actually quite disturbing, but I don't think it's something we need to worry about. I mean, I seriously doubt we'll be bumping into any real life werewolves and the only zombie around here is Zac in double history."

"I hear that," agreed Zac.

"I'm just putting it out there is all," said Meg. "I think we should keep an open mind."

"Fair point," replied Jess, "but there's keeping an open mind and there's believing in made-up creatures, so let's try and stay tuned into the sanity channel and..."

"Have you considered Satan?" asked Zac, to the bewilderment of the others.

"What?" asked Jess.

"You know, Satan – the devil."

"I know who Satan is, numbnuts. I mean what about him?"

"The thing is, I got thinking last night about the occult and stuff, and devil worshiping in particular."

"Devil worshiping?"

"Yep."

"Devil... *worshiping*?"

"Uh-huh."

"Ugh, go on then, Zac," sighed Jess in disbelief, "what about devil worshiping?"

"Well, Charlie lives in the sticks right, in a big house with no one around."

"So?"

"So, perhaps someone there is performing some ungodly rituals and bringing stuff back from the dead!"

"Well, Charlie?" asked Meg, before Jess had a chance to dismiss the nonsense.

"Well what?" Charlie replied, looking both dumbfounded and offended.

"Do you know if anyone at your place is into that sort of thing?"

"No of course not, don't be ridiculous."

"No you don't know, or no there aren't?" pressured Zac.

"No there are not!"

The bell rang indicating the end of the lesson and the whole class broke silence as they started packing away their belongings.

"Thank God for that!" uttered Jess.

The remainder of the afternoon passed in the usual slow manner and after the final class of the day, the rickety bus arrived to shuttle them home. Jess and Meg managed to secure a seat on the bottom deck, successfully avoiding the heat - and noisy simians, upstairs. They sat together, sending picture-messages to one another for fun. Charlie then arrived looking hot and bothered while nursing his head. He saw the girls and sat in front of them. "Hey Jess. Hey Meg. Where's Zac?"

"He text me just now," replied Meg, without looking up from her phone. "He's in detention."

"Detention, what on earth for?"

"Halfwit Harry dared him to climb out of a window, so he did."

"What?! Why?"

"Because Zac is an idiot who would jump off a cliff if you dared him to."

"Oh right. Did he say anything else about tomorrow in his message?"

"Let me see... frowny face, angry face, unamused face, angry face, pile of poo and... another angry face. Nope, nothing about tomorrow."

"How rude," joked Jess.

Meg then looked up and noticed the large bump above Charlie's eyebrow. "Holy crap! How did you get that?"

"What?"

"That massive lump, right there. Don't tell me you've been in a fight or something." She poked it with her finger, making Charlie grimace.

"Oh that. Just did the hammer throw in PE. Damn near killed myself!"

It was hot and sunny once again and dust took to the sky as the bus bounced along the road. As Meg was working that evening and Zac was otherwise engaged, they decided to not hang out at the den and go home. They agreed to meet Charlie at the gates of his estate shortly before midday on Saturday.

That evening at The Admiral Nelson was busy as predicted by the owners, who happened to be the twins' parents, Gary and (Big) Jessica Hewes. The pub is an old coaching inn. A charming little gem popular with the locals and passing canal folk. It remained simple and old fashioned with original outdoor toilets complete with cobwebs in the draughty roof spaces. By nine o'clock in the evening a dense blanket of cloud had reached the village and a heavy downpour was bringing relief to the parched landscape. Inside the pub it was now standing room only and at any other time, the two characters seated in a booth in one corner would have stood out like a sore thumb, but tonight, due to the many visitors, they were lost among the crowds.

Both men had bristly chins desperately in need of a shave and each wore a grubby woollen jumper with high collar despite the warm weather. One of them spoke with a London accent while the other sounded foreign. They talked quietly and sparsely as they drank their third round of real ale accompanied by whiskey.

"Don't think the boss would like us being here, Larry," said the foreign man. "We should be working the estate like he said."

"Don't worry my French friend…"

"Belgian."

"Say wot?"

"Belgian. I am Belgian, not French. It is an entirely different country you know."

"Whatever, now like I was sayin' - we've been hanging around at that damp and draughty old dump every night for two weeks and nothing's happened. A man could go crazy without his needs being satisfied. Anyway, we deserve a breather, you know before the big day tomorrow." He sipped from his pint and received a white foamy moustache which he then wiped off with his sleeve. "And just fink, in a few days we'll be rich and won't have to answer to anyone. Don't that sound just perfik?" They

clinked glasses and laughed wholeheartedly, but stopped and quietened down immediately when someone approached the table. It was Meg doing her rounds.

"Collect your empties, Gentlemen," she said not really asking permission or expecting an answer, rather just going about her job. She placed the used glasses on the tray and whilst doing so couldn't help notice the hands of the men: they were filthy dirty like those of a coal miner, complete with a black substance under their fingernails. She also noticed that one of the men — a thin, scruffy looking character, had a tattoo of a scorpion on the back of his hand, while the other man's hand seemed even more extraordinary, for it was a hand of truly incredible proportion. This hand holding a whisky glass was so big it almost appeared like a normal sized adult hand holding a child's tea cup and Meg found herself uncontrollably raising her head to look at its owner's face. She saw his broad chest that was twice as wide as the other man's and that he sat a clear two feet taller. Good manners were forgotten as she unashamedly gawped, unable to break from the trance she was in. She was about to see his face. It was…

"That'll be all, miss," said the thin man.

This caused Meg to snap out of her daze and inadvertently knock over several glasses. "Sorry, err… gentlemen," she said all in a flutter. She gathered the tray and quickly moved along, but was unable to resist stealing one last glance at the men through the crowd. They sat and watched her with unblinking eyes until she was out of sight, at which point they resumed drinking.

"Nosey young good for nothing. Hey, Pierre, how about another two beers?"

"That is not my name."

"Whatever. Now, do you want a drink or not? And hurry up, I need to see a man about a horse."

"Fine, but these are the last ones. Remember, we're working tomorrow."

4

June 21st

"Heatwave! Heatwave! Heatwave!" That's what the weather lady on TV said that morning. And she was right too, because whilst Jess sat eating her cereal at 08:15, it was already twenty-one degrees and rising without a breeze or cloud in the sky. *"High pressure, slightly cooler at the coast, but watch out if you're inland, where we are expecting temperatures to beat the nineteen seventy-six record of thirty-five…"*

Jess switched off the TV and loaded her bowl into the dishwasher. After a quick brush of her teeth and an application of factor fifteen, she gathered her belongings and set about retrieving her bike from the shed. She had dressed light: trainers with ankle socks, shorts and a white t-shirt. Her hair was tied back in a single long pony-tail, passed through the loop in her baseball cap.

She wrestled her eighteen-speed mountain bike from the shed and prepared for the hard part – getting it along the narrow path which connected her back garden to the front, between the neighbouring house. She had to turn the handle bars side-on and lift it in parts, or it would jam and add to the scratches on the brickwork. A scraping of shins by a rogue pedal was often inevitable during this delicate operation. Once successfully at the front she shouted goodbye to her mum, who was dressed in full length, oil-stained overalls, revving the engine of a rusted old lawnmower. "Mum, I'm off now… Mum… MUM!"

Mrs Birchwood turned off the noisy two-stroke motor and removed her eye protection when she eventually heard Jess shouting at her. "What's that, dear?" she asked.

"I said I'm off now, Mum."

"OK my precious, have a lovely time and don't have too many cream teas will you. Oh, and don't forget to keep your pinkie raised at tea time.

Very important that." Mrs Birchwood giggled at her own wit, but Jess could only manage a raised eyebrow in response.

"Eh… OK, Mum. Will you say goodbye to Dad for me?"

"Tell him yourself, he's right there." She gestured with a half-inch spanner toward the roof and sure enough Mr Birchwood was up there. He was shamelessly dressed in wrap-around sunglasses, offensively-bright Hawaiian shirt and a pair of equally outrageous shorts with matching flip-flops. He was precariously placing, of all things, a light-up reindeer on the flat roof extension.

"Hey, Dad. How's it going?" Jess asked, shielding her eyes from the sun.

"Oh hey, Jess. Going just fine thanks. Are you off to your friends for the night?"

Mr Birchwood was the founding member of the *Society of the Annual Neighbourly Tree-light Association*, S.A.N.T.A. An organisation responsible for such popular charitable events as the festive Santa Run, mince pie eating competition and the Mobile Santa Wagon. He also held the prestigious Village Christmas Light Competition gold award and had done so for six years in a row. He could be found from June onward, busily assembling the yuletide display on and around the family home.

"Yeah I am," Jess replied. "Will be back tomorrow afternoon at the latest."

"That's great, I'll be here if you need me. Hmm, now where is that 30mm flex?" He turned and almost lost his balance, but this had become standard procedure within the Birchwood household and neither Jess nor her mother bothered to pay much attention to his 'little accidents' any more.

"Have you had some breakfast, my little sweetie?" asked Mrs Birchwood. "Shall I make you some eggy bread?"

"No thanks, Mum. I've had something already."

"Are you sure? It won't take a minute."

"I'm fine, Mum. Thanks."

"How about poached egg then?"

"Mum, I'm fine, really. I…"

"Scrambled?"

"*Nothing*. Now, I should get going, I'm meeting the twins."

"OK then, dear. Have a great time. Oh, and watch out for the hurricane won't you."

"Hurricane?!"

"Yes haven't you heard? Hurricane Joslyn from the states. Been causing havoc across the pond apparently. It seems we're going to get the remnants of it tonight."

Jess finished saying her goodbyes and set off on her bike. Passing row upon row of people mowing their lawns, trimming their hedges and washing their already clean cars, she felt relieved to be escaping the boredom of village life for a while. She took the footpath that ran between the terrace houses to the little park behind. From there she crossed the field and arrived at the twin's house, who were already out front arguing. As she skidded to a stop there came a dog bark from the house, then out scampered Cookie - the Chihuahua-cross pup that had the heart of a lion. It was quite a rare sight to see the little dog so full of life, as he tended to spend most of the day lying around the house, either on someone's bed or the sofa. He officially belonged to Meg and lived a good life as a pampered pooch. In fact, he had not been known to eat actual dog food for several months, opting always for sausage, cheese, steak or something containing sausage or cheese or steak.

He jumped up to Jess and said good morning in his own distinctive way – with tail wagging frantically and trying his best to lick her face. She fussed over him for a moment before returning him to the ground, where he decided that Zac's shiny bike wheel would look better with some pee on it. She then stood for a moment waiting for the twins to stop arguing and notice her.

"Really, Zac," grumbled Meg, "I just don't understand why you have to fart at the most inopportune moments. Namely in front of my friends. It's so immature and annoying!"

"I'll think you'll find," Zac argued, "that you and your friends saying things like *probs* and *totes* is annoying. And even you can't deny that farting is completely natural."

"Whatever you jerk. Just promise you won't let your intellectual shortcomings ruin this weekend."
"Whatever yourself, sis."
"Idiot, drop dead."
"You drop dead."
"Get a life."
"You get a life…"

This had the potential to go on for some time, so Jess loudly announced her presence, "S'UP TWINS?"
"Hey, Jess," they both replied in a cheerful change of tone.
"You all packed then?" enquired Jess.
"Pretty much," replied Meg. "Just waiting for him."
"You still sure about this sleepover then, Jess?" asked Zac a little hesitantly.
"Oh totes," she replied smiling. "Why wouldn't I be?"

"It's just that, well, you know..."

"I... don't know. What?"

"It's just that... well, what if Charlie's place is haunted or something?"

"Not this again! What's put this nonsense into your head?"

"Nothing, nothing at all. I just remember hearing a story about a young boy who biked to the estate one foggy day, that's all."

"How did it go?"

"What, the bike?"

"The story, idiot."

"Oh, he got lost and was never seen again."

"Really?"

"Well, sort of. Well, maybe - he definitely did get lost for a few hours though. But the house being haunted is true."

"Says who?"

"Ben M, from school," replied Meg. "He broke his leg there."

"Not you too, Meg!" said Jess astonished. "Besides, Ben M didn't break his leg, Ben P did - and he did it by falling out of a tree in the park. Say, you're not scared are you?"

The twins glanced at one another and not wanting to admit that they were indeed just a little apprehensive, dismissed the accusation. "That all you taking?" asked Zac nodding to Jess' moderately-sized rucksack.

"Yes, why?"

"Oh, no reason," he replied, as he walked to the front door and retrieved a full-size army backpack stuffed to bursting point, complete with dangling pots and pans. It clanged and clattered as he heaved it onto his back.

"Ber-limey, Zac," laughed Jess. "You're going for a night in a country house, not a week in the jungle!"

Meg, who was well used to this sort of behaviour just rolled her eyes and ignored him.

"And what's that you have there?" asked Jess when she noticed Zac fastening a small cylindrical object to the side of his crash helmet.

"It's a high definition camera. I'm going to record the trip, you know, like a documentary. Might even get some hits on t'internet if we see anything unusual. I could end up famous or something. Lookout munsters, here I come!"

"You mean *monsters*," said Meg in contempt.

"That's what I said, munsters."

"Just be sure to mention us in the credits, Zac," joked Jess riding away.

Meg called Cookie over and helped him into the basket on her bike, she then set off after Jess with Zac following behind. They headed up the hill towards the upper part of the village where the change in gradient quickly became apparent. It would take a herculean effort to make it to the top of the mile-long, S-shaped road without dismounting bicycles and there were bragging rights up for grabs for anyone who could meet the challenge. Many had tried and most had failed.

After ten minutes and without anyone having to get off and walk thus far they arrived, somewhat out of breath, at the half way point - the bus drop-off beside Stanton's convenience store. They lay their bikes on the ground and Cookie was commanded to 'sit', but ended up being fastened with his leash to prevent him wondering off. The children entered the shop, sounding the bell mounted above the door as it opened notifying the proprietor he had customers. The smell of freshly baked bread filled their nostrils and they admired an impressive display of fresh vegetables, which they passed on route to the confectionary section. They selected some sweets, bottled water, one banana (for Meg), some fun snaps (for Zac), a packet of water bombs (just in case), and with nothing more they could think of taking that their host could not provide headed to the counter.

There was no sign of Mr Alexander, the owner (who just so happened to sport the longest eyebrows in the county) which wasn't unusual, for he was often busy out back. The children, therefore, opened the till and deposited the amount owed, something that also wasn't unusual for the locals. They gathered their purchases and headed for the exit, but had they noticed the newspapers on the counter, they would have seen they all shared a similar headline.

Jewellery thief The Wolf strikes again!

Once outside, they placed on sun glasses and crash helmets ready to depart. After fuelling up on cola bottles, they mounted their bikes and prepared to set off for Charlie's place. They had agreed that the best route to take would be to avoid climbing the rest of the hill to the upper part of the village and instead take the shortcut, which ran west along the old railway line from their current location. They could follow this track for a mile or so then connect with the Midsummer estate road, circumventing the uphill climb and cutting around two miles from the journey. However, in order to hook up with said railway line they would have to travel around the 150 acres occupied by the former Royal Ordnance Depot.

In its service years the depot had served as a military supply factory, having its own railway and canal connections. Today, although the railway lines have long been removed, the canal section, albeit in a sorry state, remains. To the local children it is a place of mystery, for it looks like a setting of a zombie film with its dilapidated buildings, broken windows and overgrown weeds pushing up through the pavements. It even has a colony of bats living in one of the old storehouses, which have been labelled the vampire kind by imaginative youngsters.

Jess and the twins crossed the road and travelled north alongside the depot wall. They quietly passed the main gate where they anticipated some unwanted company in the form of the resident guard dog, Brown Bess. This pooch was a thing of legend in the village and feared by all except its owner and handler - Dennis aka 'Dirty Den', the site security guard. Both owner and hound lived and worked on the site and many locals subscribed to the story that they had never left its borders. Some children would tease old Bess at the gates by banging sticks and objects against the bars. Others would even play a game in which someone would dare to place their bottoms the closest without being bit.

In one occurrence a school boy by the name of Jamal (Spotty) Smith, pushed his luck, and his bottom, a little too far after succumbing to peer pressure. He received a bite so nasty he was unable to sit down for a month. And if that wasn't humiliating enough, he was made to wear padded underwear which gave his rear-end the appearance of being inflated with helium. This canine baiting all went on of course, only until Den heard the commotion and came over shouting obscenities, at which point everyone would scarper. More often than not though, due to the size of the depot and Den's waistline, his arrival would sometimes take up to twenty minutes.

At this time, however, there was no Den or Bess to be seen so the children breathed a sigh of relief and carried on past the gate. They turned a sharp left following the depot wall as it cornered to the west where they swapped tarmac for off-road. Continuing this way was rather unpleasant to say the least, as the towering wall blocked out the sun at all times resulting in a shady, boggy and somewhat inhospitable passage. Yet this was a familiar route for the children and after carefully negotiating its puddles, exposed tree roots, stingers, shopping trollies, broken glass and that burnt-out car, they cleared the boundary wall and once again felt the warm sun on their faces.

Ahead of them and slicing through the yellow ocean of rapeseed, remained a narrow trail that used to be the old railway line, along which they would travel until they reached the Midsummer road. The recent hot weather had baked the ground dry and the surrounding air smelled like the sweetest of perfume.

Jess and Meg arrived at the far side first and stopped to take refreshment, whilst Cookie opted to drink from a thin stream that meandered nearby. Zac had lagged behind and could be heard sneezing uncontrollably, despite having taken his allergy tablets earlier that morning. "Perhaps he needs a gas mask?" joked Jess.

"We need them more like," replied Meg. "Have you smelt it when he drop's one?!"

He finally caught up and asked what the girls were laughing at between sneezes. "Oh, nothing," they replied smiling.

Reunited again they turned onto the Midsummer private road that led exclusively to the estate. This quiet, country road was barely as wide as a single car and should any vehicle meet and need to pass, they could do so only at a handful of spots. There were potholes of truly disturbing size which had to be avoided at all costs, plus some farm traffic, but other than that they made good progress and soon arrived at the western canal bridge. They stopped and waved at the boats chugging by below, not that they knew anyone, while they took on further refreshment. This spot represented the boundary of their home parish, about a third of the way to Charlie's place. It was not uncommon for people to walk and cycle out here, but seldom did anyone venture further into the countryside beyond.

With spirits and blood-sugar levels high the children set off for the final leg. They chatted and joked as they weaved along while the morning sun burned hot on their necks. Birds sang in the hedgerows and fluffy-tailed rabbits, surprised by the sudden company, would dart for cover. An hour later and the fun part arrived: two miles of winding downhill road with an elevation drop of almost three-hundred metres. It was the fabled story the children's parents had often lamented from their own youth. The cycling equivalent of a rollercoaster. And, sitting nestled at the bottom of the valley, smouldering in the haze was the Midsummer estate.

All three of them pulled out their phones and took the same picture. "That's some view," said Meg in awe.

"It sure is," agreed Jess. "Just… amazing. Don't you think, Zac?" However, all they got back from him was his dust as he took off down the hill. "Soooooooooo looooooonnng suckeeeeeerrrrrrsss!"

Meg shook her head, "He's such a gung-ho dork."

"Yeah, but it does look fun… shall we?"

"Good idea, Jess. I wanna be there when he falls and brakes something. Come on!"

They arrived, without incident, at the entrance of the Midsummer estate right on schedule, although they could go no further as the grand gates were closed and there was no sign of their host. Zac announced his arrival with a sneeze of truly biblical proportion, one that scared away half the wildlife. He then went on to sneeze an eye-popping eleven times in a row before anyone could get a word in.

"I know a rhyme about sneezing," said Jess. "It goes…"

One's a wish,
Two's a kiss,

Three's a disappointment,
Four's a letter,
Five's something better

"What's eleven?" asked Meg.

"No idea, it only goes up to five. But it's probably something along the lines of, seek medical help!"

They dismounted their bikes and peered through the gates. They could see the great building at the bottom of the long, straight road that Zac estimated to be half a mile away. From their elevated position they also saw a lake and a forest behind the house that stretched to the northeast to form another, smaller wooded area. While looking to the west, they could see the footprint of a huge formal garden, formed of many interconnecting pathways.

"Where's Charlie then?" asked Meg removing her sunglasses.

"You think he changed his mind?" supposed Zac. "Or forgot?"

Jess thought she would try ringing him and readied her mobile. She had to turn away from the sun to increase visibility as she inspected the available signal strength, but found there was no signal at all. The twins joked at her expense and pulled out their phones, only to find they had no signal either. "Suckers!" laughed Jess.

"What's that there?" asked Meg. She was pointing to a silver box mounted on a short wooden post, which resembled a buzzer outside a building used to contact its residents. Jess pushed the button, but it made no noticeable sound and there was no response. Zac then came bounding over and pushed it a few more times before banging it with his hand. After a while he gave up and shrugged his shoulders at Jess, who stood patiently watching him. "You finished?" she asked.

The tall iron gates that towered above them were topped with spikes so climbing over was out of the question. Jess turned to face the others and placed on her sunglasses. "I guess we wait."

5

At the estate perimeter there was a peaceful, unbroken tranquillity complemented only by birds singing and the buzzing of passing insects. Well, almost unbroken, apart that is from the sound of Zac, who was still sneezing madly shouting: "Curse you pollen!" Apart from that it was an unusual delight the group had never really stopped and noticed before. Leaving the others behind, Jess walked through the long grass a short way from the entrance admiring its design while she searched for a way in. The vast stone column beside her was one of two that supported the main gates and terminated the boundary walls, resulting in this being the only way in and out of the entire estate. On top of each imposing structure was a statue of a deer, lying down with its head and huge antlers facing the approach road; although it appeared that most of the antlers had broken off over time.

She carried on walking, avoiding the many rabbit holes and droppings while she ran her hand along the railings. They felt warm, hot even, as they bathed in the sunrays, when she suddenly noticed something. Someone or something had moved in the bushes on the other side. She paused to see what it was. A few seconds passed in silence then, to her delight, a beautiful red deer fawn appeared accompanied by its mother. Jess glanced to the side to see if her friends were nearby, but they were way back at the gates so she decided against calling out to them and risk scaring the animals away and to enjoy the moment alone. "Aww, hey girl," said Jess to the adorable spotted fawn. She presumed it was a girl, but was not entirely sure. Neither animal had antlers or signs of growing any, which as far as she could remember indicated a female, or doe. Plus the fact that they both lacked any noticeable 'boy parts'.

"Are you hungry?" She gently crouched and plucked a handful of long grass which she extended toward them. The fawn tentatively looked at its mother then back toward Jess, but wasn't quite sure about approaching. Jess then reached down into her pocket and grasped her phone with intent on taking a video, but this seemed enough to spook the animals who both disappeared into the bushes.

Back at the main gates, Meg sat sketching an unusual bird she had not seen before into her notebook. The specimen was slightly larger than a house sparrow but had a bluish-grey head, black mask like some miniature feathered bank robber, and bright, chestnut back. Meg loved to draw and had an inordinate fondness for animals (so said her biology teacher, who admitted to never before meeting such an enthusiastic and attentive pupil), which meant she would save an insect from drowning or move a snail clear of a busy footpath at any given opportunity. She was a gentle person, polite and caring. Seldom did she have a reason to be combative with anyone. With one exception that is.

Her brother, Zac, was a naturally gifted sportsman, a wilderness expert and technological genius - in his own mind. He was into gadgets, fixing stuff and outdoor activities, plus anything that involved mud and getting wet. He was an over-confident joker who took nothing seriously - and one who knew exactly how to infuriate several persons including his parents, teachers and sister.

The twins had recently turned fourteen, some eight months younger than Jess and four younger than Charlie. Yet despite being of the same blood, their aversion for one another was no secret and sometimes their arguments would even come to blows. Take for instance one legendary scuffle way back in primary school, when Meg received a broken arm as a result of being pushed over by Zac - by *accident* of course. Meg had taken revenge though some years later by *accidently* locking a near-naked Zac, save for a pair of crusty underpants, outside of his bedroom window after he had ventured onto the flat roof to retrieve one of his action figures. In another incident, this time in retaliation for Zac gluing Meg's hair brush to her hand, Meg had drawn a thick black moustache on her brother while he dozed, but hadn't realised she had used a permanent marker. He ended up having to give a book report to a full class the following day sporting the amusing makeup.

Zac was presently busy rummaging through his rucksack and eventually pulled out a rather sorry-looking sandwich and proceeded to take a bite from it. "Marmite butty, anyone?" he mumbled, wafting one around.

"Good God no!" replied the girls repulsed.

"Suit yourselves." He rummaged some more and this time retrieved a pair of oversize binoculars, powerful enough to see a person picking their nose for boogers on a passing aircraft. "Wow! You plane spotting?" enquired Jess.

Zac had come equipped with an arsenal of tools, gadgets, gizmos, utensils, instruments, appliances and contraptions. About enough to supply a small army. He used the massive lenses to survey the landscape ahead. "What is Charlie's E.T.A again?" he asked.

"His what?" replied Jess.

"EE-TEE-AYE. Estimated Time of Arrival. It's a military acronym."

"Oh, I see," said Meg. "In that case any minute. And does that make you a D.O.R.K in military terms, Zac?"

"Very funny! …Hey, I see someone coming up the road. Twelve o'clock."

"But it's ten past twelve," replied Meg after checking her watch.

"Not twelve o'clock as in time," griped Zac indicating ahead of himself. "Twelve o'clock as in – down there. Straight ahead!" Zac described a plump, bespectacled figure cycling frantically against the uphill gradient wearing sandals, khaki shorts and a baby-pink polo shirt. His nose bore a thick splodge of sun block and he wore on his head an Australian style bush hat. "It's Charlie, alright. Him or Indiana Jones the third. And what's he thinking wearing sandals and socks? *So* embarrassing!"

The girls squinted through the railings but saw little more than an ant-sized blot hundreds of metres away. "Whoa, those binoculars must be good," said Jess. "Here, let me see!" She yanked the glasses towards her, not realising the attached cord was still around Zac's neck and pulled him over with them. "Oh yeah," she announced. "Look at him go, he's like a little wind-up toy!" She passed the glasses, with Zac still attached, to Meg so she could see and a short while later their host arrived at the gates, huffing and puffing with cheeks as red as freshly-ripened tomatoes.

"Whoa-ha-ho!" exclaimed Zac. "Here's trouble petrified!"

"You mean *personified,* dummy," uttered Meg.

"That's what I said, petronifed!"

"Alright chaps," wheezed Charlie between breaths.

"Charlie, you're late," said Jess through the bars. "Where have you been?"

"Sorry... *phew*. Just sorting things out... *gasp*, with Auntie!"

"We still on then, Charlie?" Meg asked.

"I'll say! Auntie has even got... *wheeeeze*, the pool setup for us... and some lunch if you're hungry."

"Sounds wonderful, Charlie. Now how about opening the gates."

"Oh, yes of course. Forgive me."

Charlie went over and pushed a button on his side of the barrier and immediately the huge entrance gates began to creak and screech open. Jess and the twins then gathered their gear and crossed over into the estate with Cookie following behind. Mounting their bikes, they pushed off and were soon soaring down the open road. It was exactly one kilometre to the house along the perfectly straight boulevard, flanked its entire length by giant ornamental Cedar trees - planted over a hundred years ago for the sole purpose of grandeur. The building ahead of them in the distance grew larger and larger, until they eventually passed under an archway and entered the courtyard beyond. They arrived in front of the house on an extensive circular driveway, which permitted vehicles to turn around like a roundabout. Standing proudly in its centre on a plinth, was a life-size bronze statue of Winston Churchill, the prime minister who helped Britain achieve victory in the Second World War.

Skidding to a stop on the gravel they caught their first sight of the magnificent residence that Charlie called home. "Welcome to Chez Midsummer," he announced proudly. "Mi casa es su casa."

"Whoa, sweet digs, Charlie," said Jess punching him lightly on the arm. "Didn't realize you lived in a castle!"

"Oh, don't let the battlements fool you, I assure you it's a house underneath."

"Err, just how rich are you exactly, Charlie?" probed Zac bluntly.

"Zac!" snapped Meg. "You don't have to answer that, Charlie."

"That's OK, Meg. You see, Auntie describes us as cash poor but asset rich, whatever that means - but the house and grounds are probably worth a few mill' you know."

"WHAT?!" coughed Jess.

"Sheesh, is that all?" joked Meg after getting over the shock. "And just how many of your family live here at Hardup Hall? The whole clan no doubt."

"It's just Auntie and myself in the family, but there are a few staff who live here in the house, in the staff wing. There is Donald the groundskeeper - actually come to think about it, he lives up at the cabin. Then there is Barker - he's the butler. Mrs Blackwell the cook, oh, and the maid – a German lady who goes by the name of Fräulein Bertrümn. Heh, I call her Bertie for short." Zac smirked at the maid's name before Charlie had finished. "Careful of her though, she can be a trifle scary to say the least!"

Meg recorded these names in her notepad like a detective at a crime scene, but misspelled 'Fräulein' repeatedly, settling with *'Bertie - Maid'*.

Charlie pushed his bike over to the side of the driveway where he lay it on the ground and the others did the same. Cookie jumped out from his basket and sniffed around one of the hedges, before deciding to take a poop on the immaculate lawn which Meg had to attend to. "Sorry, Charlie!"

"That's quite alright, Meg. So, what shall we do first chaps?" He had barely finished speaking before Zac suggested his favourite pastime - eating.

"Hold on a minute," said Jess incredulously. "You just had a sandwich - if you can call it that - up at the gates. Surely you can't be hungry already?"

"Err, yeah I can!"

"Zac, you're always eating," grumbled Meg. "By rights you should be at least twenty stone!"

"Well what can I say, I'm an athlete. Now, Charlie, where is breakfast served exactly?" He threw his arm around Charlie and led him towards the entrance doors.

"Your brother is incorrigible, Meg," said Jess.

"Tell me something I don't know. I think he must have worms or something!"

Jess grabbed Charlie's arm and rescued him. "Charlie, up at the gate just now, I saw some deer. They were pretty tame. Are there lots of them here?"

"Why yes, Jess. In fact, we have had a herd on the estate for decades. It's nice that one was friendly with you like that. It's just that, well, lately they have been staying away from the house… like something has spooked them."

"Something…" Meg supposed, "like a werewolf?"

6

The children entered the house through its heavy oak door which boomed loudly as it closed behind. They dropped their bags and stood rooted to the spot in wonderment while they gazed around the vast hall. Ahead of them, a grand mahogany staircase joined the ground floor to the first, with each step lined by a narrow carpet of green bordered with black studs. The roof above must have been some twenty feet up and suspended from it was a beautiful crystal chandelier that sparkled majestically in the sunlight. All of the walls, however, were covered in dark wood panelling which gave a dim and gloomy feel to their surroundings, despite strong sunlight shining through tall windows either side of the door. Below them, the floor consisted of polished, black and white tiles encircling the slightly more colourful, but worn family crest in its centre.

"Bloody hell, Charlie!" exclaimed Zac boisterously. He spoke no louder than usual but the open space seemed to amplify his tone. "This is some kick-ass pad!"

"Zac," replied Meg. "Will you please show some decorum!"

"What, what did I do?"

"You know what, being a loudmouth as per usual."

"Sorry Mum!"

"Keep your voice down!"

"Make me!"

"Actually, just stop talking. Problem solved."

"You'd like that, but no can do I'm afraid."

Their exchanges echoed around the hall breaking the customary silence and it wasn't long before somebody noticed. "AHEM," coughed a distant voice. "I see your guests have arrived, Master Charles."

Addressing them was an elderly gentleman standing ramrod-straight, looking on with one eyebrow raised higher than the other. In contrast to the children in their shorts and t-shirts, he was dressed in full formal attire of black shoes, grey striped trousers, white wing collar shirt with black tie, plus waistcoat and jacket. He even wore cotton gloves as not to get fingerprints on the furnishings. Despite his age, which Jess and the twins guessed to be somewhere in the late seventies, he maintained a decent head of white hair which may have been parted using a set-square. He was thin and looked a little frail, but nevertheless remained a champion of etiquette, manners and grammar. A pedantic purveyor of pronunciation prowess, capable of inducing fear in others as well as any stringent school head. He eye-balled the newcomers through circular lenses so thick they magnified his eyes several times over, making them appear much larger than they actually were.

"Ah yes, Barker," replied Charlie stepping forward. "Perfect timing. These are my friends – Jessica, and the twins Megan and Zachary. Oh, and Cookie the dog too. I trust the rooms are ready as I requested?"

"But of course, sir," confirmed Barker, without showing the slightest bit of emotion or interest. "Next to your bed chamber as you desired. Should I take the luggage upstairs to the rooms, sir?" The visitors shuddered at the thought of someone his age carting their bags up the many stairs, especially Zac's, and shook their heads at Charlie.

"Err... no thanks, Barker. We can manage. Thanks all the same, mind."

"He needs to really get a baggage boy or something," remarked Zac, thinking the old timer wouldn't hear him.

"YOUNG MAN YOU JUST SPLIT AN INFINITIVE!" snapped Barker loudly, making everyone jump.

Zac first looked startled, then confused. "I split a what now?"

"Your grammar, young man," replied Barker aghast. "I am referring to your grammar!" Charlie and Jess found the whole exchange rather amusing and couldn't help but smirk a little. Barker, however, was not impressed at all. "Oh never mind. I suppose it doesn't matter anyway." He lowered his eyebrow, rolled his eyes and walked away mumbling something about the youth of today.

"He called you Master," chuckled Meg pulling on Charlie's arm. This also made Jess smile, but trying to appear to behave 'properly' like she promised her mum, she quickly restored a more straight-faced persona.

"And just who is that stuffy old geezer?" questioned Zac. "I get enough abuse from starchy suits at school thank you very much!"

"Oh, that's Barker the butler," Charlie replied. "He's been here for ages. He likes things to be ship shape, but he's a softy once you get to know him."

"Yeah, well, he's besmirched my reputation he has."

"I'll punch you in your besmirched face, Zac," warned Meg, "if you embarrass me like that again!"

"OKAY then," continued Charlie a little awkwardly. "Moving on! If you'll follow me, I'll show you up to your bed chambers."

The visitors picked up their bags and followed Charlie up the wide staircase. At the top and turning to the right was a long corridor again lined with dark wood panels, but minus the sunlight that blessed the ground floor it was noticeably gloomier. There were fifteen doors - seven on either side and one at the end some distance away. Between each door a life-sized painting was fixed to the wall space, the majority being of Midsummer family members from past generations, and centred above each painting was a brass hand clasping an antique gas lamp which had been converted to take a thin electric bulb. Along the corridor in the other direction were four doors: three of which were bedrooms for members of staff plus a fourth, closest to the stairs, which Charlie informed them led up to the attic.

"That room there is the toilet," Charlie informed them. "Just make sure you whistle or sing when you go in as it has no lock." He was joking of course, but no one got it and just looked blankly back at him. You could have heard a pin drop in the silence. "Ahem..." he continued, "all the rooms have en-suite bathrooms, naturally. Now, over here on my right is a room you can use, Zac, which is next door to my own. Jess and Meg, you can take the two rooms opposite us there. All rooms have connecting doors inside so I feel it's probably best to have girls on one side and boys on the other. You know - to avoid any embarrassing *incidents*." Charlie looked slightly uneasy and was envisaging one of the girls seeing him whilst wearing just his underwear, or worse - catch sight of the white, fluffy bunny onesie Auntie had bought him for Easter. If word got out at school about that, how could he ever hope to live it down!

Jess and Meg cheerfully pushed passed and together entered one of the rooms indicated by their host. "OH-MY-GOD!" they announced delightedly. They dropped their bags and stood looking at the large king, no - super-queen-size, four-poster bed that was simply huge compared to the beds they were used to. They looked at one another before running over and diving on top, where they lay spread-eagled making imaginary snow angels on the immaculate Egyptian silk sheets. Laying side-by-side, four feet above the ground and with ample space for another person, they gazed up at the roof of the bed which was beautifully embroidered, depicting images of wild landscapes and horses. There were even red velvet curtains affixed to the sides of the bed for added privacy. After a while they both got up and ran off into the adjoining room giggling as they went.

Cookie and the boys looked on from the doorway wondering what to make of it. "Let me show you to your room, Zac," offered Charlie. He led his only male guest across the corridor and pushed open the door. Similar to the girl's rooms, the dark wood panelling theme continued on the walls and ceiling, while the floors were devoid of any carpet revealing brown floorboards, except by the bed where a large rug lay. It smelled stuffy with a hint of furniture polish, but nothing a little fresh air wouldn't sort out.

"Tidy," said Zac acknowledging the rooms suitability. He entered with Cookie and dropped his heavy bag on a chair before taking a look around. He opened and closed a drawer or two. He sat and tested the bed then, appearing satisfied, began to unload his belongings. Once he had done all that he went over and opened the window to a view of wooded, well established landscape. He figured he must be west-facing (which he confirmed using a compass app) due to the lack of direct sunlight for the time of day. He also noticed he was quite high up, not far off eye-level from the tops of some of the tall trees adjacent to him.

Across the way, Jess and Meg had also opened their windows and were enjoying the warm sun on their faces. They talked to each other between balconies as they surveyed the grounds while their bikes baked on the gravel below. Overlooking the courtyard and formal gardens to the east, their view was simply breath-taking. They marvelled at the pristinely manicured lawns, expertly sculpted topiary hedges, plants and flowers of various colour and size - all of which were flawlessly arranged like a meticulously embroidered rug. Inside their chambers was enough wardrobe space to house dozens of outfits and twice as many pairs of shoes. There were also personal dressing tables offering, amongst other things, a large mirror and a selection of perfumes; none of which they recognised, each of which they sampled. There was even a woven bell pull next to the beds, on which a single tug would alert the servants that they were wanted.

The jovial noise made by the girls could be heard across the corridor and after a few minutes, Charlie returned to their door and knocked. He heard the sound of running and giggling from the other side which abruptly stopped. The door then slowly opened and revealed the girls, facing Charlie with deadpan expressions.

"Err... hi, girls," asked Charlie politely. "Is... everything OK?"

They nodded and informed him that, "It most certainly was," before bursting into laughter once again.

"I am glad that..." began Charlie, but he was cut off.

"Be with you in a minute, boys," they giggled, before slamming the door shut.

Zac had been keeping himself busy using the electric shoe buffer he found in his cupboard to shine some of his tools, but had been unable to find a use for the trouser press. After updating his video diary, he had taken a good look around his room and the adjoining corridor, looking behind paintings, knocking on walls and inspecting some of the unusual lamp holders. He had even used a special extendable attachment to send his camera into little holes in the skirting boards to see what was behind them, but only managed to discover clumps of dust and the skeleton of a mouse long since dead. He did, however, find one of the framed pictures to be of interest, which seemed to show Charlie's aunt and the president of the United States of America, shaking hands at some ceremony. He inspected it further with his magnifying glass, looking for evidence of digital trickery but saw none. He intended to ask Charlie about it, and commend him on his work, but when he joined him outside the girl's room there came an almighty scream from within.

"AAAAAARRRRRRRGGGHHHH! EEEEEEEEEEEEEE!"

"JESS, MEG, ARE YOU ALRIGHT?!" shouted the boys. "WHAT IS IT?!"

Zac thundered on the door while Cookie yapped furiously beside him. "Quick Charlie, unlock it!" But there was no need, because on the other side the sound of footsteps came rushing toward them and the next thing they knew, the door suddenly flew open and out came the girls at speed. They bumped into the boys and all four of them fell to the floor. "WHAT ON EARTH?!" exclaimed Charlie.

"In there," replied Meg between breaths. "A rodent! A giant hairy beast!"

"WITH FANGS!" added Jess.

Zac got spooked at this news and shuffled backward, but Charlie wasn't quite so fearful. He stood up, dusted himself off and announced, "Wait a minute," before boldly entering the room.

"Don't go in there, Charlie," said Jess. "I'm warning you!"

A tense few moments later and just as the others finished composing themselves, Charlie returned carrying a furry four-legged creature with long tail, the sight of which caused Meg to leap into Zac's arms. "WHOA!"

"It's *OKAY*, guys," Charlie assured them. "It's only Robby. My *Rattus norvegicus*."

"YOUR WHAT?!" replied the others.

"*Rattus norvegicus*. My rat - my pet rat. He must have escaped from my room again. He's totally harmless you know."

Robby the rat was the length of its owner's forearm, brown in colour and had prominent teeth that it liked nothing more than to sink into strangers' fingers. Cookie inspected it, turning his head from side to side, not sure what to make of it, but still growled bravely nonetheless. Zac then gave a scornful look at his sister, who was still firmly attached to him, before dropping her.

"Well what on earth is it doing running around our bedroom?" asked an astonished Jess on behalf of a distressed Meg. "And are there any other little *surprises* scurrying around that we need to know about, Charles?"

"Just the bird-eating spiders," he replied casually.

Three very blank and concerned faces stared back before Charlie added, "Only kidding!" at which point the disbelief and frowns slowly turned to relief and smiles all round.

Zac bumped knuckles with Charlie, "Good one, dude."

"I do, however," continued Charlie as he opened his bedroom door to show them, "have two pet ferrets. Come see."

Unlike Robby, who it seemed had the freedom of the house, these two creatures were secured in a large cage tall enough for a person to stand up in. Their home had no less than five levels connected by little steps and various colourful tubes, with an abundance of toys and accessories scattered around the place. Jess and the twins approached and admired its furry residents, well, their rear-ends at least, as they were both snuggled up in a corner fast asleep. Charlie informed his guests that the animals were long and thin, weasel-like in appearance and had tiny pink noses and ears. He then went on to add that while Doc had pure white fur, Marty was black with light brown patches.

"Aww, they are positively adorable, Charlie," said Meg. "How long have you had them?"

"About three years. They keep me company and make me laugh. I have to keep them locked-up though, because Doc once bit Auntie and made her faint. Did you know, the name ferret means *little thief* in Latin? As they tend to run off with things that don't belong to them."

"Fascinating, Charlie," observed Zac. "But if you ask me, they just look like squirrels."

"Well that doesn't surprise me," replied Meg.

"And why not?" asked Zac.

"Well, you're no wildlife expert are you? I mean, you thought the most interesting thing at the museum of natural history was a flea dressed in miniature clothing. Forget thirty-foot tall dinosaurs, millions of years old!"

"Yeah, that was pretty epic - he had little boots and everything."

"I rest my case!"

"Whatever, sis. Look - squirrels, ferrets, squirrel-ferrets - the point is I'll wager someone gets bit before the weekend is through. What do you say, Charlie? Care to take me up on that?"

"Pardon me?"

"Bet, Charlie, do you want to bet?"

"Sorry, Zac, but I don't gamble."

"Really? Then in that case, I bet a pound I can make you start by the end of the day. What do you say?"

"Hmm… … you're on!"

7

After returning Robby to his cage, Charlie led his guest's downstairs and to the dining room where cook had left out some light bites in the form of fruit, pastries and chocolate-filled croissants on one end of the enormous dining table.

"Now that's what I'm talking about!" declared Zac, who swiftly darted to the table and helped himself like a castaway after months of being stranded at sea. The others followed his lead and got stuck into the delights, before they were all gone.

"Are you hungry, Zac?" enquired Charlie, as he watched him load his plate.

"He's always hungry," replied Meg. "In case you hadn't noticed."

"Well I'm certainly a little peckish, Charlie. And it's a real treat having something different to eat; all we seem to get at home at the moment is baked beans. Take Tuesday for example - we had beans on toast for breakfast and bean surprise for dinner."

"What was the surprise?" asked Jess out of interest.

"BEANS! I'm just thankful Mum hasn't figured out a way to put beans into sandwiches!"

"Well that explains your flatulence at least," joked Jess. "I was beginning to think you had something seriously wrong with you."

"He does!" exclaimed Meg.

Much to her indignation, Zac then placed a whole muffin in his mouth and somehow managed to continue speaking. "So, you got internet fibre here, Charlie? Must be a really fast connection. What is it, couple-hundred meg?"

"Good heavens no," replied Charlie modestly. "Nothing like that, more like 56 kilobytes on a good day."

Zac stopped chewing for a moment while his brain caught up. "Wait, did you say *kilobytes*?"

"That's right. About 0.054 of one Megabyte I believe - using the phone line. The fact is we are more of a 'not-spot' than a 'hot-spot' out here in the sticks. Come to think of it, did you know there are around two million people with inadequate broadband in the UK? This affects mostly rural households because..."

"*Ahem!*" interrupted Jess. "Thank you, Charlie, we get the general idea."

"Sorry, Jess." Charlie had a habit of deep-diving into random and often seemingly pointless subjects, regularly leaving his peers wondering what on earth he was waffling on about.

"Well that explains the lack of WiFi," observed Meg, confirming the case on her phone. "I take it you're not a fan of online gaming then, Charlie."

"Err, no, Meg. It's just impossible you see."

"So... must make playing Minecraft a bit difficult, unless you play offline?"

"Mine-what?"

"You know," said Zac, "Minecraft. With the mining and the crafting and the... stuff. It's played by millions around the world. Literally millions. Mill... oh forget it. You don't know what we're talking about do you, Charlie?"

Their host shook his head completely zoned out. "I am afraid not. You see I don't get much time for cartoons between study and helping out around the house. Besides, Auntie believes in the more traditional fundamentals of childhood. You know, like long walks, shooting, knot-tying and shoe polishing. That sort of thing. Rather than relying on technology. Come to think of it, I don't think Auntie even knows what the internet is. Hence the lack of it."

"Lame," replied Zac unimpressed.

"Hey, Charlie, that reminds me," said Jess, "what about our phones, how come we don't get any signal here?"

"Oh you won't, naturally," he informed them matter-of-factly.

"And that's because?"

"Because the nearest telecommunications tower is way over at the north-west side of Daventry, atop of Harris Hill. Its coverage doesn't extend down here, never has for that matter."

"In... that case then, Charlie," Meg enquired, "when you want to update your status, what do you do?"

"Update my what?"

Zac slapped his own forehead in disbelief while the girls almost chocked on sugar-coated croissants. "Hold on a sec, Charlie," coughed Meg, "are you telling me we won't be able to update anything for as long as we're here? People will think we've died or something!"

"Well, I'm, err, not sure about that, Meg..."

"Now I know what it was like for our parents when they were kids," bemoaned Zac. "We're back in the dark ages, people!"

"Guys, *chill*," chuckled Jess. "It is what it is, so let's not overreact. I'm sure we can all manage without our phones for one whole day and night – at least I think we can. But it does mean we'll have to solve Charlie's mystery the old fashioned way."

"How's that?" enquired Meg looking dismayed.

"With pen, paper, the little grey cells in our heads - and actually walking around getting our hands dirty."

"Jesus, Mary and Joseph!" exclaimed Zac.

At that moment the kitchen swing door burst open and through it walked Fräulein Bertrümn, the German house maid. She was rather masculine in appearance and noticeably tall - nigh on seven feet tall - which caused everyone to look almost vertically upward as she came near. Her skin was as pale as death itself, yet contrasted by hair blacker than the long dresses she always wore. Her eyes were dark pools of brown, complemented by eyebrows so unkempt they joined to form one long brow. A lonesome and truly enigmatic character, she seemed to have the effect of freezing the visitors in time, who sat in silence unable to brake their gaze.

"Kinder finished, ja?" she asked quietly, which wasn't unusual, for she seldom spoke in sentences longer than three or four words.

"Why yes thank you, Bertie," replied Charlie. "Please, carry on." He then noticed the others, including the dog, remained motionless and snapped them out of it. "Come on, guys, let me show you around while it's still sunny. Its forecast storms this afternoon you know."

Fräulein Bertrümn began clearing the table and the children raised from their chairs just as the serving hatch was opened, where a friendlier face addressed them through the opening. It was Mrs Blackwell, the cook, evident by the tall white hat atop of her head. From what was visible of her, she appeared to be of medium height with a round and rosy face punctuated by a bulging, sticky-out chin. However, everyone's attention seemed to be engaged solely on the large, hairy mole on her right cheek. She also appeared to have long, bushy hair which fell to her shoulders and wore a pair of thick, red–framed glasses straight from the seventies. She addressed the children in English of sorts, but in an unusual accent which no one could quite identify. One thing was for sure - she didn't let anyone get a word in edgewise.

"Was that alright for you, Master Charles sir? Excellent. Don't worry about old misery chops over there, she has a heart of gold don't you, Fräulein? That's right, now you run along, children. Lunch will be served slightly later today at two thirty. Cold meat buffet and chips OK? Excellent. Goodness gracious, I see you have a dog! I'll see if I have any bones going. Oh well, if you'll excuse me I must get back to the grindstone. You know how it is. Come along now, Fräulein, chop chop!"

The moment she finished speaking the hatch doors slammed shut before anyone could reply, not that anyone needed to. The children looked at one another and smiled, then looked at Fräulein Bertrümn, who was looking back and definitely not smiling. They immediately wiped the smiles from their faces and made for the door quietly and in an orderly fashion, not daring to speak until they were in the hall.

"See what you mean about the maid, Charlie," said Zac softly.

"Very peculiar indeed," agreed Jess. "She's got the whole Addams Family thing going on."

"Talk about the living dead!"

"That's an oxymoron, moron," replied Meg disapprovingly. "And don't be so judgemental, both of you. I'm sure she's a lovely person whatever she looks like. Right, Charlie?"

"Quite right, Meg."

"Sorry, Meg," replied Jess sheepishly.

"I... suppose... I shouldn't mention that mole on Mrs Bakewell either then?" continued Zac.

"Idiot, it's *Blackwell!*" snapped *Meg*. "And no - don't even go there!"

A brief awkward silence followed, until Charlie rubbed his hands together excitedly. "Does anyone fancy a game of billiards? It's kind of like snooker. We also have a dart board and skittles. Or we could play a board game, Monopoly perhaps?"

"Whoa! Not if you value your life, Charlie," replied Jess raising eyebrows at the twins. She was referring to the habitual arguments of truly legendary proportion that arose each and every time they had dared play a round of the popular game. "Trust me, you don't want to go there - we'd never get an ambulance out here in time!"

The visitors accompanied by their host had a look around in the games room which immediately turned out to be a lot less interesting than it sounded. There was a well-used dart board with only one dart, a skittles table with cheese* but no skittles, and a large snooker-like table which appeared to lack any coloured balls. Against the side walls were bookshelves and glass cabinets, not solely displaying books, but also an extensive variety of embalmed wildlife. The specimens on show included a fox, badger, stoat, otter, and dozens of birds. There were also cabinets displaying countless butterflies and moths of all size, pattern and colour imaginable. But presiding over everything and proudly displayed at the very top of one of the bookshelves, was a monster of a fish well over a metre long. It was mostly brown in colour with a long jaw lined with razor-sharp teeth. Its lifeless, beady eye seemed to follow the children's every movement.

*A wooden object used to knock down skittles.

"What… the hell… is that thing, Charlie?" asked Jess gazing up at it.
"It's a Pike," he replied. "Caught in our lake right here in the estate."
"You mean that thing was real?!"
"Why of course."
"What were you feeding it?" asked Zac incredulously. "Big Macs!"
"Splendid isn't it?" replied Charlie proudly.
"Splendid, it's Fishzilla!"

Meg, however, wasn't at all impressed and felt uncomfortable in the presence of so many dead animals. "Well I think it's cruel to put the poor creatures on show like this. And it's stuffy in here. Phew, and it smells kinda funny too."

"Hmm, it does now you mention it," agreed Jess sniffing the air. "Hey Charlie, can't we do something outside? It's far too nice to be stuck indoors."

"Yeah, that reminds me, Charlie," said Zac replacing the lid on a crystal decanter, "why did you ask us to bring our swimming kit, or 'bathing clothes' as you put it?"

Charlie smiled back at them, "Get changed and I will show you. Meet me back here in five minutes."

8

Perfect. That's what it was. The alluring blue water that glistened under the sun was simply perfect and never before had anyone appreciated throwing themselves into it so much. The pool offered immediate relief from the relentless heat that had baked the country dry for the past month. So much so that once in, no one wanted to get out. The many muggy nights, stuffy classrooms and those dreadful bus trips were instantly forgotten. A distant memory, replaced with clear blue liquid ecstasy.

The pool was located at the south of the house beyond the conservatory. This ensured maximum sun exposure and caused the bordering sandstone paving to become piping hot to stand on during days like today. There were colourful body boards on hand plus a variety of inflatables that doubled as air-born projectiles. These included a giant green crocodile that became a make-shift surf board, on which Jess and Zac shared the record for the longest ride - both recorded by Zac's camera in its waterproof casing. They swam, dived, dunked, bombed, front-flipped, back-flipped, pushed, leg-and-winged and belly-flopped for well over an hour, completely forgetting that they had more serious business to attend to.

Afterwards they took in a round of croquet on the nearby lawn in just their swimming costumes. It involved hitting a wooden ball with a long wooden hammer known as a mallet, through a number of small hoops, but this soon became hot work so they returned to the pool for another dip. A short while later they were drying off on sunbeds, sipping cool drinks laden with ice and a little umbrella on top. They lay back and looked to the heavens through their sunglasses and saw airbrushed cirrus clouds, forming their distinctive mare's tails across the endless blue canvas. These were accompanied only by the odd trail left by passing airliners, thirty-something thousand feet above them. Cookie had taken up temporary residence beneath a sunbed where he lay panting to cool down, although he was now considerably cooler after Zac 'insisted' he went for a swim.

"We are totes coming here every weekend, Charlie," sighed Meg. "Right, Jess?"

"Totally. You're very lucky you know, Charlie." Only he didn't respond so Jess turned her head toward him and looked over her sun glasses. "Charlie?" She saw he looked saddened - as if this was all a dream destined to end soon. He erected a parasol next to his sunbed and sat in the shade.

"Yeah I guess, it's just, you know, this…"

"This werewolf business?" said Jess, sitting up to face him.

"Yes, Jess. It haunts my dreams. I haven't slept well for days."

"Is that why you've been dozing off in class, Charlie?" asked Meg.

"I guess. I suppose you all think I am being daft."

"Not at all, Charlie," Jess assured him. "You're our friend and we're here for you, right guys?"

The twins showed their support before Zac bleated out, "And the food!" for which he received a punch on the arm from Meg.

"Charlie," continued Jess, "why don't you tell us everything you know about you-know-what. Then we'll see what we can do about it."

The twins pulled their loungers in a little closer and while slurping their beverages through curly straws, listened to their host's incredible tale of events.

"Well the first time I saw him, err it - the werewolf that is, was two weeks ago. It was Saturday night. I remember staying up late watching some old black-and-white Frankenstein movie. It was hilarious. It also featured a werewolf, which is quite ironic now come to think about it. Anyway, it was dark when I got up to close the curtains and the window was still open, as it was a warm night you see. I could hear a noise below in the gardens. Not an animal, but rather the footsteps of a person, heavy and clumsy. And that's when I saw it."

"Go on, Charlie…"

"It… it was the size of an adult but walked a little bent over. It had an odd-shaped head I thought. It didn't see me so I just stood there watching it."

"And what exactly did it do, Charlie?"

"It was looking toward the house, into the windows on the ground floor. It was like it was searching for something. I got spooked, so I closed the window and curtains, then I got under the bed sheet not daring to look."

"Did you tell anyone about seeing it?" asked Zac.

"No, not then anyway but the following night I saw it again, only this time I ran and told Auntie, but it seemed to upset her and she didn't believe me. I've told everyone: Barker, Mrs Blackwell, and even maid Bertie, but they all thought I was dreaming. And if that's not bad enough, I'm now banned from eating sugary snacks before bedtime. No exceptions! I began to believe it *was* all a dream, until I saw it again a few nights later. This time I decided to follow it from the upstairs windows. I even took a camera to get a photo. It was raining and I moved between bedrooms to follow its progress. It made for the north-east corner, keeping close to the bushes out of sight. And then…"

"**AH-CHOO!**" blasted Zac.

"ZAC!" moaned the girls.

"Sorry," he said, blowing his nose.

"Go on, Charlie," said Jess. "What happened then?"

"Well *it* arrived at the basement. There are loading doors there, used for dropping down coal and stuff a long time ago, but it's not used anymore and the doors are always locked. You see, I fell down it when I was young and broke a clavicle."

"Ah yes, the lower leg bone," observed Zac.

"Um, I think you'll find it's the collar bone, stupid," scowled Meg.

"Don't call me stupid, stupider!" he replied.

"Zac, you go to school each day and actually become more stupid!"

"Is that a fact?"

"Yes, it is actually."

"Oh really?"

"Yes, really!"

"GUYS!" yelled Jess. "Stay focused. You were saying, Charlie?"

"Thanks Jess. The thing opened the door and climbed inside, but just as it did h-he must have caught a glimpse of movement or something, as he looked right up at the window. Right at me! I just froze. A flash of lightning suddenly lit up the grounds and I got a good look at it - and that's when I thought I was going to be sick."

The others leaned in as far as they could, hanging onto Charlie's every word. "What did you see?"

"It was a werewolf alright. It had a furry face and long hair. It wore black gloves, black jacket and jeans. I watched it climb down into the basement and close the door behind. The next morning, I thought I would have a look in the basement, for evidence or... something, but the door from the hall was locked as usual, so I went to the loading doors outside and guess what?"

"What, what?!" pleaded the others.

"The doors were locked! I tried to open them to peer inside, but just as I did there was a noise behind me; it was maid Bertie and she stood staring at me, before telling me to go somewhere else."

"But what about your camera, Charlie?" asked Zac. "You got a photo, right?"

"Oh yes, I printed it out. Here it is, but..."

Zac snatched the paper and removed his sunglasses to inspect it. "Err, it's just a black page, Charlie."

"Yes, you see in the excitement I forgot to use the flash."

"Dumb-ass!"

"Ignore him, Charlie," said Meg with notebook now in hand. "We all make mistakes. Can I just check though, you said you told everyone about seeing the werewolf, right?"

"That's right, Meg."

"Well you didn't mention this Donald the groundskeeper, in your account just now. How did he react when you told him?"

"Gosh, I completely forgot about him. And no, I haven't told him. Come to think about it, I haven't seen him around for a few days now."

"Is that unusual, not to see him?"

"Donald keeps himself to himself, there is no doubt about that, but I would expect to see him working the grounds daily. Especially at this time of year."

"Hmm," mused Meg sucking her pencil top. "How very interesting."

The sunshine that had been blazing all day suddenly dimmed as a cloud arrived overhead. It caused a dark shadow to run across the ground like someone pulling a rain-cover over the estate. Jess looked to the sky and removed her sunglasses. "Well, one thing's for sure, Charlie. Werewolves don't wear gloves."

"Or jeans," added Meg.

"Abso-frigging-lutely! Now, why don't we take a look at that basement of yours, Charlie? And we should probably have a chat with the groundskeeper too, see what he makes of all this."

"Good idea," replied the twins together.

"But after lunch, yes?" proposed Zac, concerned he may miss a meal.

"By all means," replied Charlie. "After lunch. I think we'll all need our blood-sugar levels topping up before we do anything strenuous in this heat."

Cookie then barked to notify them of persons approaching and they all looked toward the direction of the house to see who it was.

Lady Midsummer had an old-fashioned elegance and was posh without a doubt - old-school 1920's kind of posh. She approached poolside in a full-length, purple silk dressing gown complete with fluffy cuffs, collar, and matching slippers. She was plump and stood around five foot five, but well into her eighties remained a defiant gadabout, light and spirited on her feet. She sported oversize, designer pink sunglasses - the kind Elton John would die for, which she tilted downward as she eyed the children. "Yoo-hoo, Charles!" She was accompanied by Barker, who was doing his very best to keep up holding in one hand - a petite white umbrella over her head, plus a white towel draped over his forearm. In his other hand was a very tall and colourful beverage balanced on a shiny silver tray.

Lady Midsummer arrived at her lounger - the last in the row and sat down heavily making it creak under the strain. Barker then carefully placed the drink on the table beside her, adjusted the parasol so it provided sufficient shade and offered the towel to her ladyship. "Your towel, madam. And your low-fat rose and lavender elixir."

"That's all very well, Barker," she replied fiercely, "but what about my cheese and biscuits? Am I to starve? Is that what you want? Goodness gracious! Now stop fussing and go and get them if you please. Oh, and would you kindly inform Donald that the hedges need cutting. I mean look at them! Honestly, I don't know why I employ that man."

She waved Barker away, who bowed before heading over to the children to enquire if they were in need of anything. He arrived just as Zac downed his remaining half glass of ice-cold mint and kiwi slushy in four big mouthfuls. "AAAAHHH! Brain-freeze!" he grimaced, pinching the bridge of his nose.

"Serves you right," replied Meg. But she was then further mortified when her uncouth brother let out a monstrous, long and incredibly loud...

BUUUUUUUUURRRRRRRRRRRRRRRRRR----P!

"Boy that was good!" announced Zac proudly, as Meg buried her face in her hands. He looked up at the butler who was now blocking his sun, "Ah, excellent timing, Barker. Can I get another one of these please my good man?"

"Forgive me, sir," Barker gruffly informed him, "but once again your grammar has failed you. When conversing, it is *may* I. *May* I have another. Not *can* I."

"Oh, right you are, Barker," replied Zac trying to keep a straight face. "And who'da thunk it? But in that case, *may* I have another... If I can?" He sniggered as he replied and the others tried not to join him, but Barker's deadpan expression told another story. He took the glass and turned to leave. "Oh, actually, Barker," enquired Zac, "for my next drink can you make it... a werewolf?"

A brief period of silence followed between Charlie spitting his drink away in surprise and the reaction of the old man. He stood motionless, staring down at Zac with only his raising eyebrow suggesting he still had a heartbeat. After what seemed like a very long time, he eventually straightened up before stepping aside so the bright sun was once again on Zac's face. "I am afraid I do not know that particular drink, sir. Now if you will excuse me, I have more pressing things to attend to."

They all sat quietly until Barker was out of sight, at which point Charlie opened fire on Zac's behaviour. "What are you doing?! Why did you mention werewolf?"

"I was testing him of course. You know, to see if he knows anything."

Charlie thought for a moment, "Oh I see… and… does he?"

"Hard to tell."

"Zac's right," agreed Jess. "By the look of it, Charlie, your butler either doesn't know anything about your predicament, or he's a very good liar."

"Well he's certainly a toff!" griped Zac. "I'm sure he doesn't like me you know."

Meg rolled her eyes. "Can't imagine why not."

Across the way, Auntie peered out from below her parasol as another cloud passed overhead. "Oh blast the elements," she grumbled. "It looks like we're in for stormy weather, wouldn't you say children." It was more rhetorical than an actual question and before anyone managed a response, she was busy taking off her gown to reveal a bathing suit resembling one found in the Victorian era; one which the children found very comical indeed. "Does my bum look big in this?" she asked to their surprise. "Oh who am I kidding, my bum looks big in everything!"

"You, err, have a wonderful home, Your Ladyship," said Meg.

"Pardon me, dear?" replied the old lady. "Oh please, children - call me Auntie. We keep things pretty informal round here. Right, Charles?"

"Right you are, Auntie," Charlie replied, who then went on to introduce his friends.

"Delighted to meet you all," Auntie announced cheerfully. "Friends of Charles are always welcome here you know." She placed her sunglasses back on and lay down on the lounger letting out a satisfied sigh. "What a perfect way to waste time. Don't you agree, children?"

"Oh yes… um, Auntie," replied Jess. "Just lovely."

Charlie's aunt was truly larger than life and the children all felt immediately comfortable and relaxed in her presence, as if they had known her for years. She carried on talking about nothing in particular while she relaxed and enjoyed her drink. "Oh Charles, I believe cook has arranged some lunch for you all, if you are hungry."

"I sure am!" announced Zac eagerly, unable to contain his delight, or his rumbling stomach.

"Good, then run along children and don't make a mess in there. After all, you never know when the Queen may come visit."

"The Queen, Charlie?" enquired Meg.

"Um, yes," he replied, a little embarrassed. "Auntie's getting a bit old you see. She says that quite a lot."

By this time, Zac had already finished gathering his things and was impatiently hurrying the others along, but to his frustration found they weren't in such a great rush. Charlie picked up his belongings and was ready to go. The girls, however, still had several items to gather, such as sun lotions, lip balms, phones, hats, magazines, beach bags, plus various other 'junk' as Zac put it.

"That's about everything," said Meg some time later. "Now, where's Cookie got to?" They had a quick glance around and called his name, before Charlie giggled and tapped Meg on the shoulder. "Um, Meg..."

He was looking toward his aunt, for it turned out that Cookie had positioned himself at the foot of her lounger and was busy licking coconut sun oil off her feet. Even more surprising was the fact that Auntie was lying down and seemed not to have noticed. The children did their best to contain their laughter and attempted to coax Cookie away, but despite their best efforts he didn't budge an inch - that is - until Zac walked off announcing "lunch time", at which point he took off like greased lightning.

"It was nice to meet you, Auntie," said Meg politely. But the old lady remained horizontal and didn't respond, although she did make some noticeable snoring noises.

Leaving the pool area behind, Charlie and the girls entered the house by way of the conservatory. This metal-framed glass house was at one time full of botanic wonder, with specimen's native of tropical countries thriving in its warmth all year round. The same cannot be said today though, because apart for one or two common plants found in any garden centre, it sat empty and unused. Nearly all of the glass panels were brown and dirty and it was not possible to see clearly through any of them. Beside the footpath, the ground that was once kept moist and dark with nutrients was now dry, dusty and devoid of life. The Conservatory did, however, remain extremely hot under the sun and felt like entering a sauna on passing through.

"Your aunt seems nice, Charlie," said Jess, breaking out a battery–powered fan from her bag. "I'm surprised I've never seen her around the village, or in town."

"Ah yes, well, you see Auntie doesn't tend to venture outside of the grounds much these days. In fact, she hasn't for a while now."

"How long's a while?" asked Meg.

"About seven years."

Letting Charlie go on ahead, Jess and Meg dropped back for some deliberation, but before they uttered a single word they realised they were not alone. The maid, Fräulein Bertrümn, stood spraying mist over some thorny cacti, but her gaze was fixed firmly on the girls. They then noticed a bloody bandage wrapped around her hand, which she promptly removed from sight. Jess tugged on Meg's top, "Come on, Meg, lunch will be getting warm."

9

After changing back into their day clothes the children regrouped in the dining room for a buffet lunch served on gleaming silver platters. Sandwiches were perfectly triangular. Succulent cold meats were plentiful and a multi-tiered cake stand displayed tantalising sugary delights. "Oh rapture!" declared Zac salivating readily. The girls hadn't bothered to dry their hair opting to do it later after a shower, so for now wore it tied back. Meg had brought a hooded top for the moment tied around her waist, while Zac had with him his smaller rucksack. No member of the house staff was present and while they ate there was a noticeable silence, broken only by the ticking of the grandfather clock out in the hall.

"Delightfully delectable," announced Jess.

"Deliciously delovely," agreed Meg.

But Zac, however, wasn't completely satisfied, despite loading his plate so high it formed a pyramid at serious risk of toppling over. "Hey, where are the chips your cook promised us, Charlie?"

"I have no idea, sorry. Anyway, Zac, I don't think you would fit much more on your plate to be honest."

"Oh Zac," sighed Jess helping herself to seconds, "all this wonderful food and you're moaning about chips! Tell us, is there anything you *don't* like to eat?"

"Not really, well, a few things I suppose. There's that stuff that appears on Sunday roasts. What's it called, Meg?"

"What's what called, loser?"

"You know, that stuff I hate. The stuffy-stuff."

"Stuffing?"

"That's it – stuffing. Straight from the devil's bottom that is! Then there's that weird Lettice what smells like feet."

"Think you'll find that's cabbage, you cabbage."

"And those funny apples..."

"Those are onions!"

"Oh right, that explains a lot!"

After clearing their plates, Meg glanced around the room and then under the table. "Um... Zac, where's Cookie?"

"I dunno," he mumbled through a mouthful. "I thought he was with you."

"Err... he went with you from the pool to get lunch, remember?"

"I got inside and he wasn't with me. I figured he had gone back to you."

After another quick look under the table, Meg got up and started calling for Cookie. Charlie then assisted and checked the kitchen before following the girls into the hall. Zac reluctantly shoved as much salmon as he could fit in his mouth and grabbed a chicken leg before joining them. A quick search of the ground floor and their bedrooms revealed no sign of the little dog, so they agreed to split up and check outside. The girls covered the courtyard area while the boys returned to the swimming pool. They saw Auntie - now wide awake, on her sun lounger reading a novel entitled *The Lost Kingdom of Zelda Sayre*, whilst Barker was looking thoroughly miserable performing a pedicure for her.

"Barker, have you seen Cookie?" asked Charlie.

"Which one of your friends is that exactly, Master Charles?"

"The one with - wait, what? No, he's the dog - my friend Megan's little Chihuahua - he seems to have gotten lost."

"Sorry, but the animal is not here, Master Charles. Perhaps it ran off chasing rabbits."

Following a sweep of the surrounding area, Charlie and Zac returned to the main entrance and met the girls. "Any luck?" They asked. They were hoping that Cookie had returned and that the matter was closed. Unfortunately, Meg looked saddened and simply shook her head indicating they hadn't found him. Jess put her arm around her friend to comfort her. "I'm sure he's just off chasing rabbits or something. Right Charlie?"

"Yeah, I'm sure that's it, Jess," he agreed, trying to keep Meg's spirits up. "He's probably having the time of his life running around the fields.

Besides, we know he must be in the grounds at least. No doubt he'll turn up when he gets hungry. You know - I used to run away from home quite often, but I would always come back for dinner."

"A-LOSER!" coughed Zac.

"OK, Jess," Meg replied sadly, doing her best to put on a brave face.

"That's my girl, Meg. Now, Charlie, let's get down to business. Can you show us the basement?"

"Sure, Jess, good idea. But we'll go via the dining room, there are some things you should see on the way."

"It's show time," announced Zac excitedly. The others watched as he grabbed his rucksack and affixed his camera to the left shoulder strap. From here on he would occasionally speak into its microphone, stating present location and other nonsense to the annoyance of everyone else. He carried his phone displaying a digital compass to indicate direction and would have preferred to use his dedicated GPS tracker watch, but it showed no informative map of the area. He followed behind Meg, who followed behind Jess, who followed behind Charlie, who led them past the dining room table and through the swing door into the kitchen. To their bewilderment, he then proceeded not out the back door, but rather to a food cupboard in one corner of the room.

"We stocking up on supplies?" asked Zac.

"Hardly," frowned Charlie.

The kitchen was decorated mostly in white with the exception of the black granite work surfaces. A large range cooker equipped with its own chimney sat against the rear wall and had enough cooking estate for about a dozen pots or pans. In the centre of the room was a long, rectangular island large enough for preparing courses for up to twenty visitors, with various pots, pans, woks, griddles and utensils dangling above it from the ceiling. On either side of the swing door were two sizeable oak dressers each fully loaded with fine china and silver dinnerware. While above the door itself were a number of miniature bells, which Charlie informed them were the ones that rang should you utilise the woven pulls in the bedrooms.

Charlie opened the pantry door and entered signalling the others to join him. Once inside, they found it spacious enough for all of them to squeeze into at once, only without an inch to spare. They saw on either side of them were tall shelves stacked with foodstuff of various size and origin, about enough to feed the household for several months. Charlie asked Zac at the rear to close the door behind them, plunging them into total darkness.

"It's a bit early for a midnight snack, Charlie," joked Jess. There followed a rustling sound and something was knocked over.

"Please tell me you're not eating, Zac?" said Meg.

"…Nuh-uh," came a garbled reply.

"Oh my God you are *unbelievable!*"

"Just don't cut the cheese, Zac, whatever you do!" begged Jess.

"Well now you mention it," he replied. "Here, pull my finger…"

"DON'T YOU DARE!" shouted the others.

"…Eww, I can feel something damp," said Jess, moments later.

"That's my mouth," replied Charlie.

"Ouch! Someone just stood on my foot!" complained Meg.

"And who keeps pushing me?" griped Zac.

"Charlie!" grumbled Jess, "it's very cosy in here but just what on earth is going on?"

Charlie turned on a little pocket torch to see the girl's riled faces staring back at him. He then shone the light over their shoulders to reveal Zac, taking a large bite of pie. "Mwhat?" he mumbled.

"That's it!" declared Meg. "Charlie, get me the hell out of here, NOW!"

Charlie immediately set to work feeling for something on the shiny rear wall of the pantry. Shortly after he found what he was looking for. "Ah, here it is…" This was followed by the sound of a latch clicking, then a section of the wall opened away from them revealing a doorway.

"Well debug my dongle," exclaimed Zac. "A secret passage!"

The little door no taller than five feet had opened to reveal a brick-lined passageway. The girls joined Charlie to peer into it.

"What exactly is this, Charlie?" Jess asked.

"It's a sort of priest hole, I guess you could say."

"Oh, I have read about these," said Meg keenly. "A priest hole is a hiding place created to conceal, well - priests, during the sixteenth century, when Catholics were persecuted under Queen Elizabeth I. Back then a priest could be imprisoned, tortured or even killed just for being Catholic! So secret hiding places were cleverly disguised within a house to baffle search-parties. Sometimes you get double or even triple hides, so that if anyone opened the first section they would still not be able to see someone hiding in the second or third compartment. And it wasn't just for priests either. Did you know that gunpowder plot sympathisers had a secret hide in their house, not far from here in Ashby Saint Ledgers?"

"Perfectly put, Meg," Charlie replied impressed with her knowledge of the subject. "Only the ones in this house were used more in the first and second world wars. You see, Auntie, her parents and her grandparents all worked for the government, but doing what exactly I'm not sure."

"That really is a thrilling history lesson," said Zac without much interest, "but where exactly does it go?" His attention and head remained in the pantry - deep in a shelf where he had discovered some jars of caviar. He brazenly placed one in his backpack, but it just as quickly came back out when Meg saw what he was up to. "Hey!" he protested.

"UGH! For five minutes can you stop thinking with your stomach? For just five..." She stopped talking because outside the sound of the kitchen swing door indicated that someone had entered the room. Everyone froze and stood in silence. They heard footsteps, then the sound of bags being placed down.

"It's probably cook", whispered Charlie. "She goes grocery shopping on a Saturday. Quick, come this way." He held the little door open while the others shuffled through, allowing it to close gently just as the pantry front door opened. Mrs Blackwell then bounded in and turned on the light, oblivious that anyone had been there just moments before.

10

With the door closed behind them, Charlie's guests shared a tingling of excitement. They saw a long, sparsely lit corridor constructed of raw building materials, rough and unfinished, yet the air was surprisingly cool and a breeze helped prevent anyone feel claustrophobic. "This way guys," said Charlie softly. The route led away in a straight line alongside the kitchen and they were required to walk single-file due to the proximity of the walls. After a few paces it turned ninety degrees and continued for another twenty or so paces. Arriving at the tunnel end was a door in the form of a large, flat wooden board - more square shaped than rectangular - to which Charlie pressed his ear. Zac was at the back of the line and bumped into Meg when they stopped.

"Oomph, watch it clumsy!" grumbled Meg.

"Sorry," replied Zac, "but it is a little hard to see anything behind your massive derriere! Why have we stopped anyway?"

"We've stopped, chump, because it looks like Charlie is listening to a door. Oh, and I'm surprised your massive head hasn't got stuck between the walls!"

"Who has a massive head?"

"You have, fool!"

"I know you've got a massive head but what have I?"

"A massive head."

"I know you've got a massive head but what have I?"

"A massive head!"

"I know you've got a massive head but what have I?!"

"A massive head!!"

"I know you've got a massive head but what have I?!!"

"A massive HEAD!!!"

"I know you've…"

"*ENOUGH!*" shrieked Jess, unable to take any more. "Guys, you know I love you, right? But will both of you please shut the hell up!!"

After their telling off the twins managed to keep their comments to themselves, resorting to nudging and pushing one another while they waited. Ahead, Charlie was now standing on a step and had pulled open a small flap located near the top of the door, where he stood peering through a little hole.

After a few moments of precision peeping, he informed the others that the coast was clear and jumped down. Using both hands he pressed against the wooden board on one edge and opened it just enough to further inspect the room. The amount of light immediately increased, before Charlie opened it fully and stepped through.

There was a drop down of around two feet and one-by-one the others filed into the room looking around trying to gather their bearings. They immediately recognised the room as a library, because against each of the four walls were tall book shelves reaching some fifteen feet in height. In front of each section a movable ladder attached to a gold railing permitted access to the upper shelves and Zac couldn't resist pushing one along and catching a ride on it. The room was carpeted with brown and red squares, with two exits by means of doors facing one another at opposite ends of the room. Like the walls, each door was painted in green with dark purple borders and they figured that one led back to the hall, but were not entirely sure about the other. In the centre of the room was a large armchair accompanied by a coffee table and reading lamp; just perfect for settling down for a literary binge thought Meg. On the table sat a chess set with pieces carved from the blackest of ebony and the whitest of ivory, acquired decades before such a thing was frowned upon.

The doorway that had click-closed behind them was actually an impressive oil painting of George V, the once King of the United Kingdom, the British Dominions and Emperor of India. Jess gazed up at the painting, wondering if George would offer a hint to the secret tunnel concealed behind. *'What else are you hiding?'* she thought. She then tried to open it once again, but found it wouldn't budge. "Sweet, Charlie, but tell me, do your staff know about it?"

"No they don't, apart from Barker who may know, but definitely not the others."

"And your aunt, does she know?"

"Yes, she does for sure. In fact, she showed me this one and the others some years ago."

"There are others?" asked Meg.

"Yes a few more, plus numerous peeping holes and various listening vents."

"Listening vents?"

"Yes, to listen in on conversations."

"Dur," ribbed Zac.

"Well I hope no one is listening to us now, Charlie," replied Jess.

"And I certainly hope there won't be anyone *peeping* into my bedroom!" added Meg.

"Don't worry," Charlie assured them. "There won't be."

"So what exactly did your aunt do during the war, Charlie?" enquired Jess.

"Auntie only ever says she worked for the government, but I like to think she may have been a spy or something."

Charlie was about to further speculate on his aunt's colourful past when Zac called out to them. He had glided along on a ladder to the far end of the room where something of interest caught his eye. "Hey Charlie, what's up with this door?" The others joined him and it was only when asked by Zac to open it that the girls realised what he was talking about. They tried to grab hold of the handle, but discovered there wasn't physically one there. They then felt for the door edge and hinges, but to their surprise found the entire thing was merely painted on the wall. "What kind of door is that?"

"Charlie?" questioned the girls, equally perplexed.

"Ah yes, glad you asked. You see, it was desirable back in the seventeenth century to have symmetry, which meant things had to appear in perfect balance and harmony. And this is an excellent example of such a thing. You see, this door faces the real door and looks symmetrical. It's all about appearance. Fascinating isn't it?"

"Yeah, fascinating," said Zac, but lacking enthusiasm.

"Ah but there's more," continued Charlie. "Look here..." Their host directed their attention toward a section of bare wall perpendicular to the faux door. He pushed the ladder, with Zac still attached, along until he could access a brown carpet square in the corner. He stepped on it and a click was followed by a section of the wall swinging out toward them about one inch. A part of the wall painted in the same style and adorned with the same wooden dado rail was effortlessly pulled open, revealing a second hidden passageway.

"This one's a servant's passage," Charlie informed them. "It leads to the courtyard if you go right and the main hall on the left. Don't think it's ever been used in my lifetime though. Care to try it?" He gestured his friends to enter and one-by-one they funnelled inside taking the route to the left. This passageway had several small glass blocks built into the wall just above ground level, which let in a generous amount of sunlight and warmth. After just a few dozen feet they arrived first into the rear of a coat cupboard and then back into the grand entrance hall. Without stopping to catch a breath, Charlie led them across to the sitting room where they were immediately drawn to the outrageously eccentric, mustard-yellow leather sofa and matching arm chairs in the rooms centre.

"Boy, rich people sure have odd taste," said Zac.

"For once I agree with you," replied Meg. She thought she would try out the sofa for comfort, but as she sat down found it made an awkward, squeaky farting-like noise that seemed to go on for ages. "It was the chair! Honest!"

Opposite the sofa stood a formidable stone fireplace, the tallest and widest they had ever seen. Its thick mantle had been stained black in its centre after years of use and several equally black plates depicting sailing ships were displayed on top. Against both side walls were shelves stacked full of books and artefacts, plus some disturbingly eerie stuffed animals, the variety of which was not immediately obvious. An enormous potted palm plant sat either side of the fireplace and on the floor in front was a large, furry striped rug.

While the visitors nosed around the room, Charlie softly closed the door before positioning himself in front of the fireplace. Behind him on the wall was a gold-framed painting of the Midsummer house which the girls admired. They also noticed that this painting had replaced another at some point, as the blackened outline of the previous one remained.

"What's it to be this time, Charlie?" queried Zac, who was busy inspecting the rug with a magnifying glass. "Revolving bookcase I'll wager."

"How exiting!" said Meg. "Is it, Charlie? Tell us, per-lease."

"Good guess," Charlie replied, "but... well you had better stand clear of the rug, Zac. This one can be a bit... dangerous!" He reached down toward the side of the fireplace where some fire-tending utensils were held in a metal cage. Placing his hand on the thinnest loop poker behind all the others, he pulled it first sideways, then upwards towards him. There followed a mechanical clunking sound like some mechanism had been activated. Then, without warning, the area once occupied by the rug simply disappeared. It was a trapdoor and the sudden appearance of a large opening in the floor left Jess and the twins quite speechless.

"Well shiver my timbers!" said Zac amazed. They gathered around the void and immediately noticed they could hear flowing water from its depths. Zac rummaged in his backpack and retrieved a torch which he shone into the darkness, illuminating something that resembled a well, only much larger, complete with a body of water at its base. Beside them, a small section of the fireplace floor directly beneath the mantle had moved backward, revealing a ladder. It offered access into the chamber below and Charlie positioned himself to make use of it.

"You're not going down there are you, Charlie?" asked Meg.

"Of course. It's quite safe." He began descending the stairs and Zac hurried over to join him. "Trust me."

"Trust him he says!" uttered Meg. Being in confined spaces was one of her worst fears and she suddenly felt far outside of her comfort zone.

"Come on, Meg," said Jess. "You'll be fine. I'll go after you. Besides, we can always come back up."

Charlie and Zac had already reached the bottom and were calling them down so tentatively, but far too enthralled to decline, they followed. The girls arrived safely at the bottom and were met by the boys who made sure they were both alright. Looking around, they found themselves standing on a narrow, metal grill-like platform attached to a section of rock wall by heavy-duty bolts. They quickly realised that it was no typical well at all, but rather a flowing body of water.

There was sufficient luminance provided by Zac's torch to see the cylindrical construction of the chamber was around fifteen feet in diameter, by roughly twenty feet deep. Above, they could see the striped rug still attached to the volatile section of floor hanging down on its hinges. Below, the water flowing past did so at a calm yet steady pace. It seemed to follow an east-to-west route along a blue brickwork tunnel itself no taller than any of them. Alongside the flow of water was a thin walkway wide enough for a single person to traverse, similar to a canal tow path only considerably narrower.

Zac shone the torch along the tunnel in both directions where its beam was swallowed by the blackness. As he did so he leant recklessly over the guard rail. "Major bummer for anyone falling in," he remarked. Meg crept up behind and gave him a sharp shove for fun. He then returned the gesture by grabbing her and threatened to push her over the side. They abruptly stopped messing about when Charlie pulled a lever attached to the wall and a loud mechanical noise startled them. This was followed by the trapdoor suspended above, slowly jerking back to its original position, sealing them in.

"So much for going back up!" uttered Meg.

"Tell me we don't have to swim for it, Charles?" enquired Jess anxiously.

"Not unless you want to," he teased. "Alternatively, we can use the exit here..." He stepped aside to reveal a steel doorframe cut into the rock. It led into a damp, but surprisingly spacious tunnel lit by fizzing electric lights attached to the walls roughly every ten of their footsteps. The noise of flowing water fell silent after just a short distance, at which point they found there was no noise to hear at all. They yelled just to hear the echo as they skipped along until they arrived at a wooden door. Charlie pushed it open and they entered into what appeared to be a simple old garden shed, which was receiving just enough natural light for them to put away the torch.

Being the first one in, Charlie received a face full of cobwebs and hopped around frantically pulling them off, much to the amusement of the others. "Thanks, Charlie," laughed Zac heartily. "I've got it all on camera."

Behind them, the door they had passed through appeared as the rear wall of the shed and was covered by a selection of rusty hand tools suspended from hooks. A single small window let in some daylight but offered no view, as something growing on the outside had completely obstructed it. There were shelves containing more rusty tools and a potting bench with dusty soil spilled out on top, but nothing of real interest.

After spitting out the remains of cobwebs and the content contained therein, Charlie attempted to open the front door, finding he had to put his shoulder against it to get it to budge. It turned out that the entire shed had been engulfed by ivy, which had been left to grow wild for decades and could now be the only thing holding the old building up.

One-by-one they pushed through the emerald barrier and continued their whistle-stop-tour. They followed Charlie single-file along a grassy trail between the pendulous branches of weeping willow trees, until they stepped out into the open and met the footpath that encircled the house.

"AAAAAAA-CHOO!", sneezed Zac loudly, four times.

"Bless you!" said the others.

They all spent a moment picking off sticky beads, blowing away greenfly and scratching parts of themselves that had been stung along the way. Meg was the first to finish and look up to see the amazing sight ahead of them. "That must be where the water leads to."

"Whoa!" said Jess and Zac, on seeing the sight for themselves.

The scene was glorious. It was the lake located behind the house and it looked like they had stepped into a nature reserve for it was teeming with wildlife. The dead-calm water appeared like glass, creating a mesmerising mirror image of its surroundings in an alluring upside down world. There were swans, amongst other birds, in abundance and Meg excitedly pointed out and named as many types as she could like a child in a toyshop. They marvelled at the great body of water and Charlie pointed out a herd of deer at its far side, at least thirty in number, drinking at the sparkling waters edge.

Closer to where the children stood, a course of water flowed past from an outlet, presumably from the underground system they had just came from. It followed a concrete channel but the water within was presently a mere trickle and slow moving. It joined the lake some distance away where it fell a few feet creating a miniature waterfall. Behind them, a dense wall of trees hid the great house from view and they were to follow the footpath north to resume their tour. Meg yearned to stay for a while but the others insisted they carried on. They were after all, here on business.

It was a short and pleasant walk up to and around the north side of the house, where its corner section eventually emerged from the trees indicating the end of the woodland. The girls carried on and chatted happily, while Zac and Charlie lagged behind arguing over the scale of the building. They stared up toward its tall chimney stacks trying to gauge the height: one hundred feet Zac estimated. The path cornered to the right taking them alongside the northernmost side of the house - the only side shaded from the sun throughout the day. As a result, there was a green-tint to the stonework and a noticeable reduction in plant life. Shortly after they turned right again and if they continued this way they would arrive back at the courtyard. However, they didn't need to travel that far because after just a dozen or so feet they arrived at their destination: the basement loading doors.

11

Back in full sun once again, Zac broke out some bottles of water from his backpack and shared them around. The doors that permitted entry to the basement were not like doors found on any house, as they lay almost horizontally and opened upward, allowing heavy goods to simply slide down a chute into the underground room.

"This where you saw the werewolf go, Charlie?" asked Jess.

He looked a little nervous and gulped before answering. "Yes, but it's always locked, I don't know how..."

Before he had a chance to finish, Zac yanked open one of the doors, "Well it's certainly not locked now, Charlie."

"Hey look here," said Meg excitedly. She found a padlock lying nearby and picked it up to show the others.

"The shackle's been cut clean through!" observed Zac.

"Looks like our uninvited guest was determined to get in here then," said Meg. "What do you think, Jess?"

Jess was inspecting the path where she noticed dried muddy footprints leading from the gardens to the loading doors. There were multiple sets in different sizes and it appeared that the path had been used as a regular route to and from the basement. She joined the others to discuss who would go below first, but after a discussion that showed no sign of providing an outcome, they agreed that a round of rock-paper-scissors would be the fairest way to decide - the result of which was that Zac would lead the way. Charlie and Meg pulled open the second door and they all peered down into the darkness. There was no stairway or ladder to reach the bottom, after all this was a loading bay designed for dropping down heavy supplies, not people, and the only way down was to use the slope.

Zac removed his rucksack and precariously stepped up to the edge. The sun felt hot on his back and he cast a long shadow down the void where it merged with the blackness. "Watch and learn people."

"Break a leg, bruv," said Meg seemingly for luck.

"Thanks, sis."

"No seriously, break a leg!"

"Umm…" said Charlie, slightly more concerned for his friend's welfare, "maybe it would be sensible to slide down on your bottom." But Zac being Zac merely laughed at this suggestion, stating the girls could do that if they chose and with common sense firmly dismissed, he boldly began his descent down the incline. He proceeded slowly at first balancing like a tightrope walker and taking baby steps, but almost immediately started accelerating uncontrollably. He then made rapid shuffling steps to try to control his descent and ended up slipping before slamming down on his back. The others watched helpless as he slid away into the darkness.

"Zac, are you alright?" Jess called down from above. A cloud of dust rose up toward them and although they could hear Zac coughing and groaning, they could see nothing.

"ZAC, ARE YOU ALIVE?" hollered Meg.

"I think so," they heard him reply quietly.

"Ah nuts!" exclaimed Meg, disappointed.

"ZAC, ARE YOU OK?" called Jess.

"Yes, but I think I pulled a muscle."

"Whereabouts?"

"On the slope just now."

"I meant whereabouts on your body!"

"Oh right, pretty much all of them I think. Slide down on your bums if I were you."

"What was that, Zac?" asked Meg smiling at the others. "Slide down on our bums like we told you to?"

Zac had landed at the bottom with only one or two splinters and his pride to trouble him. He looked into the darkness and when his pupils had adjusted, saw he was sitting on top of a small surplus of coal which had remained at the bottom of the slope in a low fenced area.

"See if you can find a light switch," yelled Charlie. "It should be by the staircase on the wall."

"Drop my torch down will you," replied Zac. "I can't see a thing." Meg immediately picked up Zac's torch and let it slide down the slope. "Oomph!" they heard him moan from below. "Thanks for the warning!" He clicked on the torch and patted himself down. He then climbed up and out of the holding area. "Dang it!" they heard him say shortly after.

"What is it, Zac?"

"Torch just died!"

"You want Charlie's?"

"Nar, I'll be alright. Almost there now..."

Sometime later and following noises similar to a metal bucket being kicked and stuff being knocked over, Zac found the light switch and flicked it on. "Got it!" Charlie helped the girls over the edge of the slope and watched them descend gracefully and without incident. He then sent down Zac's rucksack and followed after, but somehow managed to spin around and end up on his belly. After crashing down into the pen he gingerly crawled to the edge and climbed over the fence. His glasses had been bent and blackened by his tumble, so Meg helped him to straighten them and gave them a wipe. When he put them on again the others laughed, as he had two circles of clean skin where his glasses had been, while the rest of his front half was covered in black dust. He blinked and focused on his friends noticing that Zac had also received a generous black coating, as had the girl's bottoms and palms. Around them the dust was beginning to settle and visibility slowly improved as it did.

"Everyone alright?" Zac asked between coughs.

"Fine," replied Jess. "You alright, Zac?"

"Yeah, although I think I broke my bum crack!"

"You wanna be careful – that's where your brain is isn't it?"

"Very funny!"

"Just kidding. You OK, Meg?"

"I'm good, which is more than can be said about my jumper! Oh well, are you OK, Charlie?"

"Yes, still in one piece - I think." He stopped patting himself down and gazed around. "Auntie wouldn't approve of me being down here you know."

"Because of the accident you had, Charlie?" asked Jess. "You know, when you were little."

"That's right. I was eight years old and playing at the top of the slope there. I managed to slip down and break my clavic... my collar bone - and knock myself unconscious. Auntie and the others were looking for me for hours and it was dark before they found me. The police and fire brigade were even called in! They eventually found me clutching my arm and shivering from the cold. I was missing for eight hours. After that I was banned from coming down here and the doors were locked. So please, can we keep the noise down as not to alert anyone that we're here."

"Pah, loose the conformity will you, Charlie!" replied Zac unconcerned. "Do I need to remind you we're on a mission of the highest importance here? Surely we've got diplomatic immunity. Now who's with me?" He raised his hand waiting for a show of support, but found none. "Don't leave me hanging people!"

"Come on, guys," said Meg ignoring him. "Let's check the place out – *quietly*."

Looking around they saw the basement contained several rows of wine racks fully stocked with dusty bottles. A rudimentary wooden stairway led up to the ground floor in one corner, with the light switch and archaic fuse board mounted on the wall beside it. Barely adequate lighting was provided by a number of hanging bulbs topped with little mounds of dust, but some were not working and those that were failed to illuminate into the far corners of the room. They saw a network of pipes and cables of various size, colour and age affixed to the walls and ceiling, on route to and from some other parts of the house. It felt like a creepy kind of place and was cool compared to the outside. Thankfully though, the sun shining down through the loading doors provided an increased level of light and warmth than one could usually expect, which helped lighten the mood.

"Glass of bubbly, anyone?" asked Zac, who had grabbed a bottle from one of the racks. He blew dust from its label and attempted to read its description. "Dom Champ, err something, seventy-six. Wow! It must be well off by now!"

Meg shook her head and snatched the bottle from him. "Give it here you illiterate. It's champagne - probably vintage and more than likely very expensive."

"I knew that. And don't call me illiterate. I read books."

"Err, for your information - comic books are *not* literature."

"Sure they are. Anyway they're graphic novels."

"Whatever. Like I was trying to explain - the older the Champagne the more expensive it is. Isn't that right, Charl..." But Charlie wasn't paying much attention as he had joined Jess beside a white wash basin at the far end of the room. He called the twins over.

"Does anyone have a torch that works?" asked Jess. Charlie reached into his pocket and offered up his small LED key-ring in the form of a LEGO character, but it failed to impress. "Got anything bigger?"

"Allow me..." announced Zac, who put his finger on Charlie's chest and pushed him aside. He then took off his rucksack and after some light rummaging pulled out a huge torch. A torch so big and powerful it could land an aeroplane on a foggy night. "Will this do?"

"How many torches have you got?" asked Meg incredulously.

"Aha, that's more like it!" said Jess. "Now, look here..."

She switched on the torch causing everyone to squint and turn away while their eyes adjusted to its brilliance. After a brief moment of total blindness all round, she directed the light toward the bottom of the loading bay. "See there: footprints. Dried muddy footprints."

With the improved luminance it was easy to see evidence of a busy walkway. One that continued from the coal store straight to their present location beside the sink, with only one or two detours. They backtracked following a branch off the main trail and arrived at one of the wine racks where they inspected some of the bottles. It was clear that some had been disturbed recently, as there were patches around the labels where they had been handled and the dust removed. Furthermore, there were several bottles missing from some of the slots in this section.

"Charlie," asked Jess, "could these footprints and missing bottles be the result of your aunt, or one of the staff?"

"Highly unlikely I would say. No one ever comes down here and if they did, they would use the entrance door from the house, not risk breaking their neck on the loading bay. Besides, these champagnes are for special occasions when Auntie hosts her formal parties, or at least they were a long time ago. But she hasn't had any of those for several years."

Meg took a step to one side and felt a crunch under foot. Looking down she saw the remains of a broken bottle. "Guys, look here." The others joined her and they all noticed something else too. "Is that… blood?"

Using tweezers, Zac carefully picked up a fragment of glass and held it into the light. "Sure looks like it."

"There's more here," confirmed Charlie. "A number of spots leading toward the stairs. I guess someone must have cut themselves."

They all returned to the main footprint trail and followed it back to the wash basin by the wall. "And what do you think of this?" Jess asked, shining the light on the prints that began and ended at the sink. "Come on, guys. There are no bad ideas."

"Werewolves like to wash?" answered Zac enthusiastically. You could have heard a pin drop in the silence that followed and everyone looked toward him, unable to tell if he was joking or just being plain stupid. "What?" he asked.

Meg looked at him shaking her head. "That's the worst idea ever. Even by your standards."

"Thank you, Meg," said Jess in agreement. "OK, forget the ideas, let's consider the facts. Charlie witnessed our wolf man entering through the doors up there and we have muddy footprints going to and from the sink here, but interestingly none to the stairs. So, I'd say there is perhaps more to this area than meets the eye. Wouldn't you agree?"

"You thinking secret passage?" asked Meg.

"Exactly. So, Charlie, what can you tell us about the sink?" Jess had asked with the assumption that he somehow knew what she was talking about, but he replied negatively.

"Sorry, Jess. I don't know of any passage or tunnel down here, but I do subscribe to your theory."

Undeterred, Jess shone the light onto the wall and the others set to work looking for a trigger. They pushed, pulled and tapped bricks, picked up bottles, even jumped up and down on the floor. The deep, square sink itself had two silver taps fixed to its top and its basin had turned darker over the years as it succumbed to several layers of grime. On further inspection, Meg noticed that one of the taps was stained red. "Hey, look here. More blood! Looks like someone's been using the sink."

"Big deal," replied Zac. "So someone used the sink to wash up after cutting themselves. What's you point?"

"My point, is that the sink is still covered in dust n' crap. There's clearly been no water running through it."

They all considered the possible explanation for this and a moment later looked at one another, as if they had reached the same conclusion simultaneously. Jess raised her hand and reached for the tap as the others looked on. She grasped it firmly, held her breath and turned it. Nothing happened, apart from it making a squeaking sound as it rotated and a hiss as it expelled some air. She continued to turn it until it wouldn't turn anymore. Still nothing happened. "Try the other way," suggested Meg, still confident that something would happen.

Jess turned the tap clockwise this time several rotations until there came a loud 'click', at which point the thrill of adventure made them all beam with excitement. With great anticipation they stepped back and waited for the doorway to reveal itself. In what form would it take? Was a trap about to spring? Would the very floor they stood on fall away like in the sitting room? Alas, nothing happened and everyone's shoulders dropped as the adrenaline within them dwindled.

"Maybe not then," said Jess, breaking the silence that followed.

Meg's face showed her disappointment, "I don't understand. How could it not... you know... I was sure it would..."

"Hey, never mind," encouraged Charlie. "It was a great idea, Meg. Besides, we can always..." It was at this moment that he stepped up to the sink, turned, crossed his arms and leant backwards against it. However, instead of having his weight supported he found himself falling backward. Jess instinctively lunged for his flailing arms throwing the torch aside, but ended up being pulled back with him. Together they disappeared into a black hole in the wall.

Zac retrieved the torch and restored visibility. It appeared that the sink and the section of brick wall it was attached to had moved backward, resulting in Charlie tumbling into the void accompanied by Jess, who had landed on top of him. They lay looking into each other's eyes within touching distance of noses. "Thanks for breaking my fall, Charlie," said Jess.

"My pleasure!" he groaned painfully.

The twins helped them up and couldn't help but snigger at their friend's circumstance. "Come on, love birds!" joked Meg.

"Awkward!" teased Zac.

"Oh grow up!" replied Jess, who was now on her feet patting herself down, but failing to hide her embarrassment. Charlie on the other hand, was looking rather delighted with the whole experience and Meg had to snap her fingers in front of his face to bring him around. Zac shone the torch on the opening to expose a jagged brickwork archway and they saw the section of wall, with the sink still attached, had slid backward several feet revealing an unlit tunnel. The ground below was dusty, almost sandy, and showed an unmistakable trail of foot traffic, one which continued on into the darkness. The children rejoiced at the thrill of finding the secret door and adrenaline once again pumped through their veins.

"Get in!" exclaimed Zac, snapping his fingers together.

"That's what I'm talking about," said Meg, high-fiving Jess.

"That's my girl!" replied Jess.

"SPLENDID!" shouted Charlie, super-excitedly and jumping for joy, which resulted in some odd looks from the others.

"Ahem," resumed Jess more calmly. "Shall we?"

One-by-one they crouched and passed under the opening. Zac shone the big torch along the passage which produced a brilliant beam of light for some distance, but failed to find an end. It was completely black and completely silent. The passageway had been roughly hewed from the sandstone beneath the house and was slightly, although unevenly, arched at the top; it was as if the whole thing had been tunnelled by a giant mole. Jess noticed Meg was looking a little pale and squeezed her hand. "You can do this," she told her.

Attached to the tunnel wall they saw a metal wheel and found that turning it just a little, effortlessly moved the false wall forwards and backwards. "That might come in handy if we need to get back out!" noted Charlie. And it was a good thing they noticed it too - because stepping a short distance into the tunnel triggered a foot-plate buried beneath the dirt. With a whir it sent the wheel spinning and saw the door quickly return to its closed position. There was a thud as it shut leaving them gazing into the unknown reliant solely on the torch light. Standing confined in the dark they were all a little apprehensive about continuing, but courage, determination and the company of one another drove them onward. Plus, they now shared an appetite for adventure and craved another helping.

Before continuing, Jess called them together for a huddle, "Listen guys, we're going to buddy-up for safety, you know like scuba divers do. Zac, I suggest you go first with your torch with Meg behind you. Charlie and I will follow with the little torch. Keep your buddy close by at all times. That OK, peeps?"

"Why do I have to be *her* buddy?" complained Zac.

"Because I said so. Any more questions?"

"Should we hold hands?" asked Charlie. "You know for..." The others looked at him disgusted, like he was trying to arrange a double date or something. "Or... not." While they huddled it was possible to see one another's faces, but as they broke up and formed the agreed rank they could see only the tunnel ahead. At the rear, Jess and Charlie noticed that it was so dark, it was not possible to see a hand placed in front of ones face. As a result, even walking had to be done carefully to avoid twisting an ankle on a hidden rock or crevice, or banging heads on a low section of ceiling.

The route they followed was level for some distance but after a while became a gradient taking them upward. Progress was slow as four had to make do with one decent light, with those behind more prone to stumbles. This also meant that regular calls to the torch bearer to 'hold up' were required. Only the sound of light conversation, footsteps and their breathing broke the silence and the irregular face of the tunnel walls seemed to absorb all noise, creating an unpleasant sense of confinement. After several minutes of walking with little sensation of distance travelled, worry and uncertainty began to creep into everyone's minds.

"Anyone got a pen and paper?" enquired Zac softly.

"I have my notebook," replied Meg. "Why d'you ask?"

"So I can leave a note for the CSI team – the ones that discover our skeletons fifty years from now!"

Despite the sweltering June heat above ground, down here it felt more like an afternoon in January and the gang suddenly felt considerably underdressed. "You think there's any rats in here?" asked Jess nervously.

"Bats?" replied a voice from ahead.

"No, RATS."

"RATS?"

"Yes rats. It's just that, well they give me the willies do rats."

"RATS OR BATS?"

"Oh forget it!"

More minutes passed and common sense was now shouting out telling them to turn back, but the trail of footprints continued onward and so must they if they were going to solve this mystery. Their spirits received a welcome boost, however, on the discovery of several fresh cigar and cigarette butts that had been discarded along the passage. With renewed incentive they agreed to carry on, maintaining a steady pace up until Charlie, who was walking at the rear with one hand on Jess' shoulder, suddenly walked into the back of her. She had stopped, as had Meg in front of her. "The end. We've reached the end!" called out Zac from the front line.

At last they had arrived at the end of the tunnel where huge relief was shared all round. Jess and Charlie huddled up behind the twins and looked over their shoulders to see what form the exit would take. They saw a metal ladder that led up, entwined with a giant root system which had squeezed it out of shape. Zac momentarily turned off the torch and could just make out a small ingress of light about twenty feet up. There was no other way to go so one after another they began ascending. It was a difficult climb, but thankfully not too high and in no time at all they were queuing while Zac attempted to find an exit. "What can you see?" asked Charlie from below.

"It's a door," Zac informed them. "It's made of wood. Solid oak wood."

"Can you open it?"

"There's a keyhole, I can see light shining through. Very interesting design, probably a sophisticated locking mechanism of the upmost complexity and..."

"JUST OPEN IT!" shouted Meg impatiently.

It occurred to Zac that this wasn't a bad idea, so he placed his hand flat against the panel and prepared to push. He slowly applied pressure and was relieved to discover the wooden door opened a little without much resistance, letting brilliant golden sunlight illuminate its border. He pushed a little more and squinted from the brightness. He then switched off the torch and placed his head into the gap to check the coast was clear. Once satisfied he pushed the door open and stepped out into the light.

12

Jess, Meg and Charlie followed Zac through the door into the daylight, finding they too had to shade their eyes until they had adjusted to the brightness. The immediate rise in temperature greeted them like a warm hug, charging their mind, body and spirit as if they were solar powered. They stepped out into woodland populated by giant, ancient oaks, where the green hues were as welcome on their eyes as the unspoilt air in their lungs. They had travelled around five-hundred metres and were now just a stones-throw from the estate boundary wall at its north-east side. Looking behind, it appeared they had exited through a concealed doorway which had been cut into the trunk of a giant tree. It was so well concealed in fact, that only the trail of trampled down grass leading to and from it gave any indication of its existence.

"Whoa, cool," announced Meg. "Look there, you can see the house!" Down the hill between the trees it was just possible to make out Midsummer Hall, which appeared like a miniature dolls house in the distance. Zac immediately pulled out his super-binoculars and reported that the maid and cook were having an argument in the courtyard. He informed the others who looked and saw for themselves. Each of them attempted to lip-read but failed to make out a single word. They did, however, have better success reading the body language, agreeing it was at least a very heated conversation. Jess looked last and witnessed Barker the butler appear. She watched him briskly put a stop to whatever it was the staff were disputing, before sending them back into the house. He then remained outside where he lit up a self-rolled cigarette behind a hedge.

"Did you know old man Barker smoked, Charlie?" she asked.

"He most certainly does not," Charlie replied adamantly. "I'd hang my hat on the fact. Disgusting habit!"

"What hat?" enquired Zac looking confused.

Jess handed Charlie the binoculars and he proceeded to take another look. While he did so, she held out her hand and received from Meg, one of the cigarette butts discovered in the passageway.

"Well I'll be darned," observed Charlie. He lowered the glasses and received a bigger shock, on seeing Jess holding the discarded filter toward him.

"Coincidence, Charlie?"

"Now hold on just a minute, surely you're not suggesting that Barker could, that he would..."

Zac's face lit up, "THE BUTLER DID IT? I knew there was something fishy about that old geezer. I knew it!"

"Why that's absurd," objected Charlie. "It's unfounded, it's, it's..."

"Evidence," said Meg matter-of-factly. She then took back the filter and returned it to a small plastic specimen bag.

"No one's suggesting anything, Charlie," replied Jess. "But it's food for thought, that's for sure." While she spoke a heavy, dark cloud arrived overhead and the level of light reduced noticeably. A moment later there followed a rumble of distant thunder which seemed to linger in the sky. She turned to the twins and glimpsed something over their shoulders. "Look, over there. A building."

"It's Donald McGee's cabin," confirmed Charlie. "The groundskeeper."

The cabin was just visible in the distance and a well-trodden path had been created through ferns from their present location to and from it. Looking down, they noted three pairs of dried footprints on the ground below: one was about a size ten and of a hiking-boot design; the second was slightly smaller and wider, and showed the style of a flat-soled shoe with heel; and the third set evidently belonged to a very large and heavy person which the gang estimated to be a size seventeen boot at least. These particular prints were square-toed and sunk deep into the ground in parts, much deeper than the other pairs.

Zac took a moment to record this information using his camera, with his phone placed alongside each print to indicate scale. It was at that moment they noticed the unmistakable sound of a branch snapping, in the bushes just a dozen or so feet from them. This was followed by rustling, that had to be made by something significantly larger than any small mammal. As a group they glanced at one another, before slowly making their way towards the bushes. Charlie broke off a branch from a nearby tree ready to use as a weapon. Zac grasped his torch, Meg picked up a rock and Jess made knife hands. When they were close enough whatever was hiding within made itself seen.

The thing jumped out shrieking like a stuck pig. It was human-like in appearance and of the same height as the children, but it had the hairy face of a wolf. And that wasn't all, because there were two of them. There were two werewolves. "RAAAAHHHH! ROAR! SNARL!" they cried.

The terrible creatures bounded forward while the children stumbled back screaming and shouting. They had been caught unawares and had little chance to escape. But wait, the voices of these beasts were not that of any monster, but rather of boys - boys that sounded familiar in fact. They also appeared to be rather casually and colourfully dressed.

Jess suddenly felt a little silly and stood upright out of her defensive posture. While her friends remained tightly huddled behind, she bravely approached the pair who no longer came across as any real threat. One of them even seemed to be holding up a mobile phone recording her every move. She continued closer until she was able to reach for their masks. She grasped one of the woolly faces and pulled it up followed by the other.

"SURPRISE!"

"I don't believe it!" gasped Jess. "Jake Jenkins and his partner in crime, Basher Yoga. What in the name of all things holy are you two doing here?"

Meg, Charlie and Zac who were equally gobsmacked and fast becoming majorly annoyed, realised they had been the butt of some cruel joke and made their way over. "What? What?!" questioned Zac astounded.

"Thought we'd give you a fright," sniggered Bashir in his grating laugh.

"That's right," boasted Jake, "and by the looks of you fools we succeeded. BOOM! And the best part is we took a video to put online. You'll be a laughing stock!" The infuriating pair high-fived and low-fived making silly noises, then chest-bumped laughing at the dumbstruck faces of their peers. "Totally punked - in full HD!"

"Seriously not cool boys," replied Jess.

Charlie arrived alongside her still trying to comprehend their presence. "You, you are trespassing on p-private p-property! How did you get in anyway? And how did you know about the w-w-werewolf?"

"Because, tubby, we heard you t-t-talking the other day after s-s-school," teased Bashir.

"They must have followed us to the den!" said Zac.

"That's right, *Zachary*," confirmed Jake. "And we got in here by climbing a tree, by the wall not far from here. We just climbed up and over, it wasn't hard. Then we followed some footprints. Figured they were yours like. Say... what are you chumps doing anyway? Why are you carrying a torch in the middle of the day? And why on earth are you covered in black dirt?"

"MIND YOUR OWN BUSINESS!" yelled Charlie, rustling his branch in anger. He picked up one of the crude masks and held it ahead of him. "And do I take it that you are the ones responsible for trying to scare Auntie and me? With these silly things!"

Jake snatched the mask back. "Whoa, calm your little boy-boobs down, rich boy. I've never seen or heard of your stupid aunt. Oh and for your information, this is the first time we've ever been here. Bit of a dump too if you ask me. I mean, where we sposed to skate?"

"Don't call me rich boy, or I'll..."

"You'll what, mate?" enquired Bashir, squaring up to Charlie sending him cowering backward.

Meg, who wasn't about to be intimidated, pushed the oversize bully aside. She then set upon Jake, grabbing him firmly by his yellow designer polo shirt and shouted directly into his smug face. "Was it you who took my dog? Where is Cookie? What have you done with him? TELL ME!"

"You what, princess?! We haven't seen your friggin' dog either. Now if you don't mind you're wrinkling my shirt!"

Jess stepped up as ambassador despite her hatred of the party-crashers in an attempt to calm the situation. "Now just hold on everyone..." Charlie turned and inadvertently gave her a face-full of shrubbery. "Charlie, lose the bush will you. And will everyone just shut up for a moment! Thank you. Now Jake, Basher, you said a moment ago that you followed footprints here, right?"

"That's right," replied Jake.

"And you're sure there were several prints?"

"Yeah, I guess."

"Well, none of *us* have been here before."

"So what?"

"So... Charlie, does the groundskeeper live alone?"

"Yes he does, Jess. Has done for years. Why?"

"And does he ever have any visitors?"

"What? Good heavens no. That man hates just about everyone apart from himself. That's why he's happy to live up here out of anyone's way."

"Well then," continued Jess, "unless he's made some friends recently, it would appear that we have more unexpected visitors besides these two jerks." She carried on speculating but lost Jake and Bashir's interest who began to walk off.

"And just where do you think you're going?" asked Meg.

"Well we'd like to stay and play, princess, but our work here is done. So if you'll excuse us, we'll be on our way. Besides, we've got a video to put on YouTube."

"Err, just a minute, gentlemen," yelled Zac. "Correct me if I am wrong, but doesn't the tree you used to get over the wall only work one-way? I mean, how will you get back over if the tree is on the other side?" The pair looked at one another and realised they probably should have thought this through a little better, not that they would admit it. "Your sorry faces confirm my point," continued Zac. "In which case it looks like you're stuck here, until Charlie decides to let you out that is. Right, Charlie?"

"Right, Zac," Charlie replied smugly, which angered the two boys.

"Unless or course, you would prefer it if Charlie set his guard dogs on you, in which case you'll be leaving in little bags. Right, Charlie?"

"Right, Zac!"

"*OKAY,*" replied Jake walking back over. "OK, you win. So, let us out and you can go back to playing hide and seek or whatever the hell you're doing."

Jess pulled the bullies together and addressed them almost nose-to-nose. "All in good time, boys, but for now you'll have to tag along with us. Keep quiet and do as we do, until we can throw your sorry behinds out the gates like civilised people. Right, Charlie?"

"Right, Jess!"

She shoved them backward where they begrudgingly accepted her proposal. "Oh and Bashir, do us all a favour and get some mints. Your breath smells like dog food!"

After their unscheduled interruption, the children were able to resume their investigation and quietly made their way toward Donald's cabin. Behind them lagged the two uninvited guests grumbling amongst themselves. They all followed the trail that had been created by person or persons through an area of flattened ferns, which would otherwise have been four or five feet tall. Jess, Charlie and the twins walked single file and by crouching a little were able to move unseen thanks to the surrounding cover. Jake and Bashir, however, refused to play along and walked arrogantly upright. Zac then began sneezing after just a few dozen feet and dropped back whilst he located some tissue and tried to compose himself. At the front of the line Jess followed behind Charlie, whose attention appeared to be wondering. "*Pteridium aquilinum,*" he muttered to himself.

"What?" whispered Jess.

"The ferns - it's the Latin name."

"HEY CHARLIE," shouted Jake. "What's the Latin for major dork?"

"SSHH!" shushed Jess.

"Shut it all of you," snapped Meg. "We're almost there."

"He started it," sulked Jake.

"I'll finish it!"

A few steps further revealed an empty bottle lying in the undergrowth, which turned out to be the same vintage champagne from the basement. Looking ahead, the building appeared to be a simple, single-storey log cabin with its roof structure covered in green moss owed to its shaded location amongst the trees. The main entrance was via a doorway covered by a peaked annex, which had ivy and various other climbing plants attached to every exposed piece of timber. The cabin had served as the home of the resident groundskeeper for as long as the estate had existed and lacked most modern conveniences. Parked beside it was an off-road vehicle used by the groundskeeper to maintain the estate. Parked behind that and blocking it in, was a large and very unsightly, rusty van. It was filthy and had once been white, but was now adorned with various crude remarks and images. Meg recorded the van's number plate in her notebook: GRVY TRA1N.

Continuing on, the children eventually met the narrow road that connected the cabin to the rest of the estate. They passed by the vehicles and climbed the wooden stairs as quietly as they could. The name of the building was *'Lulworth Cottage'* which was carved into a wooden board beside the entrance. They crouched beneath a side window around the corner, well away from the front door, but while this was serious business to them, Jake and Bashir maintained their jovial attitude making fun at their peer's expense. Once safely nestled in a flowerbed Jess made a pointy-up sign.

"Wait, what are we doing?" asked Bashir vacantly.

"Shut up, Basher!" whispered Jess. "Everyone else, let's take a look inside."

"Why don't you just knock on the door?" asked Jake.

"That's not a bad shout you know," agreed Zac before Jess had a chance to reply. "I mean, what if we stand up and see Donald naked, doing yoga or something with his tackle out? Man, I'm too young to see stuff like that!"

"Thanks for painting that picture," replied Meg.

"Because boys," said Jess sternly, "we don't yet know what we're up against. Trust me, it's safer this way."

"Hold on a minute," said Jake, "but why is there a naked man in there - and why the hell are you spying on him?"

"*Nobody is naked!*" replied Jess. "At least I don't think there is, so will you please keep quiet."

"But what if he *is?*" stressed Zac, growing ever concerned.

"Then close your eyes!"

On a nod from Jess they all slowly rose up to peer inside the cabin. Six curious faces - one with his eyes closed - then appeared at the bottom of the window. The glass was dirty and the sill on the inside was cluttered with objects which reduced visibility, but what they did see made their eyes widen, their jaws drop and their hearts skip a beat.

13

Donald the groundskeeper was sitting in a chair a few feet from the window bound with rope and mouth gagged. He seemed to be staring right back at the children which made them instinctively duck back down in surprise. They looked at one another speechless. "WHAT THE…" blurted out Bashir way too loudly, forcing Jake to silence him by placing his hand over his mouth. "SSSHHH!" shushed the others. Bashir nodded to Jake and asked his question again, only this time in a more controlled whisper. "What the hell is going on here?"

"Basher," replied Jake, "let me handle this… WHAT THE HELL IS GOING ON HERE? IS THIS SOME KIND OF SICK JOKE?"

"SSSSHHHH!" shushed the others.

"I suggest you keep your mouth shut if you value your life," warned Jess. "We'll explain later." After composing themselves and realising their cover had not been blown, Jess signalled up once again. Their faces then returned to the window for another look.

Donald was a scruffy recluse who didn't really belong in the twenty-first century. He knew only of old-fashioned methods of living and of working and had no knowledge of modern gadgets or their purpose. His thin ginger hair was wild and unkempt, as was his beard. His face and hands desperately needed a good wash; his teeth a good brushing. He wore scruffy clothes with shorts revealing skinny legs wrapped in socks pulled up to the knee. His age to guess at was around sixty, for his face was callous and weathered, but this man was actually ten years younger.

After Charlie waved at him a few times and received no response, they concluded that he probably couldn't see them and was sat staring at his own reflection. He also seemed drowsy and appeared to be dropping in and out of consciousness. Their faces then panned to the right after the sound of laughter caught their attention. They saw three men, sitting at a small table in the kitchen playing cards. "You recording this, Zac?" asked Meg.

"You bet your life I am."

The first man went by the name of George Kaylock, known amongst the criminal underworld as Gorgeous George, despite the numerous scars on his face. At around five feet four inches he was undeniably short and aged in his fifties. He was almost bald headed, if not for the hair clinging to the sides of his head like seaweed clings to a rock. He also had a few thin strands which he combed over from one side to the other, in a last desperate attempt to retain coverage. He was an efficient thinker and planner with an above average knowledge of many subjects and, as a result, called himself the leader of this small band of men. A fat cigar was held in his mouth between stained yellow teeth from which he sent a steady flow of smoke into the room.

The second man was Lawrence Birkenhead, aptly known by those that knew him as Burk. In his late-thirties he was tall and skinny; his long nose was of a sensitive subject to him and he had a wayward eye that often appeared out of sync with the other. He had a thick head of matted brown hair which he often kept under a hat whilst in public, to avoid drawing attention to himself. He grew up in the east end of London and was once a member of a gang known as *The Scorpians* (spelt that way) before they split. Despite being a devout catholic and of a nervous disposition, he is, by his own admission, a lifelong pick-pocket and untrustworthy thief. One who would literally sell his own mother for a pocket full of cash. He always carried Rosary beads and would rub them in times of worry, as he did now during their game of cards.

The third man was truly a giant in proportion to the others. Touching on seven feet two inches, he must have weighed in at around thirty stone at least. A Belgian by birth, he went by the name of Renard, for his full name – Rénard Rèné Dupônt, was beyond pronunciation for most of the men he did business with. Yet this was no overweight slob of a man by any means, but a strong and capable one who had been born of gigantism. He was mid-forties in years and was presently squeezed onto a chair that was so under strain it looked like it may give way at any second. He spoke acceptable English - more than could be said for his colleagues, but was a quiet person who chose to remain mute most of the time.

The three men sat playing poker and some money in paper form was changing hands, mostly towards the side of George Kaylock. Behind them on a little stove some fat sausages sizzled in a pan beside a mountain of dirty dishes. A number of empty champagne bottles matching those from the basement were littered around the entire cabin and an ashtray filled with cigar and cigarette ends was spilling over onto the floor.

"The men from the pub!" gasped Meg.

"What's that, Meg?" asked Jess.

"Those two men - the skinny one and the big one - were at the pub last night. I saw them when I was working."

"Are you sure?"

"No mistaking those two! They made me feel really uncomfortable. Look there - that one's got the same scorpion tattoo. And there on the coat rack: the very same hats they had too. I figured they were travelling through for the canal boat show or something, but now it makes perfect sense."

"What does?" asked the others.

"Why their hands were so filthy of course - it's from the coal in the basement. It has to be."

Zac had also noticed something and gulped before sharing it. "That's not all, look there in the corner." All heads turned to the direction he had indicated. It was Cookie the dog - locked in a cage but thankfully alive and well. "COOKIE!" cried Meg, standing up in full view of the window. Jess and Zac grabbed her from either side and wrestled her back down, just as one of the men looked over his shoulder.

"Let me go!" squirmed Meg. "I've got to help him!"

"Meg," pleaded Jess, "for God's sake..."

"LET ME GO!"

They abruptly silenced when they heard a creaking sound at the cabin steps. Inside the building, Burk had also heard it and jumped to his feet inadvertently banging his head on the pots hanging above. He took down a saucepan and prepared to 'welcome' the visitor.

"Calm down you big girls blouse," said Kaylock gruffly. "Now, get the door seeing as your up." Rubbing his head, Burk went over and lifted the little curtain to peer through the glass. He then slid the bolt along to unlock the door, pulled it open and stepped aside. A person entered, but their face was hidden from view as he or she wore a dark waterproof hat and coat, similar to ones used by fishermen known as slickers. Burk replaced the door, which appeared to be unattached from its hinges.

"Good evening, Frank," said Kaylock smiling, who then abruptly turned his expression to a frown adding, "You're late!"

"Did you hear that?" whispered Meg to the others. "He said his name was Frank. Charlie, what's your butler's first name?"

"Urm…"

"You don't know?"

"Sorry, but I only know him as Barker."

"Dumb-ass!" said Zac and Jake together.

As much as they tried, from their position at the window the children were unable to hear complete conversations. However, several snippets of context were audible and included: *"proceed as planned tonight"*, *"old lady and staff expendable"*, and *"stop at nothing to find the ruby."*

Meg recorded everything in her notebook, but kept getting knocked by Zac who was unknowingly crouched in a patch of prickly holly and fidgeting wildly. If that wasn't distracting enough, he then revealed he was on the verge of sneezing. "Ah… ah… AHH…" A sneeze was about to erupt. Their position might be compromised. They could be captured, tied up and left to die like poor Donald in his armchair.

Thankfully, relief came when Jess shoved her finger against Zac's nose successfully halting the outburst. The others, who had all crouched and held their breath anxiously, now slowly exhaled when they saw this quick thinking had saved them from impending doom. "Few, that was…" started Charlie, but he never got the chance to finish, for there suddenly came an almighty A-TISHO! Not from Zac, but from Jake!

"You idiot!" scolded Jess. She returned to the window and was relieved to see the outburst had passed unnoticed, as the men inside were busy arguing over something. "It's alright," she informed the others, "they didn't…" Only she failed to finish her sentence and suddenly appeared to be standing motionless.

"Didn't what, Jess?" enquired Charlie. He and the others joined her and saw for themselves that Donald was now conscious and staring right back at them. He had heard the sneeze and now saw the faces at the window. His eyes widened and, frenzied by the hope of rescue, began chair-hopping frantically towards them. Fearing they would be exposed, the children made the 'shush' finger motion back at him. They then waved their hands desperately instructing him to stop. Too late. Donald got as close as he possibly could but the chair tipped forward, sending him crashing into the cluttered windowsill and planting his face against the glass. The children looked on stunned as his squished cheek remained firmly pressed against the window just inches from them. His wide eye stared helplessly down like a fish out of water, while he mumbled madly through his gag.

There followed the sound of a chair moving in the kitchen and the children's heads whipped toward the men. They saw them all standing silent, looking back toward Donald. The children dropped to the ground like heavy sacks, prickles or no prickles, and held their breath.

"Sort that fool out," muttered the hooded person. On a nod from Kaylock, Burk and Renard immediately placed their cards face down on the table and made their way over.

Outside, the children sat silently with their backs pressed against the cabin wall. Silently, that its, until Bashir became overcome with fear and tried to scramble away on all fours. He was immediately set upon by Jake and Zac, who dragged him back and secured him, but in the frenzy one of his trainers came loose and remained precariously out in the open. There was no time to retrieve it, as Burk's face appeared at the window directly above them.

He watched intently for any activity as his breath misted the glass. He scratched his sinewy neck and rubbed his bristly chin. All the while, Bashir's bright footwear sat glowing in the undergrowth. After seeing nothing of concern, Burk eventually left the window area and joined his giant colleague, who had grasped Donald's chair with one hand and was dragging him into the middle of the room. Donald was then further secured and spun around to face the kitchen. "Trying to fone a friend were yer?" joked Burk sourly, kicking the back of the chair.

Jess once again gestured upward and the gang turned and ascended so that just their eye-line was visible above the sill. They watched Kaylock rise and slowly walk over chewing a mouthful of food. He arrived in front of Donald holding half a sausage, where he stood staring for a moment contemplating what to do with him. Surprisingly, he then leant over and placed the sausage on Donald's crotch before emitting a sharp whistle. Almost at once from a corner of the kitchen, a short, fat, slobbering dog - a British Bulldog to be precise, came lumbering over. He (undoubtedly a *he* owed to the large pair of dangling, well, you know what) was so overweight he almost walked sideways on and struggled to control his fat rear. He had also lost an eye fighting years before and his vision through the remaining one was impeded by the numerous rolls of fat on his forehead.

"Mycroft, guard!" instructed Kaylock. On this sole command the dog obediently sat between the legs of the groundskeeper and stared up at him. Poor Donald sat looking down wide-eyed and dared not move at all. He dared not even blink. All the while the mutt sat impossibly still at his feet salivating readily, looking forward to the promise of a meaty snack one way or another. Cookie then dared to yap at Kaylock, who responded by kicking the cage. "Shut it you rat," he bellowed, "or you'll be next on the menu!"

Once Kaylock and Burk had returned to the kitchen and reclaimed their seats, the giant man remained behind for a moment. He walked over to Cookie, who seemed surprisingly happy to see him given the circumstances, knelt down in front of the cage and reached into his pocket. "What's he doing?" asked Meg. Jess grasped her arm to restrain her while they looked on in awful anticipation. They watched as the man pulled a small object wrapped in tissue from his pocket. He then glanced toward the other men, perhaps to ensure he was not being observed and proceeded to unwrap… a sausage, and feed it to Cookie. "Phew!" uttered the girls.

Shortly after, Kaylock finished his conversation with the hooded man. They both then raised from the table and checked the time on their watches before the hooded man exited the building. "Right, lads," said Kaylock lighting up another fat cigar. "We go tonight, so gather your gear and don't forget your masks. We want to give the old lady a night to remember."

"And wot if she don't cooperate?" asked Burk.

Kaylock took a long pull on his cigar and expelled the smoke. "Then tonight, may just be her last."

Outside, the children crouched and watched the mysterious hooded figure walk down the road toward the house. Once they were sure the coast was clear, they remained stooped and cut through the woodland in order to avoid passing the cabin entrance. They hastened back along the trail in silence trying to come to terms with what they had seen until they entered the cover of the oak trees, where they were able to walk upright without fear of being noticed. There was a flash of lightning followed by a rumble of thunder. Not long after rain began to fall, lightly at first, but the drops were fat and exploded on contact like miniature water bombs. Jess stopped and motioned the others to carry on. She then returned to Meg who had dropped back and was standing in the rain looking distraught. "Meg?"

"What about Cookie? I can't just leave him."

Jess took hold of her hand. "Please, Meg, I know it's hard for you but there is nothing we can do right now. If *we* get caught, then we won't be able to help Cookie or anyone else. I promise we will get him back but right now we need to go. Do you understand?" Jess was sincere and Meg believed her. She acknowledged, albeit sadly, with a nod.

Together, they carried on and met the others under the cover of the mighty oak containing the tunnel entrance. Here they were sheltered from the rain which was now falling heavily all around. The clear blue sky above had been replaced by a dark and ominous ceiling of cloud that had brought with it a mighty storm. Now a safe distance from the cabin, Jake exploded. "Seriously now, what just happened back there? Please tell me it's a joke!"

"It's no joke," replied Zac.

"Dude, that guy was tied up - KIDNAPPED!"

"We know, Jake," replied Meg, "We were there too."

"Think I'm gonna hurl," groaned Bashir.

"Poor Auntie," said Charlie, "she is in grave danger. The police, we must contact the police!" This was a great idea and everyone raced to make contact. They all frantically dialled the number and held their mobiles to their heads, but just as quickly lowered them to try and figure out why nothing was happening.

"No signal!" said Jake. The others all confirmed the same and went through the process of walking around, holding their phones up at different heights trying to find some coverage. None did.

"Charlie, is there a phone in the house?" asked Jess.

"Yes of course, in the study, but... but..."

She grabbed him firmly by both shoulders. "BUT WHAT?!"

"But one of *them* - one of the gang members - the one we saw heading back to the house."

"What about him?"

"He, or she, must be a member of staff. Maybe they won't let us make the call!"

"Oh that's just perfect!" wined Bashir. "How the heck..." but Meg advised him to 'put a sock in it', which he did before walking off kicking the ground.

"Take us to the gates, Charlie," demanded Jake. "Take us to the gates and let us the hell out of here, RIGHT NOW!"

"That doesn't help Charlie's aunt," replied Jess, "or his staff."

"LIKE WE CARE!"

"Oh that's a great attitude," said Meg. "Looking after number one as usual, right, Jake?"

"The only one that matters, princess. Call it self-preservation."

"You disgust me."

There followed a moment of silence while the realisation of the events they found themselves up to their necks in hit home. Charlie and Meg sat down with their backs against the tree and Charlie lowered his head onto his arms. All around them the wind was testing the branches of the trees creating a ghostly sound as they came under strain. Not long after, the first rain drops started to filter down beneath the canopy. "What are we going to do, Jess?" asked Zac. Everyone looked at her searching for hope. For inspiration and leadership. For a way out of their dire situation.

Jess placed her index finger on her chin and considered the facts carefully. "Good point, Charlie, about the insider down at the house I mean. Based on this we have to assume that we're walking into a trap, when, or *if* we return there. Therefore, I suggest we send someone back to the village to raise the alarm - then at least we know someone will be coming to help us. Furthermore, I think those who stay, or at least one of us, should go back to the house and tell Lady Midsummer what we know, so she knows what she's up against. It's the very least we can do. Maybe we could try to contact the police too."

"And what would we do then, Jess?" asked Meg. "*If* we're able to contact the police - and we're left waiting for them to arrive."

"Well, I suppose we could hide, for one, or..."

"Or what?" enquired Zac.

"Or we could make a stand. We could try to stop the crooks or at least delay them long enough for the police to arrive."

"Bit risky, isn't it?"

"That's probably an understatement. But if you're not up for it..."

"Whoa, easy now. I never said that."

"That's what I thought. So Jake, Basher, where are your bikes?"

"Not far from the main gate," replied Jake. "Why?"

"Because someone needs to go and notify the authorities of our situation and as you two weren't on the guest list, it's unlikely your presence will be missed. That is, unless you would prefer to remain here with those crooks whilst the rest of us go for help?" The look on the boy's faces was enough to tell Jess they weren't keen on that idea. "Just as I thought. So, how long do you think it will take to get back to the village?"

"Two hours, hour and a half maybe at a push - but we should be able to use our mobiles once we're out of the valley, in about an hour."

"Excellent, that will give us..."

"Err, hold on, Jess," interrupted Zac. "I see a problem with this."

"What problem, Hewes?" questioned Jake angrily.

"I'll tell you what problem - you and Basher informing the police, be it by phone or in person, that there is going to be a jewel heist in Midsummer estate, by person or persons masquerading as werewolves no less. *That's* the problem!"

Charlie and Meg nodded in agreement and Jess realised that Zac probably had a point. Meanwhile, Jake and Bashir folded their arms in defensive body language, eager to see where this was going. Zac continued like the prosecution in a court case. "With their infamous reputation within the village of lying, stealing, bullying, unsociable behaviour, damage to public property and general lack of respect for anyone or anything, I doubt the police will believe them. No offence, boys."

"None taken!" they smirked. It seemed they had received the barrage of negative opinion as a compliment.

"Well what do you suggest then, Zac?" asked Jess.

"Well... I suppose one of us will have to go with them."

"One of us?"

"Yes."

"Who?"

There was a brief period where no one spoke and the sound of the falling rain seemed deafening. "I'll go with them," offered Meg. Jess, Charlie and Zac were more than a little surprised that she had volunteered and initially didn't like the idea at all. "The police will believe me," she continued. "There's no doubt about that."

"Why, because you're a goody-two shoes?" mocked Bashir.

"If you like," she replied calmly. His inability to offend her had started to bother him.

"Look, maybe you're right, Meg," admitted Jess, "but..."

"But nothing. I should go. Look at it logically: Charlie has to stay as it's his home and family down there. Jess, you're the leader, and Zac can help protect you if something goes wrong. Who knows, you might even find a use for some of his silly gadgets."

"But your bike," said Charlie. "It's down at the house!"

"It's OK, Charlie. I'll get a ride with Jake. Right, Jake?"

"Your carriage awaits, princess," he replied bowing as he did so.

"You just keep your slimy hands to yourself, Jake!" ordered Zac.

"And what's that supposed to mean?" Jake demanded, who swiftly walked over to Zac, chest out and stood right in his face. Zac responded by pushing him away but before Jake could retaliate, Meg stepped in between and held them apart.

"Zac, this is not the time for playing big brother. Besides, I can look after myself. Jake, just back off and stay away from him won't you. We're wasting time by fighting between ourselves. OK?... OKAY?"

The boys stood down before Jake laughed and walked off toward Bashir. "Come on, Bash, let's get the heck out of this nut house." They headed away without waiting for Meg. "LATER DORKS!"

Jess put her hand on Meg's shoulder and said her goodbye. "You sure about this?"

"I'll be fine. Just look after yourselves. Now, I should go."

"Hold on a minute, Meg," said Zac. He pulled a walkie-talkie radio from his backpack, turned it on and held it toward her. "Here, take this. It's good for a few kilometres. Let us know how you're doing. Channel six." For once he looked genuinely concerned for his sister, but he knew she was strong and independent and he had every confidence that she would get back to the village – back home, OK. She took the radio and acknowledged his gesture with a hug.

"THINK I'M GONNA BARF!" shouted Jake.

Meg untied the hoodie from around her waist and pulled it over her head. After switching the radio to channel six and placing it in her front pocket, she smiled in spite of their situation, before hugging Jess one last time. She then turned and set off into the trees.

14

Jess, Zac and Charlie stood beneath the mighty oak feeling thoroughly divided and saddened after the departure of little Meg. To add to their torment, the rain now fell in straight vertical lines and the explosive thunder seemed to culminate directly above them. The butterflies in their stomachs made it difficult to know what to do next; their legs had become heavy dead weights unwilling to move.

"This is how I felt when Zayn left 1D," grieved Charlie.

"Come on, boys," said Jess trying to raise their spirit. She placed an arm around each of them and pulled them in close. "I know it feels strange without our Meg and believe me I'm feeling it too, but it's only natural to feel this way when someone you care about so much goes away. Even more so under crazy circumstances like this. But she'll be back real soon so we need to keep our chins up, after all, we're still a kick-ass team you know. The Three Amigos. The Three Musketeers. The Three …err, I dunno - something or other. One team, one dream. So, are you with me or do I go it alone?" She squeezed them tight and their frosty faces began to thaw. In fact, Charlie particularly enjoyed the intimacy as this was undiscovered territory for him.

"What the hell," announced Zac. "I'm up for a skirmish. After all, adventure is my middle name."

"I thought it was Horace?" teased Charlie.

"Yes, ahem, well, moving on," replied Zac hastily. "You in, *Charles?*"

"To try, per chance to succeed."

"In English, Charlie."

"I'm in."

"Excellent," replied Jess. "Now boys, there is a defenceless old lady down there who needs our help and without us, well, you heard what those thugs said. So it's up to us to put things right. It's our chance to be heroes."

"Or heroines," replied Charlie matter-of-factly.

"You can be what you want," joked Zac.

"I was referring to Jess, dork."

"That's the stuff boys," continued Jess. "Right then, let's get back and find Auntie, and remember - we can't trust anyone down there."

"Not even old Barker?" asked Charlie. "I still can't believe that he has anything to do with this whole nasty business."

"*Especially old Barker*," replied Zac coldly.

"I'm afraid Zac's right, Charlie, but it's for our own good at the moment. I hope you understand."

With their plan of action now loosely formulated, they turned and attempted to enter the secret doorway only to find it couldn't be opened from the outside. "Don't suppose you have a key, Charlie?" asked Zac, but he shrugged indicating he hadn't.

"Looks like we're taking the scenic route then," said Jess. "Don't suppose you have an umbrella, Zac?"

"Sorry, Jess."

"Oh well, a little rain never hurt anyone. Right?"

"No, but I'm pretty sure lightning did!"

With no other option they set off, somewhat reluctantly, to join the road and the moment they left the shelter of the trees the rain hit them hard. It came as some relief when they arrived on the tarmac and left the grassy track behind, as it had made their legs itch no end. By the time they reached the courtyard outside of the house they were completely soaked through, so much so that their footwear squelched when they walked. They decided to keep out of sight as much as possible and used some of the topiary hedges for cover. They proceeded in this fashion toward the main entrance, but instead made use of the servant's door beside it, which allowed them to enter the house unseen.

Jess and the boys would have arrived back at the house around the time Meg, Jake and Bashir arrived at the main gates of the estate. After splitting up, they had followed the boundary wall under cover of woodland for almost a mile and were now relieved to be clear of the unyielding undergrowth. They had received a decent amount of shelter from the elements while they travelled beneath the canopy of evergreen trees; a result of which meant they remained almost completely dry. Their clothing, however, had been marked in various shades of green after rubbing against tree trunks and fallen branches, and if this wasn't bad enough, parts of them were now infuriatingly sticky with sap. With the entrance gates in sight they stepped out into the rain.

"Finally!" yelled Bashir.

"Right, let's get the heck out of this dump!" added Jake.

All that remained was to push the button and open the gates, then they were free to leave. Meg lifted the cover of the metal box housing the gate control button; she pushed it, but nothing happened. She pushed it a second time, again nothing happened. "Well open the bloody things then!" shouted Jake impatiently. He stood with hands in pockets with his normally perfectly sculpted fringe beginning to flatten onto his forehead.

"I'm trying. It's not working!" replied Meg, pushing the button with increasing desperation. The rain was now falling so hard that shouting was required in order to communicate with one another. Bashir then decided he was out of patience and came bounding over. He rudely pushed Meg aside yelling, "OUT OF MY WAY!" He tried the button for himself, but still nothing happened. He pushed it again and again, then punched it, then slapped the top and sides. He even started kicking it for good measure and only stopped when it was askew and hanging by a wire. Meg returned the shove, this time pushing him aside and inspected the box more closely. She followed the two thin cables down the mounting post towards the ground and what she saw gave her a feeling of utter dread. "It's not broken," she said ominously.

"What do you mean?" Jake replied.

"Look here. The cable's been cut."

The boys came over and saw for themselves. "The crooks?"

"Who else."

"OH COME ON!" shouted Bashir in frustration. He punched the air before burying his hands deep in his hoodie. "Great! That's just great!

Well what do we do now? Come on, little Miss perfect. You're supposed to be the smart one! Fink us up a way out!"

Meg paused for a moment wondering what to do, after all, she wasn't used to being head decision maker and didn't exactly feel comfortable being centre of attention. While she did so, the boys stood impatiently expecting an answer, which only added to the pressure making it almost impossible to think of anything. *'Come on, Meg,'* she said to herself over and over. *'You can do this. Now think, think, for God's sake think!'*

"Well?" asked the boys.

"OK, how about we radio Zac and the others? Maybe Charlie can let us out somehow. How does that sound?"

"Yeah, yeah," replied Bashir, with hope returning to his sorry face. "They can open the gates and let us out!"

Pleased she had come up with something at all, Meg unclipped the walkie-talkie from her waste and tried to raise her brother on it. "Zac, are you there? Zac. Come in Zac... Zac. Come in Zac... over."

Despite several attempts to make contact there came no reply. Eventually she gave up, returned the radio to her pocket and broke the news to the others. She then had to rack her brain some more to try and think up another option. "What about climbing the gates?" By this point Bashir would accept any suggestion and was already heading in that direction. Meg and Jake watched as he made a pathetic attempt at scaling the railings; it was like watching an overweight bear trying to climb an oily lamppost in order to reach a snack at the top.

"Too tall, too slippery and too spikey," said Jake bitterly. "And he's too fat!"

Meg turned back to Jake and let the wind blow her hair clear of her face. "Well we don't have much choice then - we'll just have to double back. I saw a tree close to the wall, maybe we can climb over it. What do you think?"

"Like you say, princess, we don't have much choice."

"Alright then, let's get going. At least we'll be out of the rain for a while!"

Together they began walking back toward the trees. "Where are you going?" yelled Bashir.

"Back," replied Jake. "You coming?"

"Back?!"

"Yes, back."

"But... the gates..."

"I'd stand clear of them if I were you, unless you want to get struck by lightning."

Bashir hastily stepped away from the perimeter and took one more look at freedom. A sudden clap of thunder further spooked him and, realising he was about to be left alone, he suddenly felt very vulnerable. "Hey guys, wait up. Guys! GUYS!"

The hidden door in the library - the one that was painted to look like the wall, quietly opened and three heads peered around it. The room was empty. Empty and silent, save for the wind howling outside. Jess, Charlie and Zac were about to step through when they heard movement and noticed someone enter from the far end. It was Mrs Blackwell, the cook, who started inspecting the books in one section. Jess motioned the boys to back up and they softly closed the door and carried on down the passageway, until they arrived at the cupboard beside the hall. Here, among the hanging coats they were able to peer through the slots in the door before exiting, which helped them remain out of sight. There was no sign of anyone and only the tick-tock-ticking of the grandfather clock could be heard.

"Charlie, we should go straight to your aunt and tell her what we saw."

"Yes of course, Jess. And not a moment too soon. With any luck, we can sit tight together and wait for Meg and the police to arrive."

"Have you forgotten the staff?" Zac asked.

"What about them?"

"Well at least one of them is in the bad-guy gang remember? An insider. A spy. A mole. We can't go shooting off our mouths and risk someone hearing us, otherwise we'll be playing straight into their hands."

They paused for a moment to consider Zac's warning. "Hmm, fair point, Zac," agreed Jess. "I guess we should just try and act as normal as possible, at least until we hook up with Auntie and..."

"NORMAL!" yelled Zac.

"SSSSHHHH!" shushed the others.

"Normal!" he continued in a whisper. "Can I remind you that there are criminals holding persons, and dogs for that matter, hostage just up the road and you want us to act normal!"

"Well, yes."

"Well that makes about as much sense as a prequel sequel remake! So tell me, how's it gonna help us exactly?"

"Think of it like this, Zac," said Charlie. "The bad guys don't know that we know. And, we know that they don't know that we know. So as long as the bad guys go on not-knowing we know, we'll be fine. You follow?"

"Right up to the bit where you said *The*."

"Look, Zac," said Jess having a go herself, "all the crooks know - whoever they may be - is that we're here as Charlie's happy guests for the weekend and, furthermore, that we know nothing about their sinister plans at this time. So... we just have to carry on making them think that."

"Just until help arrives," added Charlie.

"Right, Charlie, just until help arrives. Now, do you understand, Zac?"

"So... let me get this straight - as long as they think that... they know... that... we don't know... we know we'll be fine. Right?"

"Exactly!" said Jess and Charlie at the same time.

"Excellent," replied Zac. "Only I have no idea what I just said!"

"I give up," replied Jess slapping her forehead. "Look, we'll just have to..."

Just then one of the heavy entrance doors of the house opened and a person entered the hall. It was the maid, Fräulein Bertrümn, wearing a long, black waterproof hat and coat identical to the one worn by the mysterious person up at the cabin. The children pressed their noses against the cupboard door to observe her through the slots, when suddenly, there came a loud noise of static as Zac's radio buzzed into life.

This was followed by a voice transmitting over it. "ZAC, ARE YOU THERE? ZAC. COME IN ZAC…"

Fräulein Bertrümn stopped shaking her umbrella and snapped her head sharply to her side. The radio continued to buzz, whir and crackle and seemed deafening in the little cupboard. "ZAC. COME IN ZAC… OVER…"

"Quick, turn it off!" whispered Jess. She and Charlie frantically tried to pull the radio from Zac's backpack, almost choking him in the process. Zac reached behind himself like a dog trying to catch its own tail and they all ended up spinning around as they scrambled to silence it. At last they retrieved it, but their hands were now getting in each other's way as they jostled to turn it off. All the while the little radio continued to broadcast Meg's voice. Finally, they silenced it and returned their eyes to the door to see if their cover had been blown.

They saw the maid casually close the entrance door behind her, shutting out the storm. She then collapsed the umbrella and walked into the hall listening and looking around, where she stood for a moment in silence.

"You think she heard us?" asked Zac, in the quietest possible whisper.

"Don't know," replied Jess.

"What's she doing?" asked Charlie.

"Don't know," replied Jess.

Before anyone could utter another word, the maid suddenly turned toward the cupboard and began walking toward it. The children had no time to retreat along the passageway so quickly shuffled back against the sides of the cupboard and nestled behind some of the coats. They took a deep breath in order to maintain complete silence just as the cupboard door was wrenched opened. Fräulein Bertrümn's angry face then peered inside. She didn't immediately enter, which made those hiding within even more nervous. Instead, she simply eyed some of the hanging garments, pushing one aside with her hand. Without warning, she then raised the umbrella and violently thrust its business-end into one of the coats, missing Jess' head by an inch. She turned and thrust again, this time lower down, missing Zac's crotch by less. Once sure she was alone, the maid took off her hat and coat and proceeded to hang them up, while grumbling some words in her native tongue. She placed her umbrella against the left side of the cupboard close to where Jess was, but to her frustration, it kept toppling over. On the fourth attempt, Jess, who now desperately needed to exhale, held out a hand and grabbed hold of it. Satisfied that it was stowed away properly the maid closed the door and walked away. Only then did the children emerge from behind the coats.

Jess wore a pretty feathered hat atop of her head, while Zac was wrapped in a brown, ladies faux fur coat. They returned the items and checked to see that the hall was clear.

"Phew, that was close," puffed Charlie.

"You're telling me!" replied Zac. "She almost skewered my b…"

"Boys, zip it," said Jess, who was busy inspecting the inside of the rain coat. "Aha!"

"What is it, Jess?" asked Zac.

"Fräulein what's-her-name's rain coat."

"Bertrümn," said Charlie.

"Right."

"What about it?"

"Well, whoever the fourth person was we saw at the cabin wore this very coat, so I was interested to see who it belongs to."

"And who does it belong to, Jess?"

She showed the boys the name written in permanent black marker on the label. "Your maid, Charlie. One Adalwolfa Pickelhaube Bertrümn!"

15

Sometime after leaving Jess and the boys behind, Meg and her reluctant companions were losing spirit fast. They took it in turns walking single-file, with those behind having to stay alert or risk being struck in the face by recoiling branches. Exposed tree roots, uneven ground and relentless undergrowth had resulted in slips and stumbles by everyone, so by the time they arrived at a suitable spot to cross the perimeter, they were all looking and feeling like they had tackled an assault course.

Their symbol of hope came in the form of great knotted and gnarled Ewe tree. One with a particularly long branch at just the right height to take them up and over the wall. But while they could agree this was their best chance of escape, the enormous tree – wet, twisted and strangled by vines, would be no easy climb.

Opting to bypass its vast trunk they all tried to jump and grab hold of the branch, but found it out of reach by a fingertip. After some discussion which turned into a perpetual argument, they decided that one person would have to give the other two a foot-up and then be pulled up themselves. They were now disheartened and desperate, but above all hated the sight of one another. There was also no chivalry here, so while the boys argued over who would go first, Meg daydreamed of a warm dry sofa in her living room with Cookie sitting alongside. Her mum had brought her a hot-chocolate topped with a mountain of cream, sprinkles and little square Marshmallows. She took it in her hands and felt its warmth. She was about to take a sip, but was abruptly brought back down to earth by Jake snapping his fingers in her face. "Meg... MEGAN!"

She returned her focus and was semi-relieved to learn that she would be going first – the result of a simple coin toss. She promptly placed her muddy foot into Bashir's coupled hands ready to receive a boost. On the count of three, she was thrust upward like a rugby player in a line-out where she attempted to grasp hold of a vine attached to the branch. She found it greasy and immediately lost her grip, resulting in her dropping back down, much to the annoyance of Bashir. They tried again. This time she managed to find a firm hold and pull herself up the rest of the way. She stood up carefully, but the slippery surface and the height made her instinctively crouch back down. Looking over the side at the boys below made her feel nauseous, so she decided to stay put until they joined her. Down on the ground, Jake and Bashir quarrelled over who would go next with increasing hostility. Neither one now trusted the other and the prospect of going last had well and truly lost its appeal.

Just when it seemed their dispute may come to blows, there came a cracking sound from the bushes. "What was that?" asked Jake nervously. The sound was a very noticeable snapping of a twig or branch behind them in the woodland. Up in the tree's crown and with a vantage point, Meg tried to see into the distance to identify any movement. She scanned the immediate area as well as she could, but it was difficult to see anything among the densely populated trees and the wind made it near impossible to identify the origin of any noise. After a while she saw something and pointed toward it. "THERE!"

"What is it?" asked Bashir.

"Can't tell. There, between the trees ...THERE AGAIN! RIGHT THERE!"

Something big was without a doubt moving between the tree trunks and undergrowth, circling them perhaps. Although what it was exactly remained unclear. "IT'S COMING CLOSER," hollered Meg.

Jake and Bashir suddenly felt vulnerable, a feeling until now unbeknown to them, and found their arms involuntarily reaching to each other for comfort. Above them, Meg shuffled along the branch a little more to improve her view. Whatever was out there, it was large, larger than a man even - and longer, much longer. She wiped her glasses and looked again. She saw it walked on four legs not two as it dashed between cover. What would it do to the helpless boys below? Could it climb trees? Would it?

After a tense few moments it finally showed itself and Meg's face reflected its presence. "A deer!" she laughed.

"A deer?!" exclaimed Jake and Bashir.

It was indeed an adult stag over two metres long complete with an impressive set of antlers. On seeing it for themselves the boys let out a momentous sigh of relief and, realising that they were stood hugging, quickly pushed one another away.

"A Deer! A Deer!" sang Meg. The impressive animal strolled into view where it stood staring at the boys.

"It's just a frickin' deer!" hollered Jake, punching Bashir's arm.

"It's just a frickin' deer," replied Bashir, still in shock.

"Phew, I was almost a little worried there for a second."

"I know, right!"

"A *little* worried?" teased Meg.

The stag then let out a roar to make its presence known, startling the boys, but made no further sign it would be aggressive. "Go on, GET!" yelled Bashir in an attempt to be rid of it; a gesture that was ignored. "Dumb ass animal."

"I'm sure the feeling's mutual!" said Meg, looking down at him.

Jake shook his head and turned toward the tree. "Come on, Bash. Let's get on with it." But when Bashir crouched to make the necessary position to provide a boost, the stag suddenly raised its head bolt-upright; it had heard something and something had spooked it. Its long ears turned one way, then another, followed by its head and body. Its behaviour became erratic. It was sensing danger all around. Meg and the boys watched it in silence, their moment of relief dwindling.

"Err, Meg," whined Bashir. "What's it doing?"

Before she replied, the animal suddenly hightailed like it had been whipped across its back side. Something else was here and it was moving toward the boys at pace. This time though it was humanoid, two in fact - one thin silhouette and one much larger came lunging out of hiding like cats stalking prey. They wore masks - werewolf masks and the boys had no time to react. They were caught. Black gloved hands smothered them and long hessian sacks were shoved over their heads and bodies. They were forced to the ground, tied and left to wriggle like maggots.

Up in the tree, Meg remained unseen, for the moment at least. The rush of fear that come over her had turned her legs to jelly, so it was probably a good thing she lie clinging to the branch. It had all happened so fast. She could barely think straight let alone move. She heard the masked men convene right below her and one lit a cigarette, the smoke of which drifted upward almost causing her to cough.

"There should be one more hiding somewhere. One more plus the Midsummer rich boy, says the boss. You look that way; I'll look over there."

So the men knew of the presence of a third child, which wasn't great news for Meg. All she could do for the moment was lie still. Lie still and pray. She peered over the side and saw the men searching the area for her, working in ever increasing circles. After a while they disappeared from view completely for several minutes, at which point she considered dropping down to free the boys. However, just as she slid her hands by her side to raise herself up, the men returned. They spoke a little, then the larger man effortlessly scooped up both boys, carrying one under each arm before heading off in the direction from whence they came.

Meg was now alone in the forest. The only hope of getting back to the village and raising the alarm. Her hands were shaking, as were her legs, but there was no time to worry about that. She must carry on for the sake of her friends, for the innocent people in the estate, and last but by no means least, for her beloved Cookie. She looked up along the length of the branch and took a deep breath. She stood and raised her arms like a tight-rope walker to aid balance and took a baby step forward. So far so good she thought - it was slippery but doable. *'I can do this. I can do this.'* She reached the halfway point, no, it was slightly more than that - a few more meters and she would be over the wall, out of the wretched estate. But it wasn't meant to be.

"Well, well, what have we here?" thundered a voice from below. "A waif and stray. Slipped the net did yer little fishy?" It was one of the masked men, the appearance of whom caused Meg to lose concentration and slip down onto her knees. It was clear just from looking that it was the thinner of the two men, mask or no mask. To make matters worse he was armed with a knife, which was currently pointed in Meg's direction. He arrived directly below her and jumped in an attempt to grab an ankle and pull her down, or part of the tree to pull himself up - whichever came first. Meg was now officially freaking out and had to work hard to control her breathing and avoid hyperventilating. She tried desperately to concentrate and not loose balance, looking ahead and not down. She shuffled forward whilst the man jumped and grunted below like a crazed animal. She slipped but regained balance. She stepped again and slipped again, but this time was unable to correct herself. She fell awkwardly on the branch then toppled over the side, plummeting to the ground and landing on her back.

Her head hit the dirt hard enough to almost lose consciousness, but not completely. Then a ringing noise began in her ears. She remained on her back looking upward, unable to move as everything began spiralling. Deep, slow-motion voices became louder, then a masked face appeared in front of hers and joined the spiral. Was she dreaming? The mask lifted to reveal a large face which looked into her eyes. A giant finger then floated into view and held open one of her eyelids. It retracted and disappeared from sight. She lost consciousness and everything turned black.

16

Jess, Charlie and Zac exited the coat cupboard and huddled together in the hall. Outside, the storm sent rain streaming down the windows beside the entrance door, while Inside, there hadn't been a sighting of any staff since maid Bertrümn stowed her coat away.

"Charlie," whispered Jess, "we need to locate your aunt straight away. Where d'you think she'll be?"

"Maybe the lounge, perhaps the study... or her bedroom preparing for dinner I would say."

"Well that's helpful," griped Zac. "Can't you narrow it down a bit?"

"Sorry, but it is a big house you know."

"That's OK, Charlie," said Jess. "Just ignore Zac's sarcasms. Now, about the telephone. Where is it?"

"In the study. Over there."

"Excellent. Then let's go and phone the police straight away. It will be quicker than waiting for Meg to get to the vill... Zac! What are you doing?"

Zac appeared to be picking up items from a side table near the entrance door and sort of weighing them and swinging them around. He disregarded a small glass paperweight in the form of a deer and returned instead with a hardback book. "I need a weapon," he informed them.

"You need a *what?*" replied Jess.

"A weapon, you know to defend myself."

"And just what do you expect to do with that exactly? Bore them to death with poetry!"

"SSHH," shushed Charlie.

"Oh SSHH yourself!" replied Jess.

"SSHH!" shushed Zac at both of them.

"SSSSSHHHHHH!!!" they all shushed at one another.

Despite any planning, their failure to keep the peace resulted in the inevitable and they were suddenly interrupted by a loud voice that boomed throughout the hall. Visibly startled, they all jumped around to see who it was. They saw Barker the butler in his immaculate attire, eyebrow standing tall and shoes gleaming as usual. He stood atop of the stairs holding his reading glasses down from his eyes, while he inspected Charlie and his damp and grubby guests. "I said, I trust everything is alright, Master Charles?"

Charlie looked worryingly at Jess, who simply gestured for him to say something. "Oh it's y-you, Barker."

"And just whom were you expecting, Master Charles?"

"Oh, err, no one in particular, Barker. No one at all in fact. Right, guys? Certainly not anyone about to rob the place or anything like that. That would be absurd and..." He received a sharp elbow in his ribs from Jess which halted his rambling.

"Ahem, I hate to be a bore, Master Charles," continued Barker from afar, "only your aunt would be awfully insistent that you and your... err, *guests*, clean up before attending dinner."

There came no immediate reply, for the children simply stood frozen to the spot, seemingly unable to utter a single word in reply. They just stared vacantly up the stairs while the grandfather clock ticked behind them. Was Barker the mole they were talking about? Was he onto them? The silence quickly became deafening. That is, until Jess nudged Charlie in his side, at which point he nervously unleashed gibberish like a wind-up toy that had been given a jump start. "Oh... err, dinner you say? Yes, dinner. Isn't that nice. Exactly. Wonderful. Err, of course... um, splendid. Right you are, Barker. And um... thanks for reminding us."

Barker acknowledged with an inclination of his head and turned as if the conversation was over, much to everyone's relief. However, just as they began to stand at ease he suddenly returned and addressed them again. "Forgive me, sir, but where is the *other* young lady?"

"The other young lady," replied Charlie. "Urm, what... young lady?"

"The young lady who accompanied your present guests this very morning."

"Really? I hadn't noticed. Did you, guys?"

"No, no," they replied innocently.

"The owner of the missing dog," persisted Barker.

"Doesn't ring a bell."

"The sister, I believe, to that young man standing right there beside you."

Charlie finally turned his expression around, "Oh *that* young lady!" He looked at the others for support but found none. They just shrugged their shoulders and looked blankly back at him. He had no choice but to go it alone. "Why she's err... in the... err... urm, gone to the... err... durr - gone to the durr. The durr, durr-du-dur...durr durr durr durr durrr..."

It was no use. Charlie had evidently lost all ability to speak and become a babbling idiot, so at the same time, Jess and Zac just blurted out the first thing that came into their minds.

"*She's taking a shower!*" said Jess.

"*She's gone to the toilet!*" said Zac.

They looked worryingly at one another and tried again.

"*She's gone to the toilet!*" said Jess.

"*She's taking a shower!*" said Zac.

Realising they were not helping the situation much at all, Charlie then jumped in and clarified their story. "She's gone to the toilet... TO TAKE A SHOWER!"

Not believing the words coming out of their own mouths, they smiled awkwardly up at Barker waiting for him to leave, only he stubbornly remained frowning down at them. The ticking of the clock behind had become ear-piercingly loud and the longer the children stood around in the open, greater was the risk of them bumping into another member of staff. The clock carried on ticking, yet time seemed to have stood still.

"Why isn't he leaving?" Zac asked through grinning teeth.

"I don't know," replied Jess through hers. "But if he doesn't leave in a minute, I swear I'm going to pee myself!"

"TMI!"

Thankfully, it didn't come to that as the old butler finally turned and walked off down the corridor.

"Thank God," sighed Jess. "I thought he'd never leave."

"Me neither," puffed Zac. "Oh, and way to *remain calm,* guys."

"Well you didn't exactly help," replied Charlie bitterly.

"Look who's talking!"

"Boys, forget it, we're still in one piece. Now let's go and make that phone call... AND PUT DOWN THAT BLOODY BOOK, ZAC!"

They entered the study and rushed over to the corner desk. Charlie then picked up the heavy, rotary-dial telephone and handed it to Jess, who simply stood looking at it perplexed, for it was a world away from the compact smartphones she was used to. "What the hell is this?" she asked.

"The telephone of course."

"I want to make a phone call, Charlie, not send Morse bloody code. This is a museum piece!"

"Yes, well, be that as it may, it still works. Just dial the number."

"How?"

"Allow me..."

Charlie used the dial to input the number nine three times, which seemed to take forever, as it required revolving the disk almost a full rotation each time, then waiting for it to return to zero. Jess listened into the earpiece and tried her very best to remain patient, but nothing seemed to be happening and she became restless with worry. "Hello, hello, is there anyone there? HELLO!" She handed the receiver back to Charlie. "There's no one there!"

Charlie looked puzzled and listened for himself. He then hung up and tried again, repeating the tedious processes of dialling the three numbers.

"OH COME ON!" yelled Zac; his patience run out.

"SSHH" returned Jess.

"Don't start that again!"

Charlie returned the receiver to the base and put the whole thing down on the table. He then stood looking very puzzled. "It's dead."

"What do you mean, dead?" replied Jess.

"As in - not working kind of dead."

"DEAD?"

"Yep, dead."

"What, dead-dead?" asked Zac.

"I am afraid so."

"Well why is it dead, Charlie? And can you fix it?"

Charlie struggled to find an explanation, because the fact was he simply didn't know why it wasn't working. The old phone had functioned perfectly well for decades and there was no obvious reason as to why it had suddenly stopped. "Perhaps it's the storm. Maybe a tree somewhere has fallen on the lines."

While Charlie speculated, Zac slumped down onto the leather sofa – the noisy one that made the awkward sound. Whilst there, he happened to turn his head toward the desk and notice something beneath it. He suddenly sat bolt upright and, to the wonder of his peers, got on all fours and frantically crawled toward it like some wild animal. Jess and Charlie were left guessing as he disappeared from view under the table and began rummaging around. "Err... Charlie," came his voice from below, "do these antique telephones have to be plugged into the wall in order to work?"

"They sure do, Zac. Why do you ask?"

Zac returned holding a thin cable in his hand that appeared to have been severed. Charlie approached him, took one look at it and began pulling on the wire that plugged into the telephone base. A few pulls later the other end arrived in his hand with nothing attached. "It's been cut!" he announced ominously.

"No way," remarked Jess.

"Yes way," replied Zac.

"That's not good."

"You're telling me!"

"Right, Plan-B. Is there another phone, Charlie?"

"Yes, Jess - one, in Auntie's room."

"Perfect, then let's get going. There isn't a moment to lose!"

The grandfather clock in the hall chimed to indicate the half hour as the children hurried past. It had become unusually dark outside for the time of day owed to the storm and a barrage of hailstones were currently being unleashed forming a white blanket across the landscape. The children walked quickly but quietly up the carpeted stairs trying not to look suspicious, as they realised maid Bertrümn was now present in the hall watching them go by. "Berty," announced Charlie politely. The moment they turned the corner at the top they burst into a sprint along the corridor all the way to the last bedroom – that of Lady Midsummer.

"Auntie! Auntie! Its Charlie. Are you there, AUNTIE!" He rapped on the door as he called her name but there came no reply, so he proceeded to twist the handle and let himself in. Like three peas in a pod their heads peered around the open door to see a room twice the size of the others. There was music playing on an old record player, which sounded like some big band from the 1940's, and furnishings that resembled the contents of an antique shop.

They saw Auntie, slouched down in an armchair beside her grand four-poster bed. Her eyes seemed wide open but unseeing; her mouth hung open. Her right arm fell lifeless over the side of the chair. The children glanced at one another fearing the worst, then entered the room and hurried over. "Auntie… AUNTIE!" called Charlie, but there was no response or sign of life.

"Do you think she's…" asked Zac, pausing for a gulp.

"Think she's what?" replied Jess.

"You know... kicked the bucket."

"Oh shut up, Zac, and show some respect. ...But now you mention it, she does look a little... well you know... a bit... well... how do I put it?"

"Gone belly up?" suggested Zac.

"*Exactly*. No wait, I mean..." Charlie looked deeply concerned and hung his head down as if in mourning. "Someone should check for signs of life," suggested Jess. The boys agreed, although no one rushed to do anything about it. "Well, Charlie?"

"Well what?"

"Well she's *your* aunt." Charlie seemed unconvinced and glanced toward Zac for a second opinion. He saw Zac was firmly on Jess' side and nodded for him to proceed. Outnumbered, Charlie took a deep breath and stepped up to his aunt's side. Her lime-green dressing gown with orange frills revealed her hairy legs and accentuated her rotund midsection, which Charlie had to lean against in order to get close to her mouth. As he did so, an unexpected bottom burp was dislodged which made him leap back in surprise. "That's a good sign isn't it?"

"Don't be too sure, Charlie," replied Zac. "People who have bit the dust..."

"AHEM!" coughed Jess.

"Err... I mean, people who have *passed away* - can still fart you know. It's all to do with a build-up of gas and the decomposition of..." He stopped when he saw Jess making the chop-throat sign with her hand behind Charlie's back, indicating he should stop talking. Receiving another word of support - and a firm shove - Charlie returned to his aunt's motionless body and held his ear over her mouth.

"Can you hear anything, Charlie?" asked Jess, as she and Zac leaned in closer.

"Nothing. Wait, hold on... I hear a rumbling sound. It's getting louder." After some very peculiar grumblings that everyone couldn't help but notice, a loud and extremely un-lady-like burp was unleashed right into Charlie's face. To their surprise, Auntie then abruptly jerked back into life screaming.

"AAARRRGGGHHHH!" shouted Charlie, who stumbled backward taking Jess and Zac with him.

Lady Midsummer, who had suddenly and unexpectedly regained consciousness, now sat bolt-upright yelling right back at the children and continued to do so, until she recognised her grand-nephew and began to calm down. "Charles! What in the name of the Pope's privates? You gave me a fright! Don't you know you should not wake an old lady from her beauty sleep? You could have given me a heart attack!"

"SLEEP!" replied Zac incredulously. "We thought you were…" he wasn't allowed to finish, as Jess punched down hard on his thigh giving him a dead-leg.

"Sorry, Auntie," explained Charlie returning to his feet, "but we simply had to wake you. You see there are these men up in Donald's cabin. They have him tied up. They plan to rob the house. TONIGHT!"

The old lady swooned back into the chair placing her hand against her forehead. "GOOD HEAVENS ABOVE! Are you sure, Charles? This isn't one of your fantasies is it?"

"Yes, I mean, no. I mean – this is for real, Auntie. We all saw it with our own eyes; heard it with our own ears. Right, guys?"

"Right, Charlie," replied Zac.

"There's something else, Your Ladyship," said Jess. "We think that one of your staff maybe involved. And we also heard the men mention something about a ruby."

At this, Auntie sat upright once again and grabbed Jess firmly by the arms. "Did you say ruby? Tell me girl. Tell me everything you know!" Her eyes suddenly burned like fire and her wrinkly hands gripped onto Jess like the claws of an eagle.

"Auntie, let her go," protested Charlie. "AUNTIE!" The old lady seemed to snap out of the trance she was in and released her grip. "I'm… sorry, children. Please forgive me."

"What do they mean, Auntie?" continued Charlie. "What ruby?"

Without answering, Auntie got up and headed for a small table in the corner of the room on which stood a selection of colourful bottles. She attempted to pour herself a drink, but was so shaken she had to employ both hands to avoid spilling it. The children stood waiting patiently, yet despite the urgency, Auntie just stood staring blankly at the wall. Charlie eventually walked over and stopped the music from playing, then placed his hand on his aunt's shoulder making her jump. "Auntie, are you OK? Why don't you come and sit for a moment?" She agreed and Charlie led her back over to the armchair.

"Thank you, Charles dear. Now children, if what you say is true, then we must contact the police; we are all in great danger."

"We tried to use the telephone in the study, Auntie. I am afraid they have cut us off."

"Good Lord! Still, not to worry, children, I have a telephone – it's over there on the desk. Quick now." Zac ran over and attempted to use it, but found the line silent. He shook his head at the others. "Why those filthy rapscallions! What cunning! What slyness! Why Judas himself…"

"Don't worry, Your Ladyship," said Jess reassuringly. "Our friend Meg has gone to get the police. She left a long time ago now. They'll be here real soon."

"Oh thank goodness. I could never forgive myself if something happened to any of you over that cursed ruby."

"Auntie, *what* ruby?" asked Charlie. "You have never mentioned anything about any ruby. What is it they are after?"

"OK Charles, it looks like I can't keep the secret any longer. Go and lock the door won't you." She invited the children to sit down on her bed which had such a soft mattress they almost disappeared into it. Auntie then opened a drawer in her dresser and pulled out a box containing some old newspaper clippings and handed them around. They were all dated between 1930 and 1950, with headlines mentioning tragedy and attempted jewellery thefts at the Midsummer estate. "The ruby is nicknamed *The Sunrise* and at fifty carats, is the largest and most expensive gemstone of its type in the world."

"Carrots?" asked Zac.

"Not *carrots,* Zac," replied Charlie. "*Carats.* It's how diamonds and precious stones are weighed."

"Oh, I knew that."

"Please continue, Auntie."

"The ruby is a red beryl, also known as red emerald or scarlet emerald and is one of the rarest gems on earth. It was discovered in nineteen-thirteen in a diamond mine in Utah, America, by an archaeologist - one Thomas Jeremiah Bixby. My grandfather. On its arrival to England it was insured by Durney's of Birmingham to a value of one million pounds. And that was when five pounds was a lot of money, but its value today... well it is priceless. Thomas offered it as a wedding gift to Lady Ava Joan Midsummer - my grandmother. At the time the publicity of the ruby and their wedding saved the estate from bankruptcy, as royalty and the super-rich travelled across the globe simply to lay gaze upon its unrivalled magnificence. It catapulted the Midsummer name into the epitome of opulence.

It was a wonderful time for the family. The house and grounds were seldom without weekend guests or visiting socialites. But alas, fate intervened and Thomas was tragically killed in the last days of the Great War, just five years after their marriage, leaving my grandmother to raise two children alone. In nineteen-thirty my grandmother died from diphtheria and the ruby passed to my parents, mere children at the time. By adulthood my father, Thomas Jnr, had become corrupted by wealth and after gambling away his own fortune, almost lost the ruby - and the entire estate - to an American in a game of cards. The only thing that saved us from losing everything that night was because the yank was found to be cheating. He even tried to steal the stone before he was arrested and thrown in jail. I remember him well, a gentleman through and through, or so I thought. He had long red hair like he had been kissed by fire. A real hunk of a man, with dashing good looks and a smile that could make one faint from fifty yards. He had buttocks so firm they could crush chestnuts and..."

"AAAAHHHEM," coughed Charlie loudly.

"Sorry, children. Where was I? Oh yes, see here - there was another unfortunate incident recored in the forties, when a group of thieves attempted to steal the ruby. They were unsuccessful, but a member of staff was shot dead and half the house was lost to fire. My father eventually died a drunken, selfish shadow of his former self and my mother, Geraldine, vowed to stop this happening to her children. She announced in nineteen-sixty that she would be leaving the ruby to me in her will and not as expected to Thomas III, my brother. Over time a great jealousy grew within him, for he desired the ruby and the wealth which accompanied it. He believed it was his birth right. He became a violent envious monster consumed by resentment and bitter hatred. He took the ruby and fled.

The police arrested my brother in Birmingham where he had travelled by canal boat, before he had a chance to travel to America. He spent the rest of his life a petty criminal and died drunk and penniless in the back streets of Coventry. My mother was devastated by this and decided to prevent such a thing happening to me or future generations. She hid the ruby somewhere in the estate and never revealed its whereabouts to me. Not when we became so short of money that she sold half the contents of the house in order to feed us, and not even at the time of her death."

Auntie arose and walked over to a large, black-framed oil painting affixed to one of the walls. She pulled it aside to reveal a safe hidden behind and proceeded to place her index finger onto a little panel on its front. A moment later a moving red line scanned her fingerprint and the door clicked open. After first peering inside, she then reached in and rummaged around looking for something. While she was busy doing this, Zac happened to notice a framed photo of Auntie on a side table. On closer inspection, it appeared to be of her and the prime minister of England! They were standing side by side and the prime minister seemed to have on his cheek, a lipstick kiss in hot pink - the very same shade worn by Auntie beside him. It was even signed by the man himself.

"Psst!" Zac got Jess' attention and gestured toward the picture. On seeing it she returned an equally amazed expression. "Oh my God!"

Back at the safe, Auntie had thrown aside some sparkling diamond jewellery, plus a number of aged documents in order to retrieve a tattered old keep-sake box. She wriggled open its largest drawer and took out a small item wrapped in cloth. "It's been decades since mother hid the ruby away and I have not laid eyes on it in all of that time."

"So it's hidden somewhere?" asked Zac excitedly. "Somewhere around the house and grounds?"

"That's right, young man, but no one including myself knows exactly where. However, mother did leave me this..." She handed over the cloth to Charlie who delicately unravelled it, finding inside an iron key. It had a shaft of about three inches long with three circles pressed into its bow. More interestingly were its teeth, or notches, for they were fashioned to resemble a deer.

"It's a key, Auntie," observed Charlie.

"Yes of course it is, Charles."

"But what's it for?"

"I am afraid I don't know exactly, but it's the only clue I have."

Charlie passed the key to Zac, who immediately noticed something inscribed on its sides. "Look here, there are markings."

"What do they say?" asked Jess squinting at it. "I can't make them out at all."

Zac picked up his rucksack and retrieved his magnifying glass which he hoped would allow them to read the inscription more clearly, but to his disappointment he found it cracked. "Bummer!"

"Wait, I have an idea," announced Jess. She pulled out her mobile phone, swiped her finger to unlock it and proceeded to take a photo of each side of the key. She then invited everyone to come closer while she zoomed in on it. They saw that one or two letters were hard to make out, but eventually they all agreed on the wording which Charlie read aloud.

AFFECTION THERETO SUN

"Affection Thereto Sun. How odd! I wonder what it means. Do you know, Auntie?"

"Sorry dear."

They considered the words for a moment and a few ideas were shared, but no one came up with any viable explanation for its meaning. "What about the other side?" Zac asked. They repeated the process of scrutinising the digital image of the other side of the key, only this time it was a little more straight-forward to comprehend.

MCMXXXIX – MCMXLV

"It's roman numerals," Charlie informed them, "but I only know up to one hundred. What about you guys?"

"Four or five," replied Zac. "No wait, six ...I think"

"Tut-tut, boys," said Jess disapprovingly. "You really should pay attention in history lessons. I'll clue you in later on deciphering them but let me tell you, the numerals translate to... *nineteen thirty-nine - nineteen forty-five* ...at least I think it does."

"You are indeed correct my dear," confirmed Auntie proudly. "Precisely the time of the Second World War."

"Go, me!"

"Good work, Jess," agreed Charlie, "but how did you know that?"

"My dad taught me. It comes in handy when you want to tell the year of old films and TV programs."

"So the key has some connection to the Second World War. D'yer think?" speculated Zac.

"Perhaps," replied Charlie. "Although what exactly, I am not sure. What do you think, Jess?"

"I think... we find whatever the key fits and we find the ruby."

"Simples," agreed Zac.

"There are also these..." said Auntie, who placed in Charlie's hands two letters she had received in as many months; both demanded the return of the Sunrise ruby.

Charlie handed one to Jess and read the other himself. "This *W* character who has signed the letter, must be the mastermind behind all this. Don't you think, Jess?"

"Could be, but there is no one with a name - first or last - beginning with *W* in your staff, if I'm not mistaken. Unless of course... Auntie, what is your butler's first name?"

"Who... Barker, dear?"

"Yes, Auntie – Barker your butler."

"Of course. Let me see now. Its… um… err… right on the tip of my tongue… um… Oh what was it now…?"

"You don't know, do you?"

"Sorry, dear."

"Excellent! Charlie, what is the return address on your letter?"

"It's a P.O box, in Milton Keynes. Untraceable, unless we get the police involved."

"Hmm, agreed, but it's a little late for that right now."

Something then caught Jess' eye in her letter, something that she found a little out of the ordinary, but Zac started speaking and she decided to keep it to herself for the moment. "You know," he said, "if we found it - the Sunrise Ruby that is, we could use it to bargain with those crooks. They might even leave us alone then."

"Now hold on a minute, Zac," replied Charlie, "but don't you think that's just a little too dangerous? After all this isn't a game and I don't think we should treat it like one. Besides, Meg will be here soon with the police and that will be the end of it. If you ask me, I propose we simply sit tight and wait."

"You mean just sit and wait for those thieves to come and torture us or something? Well if that's the case, then we may as well just walk downstairs with our hands above our heads shouting *we give up!* Personally though, I would prefer not to have my nostril hairs pulled out by a red hot poker!"

"Um, that's not exactly what I had in mind, Zac. Jess, help me out won't you?"

The boys looked at her knowing that her decision would ultimately decide their next course of action. After all, she could side with only one of them. Just then there was a knock at the door. "Who…" started Auntie, but it came out in a high pitched voice so she cleared her throat and tried again. "Ahem, who is it?"

"*Barker, madam.*"

"It's Barker!" whispered Charlie to the others.

"Yes, we can hear you know!" replied Zac.

"Well what shall we do?"

"I'm sorry, Your Ladyship," said Jess quietly, "but we can't trust anyone right now. Just ask him what he wants and get rid of him."

"Now hold on a moment, young lady. Barker has been my loyal aid for close to forty years. His integrity is beyond doubt and..."

Charlie took hold of her hand and looked into her eyes. "Auntie, please. I am sure he'll understand once this is all over. If not, just tell him we tied you up or something."

Reluctantly and feeling as if she was betraying her old friend, she followed the advice of the children. "Yes, Barker. What is it?"

"Begging your pardon, madam, but it is approaching seven o'clock. Cook is preparing some dinner for yourself, Master Charles and his guests. May I inform her that you will be attending?"

Charlie nervously began repeating the message as if no one else had heard it. "He said Cook is preparing some dinner..."

"Yes, we got it thanks, Charlie," confirmed Jess. There was a pause while they huddled and considered their options. A few whispers later there was another knock at the door.

"Madam, is everything OK? Madam?"

"Oh... err, thank you, Barker," replied Auntie. "Yes, we will be down shortly. That will be all." Barker's footsteps could be heard departing from the door and everyone breathed a momentary sigh of relief.

"Auntie, why did you say we will be attending dinner? We should just wait here until the police arrive."

"Charlie's right," agreed Zac. "We might end up poisoned or something. That is, if we haven't been already!"

Auntie leant in and replied in a whisper, "Because, children, walls have ears."

She gestured with her head and without turning her body toward an ordinary painting on the wall behind her. It was a portrait of Lady Ava Joan Midsummer, grandmother to Auntie. However, there was something extraordinary about this particular painting, for the children noticed that its eyes had come to life and were looking right at them. Almost immediately, the eyes suddenly sunk backward and the lifeless, two-dimensional pair swung back in. Zac ran over and attempted to pull the painting from the wall, but it was firmly attached and didn't budge an inch. "We see yer… yer filthy beggers!" Show yourselves why don't you!"

"Forget the painting, Zac," said Jess.

"What do you mean?"

"I mean we won't be hanging around in here anyway."

Charlie looked at her, puzzled. "Jess?"

"Zac is right," she explained.

"He is?"

"I am?"

"That's right. I think it would be a mistake to sit hoping that the thieves simply leave us alone, especially now it seems they maybe onto us after all. We should find the ruby, before the bad guys do. That way at least we can perhaps use it to bargain for our lives. And, if lady luck is on our side, then maybe the police will arrive soon and none of it will matter anyway. Now what do you say boys? Are you in or what?" She held her hand out and waited for their reply. Zac, who was already on-board, thrust his hand on top of hers. "Game on."

Charlie remained hesitant, but when he glanced over to his aunt and she gave him a little wink, he made up his mind. "One team, one dream?" he asked with a thin smile.

"One team, one dream," the others replied.

Charlie pushed the bridge of his glasses a little with his index finger, then placed his hand on top. "I'm in."

17

Meg awoke lying flat on her back to see a single glowing light bulb. It dangled by its long cord from a timber roof support and had attracted a delicate moth which danced around it in wonderment, daring every now and then to touch it. She saw a roof formed of wooden floorboards, with gaps in between wide enough to let in luminance from the room above. There were cobwebs nestled into every corner of the supporting beams with many being home to some outrageously large spiders. Up top there were persons walking around. Two men were shouting at one another in a fierce argument.

"Well I say we get rid of *all* witnesses - including them interfering rats downstairs. I'm not going back to prison cos of some cocky little, snotty-nose kids!"

"And I won't be a part of killing children!"

"What's the matter? Not got the bottle, Frenchie? Too fond of the little bed-wetting scamps or something?"

"Belgian, you English dog. Not French. Belgian. How many times do I have to tell you? Besides, from what I hear, you are the only one who wets the bed around here."

"WHO TOLD YOU THAT?! ...err, I mean, that's' a lie! You garlic-eating Frankenstein!"

"Once again my English friend you are mal informed. Frankenstein was the creator of the monster, not the monster himself. It is a common misconception of poorly educated idiots such as yourself."

"Who are you calling an idiot, you damn foreigner?!"

"ENOUGH!" roared a third voice. "Will you two cantankerous clouts please SHUT UP!" The voice was gruff and seemed to have authority over the others. A deep and fierce dog bark followed which seemed to punctuate its master's command. "This job isn't paying enough for me to put up with your petty squabbling. Honestly, you're worse than those snot-rags below – I haven't heard a peep out of them. Now, Renard, go downstairs and babysit our guests. Burk ...just stay out of my sight!"

Shortly after the door at the top of the stairs opened and someone came trudging down the steps. From the sound of it, the person then took up residence on a chair not far from Meg's feet. She turned her head slowly to one side and saw a brick wall with a few decrepit shelves fixed to it. There were no items of interest, just a bunch of tinned food, many of them rusting and joined together by thick cobwebs that stirred in the draught. She turned to look the other way but found the movement made her head feel like it was going to explode, forcing her to close her eyes tight and wait for the sensation to pass. When she opened them and focused, she was surprised to see two familiar faces looking back at her. It was Jake and Bashir, or at least she thought it was. She blinked, narrowed her eyes and took another look.

It really was them - tied to wooden chairs just like poor Donald, with gags fashioned from thick tape across their mouths. They looked cold, damp and frightened. Behind them were boxes piled high from floor to roof and from wall to wall. There seemed to be no windows or other doors and she concluded that she was in a basement or cellar. Furthermore, and judging by the sound of the voices above, probably right back where they began at the groundkeeper's cabin.

"Hey, boys," she said painfully.

"Hey, Meg," they mumbled.

On raising her hand, she realised a thin blanket lay on top of her. She smelled wet dog, but it might have been her. She tried to sit up but felt instantly dizzy and had to lay back down. "Ow, that hurts!"

"Easy, little one, you have banged your head when falling from the tree. You should rest."

Meg was startled by this and her eyes widened in surprise as she lay there, unable to react much more in her present state. The voice came from the foot of her makeshift bed - an old wooden table that wobbled when she moved. She slowly sat up and looked to see who was addressing her. She saw a person sat in an old rocking chair by the base of the stairs reading a book, no wait - not a book at all, but Meg's very own notebook. She instinctively patted her pocket to see if it was there and found it was not. The man held the little book badged *Oxford Museum of Natural History* in front of his face, hiding himself from view whilst he perused the pages. "Red-backed Shrike." His voice was deep and heavy, yet somehow gentle.

"Pardon me?" Meg replied, rubbing the back of her head and feeling a lump the size of a small egg.

"Your sketch - of the bird you made. You didn't identify it. A truly delightful specimen."

"And how does the likes of you, know *that?*"

The book slowly lowered revealing an incredibly large face, one of a freak some might say, and one that was lacking emotion. The man arose from the chair and walked toward her; his footsteps like thunder made her jump with every step. Meg's face showed the same alarm as the boys beside her and she immediately regretted talking back so impulsively. The monster of a man towered above her almost banging his head on the timbers above. He leant over blocking the light which made his face seem even more frightening in the shadows. Meg moved her head away to try and retain some distance and the moment her eyes adjusted, she could make out the angry expression across his enormous face. He raised the notebook in front of her and pointed at the sketch. "Regard," he began in a heavy Belgian accent; his fingers appearing like butcher's sausages as he pointed. "Le mâle – or the male, as you have identified here, can be recognised by its blue and grey head, petite black masking, colourful back and bill of black. Did you see it near here?"

Meg didn't reply, for all she knew this may have been some sick game the man was playing. "Well if you did," he continued, "it must have been blown off course by the storms."

"What I meant, mister, was why would someone who holds people and a little dog prisoner, know so much about nature. Oh, and by the way, if you or any of your pals should dare hurt my Cookie, you will have me to answer to!"

Jake and Bashir looked on, stunned, as the giant straightened up and contemplated being told off by a minor. "What is this... Cookie?" he asked, puzzled.

"MY DOG! The one you have locked up in that cage upstairs!"

After a short pause the man surprisingly burst into loud laughter, which continued until he arrived at the other side of the table between Meg and the boys. He held in his hand a tin of rice picked from one of the shelves. "Your pet is quite safe, mademoiselle. And to answer your question, why this is simply my day job. Nature is my love and hobby - mon amour. I give you my word that no harm will come to your precious chien. I would never hurt any animal. Although I cannot say the same for little girls and little boys."

He made his point by squeezing the tin with one hand making it pop open like a packet of crisps. Meg just about managed to maintain a brave face, not wanting her captor to believe he was intimidating her. However, the same could not be said for the boys, as Bashir was now sobbing like a baby and sitting above a yellow puddle of his own doing. The giant discarded the tin and walked back toward the stairs. He picked up the notebook, climbed the steps and slammed the door behind him.

The second he was gone, Meg immediately turned and placed her feet on the floor beside the table, but feeling a rush of dizziness, had to pause for a moment and gather her balance. "Jake, Bashir, are you alright?" she whispered. They mumbled and shuffled in their chairs trying to communicate, so Meg reached over and one-by-one ripped the tape from their mouths. "I said, are you alright?"

"Better now you're here," replied Jake. "Although I think Basher maybe losing it a bit." He gestured to the puddle below his pitiful companion.

"Eww!" grimaced Meg, stepping back.

"I can't help it," sobbed Bashir pathetically. "I saw my life flashing before my eyes. I'm too young to die young. I'm too young I tell you!"

"You're not going to die, Bashir. *I promise!* Now pull yourself together for heaven's sake. We just need to think up a way out of here."

Above them, Renard the giant had exited the cabin for some fresh air leaving the other men talking, this time over shares of the job spoils. They sat opposite one another at the kitchen table, playing cards beneath a dense microclimate of cigar and cigarette smoke. Beside Burk sat Mycroft the dog, observing the games exchanges intently. "How long have we been cooped up in this cabin for anyway?" complained Burk.

"Feels like a lifetime," replied Kaylock, without looking up from behind his hand of cards.

"I'm beginning to go stir crazy I am. I tell yer, it's not natural to live in the country. Me scotches are getting stung. Me loaf is all itchy, and taking a Jimmy in the bushes just aint funny no more. Plus I've been wearing the same underwear for a week."

Kaylock showed his indifferent eyes above his cards. "I know, Burk... I can smell you."

"Hey Boss, how about we order a pizza? You know - to cheer us up like."

"Why of course. If you don't mind it being delivered by the police."

"Oh yeah, I forgot. Hey boss, tell me about that thing again."

"What thing, moron?"

"You know - the thing you mentioned about doing that stuff, with you-know-who."

Kaylock raised one eyebrow, placed a card down onto the table then picked up another before elaborating. "Like I said, with Frank out of the way, that leaves a full third for each of us. That's twenty-five percent for you of all the booty."

Burk considered the offer as he helped himself to another card. "And what..." he replied quietly, leaning in a little, "and what if old Frenchie don't agree with doing away with Frank?"

Kaylock glanced around to make absolutely sure they were not being overheard and leaned forward himself. "Then Renard might just have an unfortunate little *accident*, allowing me and you to split the loot straight down the middle, sixty/forty."

Both men returned to their natural seating posture while Burk began thinking so hard it made his eyebrows twitch, finding he had to scratch his head to aid the process along. Kaylock watched his cognitively challenged accomplice through the narrowest of eyes whilst puffing on his cigar, sending rings of smoke across the table.

"OK boss," replied Burk. "Count me in. But I get to take care of Frankenstein. How d'yer like them apples?" He proceeded to lay his cards on the table proudly displaying a straight flush.

In true poker-face style, Kaylock showed little reaction and a moment later smiled a wry smile on the side of his mouth. "Glad you're on board, Burk. And you know, you really are smarter than you look. But as for your luck, I'm afraid you haven't beaten my four aces." He casually lay his cards down resulting in his hapless associate streaming a number of profanities. "Potty mouth! Now, just remember, Burk – this conversation never happened. We don't want Frank or Renard getting wind of our little 'detour' in the schedule. Savvy?"

"Of course, boss. You can count on me. I didn't hear nothing."

"Err, say that again won't you."

"I said don't worry, boss."

"No, after that."

"I said I didn't hear nothing."

"That's what I thought you said. But do you mean you didn't hear *anything*?"

"That's what I said, boss."

"No - what you said, was *nothing*, but are you now saying you meant to say *anything*?"

"Nothing, anything – what's the difference?"

"The difference is, you moron, that one of them is a double negative."

"Come again?"

"What you just said, just now."

"What, that I didn't hear nothing?"

"Right."

"What about it?"

"You can't say *I didn't hear nothing*, as it cancels itself out."

"But I didn't hear nothing. Just like you told me, right boss?"

"*Anything*, you didn't hear *anything!* Unless of course in actual fact you are telling me that you didn't indeed hear nothing to emphasize the negative to further affirm the positive?"

"Urm, meaning what exactly, boss?"

"THAT YOU NEVER HEARD ANYTHING!"

"Ah-ha, that's right boss. Like I said – you can count on me."

"What? No, Burk you're missing the point. When I say... what I mean is... you can't... Is any of this making sense to you at all?"

"Not really, boss."

"OK Burk, then how about this: what would you say if I told you that I definitely don't think you're not an idiot? What would you say to that?"

"Why I would say - gee, thanks boss."

"That's it, I give up!"

Kaylock stood and left the table, but as he did, two playing cards fell from his trousers down through the floorboards. They landed on the surface where Meg had lay previously and she noticed that both were aces, despite the four already present upstairs. She and the boys watched from below as the cabin door opened and Renard entered from outside. Kaylock then instructed Burk to get his things ready and flicked his cigar stub into the sink. After a brief discussion, it seemed that Renard was to remain behind and *deal* with Donald the groundskeeper and the children, whatever that meant, then join the others at the house at dusk. Burk loaded six bullets into a handgun and spun the cylinder before tucking it into his waist. He and Kaylock then picked up their coats, bags and masks and exited through the door with Mycroft in tow. Although out of sight, it sounded like they had climbed into the old van parked outside, fired up its noisy diesel engine and drove away.

"Did you see that?" whimpered Bashir. "He had a gun!" Up until that point, Bashir had begun to calm down, but was now rapidly losing it again. Meg chose to ignore him for the moment and, using the metal tin the giant had crushed earlier, finished cutting the tape that bound the boys.

"What's the plan, Meg?" whispered Jake, as he stood and stretched.

"We have to warn the others."

"What? We were supposed to go and get the police, remember? We can't stand up to these people with sticks and stones when they have guns! We should follow the original plan."

"That could mean two hours at least before any help arrives – and that's if we left twenty minutes ago. Jess and the boys don't have that much time."

"But what about *us*?"

"What about us?"

"I mean, if we all end up getting caught then no one will be coming to help."

"Hmm, I suppose you're right. I guess we…"

"The radio!" yelled Bashir loudly, forgetting their delicate situation. He had noticed it sticking out of Meg's hoodie pocket.

"Dude, keep your voice down," scolded Jake.

"The radio!" said Meg, realising its significance. She had completely forgotten that her brother had the good, no brilliant foresight to give her the walkie-talkie. Oh what a wonderful brother she had. "Of course, we can warn the others from here!" She took the radio out and turned the power slider to the *on* position. Then, checking the dial was set to the correct channel, attempted to contact her brother and friends.

"Zac. Come in, Zac. Zac are you there? ZAC!

    Zac. Come in, Zac. Zac can you hear me? Over.

        Zac, Charlie, Jess, are you there? Over.

            Hello, is there anyone there?

                Hello, hello. Anybody!

                    Ugh! Why won't they answer?!"

"Maybe it's the storm," replied Jake. "Scrambling the transmission or something."

"Or maybe it's too late," said Bashir solemnly.

Meg looked at him sickened. "And just what's that supposed to mean?"

"I'm just saying is all."

"Well do me a favour - and *don't!*"

"OK, *chill*."

"And *don't* tell me to *chill!* Well that settles it. We'll just have to go and find them."

Bashir's face dropped. "You what? I'm not going anywhere near that place thank you very much!"

"I thought we were going to get the police, Meg." said Jake. "That's what your brother is expecting. And besides, whatever we agree to do, aren't you forgetting that Bigfoot of a babysitter is standing between us and the outside? We'll need a small army to take him down."

"Well boys, guess what - we are a small army. And like it or not we are in this up to our necks, with no one to dig ourselves out besides, err, ourselves. So how about we stop mincing around in the dark and do something about it?"

"Bravo!" said Jake in admiration of her spirit.

"You mean Brava," said Bashir, rather unexpectedly.

"What?"

"Brava. Its Bravo for boys, Brava for girls."

Meg and Jake looked at him gobsmacked. Who was this imposter showing some intelligence? What had they done with the real Bashir? Meg approached him and placed her hand on his shoulder. "Basher, that might just be the most intelligent thing you have ever said." He blushed thanking her and began to explain his knowledge of the subject, however, Meg abruptly cut him off. "Tell me later!" Her focus had turned to a tiny glint of light she had spotted above and behind him, just visible between some of the boxes. She shoved Bashir aside and excitedly stepped forward as far as the stack of junk would allow. She then reached up and took away a box and sure enough it revealed a small rectangular window, right at the top of the wall at ground level. It was painted over allowing hardly any light in or out, but it was a window none the less and windows can be opened. "Ha! There is hope for us yet. Jake, give me a boost."

Jake immediately crouched and interlocked his fingers to provide a step onto which Meg placed her foot. After a one-two-three count, he lifted her up and she got to work taking out boxes from the top and carefully handed them down to Bashir below. They worked silently as not to stir the ogre upstairs and would often freeze when they heard his heavy footsteps trudging around. Once suitable access had been created, Meg attempted to pull the window upward but found it difficult to open, as its rusty hinges had seized after years of inactivity. When it finally yielded, she concluded that the dimensions of the opening were sufficient for them all to climb through, albeit a bit of a squeeze for Bashir. Outside it was still raining, but Meg estimated that beyond the black clouds there was still an hour or two of daylight remaining. She asked Jake to lower her back down.

"OK boys, I need you to get to the village and contact the police like we planned. And hurry, there isn't a minute to lose." No sooner had she said this, Bashir was attempting to scale the remaining boxes like a mountain goat, until Jake grabbed hold of his jeans and pulled him back down.

"Not so fast, Basher. Meg, you're not coming with us?"

"No, Jake. I have to get to the others and help them."

"Girl, what is your problem? Help them *how* exactly?"

"I don't know, but if I can just warn them to stay out of sight, to hide at least, then they might just have a chance. And besides, Cookie is still up there with that monster. I can't leave him behind."

"You're staying in this hell hole for a chocolate chip biscuit?!" blurted out Bashir.

"Dude, that's enough!" ordered Jake.

"Look, I don't expect you to understand, boys, but I'm staying and nothing you say or do will make me change my mind. I'll be fine. We'll *all* be fine, as long as you go and get help."

Jake nodded, realising he wasn't about to talk her out of it. "Alright Meg, you go do what you have to do; we'll get to the village even if it kills us. Right, Bash?"

Bashir didn't look quite as committed, but shrugged all the same. "Wotever, can we *go* now?"

Jake crouched to give him a boost and watched his stocky friend squeeze through the little frame. He then prepared to make the climb himself, but before he did, pulled off his soiled jumper momentarily revealing a perfectly sculpted stomach. Meg couldn't help but notice and gawped at it brazenly, "so ripped!" Jake pulled his polo down and noticed her - not just noticed but *noticed*-noticed, and for some reason they suddenly found themselves gazing into one another's eyes.

"You, err, should probably get going," said Meg dreamily.

"Yeah... I guess..."

"There isn't a moment to lose."

"Nope..."

Bashir's anxious face returned to the window above and saw them standing idle. "Mate, wot *are* you doing? Let's go!"

They both snapped out of it and Jake proceeded to climb up the stack. As soon as he was in reach, he took Bashir's hand and was pulled through the opening. The window opened one last time and for one last time Jake appeared. He waved down to Meg who acknowledged. Then he was gone.

18

Jess was with Zac in his room waiting for Charlie to change clothes next door. Zac himself had finished changing a while back and was now keeping his mind busy by organising supplies in his rucksack. They had agreed to lock Lady Midsummer in her bedroom for her own protection and figured they might be able to slow the crooks down by locking as many of the doors as they could around the house. They would then retreat to the basement or one of the secret passages, depending on how things worked out, and wait for the police. Charlie was in his own room with the connecting door left open so they could see one another. There had already been an embarrassing moment earlier which resulted in Jess getting an eye-full of Charlie in his underpants. This had embarrassed him hugely, resulting in him shouting, "BEEJEESUS!" and hopping out of sight as he scrambled to pull up his trousers.

Jess had already retrieved a bag containing a change of clothes from her room and brought it over, while the boys had stood guard at her door. She had since changed into jeans and t-shirt, zip-up hoodie, and tied her hair back with clips. Her trainers, however, were the same ones worn during the day and remained wet and soggy; it was either that or wear black, sparkly evening shoes with high-heels. She stood diligently at the bedroom window looking out for any sign of approaching danger. The sun would be low in the sky now and it continued to rain thick and fast, making it difficult to see through the misted glass. A sudden flash of lightning lit up the sky and was immediately followed by a piercing rumble of thunder, indicating the storm was directly overhead. It cast shadows from the trees, creating eerie shapes that played tricks on her eyes. She would see something that resembled a person, then blink and it would be gone. Behind her, the boys were now talking to one another, but she remained deep in her own thoughts wondering if she had made the right decision by making a stand. How would she feel if something terrible happened to one of her friends? How would she break the awful news to their parents? Would she be able to look them in the eye?

"Jess..."

She did not hear her name being called, so Zac came over and placed his hand on her shoulder. "Jess, I said we're ready. You OK?"

Zac had changed into his evening apparel which comprised of hiking boots, combat-style trousers, and t-shirt with some gaming techno-babble imprinted on the front. He was munching on his modest supper - one third of a banana, trying desperately hard to imagine it was steak and chips. Jess looked at him and managed a pained smile. "Oh... yes, Zac. I'm fine. I just... whoa! What's that?" She was referring to the weird-looking, black, rubbery mask that Zac carried in his other hand.

"Night vision goggles," he casually informed her.

"Night vision goggles?"

"Yep."

"*OKAY*... and what's that on your waist?"

"Where?"

"Right there. It looks like... like a stun gun or something."

"Oh that, yeah - it's a conductive electrical weapon."

"You mean... like a stun gun?"

"Exactly, well a cheaper replica at least. But 50,000 non-lethal, ass-tingling volts nonetheless."

"Where on earth did you get it? And more importantly, what on earth do you plan to do with it?!"

"Car boot of course; and zap some bad guys if I get the chance."

Jess, like Meg, now knew Zac well enough to just go with his flow and not bother questioning why he did what he did, so she simply shrugged and carried on. She walked into the centre of the room where Charlie returned through the connecting door and met them. He was zipping up the fly on his corduroy trousers and wore a bright, knitted woollen jumper with equally dazzling leather boots. She looked him up and down as if she were his personal shopping assistant. "Err, Charlie..."

"Yes, Jess?"

"Just a thought, but haven't you got any slightly less conspicuous clothes? You know, something a little less like... um... everything you're wearing."

"Not really, but I suppose I could wear my school uniform?"

Jess looked worryingly at Zac, who simply indicated no with a frown and a shake of his head. "Err... actually Charlie, come to think of it - I do believe you look just fine after all. Don't you agree, Zac?" She nudged him in his side in order to get him to speak up.

"Oh, blates. Very... err... stylish. Very stylish."

Charlie then noticed Zac's goggles clipped to his belt. "Whoa, what's that?"

"Night vision goggles," replied Zac proudly. "Cool or what?"

"Very!"

"Surweet!"

"Totally!"

"Sic!"

"Awesome!"

"Err, boys," interrupted Jess. "If you've quite finished, can we please focus for a moment?"

"Sorry, Jess."

"Now, if Zac has everything he needs then we will proceed as planned."

"Affirmative," confirmed Zac.

"Excellent, then let's go. We'll start by locking all the rooms upstairs. Then we'll... OUCH!" Jess stopped because while they were walking she had kicked Zac's discarded shorts he wore earlier, stubbing her toe on a solid object hidden within. "Zac!" she groaned. "I nearly broke my friggin' toe! What's hiding under there anyway?"

He inspected the pockets and pulled out the object. It was the walkie-talkie radio. He also realised that it was still switched off. "Oops, I must have forgotten to turn it back on when we were hiding from Frau what's-her-name in the cupboard."

"Bertrümn," said the others.

Almost immediately, a weak, fuzzy voice came through over the airwaves - it was Meg. "...anyone there? Zac can … …. me. It's Meg. Come in, over."

Jess, Zac and Charlie looked at one another and the relief showed across their beaming faces. "It's Meg!"

"With the police."

"We're saved!"

They excitedly jumped up and down with joy and the boys chest-bumped, resulting in Charlie getting knocked backward onto the floor. For a brief moment it appeared their nightmare was over and that it had passed without any confrontation. They settled down and huddled together as Zac pressed the button to transmit. "How-do, Meg? Captain Zac here. It's good to hear your voice. You made good time, where are you now? Over."

But the response they received was not at all what they were expecting and they could immediately tell that something was wrong. "Meg, what is it? Meg, are you OK? Over." Only some of her words were audible perhaps due to the amount of electrical interference in the air, perhaps because they were close to the maximum operating range of the budget transceivers. The exchange was broken, garbled and intermittent.

"URGH, it's no good," said Jess. "She keeps breaking up!"

"Just tell her to get out of there and stay safe!" begged Charlie.

"Meg, we want you to keep safe do you hear? Don't do anything stupid. Just stay safe until the police arrive. Is that perfectly clear? Meg, can you hear me? Meg!"

The conversation they had managed to hold ended prematurely and now only the buzzing of static could be heard. Zac took back the radio and tried desperately to find an alternate channel, stopping only when Jess placed her hand on his shoulder. The news they had received was devastating, but at least it had been received. Jess and the boys knew they were on their own against armed, cold-blooded thieves. The mood changed quickly. Things had just gotten real.

Zac tossed the radio aside and lie back on the bed. "That's it then, we're done for!"

"Calm down, Zac," replied Jess, trying to console him but failing to convince even herself. "It could be worse."

"Worse? You heard what Meg said. She's out there *on her own!* Jake and Basher have abandoned her..."

"She didn't say that."

"She didn't have to! And that means *no* backup and *no* police. So tell me, how could things possibly be any worse?"

That was the last thing they said before the lights went out. Charlie walked over to the switch and flicked it on/off a few times but nothing happened. He tried the bedside lamp, as well as the bathroom light finding neither would come on. The digital clock beside Zac's bed remained stubbornly blank. "It's probably the storm," said Charlie. He was trying his very best to remain optimistic, yet his forced smile failed to mask his fear.

Jess walked over to the window and opened the curtains. Thankfully there were still maybe two hours, give or take, of clouded daylight remaining before dusk, so for a short while at least they would be able to see well enough to navigate the house. She used her sleeve to wipe a circle on the glass to improve visibility. When she focused on the path below she noticed movement and called the others over. "Boys, we've got company."

They joined her and together witnessed the same thing - the unmistakable sight of a grown man wearing a hideous wolf mask. They stepped away from the alcove and looked at one another. "What do we do, Jess?"

"Charlie, grab your keys. We lock down the place starting with the front door. Right now!"

With that said, she and the boys immediately headed toward the bedroom door. She pulled it open, but they all stopped still as a rush of fear and dread came over them. For standing in their path just a few feet away was one of the masked men. They observed one another for a brief moment, as both parties had been taken by surprise. Then, without warning, the man lunged for them.

Thankfully Jess had the quick thinking to slam the door closed and she and the boys instinctively threw their bodies against it. The door jolted violently as the man did the same, sending the children recoiling backward with each and every blow. Jess and Zac then had to share the extra strain while Charlie scrambled for his keys in order to lock it. Under immense pressure he had to find the right one out of dozens and frantically he tried one after another. Finally, he located the required key and inserted it into the slot, only for a sudden impact from the other side to cause it to fly back out. He juggled to keep hold of the key and once again managed to insert it and lock the door. Only then were they able to stand back, their hearts pounding at three times the normal rate.

After a while the thundering on the door stopped, but they stood still and quiet, not daring to move just yet. Moments passed and there came no further noise from the other side. Their breathing began to calm, so tentatively they stepped closer to listen. It remained silent.

"Perhaps he's..." Charlie was interrupted by a black leather fist smashing through the door; its fingers expanding outward in order to grab anything it could. It found Zac's rucksack shoulder strap and gripped like steel. "AAARRRGGGHHH! HELP!" he cried. He pulled away with all his might while Jess and Charlie did their best to heave him toward them, but the hand held like a vice and wouldn't let go.

"ZAC, LOSE YOUR BAG!" shouted Charlie.

"WHAT?"

"TAKE OFF YOUR BAG! THE HAND HAS HOLD OF YOUR BAG STRAP!"

"BUT WHAT ABOUT MY BAG?"

"WHAT ABOUT YOUR LIFE?!"

Zac acknowledged Charlie's suggestion and began wriggling out of the rucksack. With their combined pulling power, which almost tore Zac's t-shirt from him, he was suddenly released and they all fell to the floor.

"COME ON!" cried Charlie. They clambered to their feet and headed toward the connecting door to Charlie's room, but Zac unexpectedly stopped and returned to his bag.

"WHAT ARE YOU DOING?" shouted the others. They watched bewildered as Zac positioned himself beside his rucksack that was being forced through the hole in the door with such force it caused the wood to splinter. He unclipped the little camera that was fixed to one of the straps. "Got it!"

He joined the others and together they ran into the next room where Charlie tossed the keys to Jess and instructed her to lock the door. While she jostled to find the right one, Charlie opened the cage of his rat and asked Zac to do the same for the ferrets. He then gently released the animals into a hole in one of the skirting boards and watched them scamper away.

"Where did you put them?" asked Zac out of interest.

"Under the floorboards. Don't worry, they'll be fine - they're always getting under there."

With the connecting door and the animals now secured, the children crept toward the corridor. Together, they proceeded to quietly open the door just enough for them to peer outside. They saw the masked man violently using a crowbar to force entry to Zac's room. He stopped only when the door and its frame were almost completely destroyed and he was able to step through without obstruction. It was at this very moment the children hastened toward the stairs.

It was considerably darker in the corridor and ahead they saw the landing at the top of the staircase being illuminated to the dance of lightning. Behind, the end bed chamber of Lady Midsummer had already been lost to the darkness. "Change of plan," said Jess as they hurried along. "Let's get the heck out of here!"

They reached the top of the stairs and took a single step down, but immediately they stopped. The main entrance door at the foot of the stairs had suddenly burst open letting in the elements. From it they saw Barker the butler, struggling to remain upright against the gale. He was carrying what appeared to be a long and rather antique looking, double-barrelled shotgun, which he could just about keep pointed ahead of himself. He advanced toward the dining room with intent. Jess and the boys stood perfectly still and watched until he had gone from view, at which point they took another step down only to stop again, for they had spotted someone else. It was one of the masked men and he was carrying a silver handgun. He tiptoed from the sitting room toward the dining room door where he peered around the door frame before entering. The children looked at one another, gulped, then took another step but stopped yet again because from the direction of the conservatory came Mrs Blackwell the cook, wielding a large kitchen knife. She seemed to be in pursuit of the masked man for she too entered the dining room.

"Bloody hell, it's like spaghetti junction!" said Zac astounded. He had barely finished speaking when the sound of gunfire rang out startling them all. First the heavy shotgun: two rounds spent and the sound of a window breaking, then a single pistol shot followed by silence.

"Um, maybe we should go back upstairs," suggested Jess nervously.

"Good Idea," agreed the boys.

Side-by-side they backtracked and turned down the corridor where they immediately realised they were unable to proceed: the masked man they had evaded earlier suddenly appeared from Charlie's room. Jess, who stood in between the two boys, pulled them to a stop and they all froze together. Mercifully, the man had not noticed them, for he headed away in the opposite direction attempting to open some of the other doors. Without speaking, Jess tugged on the boy's arms and they carefully and quietly returned to the top of the stairs, where they found themselves freezing to the spot once again. This time it was the maid, Fräulein Bertrümn.

She glided like a spectre across the entrance hall until she reached the foot of the stairs – where she abruptly stopped. The children stood perfectly still and made no noise - they dared not even breathe. Below them the figure in black stood motionless like a statue, while her long, thin shadow orchestrated by lightning, leapt up the walls. Charlie's leg began to cramp up and when he couldn't bare it any longer, slowly shifted his balance to his other side. In doing so he inadvertently caused a floorboard to creak under foot and, like a hawk, the maid's head snapped up in their direction.

"TIME TO GO!" exclaimed Jess, tugging the boys backward.

"And just where d'you suggest we go exactly?" asked Zac.

"The attic," replied Charlie noticing the door. "We'll be safe up there."

"Great, then we'll be stuck in the roof unable to come down!"

"I didn't say it was a good suggestion!"

The door to the attic was just a dozen or so feet behind them and realising they were thoroughly stuck between a rock and a very hard place, they turned and made a dash for it. The masked man along the corridor had now also noticed them. He stopped breaking open doors and headed in their direction. Down in the hall, Fräulein Bertrümn had come to life and began ascending the staircase.

Zac arrived at the door first and grabbed the handle ready to open it, but found it remained firmly shut. He tried again, pushing and pulling it frantically. "Locked!" he announced.

"Charlie, it's locked!" said Jess growing increasingly anxious.

"KEY!" was all that Charlie said. He pulled the bundle that he had attached to one of his trouser belt loops using a retractable wire. "I've got it!"

"WELL OPEN THE BLOODY DOOR THEN!" screamed Jess and Zac.

Fräulein Bertrümn was now halfway up the stairs and the masked man perhaps closer, but Charlie's shaking hands were preventing him from locating the key in the lock.

"STAND BEHIND ME, GUYS," announced Zac bravely.

"Err, like we are already?" replied Jess.

"Oh right. In that case stay where you are and I'll handle our guests."

Jess watched in awe as Zac unclipped the stun gun from his belt and took a step toward the staircase. With the device held away from himself he prepared to unleash it on the closest adversary – the wolf man. "STAY BACK!" warned Zac. "STAY BACK OR I'LL ZAP YOU!" His caution did nothing to deter those approaching so he closed his eyes, held his breath and depressed the little red button. A small flash of light was followed by a fizz and a tiny puff of smoke, but nothing more.

"Is that it?" asked Jess incredulously.

"Must have forgotten to charge it!"

In desperation Jess grabbed the key from Charlie and shoved him aside. With zen-like focus, she then managed to insert it into the lock after just two fumbles. She unlocked the door and yanked it open, grabbed Zac by the collar and funnelled through just as the masked man passed the top of the stairs. Charlie pulled the door shut and Jess raised the key to the lock bringing his groin with it. She locked the door sealing them in without a moment to spare.

Part Two

19

It looked like they may have gotten away with it - that Jake and Bashir had escaped from the cabin. So far so good, thought Meg. She had heard no sound or movement from the floor above for some time, so began to delicately creep up the stairs to investigate. She arrived at the door and pushed it ajar, just enough to peer through the gap. She saw both rooms were empty, except for Donald, who remained sleeping in the chair he was tied to. His head hung back awkwardly and his mouth was still covered by tape, yet somehow managed to snore so loudly it made the pile of dishes in the kitchen shake. Not far from his side, Cookie sat alert in his cage. He had noticed his owner and was becoming increasingly excited.

Once satisfied the coast was clear, Meg slowly pushed open the door and tiptoed toward him. "Hey boy." A quick glance around revealed no one lurking in the shadows, so she unclipped the two fasteners and opened the cage letting the super-exited little dog jump into her arms. He wriggled and squirmed and licked her face frantically, as if she'd been covered in chocolate. His long bushy tail wagged from side to side so fast it created a draft.

With no sign of her captor, Meg glanced toward the cabin door and considered making a run for it, managing two whole steps before feeling a tug on her heart-strings and returning to free Donald. She approached him and gave him a nudge on the shoulder. "Mister, wake up... mister!" although he didn't respond so she tried again. "Mister, please wake up." Despite shaking him with increasing hostility, nothing happened, apart from his ginger toupee suddenly dropping into his lap. It revealed a perfectly circular bald spot on the top of his head, meaning any remaining wild hair grew exclusively from the sides and back. "Mister, come on. It's time to go!"

As Meg attempted to replace the hair piece, Cookie suddenly barked and changed to a somewhat more fearsome persona. He was looking over Meg's shoulder toward the kitchen, where someone had entered through the door.

"And just where do you plan on going, little one?"

The voice was unmistakably that of the large man whose job it was to ensure neither groundskeeper, child nor dog left the cabin alive. Without warning, Cookie suddenly sprang from Meg's arms and tore across the room toward him. "COOKIE!" yelled Meg, but it was too late. The little dog was like a mouse in proportion to the giant, but nonetheless had the heart of a lion and would do anything to protect his beloved owner. It therefore came as quite a surprise when he arrived in front of his epic quarry and simply lay down on his back with his paws in the air. The giant could have done away with him there and then if he so desired, but instead smiled, before crouching and delicately tickling his tiny chest. He spoke softly to the little pooch and, unsurprisingly, didn't seem at all troubled by him.

He stood and Meg noticed a hunting rifle slung over his shoulder, while hanging lifeless across his arm was a pheasant, presumably freshly shot. "Cookie, come here," said Meg with growing frustration. "COOKIE!" Despite her efforts he stubbornly chose to stay put. How she regretted not going to puppy training classes right now. She watched as the man pulled out a little piece of biscuit from his pocket, letting the dog smell it before instructing him to sit. Cookie immediately sat down wagging his tail and was given the treat as a reward. Meg looked on feeling betrayed. "Cookie!"

"The secret is to reward them," said the giant. "Now young lady, you sit too please."

She once again noticed the gun hanging by his side and took a seat beside Donald, treat or no treat. Donald then suddenly woke up and started panicking, realising he was still in his nightmare. Meg placed her hand upon his and tried to comfort him. "It's alright, Mr McGee, you don't have to worry. My friends have gone for help. The police will be here any minute." She knew this was a massive exaggeration of the truth as the boys had not long left, meaning any arriving help would be at least one or two hours away. Her captor, however, did not know this. Or so she thought.

The giant peered through the basement door and saw the empty chairs confirming Meg's story. He then turned, dropped the bird down onto the table and hung up the rifle on a peg. "That's a fine gun, Monsieur McGee. It shoots straight and true – but tell me, is it good for hunting children?"

Meg's face fell at the thought. "You wouldn't?"

"Wouldn't I? Well, you two just sit tight and behave yourselves and we won't have to find out. Do we have an understanding?" They both nodded; it wasn't like they had much choice. Their captor then removed his heavy coat, casually washed his hands in the sink and began stripping feathers from the bird. "Besides," he continued, "I estimate at least two hours to get to the village in this weather. Especially so, as they left just a short while ago." He raised his head to gauge Meg's reaction, who tried not to look disheartened or give away too much as she replied.

"So... you know?"

"But of course!" he roared. "I let them go. And I would have let you go too, had you followed them."

Meg glanced at Donald, his toupee seemingly on backwards, who looked back with questioning eyebrows. She turned back to the giant. "Are you going to hunt them or something?"

He lopped the head off the bird cleanly in one chop of a huge butcher's knife. "*Hunt* them! Goodness me, no. Not enough meat."

"Then... why would you let them go?"

"*Why,* little one? Let me tell you *why* - because my associates plan to kill that old lady down at the house; to kill you and your friends; him, and anyone else who could identify them, and I won't have a part in this. I am no murderer. Thief, liar... perhaps yes, but not a murderer."

"Your friends are going to kill you too, you know," said Meg gravely. "And that man, Frank. I heard them talking whilst you were out. They are going to kill you and take your share of the money."

The giant slammed his fist down on the table causing the collection of plates - and Meg and Donald - to jump in the air. He then pulled the longest knife from the chopping block and walked toward them where he held the shiny blade so close to their faces, they turned cross-eyed looking at it.

"How do I know you do not lie?" he demanded.

Donald's expression returned to that of terror and both he and Meg leant as far back in their chairs as they could. "Because..." stammered Meg.

"Yes?"

"Because..."

"Yes, yes?!"

"Because, girl guides don't lie!"

The giant steered the knife toward Donald causing sweat to drip from his brow. Had he not fainted again, he would have seen his captor burst into laughter - laughter so loud it made their hearts tremble. "Girl guides you say, young lady? Well in that case..." He proceeded to cut the tape that bound Donald's right hand, then the left, followed by his legs in the same order. He then brought the knife toward Meg but said nothing, before returning to the kitchen where he drove the blade into the table top. Meg slumped down in her chair and breathed a huge sigh of relief. Cookie joined her and together they watched the giant skilfully slice some prime cuts from the bird and toss them into a frying pan. Then, as if it were a lazy Sunday afternoon, he attentively rummaged through a little spice rack that hung above the cooker and selected something suitable for his dish. A few minutes later he had three plates laid on the table, albeit dirty and greasy ones, and carefully spooned some of the pan-fried pheasant onto each. He turned to Meg and smiled. "Now, who's hungry?"

20

The effect of someone throwing themselves against the attic door rumbled and shook its very framework. *BOOM, BOOM, BOOM!* Relentlessly it went on and with such aggression it caused dust and bits of decrepit brickwork to sprinkle down onto the children's heads. It was followed by a different sound, perhaps that of the crowbar being put to work, but thankfully this door was heavy, unyielding oak and would stand firm. After what felt like hours, the noise stopped and silence returned.

Jess and the boys found themselves standing in almost complete darkness, save for the thin ingress of light that leaked in below the door. They heard a person walk away down the corridor and, almost immediately after, someone else approach from the staircase. Looking down they saw a single eyeball staring at them through the keyhole.

"Fräulein what's-her-name?" whispered Zac.

"Bertrümn," replied the other two. They watched the round handle slowly turn and saw the door rattle. Then a voice called out, "Kinder, ja?"

"It's Bertie, alright," confirmed Charlie. The children didn't respond and after a while they once again heard footsteps heading away, allowing them a moment to breathe and compose themselves.

"She's gone," sighed Jess.

"And the wolfman?" asked Charlie.

"Gone. We're safe, for the moment at least."

"Gee that was intense!"

"That's an understatement. Oh, and Zac, the next time you think about using one of your dumb-ass gadgets, do us a favour - *don't!*"

"But..." he protested.

"But nothing! Now, who has a light?"

Charlie could be heard fumbling in the dark and his keys jingled noisily as he did so. After a while he found his little pocket torch and clicked it on, illuminating their faces from below like ghostly apparitions. They saw Zac, frantically searching for something. "Oh no!"

"What is it?" asked Jess, beginning to panic.

"I must have dropped my night vision goggles, out in the hall."

"Is that all?"

"Is that all?! I delivered newspapers for six months in order to get the money."

"You mean all those newspapers you burned in your garden?"

"Yeah, well. *Ahem*. Not all of them, just some that's all - the leaflets."

"Forget the goggles, Zac. They're replaceable – you're not. At least I think you're not. Anyway, we have a torch, sort of. Now, where are we anyway?"

Charlie turned and shone the light around. They saw they were standing at the bottom of a set of steep wooden stairs flanked on either side by dilapidated brick walls. The torch light revealed its questionable condition, highlighting countless deep cracks and crevices into which some night dwelling insects darted to take cover. Waiting at the top was blackness and the incessant howling of the wind.

"It's no luxury penthouse," said Jess ominously. "That's for sure."

"Reminds me of a bed and breakfast I stayed at in Blackpool," replied Zac. "Whose bright idea was it to come in here again?"

"Charlie's," replied Jess.

"At least I had an idea," he replied sourly.

Jess turned toward him and rubbed her hands together. "Oh well, never mind. After you then, Charlie."

"What? Why do I have to go first?"

"*Because*, you've got the torch."

He looked down at it, as if he were suddenly holding red-hot stolen property. "Here, you take it."

"I'm good thanks!"

"Here, Zac, you take it."

Zac threw his hands in the air. "Nuh-uh, I'm not going first - there might be a corpse up there!"

"What?!" gasped Jess. "Why would there be a corpse in the attic?"

"Corpses have a habit of turning up in spooky places."

"Don't be ridiculous. Tell him, Charlie."

"He's right, Jess. Just like on TV – someone's just going about their business checking out a cellar and BANG! – out pops a corpse! All corpsy and corpsified.

"Corpses don't just pop out, Charlie."

"They do if they're zombies!" said Zac.

"I can't believe I'm hearing this."

"We're just sayin' is all. Don't be surprised if we find a corpse."

"Will everyone please stop saying corpse! Now come on, Charlie. It is your house after all."

"Meaning what exactly?"

"MEANING YOU SHOULD GO FIRST!"

Charlie delayed for a moment, trying desperately to find an excuse, "Err, what about ladies first, Jess?"

"I'm no lady - and Zac sure as hell isn't."

Well then... um, what about a vote? That will be fair. You know like..."

"I vote Charlie," interrupted Jess. "Zac?"

"Charlie!"

"That settles it. You can't argue with democracy, Charlie. Now get going!"

With a firm shove from the others, Charlie gulped and shone the torch up the stairwell. He hesitated for a moment, then hesitated some more. After a while he turned back around.

"What now?" asked Jess.

"This isn't going to work - and I'm not just sayin' that. We need more light!"

"Hey, hold on a sec," said Zac optimistically. He suddenly remembered the torch app on his phone and fired it up. "Can't believe I forgot about that!" Jess then did the same and the level of light increased significantly, as did their spirit. Now armed with a torch apiece they agreed to ascend the steps together.

Tentatively they climbed and several creaky steps later arrived at the top, where they were each welcomed by a face-full of cobwebs. They spent the next minute coughing, spitting and spluttering as they feverishly shook debris and little bugs from their persons.

"BLAH, YUK! I don't usually eat cobwebs on an empty stomach!" grumbled Zac.

"First time I've heard you turn down food," replied Jess.

Shining their lights around they saw that the attic spanned a large section of the house and appeared to be rather an inhospitable place to be. Above them, exposed rafters were thick with cobwebs, many containing a selection of unfortunate mummified invertebrates. Around them and scattered about the entire floor area were white sheets, covering a variety of mysterious objects of various shape and size; they formed an array of motionless monsters that looked like they may come to life if disturbed. There were also boxes and collections of random junk in abundance, piled as high as the roof would allow in some places. There were no windows and the stairs they had come up seemed to be the only way down.

It felt uncomfortably warm despite the wind whistling through, as the old house was poorly insulated and allowed all heat from the floors below to accumulate in the roof space. Wiping his brow, Zac turned toward the others looking worried. "I wonder how long we'll have to wait up here?" He saw a tall, dusty vase beside them and drew a frowny face.

"As long as we have to," replied Jess, making the face a smiley one.

Charlie then sneezed a monster of a sneeze, "**AA-TISHO!**"

"Hay fever, Charlie?" asked Jess.

"Dust!"

"So, what do we do now?" asked Zac.

"Maybe we should barricade the door?" sniffed Charlie. "You know, to stop anyone getting up here."

"Good idea," agreed Jess, "but nothing permanent, in case we have to get out in a hurry. Zac, can you sort that while Charlie and I take a look around?"

"I'm on it."

"Good thinking, Jess," said Charlie, "but… what exactly are we looking for?"

"Something relating to the ruby. Anything that might offer some clue as to its whereabouts."

They got to work straight away with Charlie pulling a dust cover off the nearest object. It stood several feet taller than him and he yelled out in panic when a ferocious looking, stuffed grizzly bear was revealed. He stood staring up at it wide-eyed until Zac and Jess arrived at his side, thinking he had been attacked or something.

"Scaredy-cat!" said Zac.

Jess went on to open the lid of a large chest and was greeted by a real-life mouse which made her scream out. Charlie then pulled on some drapes and out flew some pigeons sending a chill down his spine. Even Zac got caught out whilst looking for some timber to lay against the door, when a cupboard he opened revealed a full size skeleton dangling from a chain. "CORPSE!" he wailed. Thankfully it turned out to be a fake - like the ones used to teach human anatomy, but it still managed to give him quite a fright.

Jess hurried over to see what the commotion was. She found Zac looking as white as the skeleton staring back at them. "Wow! Think you found the hide-and-seek winner. Didn't scare you did she?"

"Oh no, course not," replied Zac tensely.

"You sure? You're shaking like a leaf and everything."

"Don't be daft. Anyway, what makes you think it's a she?"

"Bigger pelvic cavity. For child bearing. Didn't you notice?"

"Err… yes, of course! Like you said, bigger pelvic err… capacity. I just wasn't too bothered that's all. I mean… when you're getting attacked by a skeleton you don't stop to consider if it's a boy or girl. Right?"

"If you say so," smirked Jess. "Well, if you're sure you're OK, then I'll leave you two alone."

"Just perfect, thanks!"

Jess turned and headed away leaving Zac alone with his new friend. He shone his light onto its pelvis and raised an eyebrow, then onto its face which seemed to be grinning back. "I think it's going to be a long night!"

21

The pheasant was cooked to mouth-watering perfection. Tender, succulent and simply bursting with flavour. It was proof, if proof were needed, that the man was an accomplished hand in the kitchen. Meg used her hands to eat with as there were no clean knives or forks and cleared her plate almost as quickly as Cookie the dog. Opposite them sat the giant, enjoying his meal and appearing to savour each and every mouthful. Behind them, Donald remained unconscious, but Meg had at least talked her captor into laying him down on his bed and provided some food and water by his side.

"URGH!" said Meg frustrated. "I just can't think what it is. Ask me again."

"OK," replied the giant, "but this is the last time. Now, the more you take away from me, the bigger I get. What am I?"

"I'VE GOT IT!" announced Meg after some more thought. She whispered her answer over the table.

"Well done, Megan. I knew you would get it in the end."

"Yeah, it was a tough one though, I'll give you that."

The giant cleared his plate and pushed it away to join the others abandoned on the table. He then reached into his pocket and pulled out two shiny red apples.

"Where did you get those?" asked Meg, gratefully receiving one.

"From the gardens, by the house. There are many fruits growing there. Mr McGee knows his stuff, but he could increase the variety by simply mixing male and female trees." He watched Meg devour the apple while Cookie curled up and had a nap.

"How do you know all that stuff?" mumbled Meg.

"Ah, you see, I used to be in the guides when I was a boy."

"WHAT?!"

"The guides for boys of course," he added hastily. "Back home we call it the Guidisme et Scoutisme en Belgique!"

"Oh, you mean the Boy Scouts."

"Yes, exactly. The Boys of Scouts!"

"So... mister, how did you become involved with those men anyhow? You don't seem to be like them at all."

"Please, call me Renard. It means fox in French you know."

"Oh, OK, and you can call me Meg. It means... um, Megan, in English."

"Please to meet you um, Megan." He offered his huge hand across the table and she shook it.

"So, Renard, how did you get involved with them. The crooks I mean?"

"Well, I came to England to work some time ago now - and honest work it was to start with. I was about your age when I first stepped foot in England, but already I was almost six feet tall and weighed more than most grown men. So, I did work that suited me best - physical work, heavy lifting. I settled as a farm hand doing the job of three men and that's when I learned about nature. I was given food and allowed to sleep in the barn, but it didn't pay very well."

"That sounds awful," replied Meg. "Why didn't you ask for more money and a proper room, or just go somewhere else?"

"Well you see, I am what you call an alien."

"An alien?"

"Yes, it means I am not allowed to live and work in your country."

"Oh, an *alien*."

"I could be sent home, deported. So I had to keep my head down and avoid trouble. And besides, animals nearly always make better friends than humans - present company excluded. You see you can always trust them and they will never deceive you."

Meg finished her apple, including the core and drank a whole glass of water in one. "So you were an honest farmer, then how did you end up a kidnapper and thief?"

"Well, one night there was trouble at the farm. I heard gunfire and screaming. When I looked toward the master's house I saw a masked man running away and that the house was on fire. I entered and found the owner. He and his wife had been shot, but he was still alive so I carried him outside. He thanked me, only he died moments later. Shortly afterward some of the villagers arrived. They saw a monster who had attacked their neighbour and so they tried to detain me. I tried to explain but I could not speak much English then. One of them hit me with a piece of wood - it cracked my skull and made me dizzy. I heard the police, so I fled."

"Then what happened?" asked Meg on the edge of her seat.

"I ran. I ran for as long as I could and when I couldn't run any more I walked. I walked for a day and night through muddy fields, crossing freezing streams before I arrived at a truck-stop. I climbed into the back of a lorry and, exhausted, instantly fell asleep. It turned out that the lorry was stolen shortly after by Lawrence Birkenhead - the man who tried to pull you from the tree earlier. Sometime later the doors opened. It was Burk and he took me to meet his boss, Monsieur Kaylock. He offered me food, shelter and work paying more money in one month than I earned in a year on the farm."

"But doing jobs that were against the law, yes?"

"That's right. Do you think I am a monster, little girl?"

Renard sat squeezed on the kitchen chair like a grown-up at a primary school play. He looked saddened, like he had not found his place in the world. Meg reached over and placed her hand onto his which surprised him. "No, I don't." Renard managed to smile a little without showing it too much, but then looked uncomfortable. He pulled his hand away and suddenly stood up. "Where are you going?" asked Meg.

"It's time I left."

"But... what about me and Donald? We can still go, right?"

"Of course, my dear. You go to your friends. Go home. Do whatever you wish."

"And what about you? You know the police really are on their way, don't you?"

"Oh yes, the police. Perhaps the back way out of the estate would be a good option for me then."

"But won't your business associates come back and, you know..." she made the cut-throat gesture across her neck.

"I think no, as they believe I have done this deed already you see."

"And what about my friends, Lady Midsummer and the people at the house?"

"So many questions."

"Well what about them?"

Renard paused for a moment as if questioning his own conscience. "They are of no concern to me."

He reached for his long overcoat hanging by the door, but Meg walked around the table blocking his way. "You can help them. Help me to help them." He glanced at her but turned away without answering. "So that's it," said Meg disheartened. "You only care about yourself and no one else. Not even the lives of innocent children and an old lady. As long as you're-alright-Jack, nothing else matters."

He looked over his shoulder, puzzled. "Who is this, Jacques?"

"What? Oh, nobody. My point is that you say you're not like those other men, but the fact is you *are*."

"You don't know me, little girl. Nobody does."

He turned away once again and Meg once again stood in front of him. "Well did you ever stop and think that the reason nobody knows you, is because you don't let anyone get close to you?"

"No, now please move."

"Help me. Prove you're a good human being."

"I don't have to prove anything." He walked around her, avoiding eye contact and headed for the door.

"OK, fine. Then you're a selfish coward and you should be ashamed. Ashamed do you hear me? I'm talking to you, mister!" She picked up a wooden spoon from the table and threw it in anger at his back. Renard, who was reaching for his hat at the time turned and brought his hand up as if to strike her. Cookie barked at him, but Meg didn't flinch. He looked at them both, then lowered his hand.

"I am sorry, Cherie… but I must I bid you, adieu."

On those words he opened the door and walked off into the rain. Meg hurried over and shouted out to him. "You can be better than this, Renard. You're not a bad person." Her face dropped as did her voice. "Please!"

22

From afar, the vast Midsummer estate appeared blanketed by black cloud, looming above it like a great swirling electrical smog. Jake and Bashir looked back at it in awe while they tried to catch their breath. They could see now, that the valley seemed to be somehow channelling the storm's energy, which explained the truly atrocious conditions they had endured to get where they were.

After escaping the cabin, they had returned to the Ewe tree and successfully crossed over the perimeter. From there, they had followed the wall and retrieved their bikes, then rode them as fast as they could towards Daventry. Unfortunately, they found the return journey a momentous challenge for it was almost entirely uphill, meaning progress had so far been slow. The thrilling descent made earlier seemed like climbing a mountain. Their thighs had burned like fire. Their hearts had pounded and their lungs had near burst. To add to their misery, every step and every drivetrain rotation was made against the unrelenting wind. One thing was for sure: they both deeply regretted coming out to the Midsummer estate this day.

But none of that mattered now because behind them was level ground - the top of the hill, and beyond that, sparkling on the horizon were the lights of the village. One last effort, a few dozen measly metres and they would be able to receive mobile phone signal and contact the police.

"That's it!" yelled Jake gasping for air. "We've made it. Make the damn call." Bashir let his bike fall to the ground while he located his phone, finding he had to turn around to shield his face from the elements. As he sucked in air he found, to his dismay, that it still displayed zero bars of signal.

"Well?" enquired Jake.

"It's not… there's no… I can't…" stuttered Bashir, not believing his own eyes.

Jake shook his head and rolled his eyes. "Ah for God's sake, I'll do it!" He ditched his bike and tried for himself, but no amount of walking around cursing resulted in him getting any coverage. "No signal!"

"Yeah, *I know*," replied Bashir acidly.

"I don't understand. We should have signal here. Look, we are in view of the…" Jake squinted toward the north-east where he expected to see the beacon light atop of the old Harris Hill telecom tower, but instead saw only black landscape. He climbed up onto a fence beside the road, wiped the rain and sweat from his face and took another look. Through the narrowest of eyes, he saw the reason why. "The tower! The tower has gone… vanished!"

Bashir joined him and agreed he couldn't see it either. Unbeknown to them at this moment was that the old wooden tower had earlier that very evening been struck by lightning and burned to the ground. The tower had been recommissioned several years earlier to support a makeshift mobile telephone communication transmitter/receiver, until a larger steel one could be approved. The proposal, however, had seen fierce objection by the local residents, a result of which meant it had not been given the green light. No tower meant no mobile calls - for the boys and the entire village. They looked at one another, stunned.

"CAN YOU BELIEVE IT?!" hollered Bashir. He held one hand on his head while the wind made his hoodie flap like a ships mizzen. He looked at Jake waiting for instruction, who first looked ahead to the horizon, then behind to the estate.

"We'll just have to go all the way to the village. We'll make the call from a land line. Come on, we're running out of time."

23

Using keyring-torch and mobile phone light almost every inch of the attic had been searched. Between Jess, Charlie and Zac, they had inspected almost every box, bag, carton and cupboard; as well as all the weird and wonderful items contained within. Dust covers were pulled off. Chests and crates were forced open. Creepy crawlies had scarpered for their little lives. Charlie had even painstakingly visited every object that had a lock and tried the mysterious key for size, but had so far failed to find a match.

It was hot and dusty work, so much so that Jess had taken off her hoodie and tied it around her waist. She was presently working one corner of the attic far from the boys. One particularly dusty corner containing eight oversize wardrobes. She had tackled them with gusto at first, but with one remaining and nothing to show for her efforts thus far, she was beginning to feel downhearted. She entered the last one and repeated the process of rummaging through its colourful contents. This one contained what looked to be perfectly preserved attire from the thirties and forties, including a selection of military uniforms. She thought of borrowing some for a party, or the upcoming school play - if she ever got out of here.

She continued to peruse the ladies section but her thoughts were on the key that Lady Midsummer had given them and in particular the words inscribed on it. She crouched to inspect the wardrobe floor and noticed a shoe box; it bore the name '*Robert*' and she smiled, because her aunt, Krista, had pointed out that this spelt '*Trebor*', like the mint, if reversed. A useless fact she would no doubt remember for life. This in turn, got her thinking and triggered a notion which rekindled her spirit. She once again inspected the photo of the key on her phone, zooming and panning it. '*Could it be?*' Feeling a tingle of excitement, she switched to the app that allowed her to write notes on bits of virtual yellow paper and tapped in the words from the key.

She began by reversing all the letters, but found this returned nothing comprehensible. She then proceeded to rearrange all of the letters to make other words.

HORNETS …no. *OAFS* …no. *HERE TENT* …no. *THEN TREE* …no. *SECRET*…Yes!

Secret! Secret was a great word. Now, what else could she find? She sat down in the wardrobe with only the glow of her phone for company and tried to decipher the rest. It took a while but she came up with some encouraging outcomes. *'OFF THE SECRET'; 'THE SECRET OF'*. Jess felt thrilled with the progress she had made and was thoroughly grateful the puzzle had been one of wordplay and not mathematics. Alas, as she was working on the remaining letters, her phone bleeped complaining of low battery and before she could kill the torch app it frustratingly switched off. Now stranded in the dark with the boys a good distance away, she had no choice but to feel her way all the way back to the stairs.

"You all right, Jess?" hollered Charlie.

"Living the dream," she replied, stumbling over some unseen obstacle. She set her reference point on Zac, a mere twinkle in the blackness, who was close to the top of the stairs. On arrival, she found him sat on a stuffed beaver, rummaging through a box of old comics. She sat down on the top step and started patting dust from her shoulders, but something ran across her leg so she immediately shot back up again. Zac pushed the box he was inspecting aside and sighed loudly. "Any luck?" he asked, hoping she had discovered something pivotal. Before she answered, there came a loud noise of breaking objects from the floors below, which sounded much like a shelf full of china plates being toppled over. The noises continued for quite a while and ranged from thuds and bangs to crashing and smashing. The thieves, they thought, must be turning the place upside down.

"I said any luck, Jess?"

"Oh, just a load of old junk. You?"

"Junk, apart from these comics which are quite fun. This Beano says nineteen thirty-eight, edition one. I wonder if it's valuable?"

"And that's helpful how?"

"Well, err..."

"Never mind." She went over and sat beside him. "I did, however, discover something rather interesting about the key." She grabbed his phone without asking.

"Hey!"

"Don't worry, you'll get it back. Now, check this - I figured out that if you rearrange the letters you can make some other words."

"Interesting, any rude ones?"

Jess answered with a disapproving look which was enough to get the message across. "So far I have, *THE SECRET OF*, but there's another word hidden in there I haven't figured out yet."

"Oh, OK. So what letters do you have left? But I warn you, I'm rubbish at this sort of thing."

"Let's see... we've got... *AFIONTUN*"

Zac showed the kind of face he usually reserves for physics lessons. "AFY-ON-TUN, what kind of word is that?"

"You've got to rearrange the letters, remember?"

"Oh, right. I'm with you now."

Together, they set to work trying to figure out the missing word but no matter how hard they tried, they just couldn't find a sensible outcome. Jess made an honest attempt, but Zac was more like his nan trying to find BBC One on a smart TV. "I'VE GOT IT!" he exclaimed some time later. "*THE SECRET OF FAT NONU* - it has to be! Now, just who is Fat Nonu, I wonder?"

Jess cut him the sort of look Meg would if she were here. "Err, not so sure about that, Zac. Besides you've missed an '*I*'. But at least you've got the idea."

They were interrupted shortly after by the sound of breakage and falling objects, although this time from within the attic. Looking toward one of the far corners they could see Charlie's little torch light dancing around erratically. A moment later two white doves flew from his direction and disappeared through some hole in the roof. Charlie himself eventually came bounding over carrying, no dragging it seemed, a large painting still attached to a wooden stand. He made a terrible din as he heaved the heavy frame across the attic floor, tripping repeatedly on the way and demolishing any object that stood in his path.

"We should probably help him," suggested Zac casually and without getting up.

"Meh, he's got it," replied Jess, still tapping in letters. They both grimaced at the noise as Charlie arrived next to them with a heavy, golden-framed oil painting and, in contrast to theirs, the look on his face was that of utter excitement. He stumbled and almost fell toward them, but Zac quickly raised his hands to steady him. He regained his balance, adjusted his spectacles and composed himself. He then handed his torch to Jess and used his sleeve to wipe the paintings filthy glass.

Shining the torch light onto it revealed a near life-sized portrait of a pretty, middle aged lady wearing a long red dress. She had straight, brown hair down to her waist, in which she wore a white orchid flower on one side of her head. Directly behind her was a beautiful ornate water fountain as tall as the surrounding trees.

Jess and Zac looked at the painting, then up at Charlie, who nodded toward it bursting with eagerness but said nothing. Jess and Zac looked at it once again, then at one another and then back at Charlie. This time they raised their shoulders to ask what the deal was.

"Well, here it is!" announced Charlie.

"Err, it's a painting?" replied Zac.

"That's right," confirmed Charlie excitedly. "I found it in a hidden compartment behind a wardrobe."

"A painting of your aunt, Charlie?" asked Jess.

"No not Auntie, *Auntie's mother*: Geraldine Ophelia Midsummer. My great, great aunt. See here, you can just make out her name underneath. She is the very person who hid the ruby away. And that's not all - look what she is wearing around her neck!"

Jess and Zac stood up, leaned in close to the painting and saw for themselves the magnificent Sunrise Ruby. Zac then returned to an upright position looking a trifle dismayed. He took back his phone and shone the light into Charlie's face causing him to squint. "You're kidding me, right?"

"What do you mean, Zac?"

"What I mean, *Charlie*, is that I'm pretty sure we can't bargain for our lives with a stupid painting of the ruby. What are you thinking here - cut it out and slide it under the door for the thieves or something? Gift wrapped in a little envelope?"

"There's no need to be sarcastic, Zac," said Jess.

"This is so a need!" he snapped back surprising the others. "Just look around you. We're trapped in a draughty, dusty old attic with rodents for company and murderous thieves below waiting to serve us up for dinner! I'm tired, hungry, and a little scared if I'm completely honest. *And*, to top it off, after god-knows how long spent searching for some *supposedly* priceless red gem thingy, *he* wants to play antiques friggin' roadshow! Talk about waste of time! Tell you what - why don't we just ask what's-her-face here in the painting if she can tell us where the ruby is? We might get lucky! Excuse me, miss..."

"Um..." began Charlie.

"Just... let him finish," suggested Jess calmly.

Several expletives later, Zac had begun kicking stuffed animals around the place which went flying past the heads of the others who had to duck and dodge them. "Zac!" He continued his vent of frustration, appearing not to hear his name being called. "ZAC!"

Shortly after there followed an inevitable crash as a furry airborne projectile collided with the painting, breaking its glass. It created a horrendous noise as pieces fell and fragmented into smithereens down the stairs, leaving the children wincing at every step. When silence eventually returned, Zac stood quietly and ashamedly expecting a telling off, which he thoroughly deserved by rights. However, to his relief, Jess and Charlie seemed to take no notice of him, for they had focussed their attention on the painting and were busy studying a large tear in it.

"Oops, hope it wasn't valuable," said Zac very timidly, but his peers remained totally engrossed in the painting and with a nod from Charlie, Jess pulled on the torn section like old wallpaper is pulled from a wall. It revealed an envelope fixed to the back of the frame using brown strips of tape. It was unopened, as it still bore the unbroken wax seal of the Midsummer family crest. Jess carefully reached in and took it while Zac crept over and joined them, somewhat relieved his actions had been overlooked. He watched Jess carefully pull the envelope clear from its hiding place and hold it into the light.

"Go on, Jess," instructed Charlie. With her hosts approval, she proceeded to brake the wax seal and look inside. It contained a single piece of brittle paper, on which a few lines were written in near perfect calligraphy. Jess asked Zac to come closer with his phone light, but just as he did it went out. "Battery's dead," he informed them. They then huddled to share the light of Charlie's pocket torch as Jess read the note aloud.

A memory of those who fell;

Those whose lives were turned to hell.

Only on the longest day;

Will the closing sunlight show the way.

"A poem?" asked Zac.
"Could be," replied Jess. "Or maybe... a clue."

Somewhere below them, Lady Midsummer sat at the dressing table in her bedroom, brushing the hair of her evening wig which was placed on a glass mannequin head in front of her. Her remaining natural hair was mostly grey, short and often hidden under a net used to secure her extravagant hairpieces. She had finished applying her makeup and wore an evening dress beneath her yellow silk dressing gown, ready to meet the uninvited visitors when the time came.

As agreed with the children, she had repeatedly attempted to contact the police using the telephone in her bedroom, in the event that the phone lines were restored. Alas, it remained dead. As minutes turned into hours, she was grateful to have some candle light, as well as her wind-up record player for company. After all, if Frank Sinatra couldn't get her through the night, then no one could. She found the music also helped to dull out some of the more worrying noises of the evening, such as when an unknown person tried to force entry into her room earlier. There had also been a more civilised knock at the door shortly after that and the voice of Fräulein Bertrümn had called out to Auntie several times, but she dared not respond. She was now even hearing noises coming from the attic above and wondering if the crooks were going to come crashing through the ceiling at any moment. They would, however, present themselves in a slightly more civilised manner.

Auntie placed the tall, aristocratic wig on her head and positioned it using the mirror. Whilst looking at her own reflection, she noticed a secret door softly open in the far wall behind her; a door that appeared to be a book shelf. The person who stepped through wore a long black coat, black leather gloves and a wolf mask. They were also armed with a pistol. "Good evening, Lady Midsummer."

Auntie stood bravely without showing fear. She took off her gown and checked her dress hung straight, before turning to face the masked aggressor. "And with whom do I have the pleasure of addressing, sir?" The person did not reply, but did remove their mask, leaving Auntie completely stunned and able to utter just one word. "YOU?!"

24

There was something about the painting Charlie had found in the attic. Something other than its renaissance-like aesthetics or the layer of soot that choked its elaborate frame. There was something more, something simple, just staring right back. But what?

Jess had been gazing at it now for several minutes. Studying it. Admiring it. Trying to piece the puzzle together, and it was only when Zac waved his hand in front of her face did she snap out of it. She turned to the others and suddenly looked enlightened.

"What is it, Jess?" asked Charlie.

"The word," she replied.

"What word?"

"The missing word... from the key!" She brought Charlie up to speed on her theory of the hidden message and he immediately recognised what she was describing as an anagram, as well as asking if she had found any rude words. "And I think, Charlie," she continued, "that you may have just presented me with the answer." She took hold of the torn section of canvas and returned it to its former position. "Behold, the message inscribed on the key..."

THE SECRET OF FOUNTAIN

Although as she read it aloud, something didn't seem quite right, until Charlie pointed out that perhaps it would require just a slight alteration.

SECRET OF THE FOUNTAIN

"That's it, that's it! We've cracked it!" said Jess elatedly, offering up a high five.

"GET IN!" replied the boys, slapping her hands heartily.

But their breakthrough moment was cut short when they heard a sound at the door below. It was a sniffing, scratching sort of sound followed by a bark - and not a welcome one. It seemed the noise they made earlier had not gone unnoticed.

Standing quietly, they saw a shadow appear beneath the door. The handle was turned and the door once again tested. It then seemed that no further attempt would be made to open it, as there came no activity or noise for some time. Suddenly though and just when the children were about to stand at ease, there came a gut-wrenching sound. A sound that gave them all goose-bumps - and not the good kind - and sent dread deep into their hearts. It was the sound of a mechanical monster roaring into life.

Almost immediately after, the terrible spinning teeth of a chainsaw protruded through the upper section of the door. It retracted and re-appeared but at a different angle, spitting out sawdust as it devoured the timber like butter. It retracted and returned, retracted and returned. Then it stopped.

The children froze, their hearts pounding. They saw light shining through four slots cut into the door and smelled the expelled petrol fumes. There followed a single sudden thud. A simple, sharp crack and the slots gave way to reveal the business-end of a heavy sledge hammer. It was retracted, revealing a square section of luminance in which a face appeared. It was the taller of thieves – Burk, without mask which he had presumably removed due to the heat as his face was rosy and dripping with sweat. He poked his head through the hole as if it were one of those comical boards found at the seaside and inspected his handy work. His attention then turned to the stairs where he noticed the children bunched together at the top. He grinned a wide grin showing a gleaming set of pearly teeth, including one incisor cast from solid silver.

"So there you are, kiddies!" he sneered. "You gonna' come down and play with old Larry? Hey... wait a minute... you aint' the nippers we caught earlier. Just how many of you are there?!" The children looked at one another but remained silent. "And what's that you got there?" enquired Burk, changing his tone. He had noticed the key which Charlie quickly hid from view behind himself. Jess took it from him, then stepped backward tugging on the boy's tops. All the while, the beady eyes in the face in the door followed their every move.

"Charlie," whispered Jess, "this is where you show us another way down." She looked at him praying that he knew of one, because if he didn't, they were surely done for. Charlie thought for a moment, but his concentration was broken when he heard talking at the foot of the stairs.

"What is it, Burk?" shouted a second voice. "And why aren't you wearing your mask?"

"S'only kids, boss. Free of 'em. Hiding in the attic like rats. Oh, and they seem to have a key in their possession."

"Let me see..."

The other man appeared at the door, or at least his balding head did, because whoever stood there was evidently a lot shorter than Burk. He stepped back out of view. "Ahem!" was all he needed to say.

"Sorry, Boss," mumbled Burk, who immediately fired up the hungry chainsaw and extended the hole downward. "There you go, boss."

The man reappeared with a fat cigar, for the moment unlit, held in between his yellow teeth. It was the gang leader, George Kaylock. He coughed and waved the dust away before planting his face in the hole. "Ah yes, there we are." He focused his eyes in order to examine the children but found visibility poor. "BURK, get some light. I can't see a thing."

Burk swiftly reappeared this time above Kaylock, holding a large and powerful torch which he rattled through the opening.

"That's it, Burk. Now, shine it right in the little, beady eyes... NOT MY EYES YOU IDIOT! UP THERE!" Burk once again apologised and did as he was told, pointing the brilliant beam up the stairs and onto the children. Kaylock chuckled maniacally as he watched them squirm. "Ah, Master Midsummer, I presume?" Charlie looked alarmed that he had been singled out so Jess took his hand and held it tight. "And your friends too, what a pleasure it is to finally make your acquaintance, in spite of our surroundings."

"Who are you? And what do you want?" yelled Charlie.

"You can call me, Mr Kaylock. And all I wanted, young man, was your company for dinner, but I see you prefer hanging out with rats in the dark. So, why don't you come down and get cleaned up? Then you can join your aunt at the dinner table and we can all have a nice, civilised conversation. What do you say?"

Charlie sprung forward but was prevented going any further by Jess. "If you dare lay a hand on Auntie, I'll…"

"SO THE LITTLE RICH BOY HAS SPIRIT!" bellowed Kaylock. He struck a match on Burk's bristly chin above and lit his cigar, then sent a perfect smoke ring up the stairs. "Good for you, sonny. But tell me, what exactly will you do?"

"Why I'll… I'll… I'll…"

"BAAAH-HAAHAA, AAAAAR-HAAAHAAA…" Kaylock and Burk both burst into loud laughter as Charlie stammered away, so much so it made their sides hurt. Kaylock eventually composed himself and wiped a tear from his eye. "Very amusing, young man… but also very stupid. Now, are you going to come down or do I have to come up?" Jess and the boys stood their ground and didn't move or reply, much to the annoyance of Kaylock. His tone changed; he was losing patience. "I'll ask you one final time, are you going to come down or not?"

Charlie bravely began to stutter another reply but before a single word had left his lips, Zac calmly stepped in and offered to handle the response in a calm, professional and diplomatic manner. "GET BENT, LOSERS!"

Kaylock's face twisted up with so much rage he started to resemble a pink Mycroft the dog. He took out his cigar and roared up the stairs. "WHY YOU LITTLE PUNK! HOW DARE YOU SPEAK TO ME LIKE THAT! OH!! WHY YOU!! I'LL…" After a prolonged offensive of extremely colourful language, he just about managed to calm down enough to speak without shouting. "Right then. That's the way you want it, then that's the way you'll get it. Burk will come up and get you - and mark my words, you'll be regretting speaking back to me by the time he's finished with you! Burk, they're all yours."

His furious face disappeared from view leaving a cloud of cigar smoke in his wake. Burk then immediately set about starting the chainsaw once again, jerking back the starter rope in an attempt to fire its motor. Up in the attic, Jess grabbed hold of Charlie with both hands. "Charlie, is there another way out? For the love of God, think!"

"Well..." he muttered.

"Yes?"

"Um..."

The chainsaw suddenly burst into life expelling a flume of smoke and Burk wasted no time in cutting around the doors heavy iron lock.

"Erm..." continued Charlie, trying not to notice the nightmare below, "we could..."

"WHAT?" pleaded Jess and Zac. "WE COULD WHAT?!" Mercifully, Charlie's expression suddenly changed for the better and he clicked his fingers as he enthusiastically announced, "THE DUMB WAITER!"

"The dumb what?" asked Jess bewildered.

"Waiter," replied Zac, "but frankly, I don't see how the butler's IQ level can help us out here?"

"No, no," said Charlie. "The dumb waiter is used to transport food and other stuff between floors. It's not used any more - but we might just be able to utilise it to get downstairs!"

"You mean sort of like... a lift?" asked Jess.

"Exactly."

"Great, Charlie! Where is it?"

The look of hope on their faces quickly began to dwindle though when they saw the look on Charlie's, suggesting he didn't know exactly where said lift was. "Ahem, why it is just a simple case of geometry. Now let me see..." He held up his thumb in front of him like he was trying to gauge his location, then walked around a bit. "The main chimney stack is there, the kitchen is below - there, so it must be..." He spun round with his arm outstretched and Jess had to duck to avoid getting poked in the eye. He came to rest pointing toward a stock-pile mountain of junk stacked against the west wall, a couple of metres from the top of the stairs. "There, it's behind there."

The door at the bottom of the stairs suddenly popped open and the noise of the chainsaw stopped. A filthy tattooed hand then reached around and pushed it open.

"You're sure about this, Charlie?" asked Jess.

"Of course. Well, seventy-five percent sure. Um, maybe seventy-three... point five."

Burk pushed the door open and grinned up the stairs, "Hello kiddies."

"I suddenly like those odds," declared Jess. "COME ON!"

She and the boys ran to the pile and began picking up anything and everything they could before systematically launching it down the stairs. This worked in their favour, as it quickly formed a mass of problematic obstacles which caused Burk to trip, stumble and fall as he attempted to ascend. A squeaky dog toy bounced off his head followed by an avalanche of marbles flooding the stairs, resulting in him being ferried right back down to the bottom. What remained of the attic door quickly became wedged shut with falling debris and Burk found himself being buried beneath the relentless torrent of surplus items. A selection of fishing rods, nets and old buckets came next, entangling him. This was followed by several cardboard boxes stuffed full with Christmas decorations; all spilled their contents on impact. The barrage went on. Ladies shoes and men's clothing, a mirror; model ships, a Stradivarius violin; an old hoover complete with dust; a surf board and wetsuit, an incredibly heavy diver's helmet; a mannequin, bundles of old newspapers and a collection of garden gnomes were just some of the items hurtled down the stairway.

After an exhausting and bruising effort resulting in just three steps climbed, Burk's leg became hopelessly knotted in an old skipping rope. He attempted to pull himself free, but on stepping forward managed to wedge his other foot into the frame of a rocking horse. The children had almost cleared the way to the rear wall and had just one more thing to move: a life-size, stuffed Alaskan moose complete with antlers. They stopped for a moment pondering the bizarre situation they were in, but the angry grunts from below quickly refocused their attention. They nodded to one another and got to work.

Jess and Zac stood either side of the object which was the size of a racehorse in proportion, while Charlie positioned himself at its rear end. "Ready? then… HEAVE!" They pushed and shoved for their lives and the creature screeched and rumbled across the floor. The ominous noise it made caused Burk to stop and squint up into the darkness, as his torch remained out of reach. What he saw made his jaw drop in horror, for slowly edging toward the top of the stairs was the silhouette of a colossal horned beast emphasised by Charlie's little torch at its rear.

"*Burk, why have you stopped?*" yelled Kaylock.

Burk tried to reply, but found the words didn't want to come out. "M-MO-MO-M, MO-M-MO-M…"

"*STOP BABBLING YOU INCOMPETENT IDIOT! NOW TELL ME, WHY HAVE YOU STOPPED?!*"

"**MOOOOOOOOOOOOOOOOOOOOOOOOOOOOOSE!**"

Burk frantically tried to scramble toward the door, but still firmly restrained he fell face-first into the junk. He flipped over and saw that the great creature had reached tipping point and now balanced on a knife-edge on the top step. Burk remained motionless, afraid that any movement may trigger his unconventional demise. "OK, children," he said shakily. "Nice children. There's no need to do anything silly now."

Up top, Jess and Zac had joined Charlie at the rear and hadn't paid much attention to Burk's pathetic whimpering. "Charlie, would you care to have the honours?" asked Jess, waving her hand around as if she was addressing royalty.

"Why thank you, ma'am. Indeed, I would."

With the formalities out of the way, Charlie royally slapped the beasts hide and sent the mighty moose on its way. Its huge antlers were torn from its head as it was forced between the walls by its own weight and the racket it made could be heard from every room in the house. Kaylock briefly appeared in the doorway to see what was going on, but immediately retreated when he saw what was bounding down the stairs. Burk wiggled desperately trying to release his ankle and avoid the insurmountable object but he went nowhere. His face showed absolute fear. He realised he wouldn't make it and lie still. "**Mammy!**"

25

The almighty thud that followed shook the entire first floor bringing several paintings off their hooks. The children looked down and saw the stairway completely blocked by the moose, which had wedged itself firmly between the walls and the mound of junk. And, stuck somewhere beneath it but completely hidden from view, was Burk.

"That should hold them a while!" said Jess, dusting off her hands. The boys smiled back, proud of their achievement and the impressive mess they had made.

"A little unorthodox," added Charlie, "but affective none the less."

"Hell yeah!" agreed Zac.

Not wasting a moment, Charlie turned and shone the torch toward the rear wall. Sure enough there existed a square opening in the brickwork, about four feet tall by four feet wide. They hastened over to peer inside and instantly felt a cool draft on their faces. It was nothing more than a black hole, until Charlie directed his light and they saw they were at the top of a narrow lift shaft. There was little else to see, except for two blackened ropes which rose up from the darkness and looped over a metal wheel above them.

"Don't suppose there's a button to call the lift?" enquired Zac.

"There is," Charlie informed him, "in the kitchen, but it no longer works."

"Excellent, so how do we get down exactly?"

Charlie handed Jess the torch and leaned into the shaft, stretching as far as he could to try and reach the rope. It was just beyond the tip of his fingers and the moment he grabbed hold he began to fall, but found himself hauled back to safety by the others. "Thanks chaps!" he gasped. With both hands he then pulled down on the rope over and over, causing the old wheel above to creak and squeal under the strain. After several repetitions something became visible in the shaft below. A few more hoists brought it up to the top.

Jess and Zac were left speechless as they lay eyes on the rickety wooden crate which looked like it would struggle to transport a sack of potatoes, let alone one of them. Their personal concerns would have to wait though as there were developments at the foot of the stairs, where it sounded like an attempt to free Burk was under way by Kaylock and a third person.

"Ladies first then," suggested Charlie politely, not forgetting his manners.

"Can't we all go together?" fretted Jess.

"Unfortunately not - she won't take the weight I'm afraid. And besides, it is far too small for all of us. We'll simply have to go one at a time." Jess reluctantly climbed inside, shuffled around to face the others and sat crossed-legged with her head tilted to one side, which was the only way she could fit in. "Now then," instructed Charlie, "just use the rope like I did to lower yourself to the bottom. You won't be able to see much on the way, or anything for that matter, so just try to remain calm."

"REMAIN CALM!" returned Jess. "Charlie, are you *crazy*?!"

"That's the spirit!" he joked.

Failing to see the funny side, Jess firmly grasped hold of the rope, took a deep breath and prepared to descend. "Oh, what should I do when I get to the bottom, Charlie?"

"You'll be in the kitchen. I suggest you get over to the pantry and stay put 'till we join you. As soon as you climb out of the dumbwaiter, we'll haul it back up." Charlie wiped his forehead and unknowingly marked a thick black line of grease across it which made the others smile. "What?" he questioned, wondering what they could possibly be smiling at in a moment like this.

"Tell you later," Jess replied, as she started pulling up on the rope sending the crate down the shaft. The boys watched as their friend disappeared steadily into the blackness.

Despite zero visibility, Jess found it surprising easy to travel down in the crate; she just had to use the rope to control her speed of descent and ignore the pungent stench of oil associated with it. Her breathing echoed loudly in the cramped space and she tried to imagine she was relaxing on a beautiful sandy beach, rather than being wedged in a little wooden box. In no time at all she reached the bottom with an unexpected jolt - unavoidable when you can't see where you're going. She immediately noticed a change in temperature and felt a refreshing breeze.

The access to the dumbwaiter was concealed by two small wooden doors about five feet above ground. They opened from the middle and a thin gap permitted Jess to see into some of the kitchen without opening them. She gently pushed on the doors and peered out. The kitchen was silent but had been completely turned upside down as every pot, pan, utensil and item of cookware was now strewn across the floor. Drawers had been opened and the contents tipped out. Even the dressers that had recently displayed fine china collections had been toppled and lay face down. It was also evident that the ground floor was without electricity, as the dull luminance came from the outside, while the breeze, she noticed, was provided by the wind blowing through a broken window - one with shotgun pellets in the surrounding wall.

Once happy that no one was around, she carefully climbed out of the crate and saw it immediately rise out of sight behind her. She gulped and closed the doors ready for the next person to come down, then carefully made her way across the minefield of kitchenware toward the pantry. The going was treacherous and riddled with danger, as any trip, stumble or crunch would undoubtedly alert someone to her presence. Yet despite her vigilance and after just a few paces, a piercing clap of thunder made her jump and her sudden reaction sent a silver spoon gliding across the tiled floor. It finally came to a stop after spinning for what seemed like an eternity, leaving her waiting to see if she would be discovered. Half a minute passed and there was no sign of anyone. Half a minute more and she dared to breathe out. "Nice going, Jess," she uttered to herself.

She controlled her breathing before taking another step and noticed a back door just a short distance from where she stood, but there was no easy exit that way as a heavy oak dresser had been placed against it. She carried on and carefully tippy-toed half the distance to the pantry when something caught her attention: a kind of knocking sound coming from the dining room. The swing-door that connected the two rooms was closed but the serving hatch remained open, meaning passing it was required.

She cautiously crept forward when, without warning, the lights came back on. Whatever had caused the power to go out had apparently been fixed as the kitchen appliances all whirred back into life. Jess suddenly found herself standing vulnerable in the open under bright florescent lights. She stepped forward and to the side to avoid some broken glass, taking care to keep her balance. Through the serving hatch the dining room wall came into view, on which hung the heads of some unfortunate animals hunted in the wild. Another step and the door that led to the hall was visible, a little further and the table would be in sight. She stepped again but stumbled on a piece of china, breaking silence. "Dang it!" She then happened to look through the hatch and notice two faces staring wide-eyed back at her. It was Lady Midsummer and her butler, Barker, tied to chairs beside the table; the knocking sound stopped now they sat still. A little surprised to say the least, Jess wondered for a moment what to do. Could she rescue them? Should she?

There followed a bump in the dumbwaiter behind and Charlie, who had avoided going last with a win of rock-paper-scissors, pushed the doors open and looked out.

"Psst, Charlie, c'mere," whispered Jess. He acknowledged by nodding and squeezed awkwardly out of the frame. Then, just as before it disappeared up the shaft for another trip. After several clumsy stumbles he arrived at her side where she placed her hands on his shoulders. "Charlie, promise me you won't freak out."

"Why, what is it?"

"Just *promise!*"

He agreed and Jess pointed through the hatch. "AUNTIE!" shrieked Charlie. Jess immediately placed her hands against his mouth to silence him and didn't let go until he had calmed down. "Oh God! What do we do, Jess?"

She thought for a moment, unsure how to proceed. If they attempted a rescue they could end up being caught in the process. It might even be a trap - and the unfortunate old folks were the bait. Well, regardless of what was right and what was wrong, she let the battle of her conscience ere on the side of humanity. After all, they had vowed to help Auntie and she was the reason they had returned to the house in the first place. "OK Charlie, but let's be quick. We don't want..."

She didn't finish her sentence, as there suddenly came an ear-piercing screech from the direction of the dumbwaiter. This was followed by a deep, foreboding rumble which caused the cutlery on the floor to jump around and the bells on the wall to ring. Jess and Charlie looked ominously at one another, as did Auntie and Barker. Then, as if an earthquake had struck, a thunderous boom and an explosion of dust saw Zac come crashing out onto the kitchen floor. He was joined by the rope from the shaft which coiled next to him like a giant snake. He landed face-first into a bunch of ceramic pots sending them sliding into the smashed china like curling stones on ice. The noise it created must have echoed around the entire house and most of the gardens.

Zac shot up visibly shaken by the experience and saw the others. They looked back in disbelief, for he appeared blackened from head to foot. A brief moment of calm followed while they waited to find out if their position had been compromised. It was. A dog barked - the same bark they heard in the attic. Mycroft! The mutt then appeared at the dining room entrance and immediately noticed the children through the hatch.

"Don't move, Jess," instructed Charlie. "He can't see us if we don't move."

"It's not a friggin' dinosaur, Charlie!"

The dog immediately began barking. He then bolted, as well as he could, to the kitchen door and attempted to push it open, with only some heavy pots on the other side preventing him from doing so.

"Leg-it, boys!" exclaimed Jess. She grabbed Charlie by the arm and bolted for the pantry door.

"Try to stay calm, Auntie," yelled Charlie as he was dragged away. "The police are on their way!"

Zac waded toward them and sent a barrage of kitchenware flying in his wake. By the time he reached the hatch there was another face in the dining room - that of George Kaylock. He saw Zac, staring back at him like a rabbit caught in the headlights of a car. "BURK, GET IN HERE!"

Burk arrived almost immediately holding some tissue against his bloody nose. He also appeared to have received a nasty, swollen eye from his experience upstairs. He saw Zac and erupted. "YOU! Look at my face! You did this to me, you 'orrible little scamp! Well guess what, now I'm gonna' do to you what you dun to me!"

Zac hurried out of view to join the others whilst Burk picked up a large knife and followed after. He violently kicked open the swing door, which immediately swung back toward him and slammed into his already sore nose. He was sent recoiling backward and the knife he held went soaring through the air, sticking firmly into the door frame inches from Kaylock's head. This in turn caused a knee-jerk reaction from Kaylock, who fired off a round from the antique shotgun he had taken from Barker, sending him flying away into the hall. The buckshot from the gun brought down the largest and heaviest of the stag heads mounted on the wall with an almighty crash and this was followed by a large section of plaster board collapsing, covering poor Auntie and Barker in white dust.

"*What on earth is going on?!*" a voice yelled from the hall. There followed some shouting, then Kaylock staggered back into the room in a daze. Auntie's massive beehive hair-do was now full of pieces of debris and little clouds of dust fell each time she moved her head. Beside her, Barker sat with chunks of plaster on his usually impeccable shoulders.

"Good heavens!" fretted Auntie. "If the Queen saw this mess, well I…"

"Fear not, madam," Barker reassured her. "It's nothing a little polish won't fix."

"Shut it, you old badgers," ordered Kaylock. He wiped his face to clear his head while smoke poured from the end of the old shotgun. "BURK, YOU IDIOT!" He intended to pass on the telling off he had received from his superior to his inferior, so immediately walked over to his mindless minion and brought up his hand ready to strike. Burk cowardly flinched holding his hands against his face, so Kaylock instead kicked him hard up his rear end. He then punched him twice on his arm. "Two for flinching!"

"I'm sorry, boss. I'm sorry!" wailed Burk.

"Shut up you babbling baboon! Now get in there before those runts escape again!" Burk continued apologising whilst Kaylock pushed him into the kitchen and followed behind. "Well, where are they?"

"In there, boss. Trapped like rats they are." Burk gestured toward the pantry as he rubbed his sore parts.

"Good. I'll take it from here. If you want a job doing you have to do it yourself. Right, Mycroft?" The dog barked and accompanied his master over to the corner. He then waited patiently as Kaylock placed an ear against the door. "Little ones, we know you are in there, won't you come on out? No harm will come to you. I *promise*." He smiled a wicked smile at Burk who did the same as they waited for the children to beg for mercy. "Children... are you coming out?"

There was no reply and the men's faces quickly returned to frowny once again. Kaylock stepped back and raised the long shotgun toward the door. He then nodded at Burk, who acknowledged and opened it just enough for Mycroft to run inside. "Get 'em boy!" yelled Kaylock. "Make mince-meat of 'em!"

"Save some for me, Mycroft!" laughed Burk cruelly.

Their laughter soon died down though when they realised there seemed to be little sound of suffering coming from the other side. None at all, in fact. They glanced at one another wondering what to make of it. A moment later they both reached for the door at once causing a jam. "Get back you fool!" ordered Kaylock. He yanked open the door and was amazed to find no one other than Mycroft, tucking into some twiglets he had managed to spill onto the floor. As for the children, well, they were nowhere to be seen.

Both men entered the pantry and tried to understand what had happened. "Well, Burk? You said you saw them go in here. You said they were trapped like rats. Have you been drinking that expensive champagne again? ANSWER ME!"

Burk stood totally dumbfounded. "But, but, but..."

"OH SHUT UP YOU BLITHERING NINCOMPOOP! You are without doubt the most counter-productive clown I have ever had the misfortune of working with. Really, I don't know why I employ you."

"It's because we're related, remember? Your mum and my dad…"

"I said SHUT UP!" Kaylock once again held up his hand to strike, but Burk flinched so quickly he ended up banging his head on the shelves behind.

"Serves you right! Now, get out there and don't come back without those children. Savvy?"

"Yes, boss. Of course, boss. Right away, boss."

"WELL GO ON THEN!"

The hapless Burk hurried away leaving Kaylock to take a moment to compose himself. He noticed the jars of caviar and was about to help himself, until Mycroft floated an air biscuit that is. "Seem to have lost my appetite!"

26

The library had not avoided a trashing either and was now just a riot of displaced books. Even the grand painting of old King George had been callously cut from its frame, leaving nothing more than bare wood behind.

"Poor Auntie and Barker," grieved Charlie. "I can't believe they have been treated like that."

"I know, Charlie," empathised Jess. She looked over his shoulder at the state of the room. "Whoa, I can't believe the mess those scumbags have made."

"And I can't believe how hungry I am!" groaned Zac, who received a very disapproving glance back from the others. "What? Oh right. Sorry, Charlie. Well what do we do now?"

"The fountain," replied Jess. "You know, from the painting."

"What about it?"

"The painting showed Charlie's great-great aunt standing in front of a fountain. On top of that fountain stood figures from the war – soldiers to be exact, like a sort of memorial or something. Charlie, I believe the ruby is hidden somewhere in or around that fountain."

There was a moment of pause while Charlie considered the information, then his eyes lit up. "OF COURSE!"

"SSSHHH!" shushed the others.

"Sorry, I mean, of course - the commemorative fountain. I had completely forgotten about that."

"Excellent, so where is it exactly?"

"West of the house, beyond the gardens. About half hour walk as the crow flies. It's the very last bit of the estate before the fields."

"Half hour, but we don't have half hour!" stressed Jess.

"We could go by bike," suggested Zac. "If we can get to them that is."

"We sure could," agreed Charlie. "And we can exit the house via the servant's passageway. No one will see us and the bikes are right out front."

"That's a great idea," said Jess. "We'll get there in no time on two wheels. Come on then. It's not safe to hang around here."

Trudging over the piles of antique books and avoiding any toppled ladders, they headed toward the far end of the room and used the floor plate to activate the hidden door. Charlie entered first and the others were about to follow, when a familiar voice shouted out to them. "SO HERE YOU ARE!" It was Burk, with crowbar in hand, and without warning he started running over to them, fuming like an angry bull.

"QUICK, GET IN!" yelled Charlie. He offered his hand and pulled Jess inside, followed by Zac who dived through crashing into them. They just managed to kick the door closed as Burk slammed into it, making the wall tremble and almost dislocating his shoulder in the process. They could hear his dull rantings through the wall so wasted no time in heading toward the exit at the front of the house. They found, however, that while the door was unlocked it would not open, for something was preventing it from swinging outward no matter how hard they tried.

"Now what?" asked Zac.

"We'll have to go back to the hall," replied Charlie. "Maybe we can use the front door."

"And if we can't?"

"We'll cross that bridge when we come to it," said Jess. "Come on."

They immediately made their way back along the passageway and reached the spot where they had evaded Burk just moments ago. It all seemed quiet, so with a nod from Charlie they started tip-toeing passed. Almost straight away a sudden thud startled them, stopping them in their tracks. It happened again and a large crack appeared in the wall beside them. With renewed urgency they rushed toward the other exit arriving at speed into the little cupboard. They bundled inside, inadvertently knocking coats and hats from their hooks before squeezing together to survey the hall.

They saw carnage. Items of furniture, objects, books and papers strewn across the floor. Yet there did seem to be some order, as several large tubs appeared to be loaded with items of value, including a number of rolled-up paintings crudely tied in their middle by rubber band. It had become a staging area, for filtering valuable antiquities from worthless sentimental junk.

Their eyes turned to the left when they heard shouting coming from the direction of the kitchen, which sounded like Kaylock. This was followed by a dog bark, which sounded like Mycroft. Once happy that the coast was reasonably clear they agreed to go for it. They exited the cupboard and filed around the corner toward the front door, only to find it had been blocked by a heavy piece of furniture. "Chuffing hell!" exclaimed Zac, as loudly as was safely possibly.

"My sentiments exactly," agreed Charlie. "So what now?"

"What about the windows?" asked Jess, thinking on her feet.

"Locked - and I don't have the key."

"We could smash them?" suggested Zac.

"Too noisy," replied Jess.

"What about the basement then?"

"Also locked," replied Charlie. "UREKA! But I do know of one way out - the trapdoor. They won't have blockaded that!"

On entering the sitting room, they were shocked when they saw what it had become. The wonderful eccentric yellow sofas had been upturned and slashed, their stuffing thrown all over. The tall plant pots had been cracked open and every item from every shelf had been ruthlessly slung across the floor. Even the beautiful painting above the fireplace had been pulled down and its ornate golden frame broken into pieces.

Charlie stood staring at the mindless destruction before him and his emotions began to get the better of him. Jess took his arm and lead him into the room where they both helped Zac lift one of the sofas clear from their designated exit. Just as they finished, there came an awful racket from the hall: Burk had exited the coat cupboard and ploughed into the surrounding clutter. The children held their breath praying he wouldn't join them. They listened to him kicking objects around and shouting profanities, then it sounded like he had entered the study next door and that perhaps he may pass them by. But their hearts sank a dreadful moment later when he appeared at the sitting room doorway.

"Well, well, well. What do we have here? None other than the resident house rats." He entered the room and closed the door softly behind. He then locked it and withdrew the key, preventing any escape. "Thought you could hide from me, did yer? Well the gloves on the other foot now isn't it!" Jess and the boys looked at one another and bemoaned not locking the door themselves. Appearing pleased with himself, Burk proceeded to pull out a pistol which he used to scratch his head. "Now kiddies, you just hand over that there key and tell me where the ruby is. Then maybe I might let you go. What d'yer say, sound fair?"

His wild eyes seemed to look in two different directions at once and his nose was red and swollen, with bits of tissue protruding from each nostril. He approached while jerking the crowbar aggressively, prowling left and right as if to herd the children together. They could only retreat, stumbling over the clutter until their backs bumped against the fireplace. Realising they were trapped, Jess took the key from her pocket and clutched it tightly to her chest. Burk gazed at it, as if it were the priceless jewel itself and was about to reach for it, when there came an attempt to open the door behind him.

"Burk, you in there? What's going on?"

"S'all right, boss. I've caught the wee kiddies - and they're about to tell me everything."

"Burk, you imbecile, let me in right now! You're bound to mess it up somehow or another. You hear me?"

Kaylock thundered on the door but Burk appeared to ignore him. He returned his malignant attention to the children. "Now then, no more messin' about, you lot. That key if you please."

"What do you think, Charlie?" asked Jess. "Should we let him have it?" She glanced toward him and gestured toward the rug with just her eyes. Charlie nodded ever so slightly to show he had understood and slowly moved his hand into position. Jess then held out the key toward Burk. "You want it? Come and get it."

Burk seemed pleasantly surprised at what little resistance the children had put up and stood relishing in an increased feeling of dominance. He tucked the crowbar under his arm and stepped closer, holding out his grubby hand to receive the key. He arrived onto the edge of the rug. One more step they were able to smell his cigarette scent and incredible body odour, built up over days of sleeping rough in the back of a van. His outreached fingers were now just inches from Jess'; his good eye transfixed on the object she held. He took another step...

"NOW, CHARLIE!" shouted Jess.

Charlie immediately pulled aside the trapdoor release trigger sending Burk plummeting through the floor. In desperate reaction a shot was fired from his pistol, which destroyed the chandelier attached to the ceiling. Burk's terrible scream faded as he fell and was silenced only when he splashed into the water below. The children looked at one another, part shocked, part delighted and gathered around the void. They saw Burk surface before he was carried away by the current.

"Well boot my botnet!" exclaimed Zac.

"One down, three to go!" said Charlie matter-of-factly, and perhaps just a little smugly.

Behind them, the attempts by Kaylock to enter the room suddenly escalated into a loud gunshot, which startled everyone and resulted in a large section being blown from the door's centre. Kaylock's furious, cigar-smoking face then appeared in the gap and set eyes on the children.

"Quick, down the well!" yelled Charlie. Without wasting a second they one-by-one crouched under the mantle and descended the ladder, zipping down it like a fireman's pole. At the bottom, it was apparent that the volume of water had swollen immensely and was now surging past with incredible energy. They also noticed that there was no sight nor sound of the unfortunate Burk.

"He might be alright," said Zac, although he didn't know and he certainly didn't care. The others looked at him, not sure how to respond. They then looked up and saw Mycroft the dog staring down at them. He was joined by Kaylock, carrying the antique shotgun with smoke still discharging from one of its long barrels. It was evident from his expression alone that he was amazed on seeing the underground chamber, along with the faces looking up at him from its depths. He also seemed more than a little annoyed at the unexplained disappearance of his number two henchman, not to mention the missed chance of capturing the children and recovering the key.

He saw those below dare to take a step toward the exit and, realising they were trying to make a run for it, readied his weapon. The children had little time to react as Kaylock raised the gun and nestled the stock into his shoulder, but by the time he had aimed the muzzle and fired, all had dashed through the archway. A fiery blast of gunpowder from the end of the barrel was followed by sparks, caused by buckshot ricocheting off the metal platforms, while the discharged round created an almost deafening boom that resonated down the well and deep into the tunnel. Kaylock himself was sent recoiling backward where he collided with one of the sofas and tumbled over it.

Jess and Zac were already a safe distance away but stopped when they realised Charlie was not with them. "CHARLIE!" hollered Zac. His voice echoed along the lonely tunnel but there came no reply. They rushed back with a dreadful anxiety burning inside and were relieved to see that Charlie was fine; he had returned to shut the trapdoor, preventing Kaylock and anyone else from following them.

"CHARLIE!" yelled Jess. "What are you doing? Just leave it!"

"Don't worry," he replied surprisingly calmly. "Kaylock's fired his two rounds - now he's got to reload."

Above them, Kaylock was indeed out of ammo and scrambled to load red tubular cartridges into the gun, dropping several down the void in the process. Charlie placed both hands on the lever and pulled down hard on it. Immediately its mechanical workings cranked into life and the trapdoor above started to move. By the time it had closed halfway, Kaylock had successfully loaded one cartridge and was about to add a second. When it was just inches from closing they were losing sight of him, but still he raised the muzzle ready to fire. He set his sights on Charlie and placed his finger on the trigger. Charlie stood his ground, for there was no chance of running now. Kaylock's face was wild, frenzied and beyond reasoning, so it came as a great relief when he suddenly disappeared from view as the trapdoor slammed shut.

Charlie relaxed his shoulders and wiped sweat from his brow. "Check and mate," he announced proudly.

The fear on Jess and Zac's faces was first replaced by smiles, then they laughed in disbelief. Jess then immediately ran over and gave Charlie an enormous hug, almost squeezing the life out of him. "You could have gotten yourself killed, you daft sod!"

"Sorry, guys," gasped Charlie unable to inhale.

Jess released her bear-hug but for the moment kept him firmly in both hands. "JUST… just be careful, that's all. Promise?" She felt relieved that Charlie was unhurt, but also angry he had taken such an enormous risk.

"OK mom," he joked.

"Cheeky!" replied Jess shoving him away.

"You did good, Charlie," said Zac. "You bossed it. In fact, you totally rocked, big time!" He offered up his hand, which Charlie took and pumped affectionately. "But boy was it close!"

"*Too* close!" added Jess.

"I had it under control," replied Charlie. He stood wiping his glasses experiencing a level of self-confidence like never before. He felt like he had become a secret agent or something. He could walk on water right now. He could halt the tides. There was literally nothing this boy couldn't do. Heaven help the next bully who tried to give Charles Waldorf Midsummer III an atomic wedgie!

"Err, Charlie…" Zac waved his hand in front of his friends face repeatedly, yet he remained totally vacant with the 1812 overture blasting inside his head. "CHARLIE!"

Charlie snapped out of it, returning to reality with just his ego left in the clouds. He restored his cracked spectacles to his nose and looked at the others. "Right then, shall we check this fountain out?"

Jess looked at him like a doctor looks at a patient. "You sure you're OK, Charlie?"

"Of course. Never been better."

"OK boys, then let's go find that fountain."

27

Charlie pushed between the wall of ivy that concealed the old shed and sucked in the freshest of air, cleaned of its residual pollution by the downpour. The others joined him and did the same, taking a fleeting moment to revel in freedom. It had just about stopped raining and the wind had died, but there was still enough cloud overhead to keep the evening sun from shining through. The last rumbles of thunder were now miles away and the sound of birds singing gave them all a welcome feeling of calm. However, they knew this was merely the eye of the storm, for in little under one hour it would be dark and there was still no sign of anyone arriving to rescue them.

They proceeded single-file along the grassy trail until they arrived at the footpath overlooking the lake. Once here they were reunited with the sound of flowing water and saw it now surged along the concrete channel at speed. And this wasn't the only thing they were reunited with, because a few hundred yards away they noticed movement and realised it was Burk, or at least they assumed it was. It appeared that he had been carried the entire length of the water system from below the sitting room and deposited into the lake. He was of no immediate threat though, as he presently stood at the bank of the water knee-deep in the thickest, sloppiest of mud attempting, somewhat unsuccessfully, to free himself. Jess and the boys enjoyed watching him hopelessly trying to free his legs from the suction and repeatedly topple over. In fact, he was so muddy he was almost totally unrecognisable and, to add insult to injury, he was being aggressively assaulted by a number of angry swans.

Deciding to leave the calamitous Burk to sort himself out, the children set off north and in no time arrived back at the courtyard. Once there, they positioned themselves behind a topiary hedge while they surveyed the immediate area. All seemed quiet and they saw why they were unable to open the servant's door earlier: the huge white van belonging to the crooks had been parked with its bonnet just inches from it. Furthermore, the vans rear doors had been left open ready for loading from the house main entrance and it now had a large, colourful sign attached to its side that read: *'Sherlock's Home Removals: The Careful Movers'*. They also noticed the bronze statue of Winston Churchill in the courtyard had been knocked over, presumably a result of careless driving.

"Hmm, the plot thickens," mused Jess.

"Well before it gets as thick as that mud back there," whispered Zac, "do you think we can get something to eat? My stomach is rumbling like crazy."

"Tell you what, Zac, if I see a burger van, rest assured you'll be the first person I tell. OK?"

"Chance would be a fine thing," he replied woefully.

On the other side of the driveway, their bikes lay exactly where they had been left on arrival. Unfortunately, one of them - Charlie's by the look of it, had been driven over and its rear wheel was bent irreparably out of shape. Jess gave the boys a nod to proceed and together they hurried over and retrieved their respective transport, with Charlie having to borrow Meg's Twilight Sparkler. They set off across the gravel and joined the footpath that would take them to the gardens in the west.

Charlie led them at speed over the croquet lawn, then passed the swimming pool and conservatory and beyond. Shortly after they passed under a stone arch flanked on either side by a life-size, shiny metal elephant, indicating the beginning of the formal gardens. They entered into an open area surrounded by tall brick walls, which was further divided into several rectangular raised beds, each full of thriving fruit bushes and vegetables. An exit at the far end would take them into the next section and each section they passed through was different. Some were square, some were circular, some were long and thin, and they would have to pass through dozens of such sections before reaching the fountain at the most westerly edge of the estate.

They traversed the intricate trail of footpaths finding some were several inches underwater and many were littered with fallen branches. In one memorable section they crossed over an arched bridge, which took them across a pond containing the biggest and most colourful fish Jess and Zac had ever seen, although there was no time to admire them. They carried on and learned the hard way that caution was required, as Charlie would occasionally and without warning skid to a stop, causing a sudden collision. He would then back-track and take another direction; not that he would admit to being lost. One moment they would find themselves confined to a maze of hedges or high stone walls, whilst on turning the next corner they might be in a lengthy, tree lined promenade along which they could hit full cycling speed.

After some pretty intense cycling they arrived thoroughly out of breath at the final section, in the most western edge of the Midsummer estate. They were all peppered by countless spots of mud from the journey, particularly on their lower legs and up their backs, but not even their fronts and faces had avoided a spraying. They dismounted their bikes and let them fall to the ground, then followed Charlie over to an old wooden door set in a brick wall. He used a key from his collection to unlock the rusted padlock and pushed it open. They all passed through and found themselves facing another much taller wall - the lightest of grey in colour and constructed of smooth stone blocks. Just from looking, it was apparent that this wall hadn't been assembled in a straight line, but was instead curved like it may be encircling something. Charlie led his friends alongside and after a while it seemed they might walk a full circle, finding themselves back where they started. However, after just a few more steps the wall suddenly ended and they entered an open area with a grand, ornamental structure in its centre.

The fountain was a beautiful, ornate piece of stone architecture set on three tiers. At ground level, a vast column rose from the water and held up the first circular platform, on which stood four life-size stone soldiers. They faced outward, their heads hung down as if mourning and together they formed part of the central column supporting the highest tier. At the very top stood a statue of a deer, standing proudly, high above the ground.

The fountain and its basin were situated in a spacious, circular court, bordered by the semicircle stone wall running along its north, east and south sides, but remained open to the west. There were a handful of statues and a sundial, plus two stone benches with no backs. These permitted a person to sit and face the impressive structure, or to turn the other way and admire the views beyond the boundary wall where fields stretched to the horizon. Yet for reasons unknown, neither the court nor its contents had been well maintained and had fallen into decay. Many statues were missing limbs while others had turned green, encased by tenacious climbing Bindweed. The court floor was blanketed by weeds and tall grasses, but were held in uniform divisions by impenetrable segments of rough stone – the foundations of an ancient structure long since perished.

"It's very tall," said Jess, gazing up toward the top of the fountain. The clouds passing by overhead gave the illusion that the whole thing was about to topple over and they couldn't help but lean off-balance for as long as they stared upward.

"Whoa, check that out!" said Zac enthusiastically.

"Check what out?" replied the others looking around.

"Here on my finger - a completely black booger! Must be from the coal in the basement. How cool is that?!"

Jess looked at him disapprovingly, then noticed Charlie inspecting his own nasal cavities. "Charlie!"

Returning their attention to the fountain, it quickly became obvious that it didn't appear to have been used for a very long time, as the only water in its extensive base was green and full of rotten matter. A quick sniff confirmed it didn't smell too great either. Even the statues towering above them were covered in a thick crust of bird droppings. In fact, just as they noticed this, two pigeons happened to land on the top and add their personal contribution to it.

"Must be the communal toilet for the birrrrrr…" Zac began to say, but before he dared finish, a number of unusually large crows arrived at the scene cawing aggressively, resulting in the two pigeons immediately departing. The crows did not offer chase, but instead came to rest on the arched wall overlooking the visitors.

"Whoa," uttered Jess.

"There must be at least twenty of them," observed Zac. "Maybe more." They spoke quietly to one another and didn't move, fearing they may trigger an attack of some kind.

"Um, perhaps now is not the time to tell you this," muttered Charlie through the side of his mouth, "but did you know, the collective name for a group crows - is a murder?" The others turned toward him in disbelief.

"Jess," said Zac softly, "please instruct Charlie to come over here… so I can kick him up the arse!"

"Don't worry, Zac. I've got it covered."

Thankfully, no such action was required as the crows just carried on looking down, cawing occasionally and nothing more. Jess then noticed that the arched wall facing them was actually dotted with hundreds, if not thousands of tiny holes, each one set in a small metal plate. On closer inspection and under the scrutiny of the many black, beady eyes, they were confirmed to be keyholes.

"Look there. There is some writing in the middle." said Charlie pointing to some characters etched in the very centre of the wall. "It's the roman numerals again. Do they match the key?"

Jess rummaged in her damp pocket, retrieved the key and held it up in order to improve visibility.

"It matches," she confirmed, feeling a flutter of excitement.

"Result!" declared Zac launching his hand for a high five, but realising he had startled some of the resident crows, slowly lowered it back down. "Sorry!"

"Let's find where the key goes first, Zac," replied Jess. "Then I'll high-five you all night long."

While they talked, Charlie quickly did the mental math and look concerned. "You don't expect to try the key in all of those holes do you, Jess? We could be here for days."

"Do you have a better idea?"

"Well, no. Not really, but..."

"I have an idea," announced Zac.

Jess looked at him questionably, "Really?"

"Sure, why's that so surprising?"

"No offense, Zac, but what you normally have is the exact opposite of a good idea."

"But an idea none the less!"

"Yeah, go on then. What is it?"

"Why don't we have a look around? We might have missed something."

"That's your big idea?"

"Yep, and besides, those birds are givin' me the willies!"

As no one had any better suggestions they went with Zac's idea and began examining the area. Jess made her way around the perimeter wall of the fountain and noticed it was intricately carved and decorated its entire circumference. It depicted a sort of perpetual vine, with angels and soldiers being carried along; and that wasn't all, for there were also what appeared to be keyholes similar to those in the arched wall, scattered here and there amongst the decor.

Charlie, who had followed the wall in the other direction, met with Jess and crouched beside her. Zac, meanwhile, was nearby hanging from the arm of a statue of the Greek deity, Ares, hoping to trigger a secret passage or something.

"Are those…" asked Charlie.

"Keyholes," Jess replied. "Yes, I believe they are." She tried the key in some of the slots, but found that even though it inserted fully she was unable to turn it either way. Despite Charlie's rational concerns, she then went over to the wall and tried a few of the holes there but had the same outcome. She did, however, notice that directly below the roman numerals, one of the metal plates was ever so slightly different from the others. She gave it a wipe and saw it displayed a sun with a face, with the recess in its mouth being the key hole. "Interesting," she said to herself. She located the key into the hole and turned it. Above her the crows watched her every move, waiting to see if their secret would be discovered. Nothing happened. "Pah, this is hopeless. There must be hundreds of friggin' keyholes. We'll never find the right one in time. We must be missing something. Some piece of the puzzle."

While she and Charlie stood pondering the life-sized enigma that stood before them, Zac had turned his attention to the sundial located between the stone benches. It was formed from a single piece of perfectly cut Purbeck stone, with a large, bronze face plate on top. The thing was, instead of displaying numerals, it merely had an image of the sun in its centre. "Hey, look at this!" Zac called to the others.

"It's a sundial," said Jess on arrival. "So what?"

"So… look at its top - it has no numbers. Doesn't anyone else think that's a little odd?"

Jess wasn't too sure, but Charlie's eyes lit up and he grabbed Zac firmly by the shoulders. "Zac, that's brilliant!"

"Awesome!" replied Zac.

"Err, why is it brilliant, Charlie?" asked Jess.

Zac's brain then caught up with his mouth and realised he didn't know either. "Yeah why is it, Charlie?" But neither of them received an answer, as Charlie began enthusiastically moving around surveying the dimensions between the fountain and sundial with his thumb and index finger. "What *is* he doing?"

"I have no idea," replied Jess.

They called his name several times but he remained engrossed in his thoughts and didn't respond. He quickly made several trips around the court seemingly oblivious to those around him, marking random lines on the ground with a stone as he went. Even Zac, who was now standing on top of the sundial, was wondering if Charlie had finally lost his marbles and was destined to spend the rest of his days gibbering in a padded room.

"Charlie..."

"CHARLIE!"

He finally stopped and focused on the others for the first time in several minutes. Jess noticed his eyes were wild and energised, as was he. "Charlie, for heaven's sake what is it?"

He hastened toward them bursting with excitement. "The note!"

"What note?" replied the others.

"*THE* note."

"*The* note?"

"Yes, *the* note."

"Of course," said Jess suddenly understanding. She patted her pockets to find it. "The note from the attic, how could I have been so stupid?"

"Well..." began Zac.

"RHETORICAL, ZAC!"

Charlie arrived by their side and surprised Jess by throwing his arms around her.

"Whoa, now he's on the pull!" said Zac amazed.

"Charlie!" said Jess pushing him away. "Pull yourself together!"

"The note! The note!" he repeated over and over.

"Yep, he's lost it!" concluded Zac, but Jess' eyes now showed equal appeal as she tuned into Charlie's line of thinking.

"The meaning of the note," she said. "You worked it out!"

"Yes, at least I think I have. Show me the words again."

The paper was damp and the ink had run making it hard to read, but nevertheless, Charlie adjusted his glasses to inspect it. "Now let me see, a memory… fell, turned to hell …ah, here we are - the longest day…" He and Jess read the final line together, "…will the closing sunlight show the way!"

They both now understood entirely but Zac was still frustratingly tuned out. "Can somebody per-lease tell me what is going on?"

"Don't you see?" asked Charlie. "Only on the longest day, will the closing sunlight show the way. Well today *is* that longest day - June twenty-first - the Summer Solstice! And… if I am right, then the last light of the day will show us where the ruby is hidden."

"But how?" questioned Zac.

"Well, I err, don't know exactly, but I suspect by some sort of meteorological alignment."

"Meaty what now?"

"Alignment. Allow me to explain, Zac, and let me know if you get confused. Now, utilising the Gregorian calendar…"

"I'm confused!"

"*OKAY*… how about this - if you wanted to find north at night, what would you do?"

"North who?"

"North, as in direction or compass point."

"I'd use an app on my phone of course."

"OK, but what if you didn't have your phone?"

"Why wouldn't I have my phone?"

"Just say you didn't. What would you do?"

"Then I'd use my compass."

"And if you didn't have your compass?"

"I'd ask someone."

"Ah-ha! And if there was no one around to ask, what could you do?"

"I give up, Charlie. What could I do?"

"Why you could navigate by the stars!"

"I could?"

"Of course! You could find the plough and use that to find the North Star – they line up. Alignment!"

"And... what's your point exactly?"

"*My point*, my simple friend, is that at the precise moment - a result of the earth reaching its maximum axial tilt in the northern hemisphere - the sunlight will..."

"Align and reveal the hiding place of the ruby," said Jess. "Good Lord I think you're right, Charles Midsummer! That's got to be it, it's just got to be! Oh I could kiss you!"

Zac jumped down and placed his hand between their faces to prevent any further sickening signs of emotion. "Assuming, that is, that you are indeed correct, *and* we are in fact in the right place *and* at the right time."

"Well, yes. I suppose so," replied Charlie.

"Yeah, alright then. So when can we expect the last sunlight exactly?"

"Sunset today is at approximately... nine-thirty."

"And what time is it now?"

Charlie looked at his watch and seemed disappointed when he replied, "Nine twenty-two"

"Nine twenty-two already!" exclaimed Zac. "Well that's not good. I mean, we haven't seen a wiff of the sun since lunchtime and no sun means no finding out if you're right, Charlie."

Like it or not, Zac's words were true and a look of disappointment fell across everyone's faces. "And I've missed dinner," Zac grumbled gloomily.

For a minute no one spoke. Even the crows seemed to be respecting their emotions by remaining silent. Jess and Zac sat down on one of the benches and gazed into nothingness, but Charlie refused to give in so easily. He suddenly got up and started walking around the fountain, picking up sticks and stones and throwing them against it. He then picked up a large branch and beat some defenceless statues to within an inch of their little stone lives. He even began pulling up helpless weeds and pulled them to pieces, all the time shouting and hollering to the sky. "BUGGER OFF YOU DAMN CLOUDS! DO US ALL A FAVOUR AND GET LOST WON'T YOU! YOU CAN DO IT SUN! COME ON, TRY! TRY DAMN YOU!"

Jess called out to him but it was no use, he was completely engrossed in doing whatever it was he was doing. She watched him beaver away, not sure what to make of it, while Zac tossed little stones into the fountain. "Shame isn't it, Jess? To have gotten so close and to fall at the final hurdle." He scanned around for another stone to throw. "Don't you think, Jess?" He sat up and realised she was no longer at his side. To his complete surprise, he saw that she too had started dancing around the fountain like some nut job. "WHAT *ARE* YOU DOING?" he shouted to them.

"TRYING TO GET THE SUN TO COME OUT OF COURSE!"

Oh right. Of course. Obviously that's what they were doing. Now feeling like the odd one out, Zac simply thought - what the hell! He stood up and joined in wailing and yelling like a man possessed. He even threw in some sic Irish dance steps for the heck of it.

The crows, who had taken flight the moment Charlie went berserk, were now circling overhead and cawing loudly as the children energetically performed their call to the weather gods. Several minutes later, Jess and the boys were beginning to run out of steam, but then something happened that made them stop and stare in wonder. By some miracle it seemed that their unconventional prayer had been answered, because far behind them there came an unexpected break in the clouds and they suddenly found themselves accompanied by their shadows cast from the setting sun.

Above the arched wall and high in the sky, a bright, colourful and unbroken rainbow burned across the blackness, indicating without doubt the presence of the magnificent sun. They looked at one another and laughed. They laughed out loud in disbelief, but dared not move in case it somehow jinxed their efforts. They felt a sprinkle of rain on their faces, yet the sky to the west remained clear and the red sun sat firmly nestled on the horizon.

"It's a miracle," puffed Jess. "A miracle just for us!"

"Quick, what time is it?" asked Zac.

"Nine twenty-nine," replied Charlie. "And fifty seconds."

"It's now then," said Jess. "Right now or we wait another year."

"If we live that long!" joked Zac.

They watched their shadows grow and travel across the ground. Several minutes passed and the shadows started to fade, yet their hopes remained strong. Then something happened. Some last thing was happening. The fire in their hearts rekindled and grew. Their spirit returned. Their hope regenerated. They stood and watched a light being born - a brilliant light reflected from the sundial and onto the fountain. It began creeping upward. Up and up it went this little miracle of light and the children's eyes followed it daring not even to blink. It met with a hole in the fountain, permitting the light to travel beyond and strike the wall behind. It was now just below the metal plate which bore the face of the sun and slowly rising. Charlie and Zac positioned themselves on either side of the fountain, while Jess ran over to the wall and stood beside the light. It crept higher and eventually struck the plate making it glow a bright yellow glow.

"Now Jess!" shouted the boys.

Jess slotted the key into the little hole and turned it just as she had done earlier. A second after the sun dropped below the horizon and the light it had sent to that exact spot disappeared for another year. She turned to her friends and waited for something to happen. They stepped back and looked around in case they were missing something, only nothing changed, nothing happened. They shrugged their shoulders and wondered, just for a moment, if perhaps they had got it wrong.

But then there came a sound. A mechanical sound started coming from all around and they felt a tremble beneath their feet. Something caused the water in the fountain basin to ripple, then a deep, dull grinding noise was followed by the sudden birth of a whirlpool, into which the water held therein disappeared as if someone had pulled out the plug. The moment it had drained they witnessed a heavy stone block the height of a door, rumble aside in the fountain centre revealing a heavily rusted gate. They had found the hiding place of the Sunrise Ruby.

"Well..." began Zac.

Both Jess and Charlie looked to him to hear which comical remark he would make this time, however, he simply gulped and replied that in this particular instance, he had nothing.

"I'll take that high five now, Zac," said Jess, and they heartily slapped hands. Zac and Charlie then chest-bumped, only this time Zac was the one knocked down. They were about to step over the basin wall when they heard a sound coming from the direction of the gardens.

"Is that…"

"A bell?"

"…It is, and there's a voice…"

"And a dog bark."

"Sounds like…"

"Meg."

"…And Cookie."

"Meg and Cookie."

"MEG AND COOKIE!"

28

The old boneshaker Meg rode barely qualified as a bike by modern standards. Sure it had two wheels and pedals and stuff, but it was way too big for her and looked like it had been borrowed from a museum. It also didn't help that it had just one gear, no brakes, bald tyres, a seat fashioned of solid wood and that it seemed to want to turn in the opposite direction than was desired. Nevertheless, she sliced through puddles and arrived at speed at the spot where the others had left their bikes, inadvertently crashing into them.

"Jess, Zac, Charlie, it's me!" she called out happily. She could hear the others calling her name but couldn't see them just yet. She ditched the bike and let Cookie lead the way, who immediately got the scent and efficiently led his owner to the fountain. She saw her friends and brother and ran toward them to embrace their open arms.

"Meg, thank goodness you're safe!" said an elated Jess. "And Cookie too. How are you and how is your head?"

"Are you OK, Meg?" asked Zac grabbing her by the arms. "Did they hurt you? What happened back there?"

"The police, Meg, where are the police?" enquired Charlie.

"What did they do to you?"

"How did you escape?"

"Where are Jake and Basher?!"

The barrage of questions came thick and fast and Meg struggled to find a gap to get a reply in. She used her sleeve to wipe the speckles from her glasses as best she could and took the time to catch her breath. "Guys! I'm fine, really I am. And no they didn't hurt me. We got caught and taken back to the cabin, but managed to escape. The men there, they had guns, I tried to warn you… but the radio…I couldn't…"

"It's OK, Meg," said Jess. "We're all fine and thankfully you are too."

It was then that Meg noticed the sorry state of the others: grubby, stained with black marks, speckled with mud and dirt, and that Jess' hair looked like she had been pulled through a bush or something. "So... what happened to you then?"

"Well..." began Charlie.

"It's kind of a long story, "interrupted Zac, "but you did send for the police, right?"

"Yes, well, eventually. Bashir and Jake have gone for help, but only after we escaped. An hour or so ago. We can expect the police around ten thirty, maybe eleven. I take it you couldn't use the telephone at the house?"

"'Fraid not, the crooks took care of that."

"Ten thirty is only an hour away!" said Charlie hopefully. "Give or take a bit."

"Err... yes," replied Meg, a little less hopefully and almost mumbling to herself. "If they made it."

"*If* they made it?" questioned Zac. "Why wouldn't they make it?"

"Well... one of the men, you know, the big one I saw at the pub. The one who held me captive. He... well, he had a hunting rifle."

"A RIFLE?!" yelled the others.

"But I don't think he used it - on Jake and Bashir that is. In fact, I believe he let them go."

"And what makes you so sure?" asked Charlie almost freaking out.

"It's kind of a long story also. You'll just have to take my word for it for now. Besides, he let me go and the groundskeeper too. That must count for something."

There was a moment of pause while everyone digested the news and considered the next step. Meanwhile, the crows that had been circling overhead once again came to rest on the arched wall, ready to observe the next round of action.

"OK Meg," replied Jess grasping her hand. "If you say things are cool then that's good enough for us. Right, boys?" They mumbled their agreement half-heartedly, after all, it wasn't like they had much of a choice. Jess then gave Meg another hug before bringing her up to speed on the events that took place in the house, the lost ruby, plus the discovery they had just made. As a foursome once again, they stepped into the base of the fountain to inspect the secret doorway. Charlie picked up Cookie to help him over, but hadn't anticipated receiving a barrage of licks to the face, or being beaten by a fluffy tail at a rate of a thousand wags per minute. In the basin, the floor below them was coated in rotting vegetation which created a squelchy, slippery surface - plus a very unpleasant odour.

"Phew, is that you, Zac?" joked Meg.

"Funny," he replied, only without laughing.

"It sure is good to have you back, Meg," laughed Jess. "We've missed you keeping Zac in check. He's been right tetchy since you've been gone. Hasn't he, Charlie?"

"Not half!"

"Yeah, he always gets hangry," continued Meg. "Always has. He's like a baby on four-hourly feeds."

"Um, I'm right here you know," griped Zac. "Come to think of it, if you have any food, I'm starving!"

"Sorry, bruv. But I did have pheasant for supper, if that makes you feel any better."

"Yeah right. A likely story."

They arrived at the door and peered into the blackness. "So... Jess, you think the ruby is in there?"

"That's right, Meg. It has to be."

"It does, doesn't it. I mean - it would be way too easy for us to find it on display, sat on a velvet cushion in one of the rooms."

"Yeah, but where's the fun in that?"

"Hey, Meg," asked Charlie. "Just out of interest, but how did you know we were here exactly?" He returned Cookie to the ground and wiped the dog saliva from his mouth.

"Oh easy, really. After Renard let me go, I borrowed Donald's bike to travel down from the cabin to the house. When I arrived I could hear the noise you were making from the courtyard. And that murder of crows circling in the sky - led me right to you."

"Told you," said Charlie grinning smugly to the others. "About the murder, I mean."

"I'll frickin' murder you, Charlie!" warned Zac, who made like he was going to wallop Charlie, who blinked and received instead two punches on the arm for flinching. The boys then engaged in a little friendly tussle and Zac found himself placed in a headlock by the remarkably confident Charlie. The girls smiled at one another and rolled their eyes in the usual manner. However, their jovial behaviour was interrupted when the crows suddenly took flight once again, only this time they didn't hang around. Without the extra company it suddenly became eerily silent. Even the cheerful chirping of the little birds seemed to have stopped.

"Err, you know," began Jess softly, "that Meg said she could hear us from the courtyard."

"Yeah, so what?" replied Zac.

"Well do you think that, just maybe, someone else may have heard us too?"

"It's possible," said Charlie. "Why do you ask?"

"Bee-cause… I think… there's a chance… that we are no longer alone."

"I think you may be right my dear!" The loud voice startled them all for it was not one of their own. It was a voice they feared. A voice of dread. It was the voice of George Kaylock, who suddenly appeared from one end of the wall - the same spot as Meg before him. He held across his arms the long shotgun - this time fully loaded, and at his feet was the dreaded, drooling hound of hell, Mycroft. Little Cookie put on a fierce front showing a sharp set of teeth, but one bark from the larger dog quickly silenced him. The children instinctively grouped together and considered running, until a second person emerged from the other end of the wall behind them. It was Burk, who appeared covered from chest down in mud and feathers.

"Oh fu……dge," said Jess.

"Dang it!" agreed Charlie.

"He's like a turd that don't wanna flush!" added Zac.

Meg took one look at him and had to blink and look again, thinking perhaps her knock to the head was causing her to hallucinate. "Err…" she whispered to Jess.

"Tell you later!"

"Interesting conversation you had there, kiddies," sneered Burk. "Sounds like that stinking foreigner's gone turned traitor. Don't you think, boss?" He crossed into the basin and slithered toward them wielding a rusty gardening fork, similar to the ones from the shed. He came closer and with each step he took, water squelched from his saturated boots.

"Yes it does indeed," replied Kaylock. "Or perhaps our monosyllabic comrade has gone soft? In either case, it makes him about as much use to me as a chocolate fire extinguisher. Still, never mind. It does after all mean less spoils to share around. So, now we know the purpose of that troublesome key, what shall we do with these troublesome rug rats?"

"Let me have 'em, boss," pleaded Burk. "I'll carve 'em like a roast on Sunday, just how Mycroft likes it - with plenty of stuffing."

"Not *stuffing*!" exclaimed Zac in absolute terror.

"Yes, stuffing, you little punk!"

"Phew, someone needs a shower," said Jess, wafting her hand in front of her face. "That or a breath mint."

"What did you say, cupcake?!" snapped Burk angrily. "I know, perhaps I'll start with the mouthy one here. What d'yer say Mycroft?" The dog barked to show his approval.

"That your boss is it, the dog I mean?" Jess' snappy insults surprised her peers and infuriated Burk.

"WHAT?! Why you little..."

Before he could act, Charlie bravely placed himself in front of Jess shielding her from harm. "You dare lay a finger on her and you'll have me to answer to, you brute!"

"Yeah and me!" announced Zac. "Apart from the brute thing, I wouldn't say that."

"You'll have to deal with me, too!" said Meg.

"Oh yeah?" challenged Burk.

"Yeah."

"OH YEAH?!"

"YEAH!"

As the tension reached boiling point someone else joined the fray. "KAYLOCK, CALL OFF YOUR DOG!" It was a female voice and both the children and crooks turned to see who it belonged to. The mysterious person arrived wearing the same black, slick rain coat and hat the children had seen at the cabin earlier. This time though, her face was hidden behind one of the hideous wolf masks. "Call off your dog I said."

"But he's right here next to me, Frank."

"Not that dog you fool, that one has a brain. I mean that clown over there. I don't want those children harmed. DO IT NOW!"

Kaylock issued the command and Burk grudgingly stood down, allowing the children to breathe a sigh of relief. Jess, however, immediately restored her position at the front of the huddle and surprised the others by addressing the as yet, unknown person. "I wondered when you were going to show up."

"Jess, what are you doing?" whispered Charlie.

"Solving this mystery," she replied quietly, before raising her voice once again. "It's obvious now who the evil mastermind is behind all this."

"Is it?" asked Zac.

"Of course! We know that the raincoat you are wearing is the rightful property of maid Bertrümn, as her name is written on the inside. The thing is, it's clearly way too big for you. Still, you like to borrow it anyway, so people would think it was her skulking around the grounds. I suppose she was the obvious choice to incriminate thinking about it: she hardly ever speaks, keeps herself to herself and has a general dislike of pretty much everyone. Is that why the two of you were arguing outside the courtyard earlier today? Was she on to you? Oh, and let's not forget that maid Bertrümn wouldn't be caught dead wearing box-fresh running trainers like the one's you're wearing. So that leaves three members of staff: Barker, well he's presently tied up beside Lady Midsummer, and Donald the groundskeeper has been detained at the cabin for several days. I'm no mathlete, but I'm pretty sure that leaves just one person - Mrs Blackwell."

"Is it true?" asked Charlie astounded. "Is that you, Mrs Blackwell?"

The mysterious person removed their hood and mask revealing a head of bushy brown hair, chubby red cheeks, sticky-out chin and a large hairy mole on one cheek. It was indeed the cook, Mrs Francis (Frank) Blackwell.

"Well deck my halls," announced Zac stunned. "Mrs Bakewell!"

"It is you!" said Charlie crossly. "So you're the one behind this reign of fear and intimidation and... and..."

"Yes, yes. It's me, blah, blah, blah. Well done to you all. And let me start by saying that I really must congratulate you on finding the hiding place of the ruby. I confess that even after discovering all of those pointless doors and passageways scattered around the house, I had no notion of this impressive contraption. But then again you had something that I didn't - the trust of that crazy, antiquated old granny. And you are right also, about the maid - fascinating lady... or should I say, man-lady. She just made it too easy for me with her grim appearance and unsocial behaviour. But if you're looking for some sort of prize, for figuring things out, then guess what? You're in luck!"

Zac's eyes widened and he looked hopefully at the others, until Meg frowned and shook her head at him.

"What do you mean, we're in luck?" Charlie tentatively enquired.

Mrs Blackwell walked alongside the perimeter of the fountain basin inspecting both its design and contents, with Kaylock following closely behind. "What I mean, girls and boys, is that you get to go into that hole and retrieve the ruby for me. And your reward? I let you go free."

"Get it yourself why don't you. You, f-filthy rapscallions!" stuttered Charlie, but his brave gesture only amounted to making the crooks smirk.

"Oh come now, Master Charles. With or without your extensive education, I think you'll find it a fair trade. You and your friends, your aunt and the staff - all released completely unharmed. All for one little teensy weensy piece of crystallised carbon. Now, I propose that two of you go and retrieve it, while the other two wait here. Think of it as an insurance policy, in case you think about heading for the highway."

"And if we refuse?" asked Meg.

Mrs Blackwell turned her head toward Burk and nodded. He acknowledged by pulling Zac out of the group and placed him in a headlock. "STAY WHERE YOU ARE!" she shouted to the others as they braced themselves. "But you won't refuse, will you? Now, Lord Toffee-Bottom and Princess Peach here will go and find the ruby, AND DON'T

TAKE ALL NIGHT ABOUT IT!" She had indicated that Meg and Charlie would be the ones to venture into the fountain, who anxiously looked at one another and gulped.

"Wait," said Jess stepping forward.

"Yes?" asked Mrs Blackwell.

"Meg banged her head earlier - and she's claustrophobic. She should stay and rest. I'll go in her place."

"Very well my dear. We are not animals here, well, most of us aren't. So, blondie, go join your brother and keep him company."

"Lucky me," groaned Zac from his choke-hold. "Oh, and no offence mister, but you really stink!"

Mrs Blackwell raised an eyebrow and looked Burk up and down. "Yes you're right, he does. Now, Mr Kaylock if you please, I want that ruby!"

She turned and left the area, leaving the children in the hands of her heartless underlings. "Right you 'orrible lot!" barked Kaylock. "You heard the lady - two to go and two to stay. Oh and if you don't mind we'll start by searching you all, in case you are hiding anything."

Under the watchful eyes of their captors the children were forced to empty their pockets. Burk then patted each of them down to ensure nothing had been held back; his repugnant stench made their eyes water as he did so. Their phones were dropped into the sludge and stamped on ensuring they could no longer be used, followed by the walkie-talkie radios, Zac's micro camera and the pocket torch. Even loose change was greedily seized from wallets and purses. After this the children were ordered to split up and the twins were made to sit on the fountain wall where they were tied back-to-back.

"Right, let's get on with it," ordered Kaylock, as he sat on one of the benches lighting up a cigar.

"Can we at least have the torch?" asked Jess, pointing to the little object almost submerged in the slime. Burk looked to his boss who gave his approval and Charlie walked over and retrieved it. With fear and frustration boiling over inside them, Jess and Charlie took a last agonising look at their friends and turned toward the doorway.

"We believe in you!" Zac shouted out to them.

"Quiet, mouthy!" instructed Burk. "Else I'll slap you upside the head."

"But I'm allergic to being slapped. Doctor's orders!"

Despite his medical condition, Zac received a hearty slap across the back of the head for his sassiness and, much to the satisfaction of Burk, he bonked heads with Meg in the process. Jess and Charlie made their way toward the fountain centre and stepped over a small iron grill, evidently where the water had drained through. Ahead of them was the rusty gate which had been revealed earlier. They found it unlocked and were able to swing it toward them and step inside. There was no passageway, corridor or ladder behind, but instead an opening in the ground where a set of spiral stone steps descended into the very foundation of the great structure. The sun had now long set leaving only dwindling twilight, but peering down the stairway revealed a much blacker black which filled their hearts with dread.

"Here, Jess," said Charlie, "why don't you take the torch."

"You're not turning chicken on me now are you, Charles Midsummer?"

The little Darth Vader pocket torch wasn't much, but it had already proved itself invaluable on several occasions. He handed it over and they both turned one last time to look at the twins, who could only manage a forced smile in return.

"Ready then, Charlie?"

"Ready as I'll ever be," he replied, and without further delay they took their first step into the unknown.

29

The steps were fashioned from stone and varied only between grey and dark grey in colour. They were shiny and smooth and surprisingly dry, apart from a steady trickle of water that had formed a green algae trail down the length of the central newel. There was no handrail and the steps were steep forcing them to walk single-file. In fact, the steps were so steep that with Jess just a few paces ahead, Charlie was able to look down onto the top of her head. There were occasional cobwebs early on and it was necessary to remove them by hand to avoid getting a face-full. They used the cold sidewalls for support as they spiralled deeper and found they were already completely reliant on the torch light. It was deathly silent, but they could hear the sound of whining echoing down from above; it came from Cookie, who lay at the top of the steps eagerly awaiting their return.

"Tell you what, Charlie, if I see one more damn cobweb in the rest of my life, it'll be one too many!"

"Tell me about it," he agreed. His curly hair was beginning to gather them like candyfloss gathers on a stick. "Say Jess, did I ever mention I was claustrophobic?"

"You're joking, right?"

"No, for reals, but thankfully just a little."

"Well in that case, Charlie, you should tell me all about it one day. One lovely sunny day, out in the open. By the pool or in the park with…" She heard a squeaking sound from below which made her pause forcing Charlie to queue up behind. It was followed by another sound of an object splashing into water. "Err… did I ever mention that I'm scared of rats?"

"How interesting, although strictly speaking there really is no need to be you know. They are fascinating creatures after all. Take Robby for instance - he's really intelligent and very affectionate. He even gets all depressed if I am gone for too long and…"

"Don't get me wrong, Charlie. I don't mind nice, friendly little pet rats, it's the ones living in sewers that look like stray cats that give me the heebie-jeebies!"

"Yes, well, that's understandable I suppose. Now, shall we continue?"

Back up top, a clear sky had revealed itself overhead and a bright full moon provided enough silver luminance to see without torch light. Kaylock sat peacefully puffing on a cigar while Burk, who was far too tense to relax, irritatingly walked back and forth muttering things to himself. "BURK!" snapped Kaylock angrily. "Will you please sit down!" Burk did as he was told and sat beside his boss, however, it wasn't long before he started fidgeting and the irresistible urge to move made his leg bounce up and down. "Do you mind *not* doing that?" asked Kaylock. "I am trying to think." Despite doing as he was told, Burk couldn't resist picking off feathers and scratching dried bits of mud from his person. This in turn released a pungent odour into the air, which in turn resulted in Kaylock moving to the adjacent bench.

A short distance away the twins were living out their own worst nightmare – being stuck next to one another. Zac sat agonizing over eating food that Mrs Blackwell had prepared for them and whether or not it had been poisoned. Meg, meanwhile, was doing her very best to ignore him. "But how do we know it wasn't?" he fretted. "Some poisons don't smell or taste of anything. I tell you, its culinary terrorism what she's done!"

"Oh shut up, Zac!" replied Meg unsympathetically. "Anyway, you ate the most, so with any luck you'll go first."

"Thanks, that's very reassuring."

"It is to me!"

"Well if I do get through this, I'm cooking all my own food from now on."

"Good luck with that, you couldn't boil water!"

"Whatever."

"Tell you what, Zac, if you wake up in the morning, dead, then you know it was definitely poisoned. OK?"

"Very funny. I see that bump on the head hasn't affected you. You're still the Duchess of Dork."

"And you're the Grand Duke!"

"Lame."

"You're lame."

"That's it, I'm not talking to you."

"Woo-hoo. Lucky me!"

"WILL YOU TWO PIPE DOWN!" shouted Kaylock from across the way. He had sat listening to the twin's bicker for several minutes without a moment of peace. "Honestly! All the kids in the world and I have to kidnap you two!"

"You're welcome," sulked Zac.

"I SAID SHUT UP!"

Beneath their feet and after a lost count of the number of steps taken, Jess stopped and informed Charlie that they had arrived at the bottom. She didn't immediately carry on though, causing him to wait behind. "What do you see?" he asked.

"Err… you might want to come take a look."

He carefully stepped down and squeezed in beside her, but she stopped him from stepping any further and shone the torch light down to indicate why.

"Oh!"

The last steps led into a spacious chamber, but its floor was submerged under impenetrable black water. A single opening existed in the roof through which a beam of silver moonlight shone down, as well as a steady trickle of water. The side walls comprised of a series of tall archways with half columns supporting a podium below the roofline, while away from the walls and at a symmetrical distance from one another, were six free-standing columns that grew out from the water to support the roof. What existed at the far end was for the moment unknown, as the torch light failed to reach that far.

"Could be worse I suppose," said Charlie optimistically, but just as he did, a large rat - the sort that looked exactly like a stray cat - casually swam from a hole in the wall away into the darkness. Jess flew up against Charlie and gripped his arm tightly.

"Ouch, Jess. You're hurting me!" he grimaced.

"Sorry, Charlie, is that better?" she loosened her grip to a mere firm grasp and tried to compose herself.

"Much better, thanks."

"Good, now don't say anything silly to jinx us again. *OKAY*, Charlie?"

"What, like - I suppose it could be worse?" No sooner did he say this the torch went out, plunging them into complete darkness save for the thin column of moonlight shimmering on the water.

"My bad," said Charlie from the blackness.

"Yes, Charlie. Exactly something like that. Now stand still won't you while I knee you in the nards!"

Thankfully for Charlie, a quick shake of the torch brought it back to life and the first thing it highlighted was Jess' angry face frowning back at him.

"Sorry, Jess."

Like it or not, there was no other option for them besides entering the chamber so together, like toddlers at their first swimming lesson, they continued down the steps into the water. It was cold, but not too cold, after all this water had been baked under the warm sun for several days and was also relatively clear of smelly debris, which had remained in the fountain basin as it emptied. They arrived onto the floor to find the water reached just above waist height.

Holding their arms up they proceeded carefully, as underfoot there were plenty of objects providing ample opportunity for a twisted ankle. A dozen or so paces forward they arrived between the first two columns and immediately carried on toward the next. Their movement, although steady, disturbed the water enough to send waves ahead of themselves and they soon noticed another swimming rodent up ahead. This one was doggy-paddling, the sight of which caused Jess to abruptly stop. Charlie managed to settle her nerves and get her moving once again and kept conversation going to lighten the mood by listing a bunch of rat-friendly facts.

By the time they reached the middle columns they could no longer see the stairs behind them and still nothing in front. They did, however, begin to notice a muffled squeaking sound from the darkness ahead. On arrival at the final columns, a room began to come into focus directly ahead of them. It was separated from the main chamber by a single archway identical to the ones in the chamber, only this one had a carving of a grotesque face in its centre. Written below it were the words *Beware Greed*. The room itself appeared to be much smaller in size with no other exits or windows. It too was flooded and a large, free-standing rectangular block of stone seemed to float in its centre.

Charlie's seemingly endless knowledge of rodent-based facts continued, "...the Romans considered them to be good luck and..."

"Charlie."

"Yes, Jess?"

"Time to focus, this is it."

After tentatively wading a little closer, it quickly became apparent that the large stone block beyond the arch was in fact an oversize coffin, or sarcophagus, and the realisation that they were in some sort of tomb made a chill run down their spines. To make things worse, they also noticed several rats swimming around the area, appearing and disappearing from holes in the walls.

"Our Father..." said Jess softly, "who art in heaven, if I get through this without getting rabies *or* the plague, I promise I will try harder at school. Heck, I'll even try and like Mrs what's-her-name's math lessons! You know, her with the sandals and long toe nails. For ever and ever, amen."

"Steady on, Jess. Nothing is worth that sacrifice!"

"Yeah, perhaps you're right."

On these words they boldly stepped forward and immediately made contact with an unseen step beneath the water. It made Charlie trip and fall forward, grazing his shins and soaking him up to the neck. He managed to hold a flailing arm above water, which Jess grabbed tightly and used to pull him up.

"Then again!" he spluttered.

It turned out that there were actually three steps submerged in front of the archway, curved in shape like semi-circles, and once Jess and Charlie had climbed them and entered the smaller room, they found they were only ankle-deep in the water.

"Bit macabre, isn't it?" noted Jess.

"I'll say," replied Charlie after gulping. "And I suppose if the ruby is down here, then it must be in there."

They positioned themselves on one side of the huge stone object which was as tall as their chests and twice as wide. On closer inspection, they saw that its raised surface was actually a layer of brown organic matter which seemed to spill onto the surrounding floor.

"Ugh, it stinks!" exclaimed Jess. "What is it?"

To her horror, Charlie immediately scooped up a handful and inspected it further, like a toddler looking for earthworms in soil. "Smells pooey," he said matter-of-factly.

"I could have told you that, Charlie!"

"Indeed, but the question is... what's pooing it?"

He looked at Jess who looked questionably back while hiding her nose behind her forearm. Something small, the size of a raisin or two, then dropped from above onto the mound and they both raised their heads to see where it came from. The torch light revealed a number of small winged creatures, some hanging from the roof, others flying around high above them.

"Aw, little birds," said Jess.

"Not birds, Jess. Bats."

"BATS!"

"SSHH, you'll spook them."

"Bats! Should we freak out? Cos I'm freaking out!"

"No, they're long-eared bats. Totally harmless."

"You sure? I mean, you're sure they're not the vampire kind or something?"

"Quite sure, Jess."

"Well that's a relief. But I don't know what's more disturbing: flying mice or you rooting through their poop!"

"Speaking of which…"

"You're not?!"

Before Jess could so much as look the other way, Charlie proceeded to push aside the mound of droppings from atop of the sarcophagus, which splashed onto the floor and up their legs. When its stone surface was finally revealed, he used his other arm to wipe it and inspect its markings. They found it showed the two rutting stags of the Midsummer family crest, as well as some words below.

Those who are unhappy without wealth, Cannot find happiness with it

"One last warning I suppose," said Charlie. "From my great, great aunt Geraldine."

"Seems like sensible advice to…" Jess began to reply, but a squeak from the direction of her feet led to a rat brushing up against her calf and she suddenly turned very pale very quickly. "OHMYGOD! Think happy thoughts, think happy thoughts…" she said over and over, and didn't stop until the rodent climbed into a hole in the base of the sarcophagus.

"See, that wasn't so bad, was it?" joked Charlie, but the look he received back made him think otherwise. "Ahem, they must be attracted to the guano."

"Guano?"

"Bat droppings."

Jess suddenly looked like she was going to chuck. "Rats eating bat crap?! You sure know how to show a girl a good time, Charlie."

"Actually they've got good taste. It makes an expensive coffee you know."

"You're kidding, right?"

"Nope."

"Think I'll stick to tea!"

The sarcophagus didn't appear to be locked or even to have a lock. Instead, it seemed that its lid was simply held firmly in place by its own weight. Charlie attempted to push it, but succeeded only in making himself go bright red in the face. Not wanting to seem weedy in front of Jess, he adjusted his stance and tried again. He grunted and strained valiantly - and farted in the process, but despite his very best efforts failed to shift it.

"Jess, I'm going to need your help," he puffed.

"You sure, Charlie? I thought you nearly got the better of it that last push. You know, when you went all pink and that."

"Jess."

"No really, I saw it move a tiny bit..."

"JESS!"

"OKAY, OKAY! But if I get bit by something, you'll be the first to know about it!"

Charlie smiled back at her, "That's the spirit. Now, stand here next to me and on the count of three, push against the lid as hard as you can." Jess took her place as instructed, then placed the torch in her mouth and both hands on the seal. "Ready?" he asked.

"Mm-huh!" she mumbled.

"Then on three..."

"Wait," said Jess, spitting out the torch. "Do you mean push on three or just after three? Like one-two-heave, or one-two-three-heave?"

"Err... push on three," Charlie decided for no particular reason.

"Right you are."

"OK then. One... two... THREE!"

They both heaved with all of their might against the stone slab and were overjoyed to discover that it shifted a little. They counted to three and tried again, this time pushing it far enough for it to topple off the other side. It thundered down onto the floor creating a huge splash and a deafening boom, followed by a shower of droppings from above. Jess shone the torch onto Charlie and they looked at one another straight-faced, as if they had just broken a priceless museum piece and were waiting to see if anyone had noticed. They smiled a little and managed a giggle, realising they had gotten away with it.

30

"WHAT WAS THAT?" shouted Burk jumping to his feet. He had felt the tremor and heard a boom, as had the others up top.

"Sounds like our little worker bees are doing their job," replied Kaylock casually and without getting up. "Still, you had better get down there, Burk. After all, we need to protect our investment, don't we?"

"What, me, go down there?" questioned Burk fearfully. "You're avin a laugh, right?" He looked at his boss in the hope that he was, but the grim face staring back at him completely devoid of any cheerfulness whatsoever made him think again. "But why do I have to go?"

"*Because*... it only takes one of us, of course."

"Well you could..."

"I've got to stay here and watch the children."

"But I could..."

"No you couldn't. Now get moving."

"Uuugghh, where's that French oaf when we need him anyway? This is the sort of thing he should be doing. Going down into rabbit holes..."

"Burk, you imbecile, stop wasting time and for heaven's sake show some backbone! I want to be gone before the sun comes up you know."

On these words of comfort, Burk stepped over the little wall into the fountain basin and sulked toward the centre. "Hey wait," called out Kaylock. This instantly cheered Burk up for he hoped his employer had undergone a change of heart. Unfortunately, that wasn't the case, as Kaylock instead stood and located a silver flip-top lighter in one of his pockets and tossed it over. "You had better take this - might be dark down there." The look on Burk's face immediately turned from hopeful back to pitiful and he reluctantly turned and continued on.

"Break a leg," uttered Zac as he passed by.

"What did you say, you little brat?"

"Oh, err... make... it... Meg. Make it Meg. You can make it Meg. That's what I said."

Standing beside the open sarcophagus, Jess and Charlie found they could hear an odd sound that neither one of them could identify. Beside an occasional squeak there seemed to be a grinding noise, not one of machinery, but rather one a hamster would make chewing to escape its plastic prison; only here it sounded like there were a thousand hamsters. There was also a very noticeable increase in offensive odour, enough to bring on the gag reflex and make them both want to puke. They braced themselves as best they could and each held a hand across their mouth before leaning over the edge.

They saw a truly ghastly sight: rats and lots of them. They were packed in like sardines in a can, but somehow managed to move around freely like bees in a busy hive. They hadn't been alarmed by the sudden removal of the roof of their nest, or by the scent of two humans standing nearby, but the sudden light from the torch made them scurry like crazy and they desperately started jostling to escape the intrusive luminance. Almost immediately, rats of all sizes started flowing out from exit holes dotted around the sides of the sarcophagus. They streamed out like liquid from a punctured carton, squeaking and squealing to raise the alarm. One brushed against Jess' shin, followed by another and she sprang to the side almost knocking Charlie off his feet. They both retreated backward until they bumped against the wall behind.

"Quick, Charlie!" gasped Jess. "You're the rat whisperer, sing them a lullaby or something!"

"But I don't know any lullabies!" Charlie was quite taken aback when Jess suddenly grabbed him and screamed in his face, but in doing so, she noticed that in the wall behind him was a little alcove, high above the water line and wide enough for them both to stand in. "Quick, up there!"

They climbed up onto the ledge and turned to watch the rodent exodus. Rats were still filing out from the sarcophagus, while the archway that led to the main chamber had become a four-lane motorway for swimming vermin. Some were disappearing into gaps in walls, while others were attempting to climb their way out. One or two had even managed to reach the spot where Jess and Charlie were hiding out, but found themselves kicked back into the water.

This all came as quite a surprise to Burk, too, who was halfway down the stairs using the lighter to provide a meagre luminance when the army of rodents decided they wanted out. He was first spooked by some bats whizzing by, but that happened so fast he didn't see a thing. He then heard the noise from below long before he caught sight of anything coming toward him and naturally panicked. His jerk reaction caused him to drop his gardening fork which rattled away down the spiral, and also the flame to extinguish, plunging him into darkness. Desperately he thumbed the little wheel sparking the flint but it wouldn't catch, meaning he saw his first sign of the things around his feet in strobe affect. He had little time to react and less time to flee, so he did the only thing he could besides laying down and becoming a human carpet. He stretched out his long legs and arms against the newel and side wall, then lifted himself clear off the ground. Spread-eagled he saw nothing, but he heard the frantic squealing of creatures passing below him. He bit down on his rosary beads and prayed.

Above ground, Kaylock sat quietly picking dirt from under his fingernails using a pen knife while Mycroft lay at his feet. It was peaceful and the only sound was provided by the distinctive chirping of crickets in the surrounding grasses as they rubbed their tiny wings together. With little else she could do to pass the time, Meg had turned her attention toward the night sky. She gazed in awe at a cosmic display unlike anything she had seen before. "Fascinating, aren't they?"

"What are?" asked Zac, who was still focusing solely on trying to wriggle free.

"The stars. I've never seen them so clear. Makes you realise doesn't it, about how insignificant we are on this rock called Earth. Arguing over who owns what piece of land; fighting over who's god is the best. Did you know, it takes a perfect set of conditions to create a star? Dust and gas, incomprehensible amounts of pressure and energy. Add some gravity, swirl them together for a while and boom! A star is born. Yellow dwarfs, red dwarfs; giants and super giants, but even stars don't live forever. Sure, they have a long lifespan - several billions of years in fact, but eventually they tire, start to lose their glow. Then one day when their time comes, they become stardust once again. Makes you think, doesn't it? …I said it makes you think, doesn't it, Zac?"

"Sorry, did you say something?"

"Never mind. What are you doing back there anyway? Feels like you're sitting on an ant's nest."

"*Trying* to get out of these ropes of course."

"They're plastic cable ties, Zac. You're not going to do it."

"Oh yeah, like when you said I couldn't go down Daventry hill on my skates?"

"I said you *shouldn't* go down Daventry hill on your skates. And I seem to remember you crashing into someone's pond and cutting your leg open. Remember? We had to go to hospital - and they wouldn't let you in cos you were so mucky. Oh happy times."

"Yeah, *hilarious*. But winners never quit, and quitters never quit."

"You mean *win*, and you're an idiot who doesn't know when to quit!"

"If I can just…" He frantically twisted and squirmed one last time before finally giving up and accepting defeat.

"Told you," said Meg smugly.

"I hate it when you're right."

In the silence they realised the sound of the crickets had been replaced by a dull squealing. Cookie and Mycroft then raised their heads toward the fountain centre and Kaylock stopped tending to his nails. "What is it boy?" he asked his faithful dog who stood whining and turning his head from side to side. They didn't have to wait long for the answer either, for suddenly the mass of rodents surged through the doorway like a river bursting its banks.

"WHOA!" exclaimed the twins.

The rats bolted from the fountain centre toward the perimeter and had no trouble scaling the little wall. Cookie jumped onto Meg's lap and barked bravely, but Kaylock's reaction was to leap up onto the bench and didn't bother to help Mycroft, who ended up fleeing into the bushes.

Now free of any resident vermin, Jess and Charlie returned to the sarcophagus and once again leaned over to see what remained inside.

They saw the by-product of a nest and little more in the form of dirt and waste, plus the unpleasant smell that went with it. Charlie didn't hang around and proceeded to roll up his sleeves ready to investigate further.

"You're not, are you?" asked Jess.

"Needs must I'm afraid. We'll have to shift some of this if we're going to find anything." On these words he promptly thrust his hands into the muck as if it were a lucky dip and rummaged around. Jess watched him extract handful after handful and launch it over his shoulder. "You know," he puffed, "this would take half the time if you helped."

"You want me to stick my arms - in there?"

"Yep, its only biodegradable object matter after all."

Jess knew that Charlie was right, she just didn't want to accept it. However, for the sake of speeding things along for her friends she reluctantly placed the torch on the side of the sarcophagus and rolled up her sleeves. She then slowly slid the tips of her fingers into the warm muck, but quickly withdrew them. "I can't do it," she declared, but Charlie was a man on a mission and he grabbed her hand and shoved it into the gunk up to her wrist.

"There, you've done it!"

"I'll get you for this, Charlie," she joked without humour. "Oh my days, that is *nasty*!" She tried to imagine it was simply potting compost from her dad's greenhouse, as only then could she become accustomed to the job at hand and avoid hurling. She remained relatively calm and it was only the discovery of the occasional undigested animal bone that made her want to run a mile.

After removing several large clumps, they started to reveal the top of a curved object, at which point Charlie climbed inside to improve access. They continued to dig around it like they were uncovering treasure buried beneath sand at the beach. There was no sign of any human remains, which came as a big relief and in no time at all the pair had halved the amount of muck from within the sarcophagus.

They had exposed a single large box in its centre - a rusted metal chest. It seemed to be secured and would not move, that or perhaps it was just too heavy to budge. Jess picked up the torch in order to improve the light and nodded at Charlie to proceed. He reached down and removed its central fastener, but found the lid so stiff they both had to pull it open. It was a treasure chest, plain and simple. Filled to the top with sparkling gold, silver jewellery, diamonds, pearls, and an abundance of precious gems. And, sat on the very top like a cherry on a cake was one large, red gemstone, bigger and more magnificent than anything else. It was unmistakable. It was the infamous, Sunrise Ruby.

"Whoa!" said Jess. "That's a lot of booty."

"It sure is," replied Charlie, who found himself instantly spellbound. He wiped his filthy hands on his jumper then reached in and delicately picked up the single gem glistening back at him, cradling it softly as he marvelled at its billion-year old brilliance. Just imagine the wealth and power this single object could provide he thought. Jess called his name several times, but it was only when she gave him a nudge that his trance was broken.

"Charlie, I asked if you're OK?"

"What? Oh, yes. Yes of course."

"You were kind of spaced out there. Thought I'd lost you for a moment."

"Sorry, Jess. I guess I was a bit overwhelmed by everything, that's all. I'm beginning to understand how so many lives were ruined by this cursed lump of oversize jewellery. Here, you had better take it. Now what about all the other loot?"

"Leave it. We need to get that cursed lump up top and save our friends. Besides, it's only money after all. Right?"

"Right!"

Jess helped Charlie over the side and they turned toward the exit where their torchlight revealed they had company. "Not just any money, kiddies, *my* money." Burk passed under the archway and joined them in the little room. "Well, well, well. You have been busy. But then again you're quite at home down here with the rats, aren't ya?" He wasn't interested in holding conversation and proceeded directly to snatching the ruby from Jess. He held it in front of his flickering flame and inspected it, but when he noticed the chest full of treasure behind them his eyes really lit up. "Jesus, Mary and Joseph!"

With jaw gaping he surprisingly placed the ruby back into Jess' hand and walked between them toward the sarcophagus. He had become hopelessly fixated, not by the Sunrise Ruby, but by the chest full of glistening treasure. He calmly placed the lighter down and, unable to control himself any longer, jumped inside.

Knee-deep in the muck he began scooping up handfuls of the loot letting it run through his fingers. "I'm rich! RICH!" He did this several times over and each time he did, Jess began to notice a slight mechanical tick coming from the direction of the chest. It was like a switch of some sort was being activated and deactivated. She then heard a creaking sound and saw movement in a groove above the archway. Shining the torch that way she saw what looked like the spikes of a portcullis, hanging ready to drop, and it appeared that disturbing the precious objects in the chest seemed to be making it twitch.

She nudged Charlie and gestured toward it; his face immediately showed his concern. "Err... excuse me, mister, but..."

"SHUT IT YOU PARASITES!" snapped Burk furiously. "Can't you see I'm busy? Busy counting my gold. My precious, beautiful gold. And it's all mine."

"But, mister..." pleaded Jess.

"I SAID SHUT YER CAKE-HOLES, OR ELSE!"

Jess and Charlie weren't going to ask a third time and started side-stepping toward the exit. Burk was now rummaging deep inside the chest, pulling out its contents and feverishly filling his pockets. All the while the mechanical ticking was increasing and had Burk not been so obsessed he might have noticed it himself. The portcullis was now ominously swinging from side to side knocking against the arch, so without delaying, Jess and Charlie got as close as they could and prepared to jump.

It happened when Burk's pockets were stuffed so full of valuables he was using his jumper as a pouch to store any surplus. The chest, now relieved of its weight, suddenly popped upward and the portcullis started juddering down. Jess and Charlie leapt into the main chamber, landing up to their necks in the water and extinguishing their torch for good. By the time they had turned around the portcullis had lowered halfway, but Burk had only just realised what was going on.

"PREPARE TO BE PUNKED, PUNK!" shouted Charlie.

They saw the panic on Burk's face who let his jumper fall loose, spilling its contents into the muck. He scrambled out of the sarcophagus and bolted toward the archway, dropping a breadcrumb trail of priceless gems in his wake. But it was too late. The mechanical gears that controlled the portcullis were now spinning freely and it slammed into the water just as Burk threw himself against it. He wailed and screamed and tried to lift the heavy latticed grill, but failed miserably.

"You have the ruby, right, Jess?" asked Charlie.

"Sure do," she replied, showing that it was firmly in her grasp.

"Good, then let's go save our friends. The police will take care of him later."

"POLICE?!" yelled Burk who had already resorted to begging. "Whoa, whoa, what d'yer mean, police? You know I was only kidding, right? All that talk about feeding you to the dog; the crowbar and the, ahem, chainsaw, well that was just a bit of fun. What's up, can't you take a joke?"

His manner just as quickly turned sour on realising his pleas for help were falling on deaf ears. Jess and Charlie set off toward their one and only reference point - the thin shaft of moonlight, and in no time at all both Burk and his little flame were swallowed by the darkness. His endless torrent of verbal abuse did actually come in helpful though, as it enabled them to retain some sense of direction as they waded back toward the stairs. They walked side-by-side, linking arms to ensure they wouldn't become split up and held up their free hands in front of them to feel for any obstacles.

"Prepare to be punked, Charlie? What was all that about?"

"Oh that - must have heard someone say it on TV. Thought it sounded dope, you know."

"Dope! What are you, Will.I.AM now?"

"Yeah, not quite my style I suppose. Anyway, talk about major fail for what's-his-name back there."

"That's an understatement. Still, shame about all that booty being left behind, Charlie."

"I wouldn't worry about it too much if I were you, Jess."

"Why is that?"

"It was all fake."

31

In an attempt to prevent any further unexpected gatherings of nature, Kaylock had lit a small fire using whiskey from his hip flask and was attempting to burn anything he could lay his hands on. He nervously tended it as if a pack of hungry wolves were waiting in the shadows, but found that most things were wet through and just created a lot of smoke.

Across the way, Cookie lay vigilantly listening out for signs of persons returning, like he had done for some time now, and just when the twins began to fear the safe return of Jess and Charlie, the little dog lifted his head and wagged his tail. "What is it, boy?" asked Meg. She looked toward the fountain centre and saw a figure rising from its depths. She closed her eyes and prayed it was her friends and not Burk. When she dared to open them, she saw two familiar, grubby figures. "Jess, Charlie!" Zac turned his head to see for himself and broke into a wide smile, while Cookie hopped down and ran over to greet them.

The moment Kaylock noticed he dropped the stick he was trying to burn, stood up and flicked away his cigar. "Bit wet down there was it kids? You look like a couple of sorry crustaceans washed up after a storm. Still, I take it you have the ruby?"

"We're fine, *thanks*," replied Jess.

"DO YOU HAVE THE RUBY?!"

"First let our friends go!"

Kaylock steamed toward them but stopped at the perimeter wall, reluctant to cross it and get his shoes wet. "This isn't a game, Little Miss Ditzy. Now show me the ruby, then I'll think about releasing your friends."

Jess held out her soiled hand to reveal the gem, which drew everyone's attention like bees to nectar.

"Holy cow!" exclaimed Zac.

"Whoa!" gasped Meg.

"Now let them go," Jess demanded. "Or I throw it!"

She and Charlie stood their ground, held their nerve and didn't let the fear they felt in their stomachs show on their faces. All the time the grim face of George Kaylock, devoid of emotion, stared back. An uncomfortable silence followed, but the stalemate was eventually broken by him grinning the very slightest of grins. He took out another cigar from his breast pocket and joined the twins, where he proceeded to strike a match against Zac's head and light it, much to Zac's indignation. He casually puffed until the end glowed red and discarded the match, then pulled a small knife from his pocket which, to everyone's relief, he used to cut the ties that bound the twin's wrists. They immediately stood and ran over to be with Jess and Charlie. "Thank God you're OK. What happened down there?"

"Did you see that man who went looking for you?"

"And what's with those rats?!"

"IF YOU'VE QUITE FINISHED!" grumbled Kaylock. "We have business to attend to, so skip the sentimental drivel and give me the stone. NOW!" Cookie ran over and barked bravely at him but had to flee to avoid getting kicked. Kaylock then held out his stubby fingers and waited to receive his prize. All eyes turned to Jess, who, on a nod from Charlie, went over and placed the ruby in his palm before retreating.

Initially, Kaylock didn't seem at all impressed by the magnificent gem, neither did he appear even slightly captivated by it as so many others had been before him. Instead, he simply held it up to the moon and briefly studied it, before tossing it into the air like a tennis ball and letting it fall into his pocket. If he had been handed a cheap glass imitation, it seemed doubtful he would have noticed the difference. "Good," he announced. "Now I can get paid and go home. Oh, I almost forgot. Where is that idiot, Burk?"

Jess and Charlie looked at each other wondering what on earth they would say. The fact was, they had kind of hoped the subject wouldn't have been brought up at all and that Kaylock would simply forget about his cumbersome colleague on receipt of the ruby. "Well?" pressed Kaylock.

"He's um..." mumbled Charlie, looking worryingly at Jess.

"He's what?"

"He's err, err…"

"He found some more valuable jewellery," said Jess out of nowhere, "and he's spending a bit of time examining it. Said he'd catch up."

It was an acceptable effort to conceal the truth at such short notice and they anxiously watched Kaylock sucking on his cigar, considering their story as he looked for any tell-tale sign they were lying. He saw Charlie fail to hold eye contact and that Jess' mouth twitched the tiniest amount. A moment later he gave his reply - and not the one they wanted. "A likely story!" he roared. "Knowing that cognitively constrained clot, he's probably got himself locked in a box or something daft."

"Close guess," whispered Jess under her breath.

"What was that, Miss?"

"Oh… err, I said, gee - I hope not."

"That's what I thought. Right then. Now let me tell you what is going to happen: we're *all* going to go down there and locate Burk - together, and if it turns out you were telling me porky pies then I promise it will be you that won't come back up. And I don't make empty promises. Do I make myself perfectly clear?"

At this point, Meg and Zac looked concerned, but not half as much as Jess and Charlie, who knew full well they were in big trouble if they returned to the chamber below. Kaylock tossed his cigar away, rolled up his trousers and stepped over the perimeter wall. His flat-soled Italian shoes offered little grip on the sludge and he slipped repeatedly on his way to the centre. With a gesture of the shotgun he herded the children toward the doorway, who reluctantly obeyed, but just as Meg placed a foot on the top step there came a noise which made them all pause.

"*Psst!*"

It came from one end of the arched wall - the north side, and was noticed by all those present. Kaylock turned and squinted in that direction, but saw nothing and dismissed it. He was about to return his attention when the noise returned, louder and more unmistakable than before.

"*PSSSST!*"

Kaylock again halted and again he looked to see what was making the strange noise, but still he saw nothing. "Renard, is that you?" he asked. "Frank?"

"*PSST!*" it sounded again.

"WHO'S THERE? YOU HAD BETTER SHOW YOURSELF. I HAVE A GUN YOU KNOW!"

"*Come 'ere,*" whispered the voice.

Infuriated and perhaps a little spooked, Kaylock headed at speed back to the perimeter to investigate. However, his haste caused him to slip and his legs suddenly flew skyward before he slammed down onto his back in the slime. He awkwardly returned to his feet like a fledgling on ice and tried to compose himself, pulling the damp wedgie from his butt crack. "You kids stay where you are!" he blustered in an attempt to restore authority. He stepped over the low wall then, checking the gun was loaded, set off with the barrel aimed ahead. The children could only watch and wait for events to unfold. They saw Kaylock squelch toward the wall where he stood with his back to it like a soldier, albeit an overweight and out of shape one, on special ops. He waited, then pounced around the corner.

"HA!"

He saw nothing and was not confronted so relaxed his combat-ready stance. "WHO'S THERE?" he demanded. "SHOW YOURSELF, OR I'LL SHOOT!" There came no reply, so after pulling his trousers up at the waist he continued around the end of the wall out of sight.

Just when the children considered running there came an almighty scream - Kaylock's by the sound of it, then a shot was fired. This was followed by Kaylock returning to view, only this time on his hands and knees and it was plain to see he was utterly terrified. Someone or something was pursuing him and it wasn't long before the moonlight began to highlight an object emerging from the wall. It was the long barrel of the shotgun followed by the person holding it; only there seemed to be something very odd about this particular person. It was hard to make out in the darkness, but whoever or whatever it was, appeared to have a humanoid body but the head of a large, horned animal. Touching on eight feet tall it wore a long, black leather coat and quickly bore down on the hysterical Kaylock. It used one if its heavy boots to kick his rear, sending him face-first into a puddle where he spluttered and coughed before rolling over like a dog performing tricks. He saw staring down at him only lifeless pools of black instead of eyes. "W-what are you?!"

Remaining silent, the hunter lowered the gun barrel until it was pointing at Kaylock's crotch, who then promptly closed his eyes and started repenting his sins. But then, in an act of mercy perhaps, the hunter stepped backward and motioned for Kaylock to rise. In a state of utter fear, he clambered to his feet, wheezing as he sucked in air. His bottom lip quivered uncontrollably and his hands shook. He was then instructed to leave by a single gesture of the gun followed by a grunt and didn't wait for the beast to change its mind. He turned and ran as fast as his short legs and battered lungs would allow.

The children watched Kaylock hobble away and rejoiced, for his departure came as an enormous relief to them; and they had thoroughly enjoyed seeing him being taught a lesson. Then they quietened down and turned their attention to their unconventional saviour, hoping that it wouldn't be hostile toward them. Their worries were instantly dismissed though when the stranger threw aside the shotgun and removed the frightful head piece to reveal a familiar face.

"Fräulein Bertrümn!" announced an astonished Charlie.

"Fräulein Bertrümn?!" questioned Jess and Meg.

"No way!" exclaimed Zac.

The maid, who merged with the darkness seamlessly courtesy of her hair and attire said nothing, but instead just smiled a wide toothy smile back at them. Cookie immediately stopped his yapping and ran over with ears down and tail wagging. Then Charlie rushed toward her and after clearing the fountain wall in one jump, affectionately threw his arms around her mid-section. She, however, seemed a little less enthusiastic in her affections and looked uncomfortable with the young man attached, but did manage to pat his back once or twice. "Master Charles, kinder, thank goodness I find you, how you say, in one piece, ja."

"BERTY!" said Charlie amazed. "But how? Why? What? I mean…"

"You were in sticky situation. I save you. Is good, ja?"

"Ja, err, I mean, yes. Wonderful. Isn't it wonderful, chaps?"

"Hey, hold on a minute…" said Zac dubiously. "We thought you were one of them!"

"My dear boy, whatever gave you that idea?" she asked pushing Charlie an arms-length away.

"Well, you were always giving us the cold shoulder for one," said Meg. "You know, like staring creepily at us, giving us the silent treatment. That sort of thing, right guys?"

"That's right, Meg," agreed Jess. "Plus we saw you sneaking around the house. And then you came after us and tried to force the door open to the attic!"

"And let's not forget that bandage on your hand," said Zac, "which was a result of you cutting yourself in the basement, no doubt. You must have known about the secret passage there and everything. Your blood was even on the tap! How do you explain that, *Fraw-line?*"

"My dear kinder, please to listen. I will be honest with you now und there really is nein way to put it lightly, so I will just come out und say it. I just, well, I am just hating most people you see. Especially kinder."

The children looked at one another dumbfounded while she continued. "You come to the house, messing up the place und judging me like all the others. Honestly, I have enough to do keeping things tidy without running around after a group of kinder. But I would never hurt anyone und especially not kinder. You are understanding, ja?"

Zac leaned over to Meg and whispered in her ear, "Why does she keep calling us kinder?"

"It means children, in German."

"Oh right."

"Und as for my behaviour in the house," continued the maid, "well I was simply afraid, that is all. I wanted to warn you. To protect you, ja, only you kept running away und I could not shout for fear of being found by those men. I try also to help the Lady Midsummer, but she too would not allow me."

"And the cut on your hand?" asked Meg.

"I don't deny it was from the basement - I have a key und I am allowed down there. I see also the monster at night visiting und so I investigate. I cut my hand while picking up the glass und tried to clean using the sink, but it didn't work. I mean – there was nein water."

"So... you didn't know... about the secret tunnel?"

"What secret tunnel?"

"Well that explains a lot," replied Zac seemingly satisfied.

Charlie also appeared convinced that she was on their side and, furthermore, that her recent actions had vindicated her of all and any suspicious behaviour. The girls, however, were still sceptical so Jess called the others in for a huddle to debate the maid's account of events. They all agreed that the accused was indeed a very odd character, but that alone did not make her a bad person. They also agreed that her behaviour had been 'unconventional', but the fact remained that she had saved them from a terribly ordeal - and that had to count for something despite her open dislike of children. After much deliberation, plus the approval of Cookie the dog, they reached a unanimous decision and broke up to deliver their verdict.

"What the hey," announced Zac happily. "Hooray for maid Bunting!"

"Bertrümn," corrected Charlie.

"Sorry, *Bertroom*."

"*Bertrümn!*" said Meg and Jess.

"Right, whatever - hooray for the heroic house maid - and welcome to our gang!"

"Here, here!" agreed the others.

Bertie smiled back openly, for she was experiencing a feeling never felt before. She sensed a bond with the children and for the first time in her life, didn't feel she had to worry about being teased due to her height, her crooked teeth, or her peculiar and surprisingly unpopular unibrow. Meg approached her and warmly took her black nail-polished hand. "Thank you, Fräulein, for what you did. We truly owe you our lives." But perhaps not quite ready for physical interaction just yet, Bertie coughed and withdrew her hand informing Meg that, "It was nothing - ja."

"And what about this hideous head piece, Bertie?" asked Charlie, as he gave it a kick and Cookie growled at it.

"Oh that," she replied. "It's just one of the deer heads from the dining room. It came in useful, ja?"

"It most certainly did!"

"Totally freaked old Kaylock out," added Zac.

"We should get back to the house," said Jess rubbing her hands together to warm them. "We need to be there when the police arrive."

"Good idea," agreed Charlie. "And with any luck the crooks might be gone already, now that they have the ruby."

"Sweet," boasted Zac. "It will be like storming a castle after the army has fled - just the way I like it!" He and Charlie high-fived and made light of the situation.

"So… you mean… that's it then?" asked Meg, daring to believe their ordeal was over.

"Yes, Meg," replied Jess taking her hand. "We did it. It's over."

"Thank God, for a minute there I thought…" She didn't finish speaking as she was watching Fräulein Bertrümn, who was suddenly behaving a little strangely. "Fräulein, are you OK?"

The boys sensed something was wrong and joined the girls. Together they watched the maid walk slowly away, totally transfixed on something. Unbeknown to them all, events were about to take an unexpected change in direction.

"Err… this ruby," asked Bertie, "is it red?"

"Why, yes," replied Charlie still in high spirit. "Why do you ask?"

"Und is it large und alluring?"

"Yes, I suppose it is, but…"

"Und is it strangely hypnotic und mysterious? Priceless beyond compare?"

"Yes, YES! Why, Bertie?" begged Charlie.

The children watched as the maid crouched and retrieved something from the puddle where Kaylock had taken a bath earlier. She then arose and turned to show them what she had found. Their reaction was that of absolute disbelief, for cupped delicately in her hands was the unmistakable blood-red Sunrise Ruby, presumably dropped from the pocket of Kaylock as he floundered in the water. "Kinder, I think the bad guys may not be leaving just yet."

They gathered and marvelled at the priceless gem that lay sparkling in the moonlight; the innocent object that could make them all rich beyond their wildest dreams. It wasn't hidden behind six inches of bullet-proof glass or buried in an underground safe. It wasn't guarded by a dozen policemen with attack dogs or surrounded by laser-sharks and cages, but right there in front of them.

"Spec-tac-u-lar," said Zac.

"Truly magnificent," agreed Charlie. They both gazed upon it and fell under its spell as if they had been hypnotised.

"Snap out of it boys," said Jess clicking her fingers in their faces. "It doesn't belong to us."

"She's right," agreed Meg. "We should return it to the house and use it to ensure the welfare of Lady Midsummer. Looks like we're not out of the woods after all."

"And what makes you so sure the crooks will let them go free?" questioned Zac. "How do you know they won't kill them, and us, the moment we hand over the Sunset?"

"Sunrise."

"Exactly."

"I don't, *Zac*, OK? So do us all a favour and stop being so negative."

"Well excuse me, Miss Glass-is-half-full, but can I remind you that our lives are on the line here too?"

"Don't you think we know that already? Perhaps if you thought before you spoke, that might help."

"Perhaps if you shut up, that would help."

"Zac, don't speak to your sister like that," said Jess.

"Don't tell him what to do!" returned Meg angrily.

"WHAT?" gasped Jess.

"You heard me."

"I'm *trying* to stick up for you, in case you hadn't noticed."

"Thanks, but when I need your help, Jess, I'll ask for it."

"OK fine, some bestie you are!"

"Fine!"

"FINE!"

The air quickly turned sour as the day started to take its toll on everyone and Charlie and maid Bertie were left watching as the others clashed and quarrelled over nothing. "Guys!" Charlie's attempts to get his friends attention failed, as they were far too engrossed in their petty squabbling to hear him. Then maid Bertie tried. "Kinder, KINDER!"

It was no use, it seemed nothing would stop them arguing. Well almost nothing. What eventually did catch their attention and cause them to instantly shut up, was Charlie firing a round from the shotgun into the air. It created a heart-attack inducing boom that caused everyone else to cower in shock.

They watched as Charlie efficiently checked both barrels of the gun were empty before tossing it into the nearby hedge. He then returned to try and speak some sense to them. "Guys, what are you doing? You're squabbling when we need to be working together!" Jess and the twins suddenly felt very sheepish and looked awkward when they realised that Charlie was right. "We shouldn't be fighting amongst ourselves, not when we're this close to the end. We're better than that and you know it. Don't you know it?"

"You're right, Charlie," said Jess. "I'm sorry guys, you too, Charlie."

"I'm sorry, too," said Meg. "Sorry everyone."

They all turned toward Zac awaiting his apology, but found he stood stubbornly with his arms folded. He eventually did mutter something, but so quietly that no one really heard it.

"What was that, Zac?" asked Jess.

"I'm sorry," he replied, but again very quietly.

"Didn't quite hear you," said Meg.

"I'M SORRY! Happy now? Sorry, sorry, friggin' sorry!"

"Good lad," joked Charlie, at which point everyone managed a smile, including Zac.

"Look," began Jess, "I'm going to take the ruby back to the house, to make sure Auntie and Barker are OK - and I completely understand if anyone doesn't want to go back there after all we've been through. I suggest that those who don't come with me go to the entrance gates and wait for the police."

"Are you kidding?" replied Charlie. "And let you have all the fun! Listen guys, I know things have gotten a little funky today…"

"That's an understatement!" interrupted Zac.

"Indeed it is, Zachary, but this has without doubt, been the greatest day of my life!"

"It has?" queried Meg looking puzzled.

"That's right, Meg. You guys have shown me what true friendship is. What trust and courage really mean."

"We have?" asked Jess.

"Yeah you have! And if I had to do it all over again, I wouldn't change a single thing."

"You wouldn't?" asked Bertie looking equally puzzled.

"No, Bertie, I wouldn't. In fact, I've never felt so alive, so self-assured, and it feels like a million bucks. I know we've all been through a lot, but we've been through a lot, *together*, and I say we finish it *together*. Together or not at all. The four Muska-whatsits. The Four Ninja Turtley-Dudes. Now, what do you say?" He enthusiastically thrust out his hand and waited for his peers to show their support, or not as the case may be. Meg was the first to place her hand on top of his, followed by Jess, then maid Bertie and finally, Zac. Even little Cookie ran over and tried to reach up to show he was in. "Nice one guys," said Charlie proudly. He then noticed Fräulein Bertrümn sniffling which was very unusual. "Are you… crying, Bertie?"

"What, me?" she replied, wiping her eye and dismissing the accusation. "Of course not. It is the fever of the hay, ja."

"Oh, right," replied Charlie smiling to the others. "For a minute there I thought…"

"Don't be ridiculous!" She composed herself and adjusted her coat. "Now, if you are all ready, kinder, then let's kick some Gebäck!"

32

Before returning to the house the children took a moment to retrieve the personal belongings they had been forced to give up earlier, searching in particular for their mobile phones. Unfortunately, and much to their disappointment, they found them forever beyond use after being submerged in the water. The screens were also either cracked or chipped or both and Meg's was even split into two parts - held together by some thin wires and bits of circuit board. At least Zac had some luck, for after sifting through the gunge on his hands and knees managed to locate his micro camera, finding it fully operational. "Result," he announced cheerfully. He turned and noticed the smoking remains of the fire which gave him an idea. He walked over and pulled out a half-burnt piece of wood before returning to the others. "If we're gonna' do this," he told them, "then let's do it properly!" He used the charred end to blacken his palm, with which he smeared a thick black line across his face before proudly showing the others. "What d'yer think?"

"Well this is awkward," replied Meg. "Don't tell me, Zac, you've actually gone mad or something."

"No, not mad, Meg," said Charlie. "In fact quite the opposite I believe." He stood in front of Zac and gestured him to proceed. "Correct me if I am wrong, but it's war paint - like the Celtic warriors applied to make themselves look more ferocious and intimidating in battle. Absolutely terrified the Romans. Worked a treat for the Native American Indians too. Right, Zac?"

"Well... I was going to say camouflage - like in Call of Duty, but that sounds much better."

Charlie was decorated with two black lines on either cheek, plus zig-zags across his forehead. To the surprise of the others, he then proceeded to tear the sleeves from his jumper and tie one around his head.

"They've completely lost their minds," observed Jess.

"Yep," agreed Meg.

"I mean, what's the point?"

"Beats me."

"It's ridiculous. It's…"

"Me next!" exclaimed Fräulein Bertrümn, pushing between them.

"Fräulein!" asked Jess. "What *are* you doing?"

"Looks like fun!"

"But why?"

"Who cares why! I give up trying to understand you Brits a long time ago. With your fishes und chips, und Ants und Decs. Totally cuckoo, ja!"

The girls looked at one another - their faces dirty and grimy from the events of the day. Their clothes soiled; their mascara just a blur of its former self. Their hair, well, the less said about that the better. Jess raised her hand and rubbed a clean spot on Meg's cheek. "Suppose she's got a point."

"Yep."

"What the hell. We can't look any more of a mess, right?"

"Nope," agreed Meg with a smile.

"Come on then!"

Once primed for the final campaign, the micro army of braves left the fountain area in high spirits and set off back toward the house. Beneath the moonlight they returned to the gardens and crossed the path to retrieve their bikes, where they immediately realised they had a problem: one bike was missing and the tyres of those remaining had all been slashed. Ironically, only the rusty boneshaker that Meg arrived on remained in working order.

"Those filthy scoundrels!" protested Charlie.

"I could think of some other words to describe them," sulked Zac. He was crouched beside his prized twenty-four speed, full-suspension, disc-brake mountain bike, grieving passionately as if he had lost a family member. "Oh the pain, the pain!"

"Oh get over it, Zac," said Meg. "It's only a bike! We'll just have to walk I guess, unless we can all squeeze on that thing." She gestured toward the antique on wheels, but the others didn't seem too keen on that idea.

"Holy crap!" exclaimed Zac. "You escaped from those crooks and rode here on that! How on earth did you manage it?"

"What, to escape?"

"No, to ride that bike!"

"Worry not, kinder," announced Bertie. "I have idea. Please to follow me, ja."

She briskly walked off, not in the direction of the house or the door they had just passed through, but instead, toward one corner of the garden and its boundary hedge. The others tentatively followed and wondered if she might soon realise it was a dead end and come back. However, the Fräulein didn't come back and to their complete surprise she suddenly disappeared into the darkness. They rushed over to see where she had gone, but there was no immediate sign of her. The tall evergreen box hedge simply seemed to have absorbed her.

"Where'd she go?" whispered Jess.

"Damned if I know," replied Meg.

"Bertie," called Charlie. "BERTIE!"

There was no reply and they began to question if she was coming back at all, until the Fräulein - or at least her head - suddenly appeared from the hedge startling them. "Gutentag kinder!"

"Bertie!" replied Charlie crossly. "Where on earth did you go?"

"Shortcut," she informed him, stepping out into full view once again. "Come, I show you, ja."

The children, this time following closely behind, watched her walk into an opening in the hedge - an opening that wasn't visible if you looked at it straight on, but from the side was clear to see *if* you knew where to look. It took them along a narrow passage cut into the middle which they likened to strolling along inside a maze. After a while it turned sharply to the right and led them out on the other side, where they found themselves standing on a wild grass track. The Fräulein explained it was a maintenance route used by the groundskeeper and that it ran alongside the landscaped network of gardens, all the way back to the main approach road.

"This will allow us to get back to the house more quickly," the resourceful maid informed them. "Und *this*… will get us there even quicker!"

She stepped aside to reveal a rugged, four-wheeled off-road buggy, used by said groundskeeper to transport things around the estate. It had no doors and only two seats, with a soft removable roof in place of a fixed one. Its wide, chunky tires were made for gripping in the muddiest conditions, which explained the deep pair of tread marks in the ground below, and a large, enclosed metal trailer was attached behind it, used for transporting bulky items and garden waste.

"Well index my database," uttered Zac in awe.

"Surweet!" agreed Meg.

"Oh Bertie. I could kiss you!" announced Charlie whole heartedly, which had the effect of making the Fräulein seem quite repulsed. "Or… maybe not."

"Awkward!" teased Zac who was enjoying watching Charlie squirm.

"SHOTGUN!" shouted Meg, announcing her claim to sit in the bucket seat alongside the driver. Her peers kicked themselves for letting someone else beat them to it, as it now meant they had to ruff it in the trailer. So, while Bertie squeezed her long body into the driver's seat and Meg joined her, the others, including Cookie, climbed into the cage behind.

"Pee-yew! What *is* that smell?" asked Jess. "It's gross!"

"Yeah, it is a bit ripe now you mention it," agreed Zac. "Although I actually thought it was you two. Smells like…"

"It's probably manure," said Charlie, as matter-of-factly as ever.

"What?" replied Jess disgusted.

"You know – manure. Cow poo. It's used for the gardens to feed the flowers and stuff."

"I know what manure is, Charlie. I'm just not OK with sitting in it!" She looked like she was going to chunder and expressed her desire to get out, but before she had the chance, the driver flicked a switch and the buggy's headlights lit up the darkness ahead. They then jerked forward causing Jess to fall back onto her bottom, much to the amusement of the boys.

Despite the sudden acceleration there was hardly any noise, as the buggy was a model Chitty-E, which meant it was battery-powered and didn't run on petrol. This gave them the added benefit of being able to approach the house without being heard.

Cruising along at a top speed of twenty miles per hour meant the journey should only take a few minutes, which came as great news for those in the trailer, who were being bounced around as if they were on some extreme fairground ride. Up front the driver and passenger enjoyed seeing a variety of moths and nocturnal mammals darting in and out of the headlights. Behind, the boys enjoyed watching Jess try to block out the pungent smell by burying her head in her jumper. At one point, she even tried holding Cookie against her nose, preferring the essence of wet dog.

In no time at all they cleared the trees and joined the approach road that linked the estate entrance to the courtyard, where Bertie slowed the buggy and killed the headlights. If they turned to the right here they would eventually arrive at the main gates and their adventure could potentially be over, but instead they turned to the left and continued toward the lights in the distance. Advancing no quicker than walking-pace, they surveyed the scene ahead and watched the house grow larger as they came nearer. Bertie turned off the road before the bright lights atop of the arch and stopped behind a row of fir trees. Cookie jumped out first and went off sniffing, while everyone else travelled closer on foot and grouped behind a bunch of hollyhocks. A moment later, five painted faces rose up to survey the house.

The time was now 11:20pm and their short journey had taken less than ten minutes to cover from fountain to courtyard. Crouched in their present location, they could see the main entrance doors were now open revealing a glowing luminance from the inside. A moment later they saw Kaylock appear, ferrying items between house and transport. Although he wasn't packing them in carefully like the logo on the side of the van suggested, but rather hurling them in with complete disregard. As he laboured, Mrs Blackwell arrived, who seemed to shout at him angrily and even though the children could not hear them, their body language told its own story.

"She's probably just found out about the ruby," said Jess.

"And she wants him to go back and get it," said Meg.

"But he's had enough adventure for one night," said Charlie.

"And probably needs a change of underwear!" added Zac.

"Hmm, no sign of the police then," observed Meg. "I wonder what the heck is taking them so long?"

"Maybe Jake and Basher got caught or something," replied Charlie.

"Maybe Jake and Basher simply forgot about us," added Zac.

"They'll be here," said Meg confidently.

"What makes you so sure?"

"Just a feeling."

"Well wherever they are," said Jess, "it means it's up to us to help Lady Midsummer and old man Barker." She retrieved a bamboo cane that was propping up a sunflower and used it to draw a crude schematic of the house's ground floor in the soil. The others watched as she added detail utilising pebbles to represent Auntie and Barker, small stones for themselves, and prickly pine cones for Kaylock and Mrs Blackwell. She then began to describe the pending assault. "OK everyone, we're going to split up…"

"Wild Strawberry, anyone?" interrupted Charlie, offering a handful around.

"I will actually, thanks. Now, we…"

"I could really do with my night vision goggles right now," interrupted Zac squinting toward the house.

"Excellent, Zac," continued Jess, "and thanks for butting in. Now, we'll…"

"Or even my binoculars."

"Again, Zac, thanks for interrupting! I guess we'll just have to make do without your stupid gadgets - just like the Celts and Native Indians probably did."

"Sorry, Jess. I just tend to talk a lot when I get nervous."

"That's quite alright, Zac. Now…"

"That's procrastination," announced Charlie. "It means you delay doing things - by talking in your case."

"Really?" replied Zac. "How interesting. I always thought…"

"AHEM!" coughed Jess loudly. "Will you please conduct your therapy session another time, boys? And for now - shut the hell up!"

"Sorry, Jess."

"Right, like I was saying…" she pointed one end of the cane at the kitchen section on the plan, "…we know that the outer kitchen door, here, is blocked."

"Is it?" asked Charlie.

"Yes, I saw it. And we know that Auntie and Barker were last seen tied up in the dining room, here."

"Were they?" questioned Meg.

"What? Yes! Take my word for it. So our entry point options are: front door - here; conservatory - there; secret trapdoor passage - there or basement… here."

"Well, Kaylock's got the front door covered," replied Meg. "So that's out."

"And conservatory idea is nein good," said Bertie. "Door is blocked. I saw it with my own eyes, although you can perhaps pull open windows from the outside. But what of this secret trapdoor you speak of?"

"Oh, err, nothing Berty," replied Charlie. "Besides, the you-know-what door might be a little noisy anyhow - the crooks would hear us coming. And I feel the basement is just too risky. We could end up cornered pretty easily. Trapped like rats as it were."

"That settles it then," concluded Jess. "Charlie and I will enter through the conservatory - here."

"And what will you do once you get inside?" asked Zac.

"We'll go to the dining room and attempt to free the old folks. It's up to you guys to keep Kaylock on his toes, try and keep him away from us the best you can. We can meet back here if we need to."

"Und what of the crazy cook, ja?" asked Bertie.

"We'll just have to do our best to avoid her."

"Should we synchronise watches?" asked Zac.

"Err, sure. Why not."

"Excellent, I've always wanted to say that."

"But what if something goes wrong?" asked Meg.

"What, synchronising watches?" replied Zac.

"No, you mug, with the plan."

"If something goes wrong," said Jess, "then we have the ruby. If things turn pear-shaped, we'll use it to bargain with."

"And where's the ruby now?" asked Zac.

"In my pocket," replied Charlie. He checked but it wasn't there and he suddenly looked worried. He then checked his other pocket and found it, to everyone's relief.

"Wait, what about the gates!" asked Meg out of the blue.

"What about them?" asked the others.

"I just remembered - when we tried to leave earlier - the gates were locked and wouldn't open. The control box was all smashed up and everything. How will the police get in when they arrive?"

"Good thinking, Meg," replied Jess. "Fräulein, do you think you can fix the gates and get them open?"

"Is rindfleischetikettierungsüberwachungsaufgabenübertragungsgesetz my country's longest word?" There was no reply - only some very blank faces looking back at her. "Believe me, it is. Und don't worry about these gates. I was once gas rigger in Baltics – we worked with metals in temperatures so cold it would freeze your Pinkels off! I will get them open, even if it kills me, ja."

Jess looked wide-eyed at the others, who looked the same. "Right, err… OK. Excellent, then… Meg, you ready?"

"Does Mister Kipling, know about cakes?!"

"That goes without saying. Ready, Charlie?"

"Does Dmitri Mendeleev, know about the periodic table?!"

"I'll take your word for that. And Zac, are you ready?"

"Did the Earl of Sandwich invent the baguette?!"

"Close enough. Then good luck everyone."

Those who had watches synchronised them, after which they all arose from cover and split up. Jess and Charlie headed toward the swimming pool while Bertie climbed back into the buggy and set off up the road. Meg, Zac and Cookie used the cover of darkness to advance toward the courtyard, coming to rest behind a low hedge. They were to wait until exactly 11:40pm, in order to allow Jess and Charlie enough time to reach the conservatory. Then they would begin their assault on the main entrance.

"I'm not going to die! I'm not going to die!" mumbled Charlie over and over.

"Charlie!" whispered Jess. "You're not going to die. So kindly put a sock in it."

"Sorry, Jess. Nerves must be getting the better of me."

They arrived pool side and passed the lounge chairs they had relaxed on earlier that very day. Most of them were upturned and had been forced into a corner by the gales. Any surviving parasols were torn and battered, and there was no sign of the inflatables or body boards - apart from one stuck high in a tree. The outdoor lights were off and the water had taken on the appearance of smoked glass, reflecting the moonlight like a mirror. It seemed almost unbelievable how much things had changed in such a small amount of time. Their brief moment of leisure now seemed like a delicate bubble that had long since burst. They continued and came within sight of the conservatory. It wasn't lit either, but they could see the lights from the hall beyond. There was no sign of the crooks, so they kept low and headed toward the entrance.

Peering through the grimy glass they saw the doors had indeed been blockaded as Bertie had informed them. Charlie then saw a small creature darting across the floor which disappeared behind some plant pots. "Robby!"

"Shhh!" shushed Jess, frowning back at him.

"Sorry, Jess, it's just that I saw Robby the rat. Looks like he's evaded the crooks too!"

"I'm happy for you, Charlie, truly I am. Thing is, I've seen enough friggin' rats for one day thank you very much. Now, try and focus will you. It's almost time."

They crept along one side of the conservatory where they found the ground saturated courtesy of a large rain barrel overflowing. They attempted to open some of the windows without success as all were secured. They then tried the other side and were relieved to discover one which did pull open; it seemed the piece of metal used to secure it was missing preventing it from being locked. Jess pressed the button on her watch to illuminate the dial and noted the time. They had twelve seconds remaining.

"Ready, Charlie?"

"For reals?" he replied nervously.

"For reals."

"Ready as I'll ever be... I think... well almost. Kinda."

"That's my boy. Now, let's finish this."

33

Meg silently observed Kaylock lifting-and-shifting precious items from house to van whilst Zac answered a call of nature in the bushes. She thought their target looked uneasy, paranoid even, and saw he was sweating profoundly. Undoubtedly a result of him doing the dog-work of his absent colleagues.

"Did I miss anything?" whispered Zac on his return.

"No. And what took you so long?"

"Sorry, but there was no toilet paper."

"You didn't?"

"I'm nervous, OK! And it's not like I can just stroll indoors and use the loo."

"Fair point. That ship has sailed."

"What ship?"

"Never mind. What's that you have there?"

"Oh yeah, I found these on the way back." He dropped some large pebbles onto the pile of stones they had gathered to use in their assault.

"Nice. How much time do we have left?"

"Twelve seconds."

"OK then. Let's do this."

After arming themselves and limbering up, they anxiously watched the seconds count down like paratroopers about to make a jump.

"Ready, Meg?"

"Hell yeah!"

The time ticked over to 11:40 and they commenced their wave of attack. The unsuspecting Kaylock was wiping his brow after having just dragged a large and seemingly heavy tub to the rear of the van, when a stone hit him square between the shoulders. "YEEEOW!" he wailed in pain. "WHAT THE?!" He turned just as another bounced off the van beside him, denting it. Another then hit him on his foot making him hop around in pain. "WHO IS DOING THAT?!" he thundered.

Looking toward the gardens he saw a large pebble coming his way and managed to duck just in time, narrowly avoiding being hit on the bridge of his nose. Realising he was under attack, he kicked aside a priceless Ming vase and dived into the rear of the van. The barrage of stones continued to ding off the bodywork pinning him down and when he dared peer out from the behind the door, he would hastily withdraw as an unidentified object zipped past.

There followed some rummaging from within the van and soon after, Kaylock's fretful face appeared in the passenger seat. Almost immediately, a dead-eye shot from Meg saw a stone hit and crack the glass beside his face.

"Whoa-ha-ho! Great shot, Meg!" yelled Zac.

"You too, bruv," she replied hurtling another pebble, this time almost completely smashing the windscreen.

South of the house, Jess and Charlie had successfully managed to infiltrate the conservatory and reach the hall unnoticed. There had been a sensitive moment earlier when Charlie sat on a cactus as he climbed through the open window, but thankfully, Jess had been on hand to 'defuse' the situation. They surveyed the hall and heard the metallic dings of the First-Hewes artillery raging from the courtyard. It appeared their plan was working, as there was no sign of Kaylock or his associate. Charlie had a quick check of the library and found it empty, so after nodding to Jess, they both tiptoed alongside the wall to the dining room.

Arriving at the door they peered around it and saw Lady Midsummer and her trusty butler, Barker, as they were earlier: bound to chairs on one side of the long table. They were now cruelly gagged with heads hanging lifelessly down and on first glance Charlie thought the worst, until Jess pointed out they were breathing at least. There was no sign of Mrs Blackwell and beyond the dining room the kitchen lights were switched off. Jess remained close to the door keeping a weather-eye on their escape route, while Charlie rushed over to help. "Auntie, Barker, are you OK? It's me. It's Charlie." He shook his aunt just enough to wake her, then

Barker too, and a moment later they both came around. "Auntie, it's me, Charlie. We've come to rescue you."

The initial reaction of the elderly couple was that of astonishment, because even though the voice of the scruffy irregular beside them was familiar, his appearance left him quite unrecognisable. They thought perhaps a Dickensian orphan had come to their aid. Still, Auntie's eyes suddenly opened wide as she realised her beloved grand-nephew was alive and well and standing before her. Rather worryingly though, she just as quickly frowned and started mumbling loudly as Charlie attempted to untie her bindings.

"Fear not, Auntie," Charlie bravely assured her. "You're going to be just fine." But Charlie's words did little to calm her and she began rocking the chair from side to side, gesturing with her head toward the kitchen.

"Um, Charlie..." said Jess warily. She was beginning to get the message that something wasn't quite right, unlike Charlie, who wasn't paying enough attention to notice. He just carried on untying his aunt and talking right back to her.

"Auntie, you'll never guess what? We found the ruby! We found the Sunrise Ruby!"

"Mmmmmm mmm!" mumbled Auntie. Barker then joined in too and like a comedy double act, they frantically hopped on the spot as if their chairs were on fire. "Mmmmmm mmm! Mmmm mm mm MMMMM!!"

"I know, Auntie," continued Charlie. "I couldn't believe it either. And then it was taken from us and then we found it again - lying in a puddle of all places! Can you believe it?" He finished untying the rope from her hands followed by the gag from her mouth. "Now, Auntie, what is it you're trying to tell me?"

The old lady wasn't given so much as a chance to adjust her false teeth, as the kitchen doors suddenly swung open and Mrs Blackwell casually stepped through. She held in her hand a pistol encrusted with diamonds and it was pointed toward them. Charlie took one look at it and gulped. "Oh dear!"

Outside in the courtyard, Meg and Zac had thrown so many stones their arms hurt, but were now running dangerously low on ammunition and wouldn't be able to keep Kaylock supressed for much longer. Their efforts had resulted in the van being peppered with so many dings and dents, they figured it may have been put out of service. However, any damage sustained was proven merely cosmetic, when the noisy old diesel engine fired into life and coughed out a cloud of black smoke from its exhaust. Kaylock was attempting to leave and without sitting up to look out of the cracked windscreen, he forced the vehicle into first gear, floored the pedal and rapidly accelerated away at eight thousand rpm. The spinning wheels dug a deep groove into the gravel stones and a number of delicate antiques instantly fell from the open doors at the rear. The twins arose from their cover and threw everything they had as fast as they could, but Kaylock left at such speed he quickly cleared their range.

Meg instructed Cookie to sit and for once he obediently obeyed. She and Zac then followed on foot and watched the van speed across the lawn and plough through a flower bed before bouncing onto the approach road, at which point another load of valuable items spilled out. From here, the twins expected Kaylock to simply drive up the road and be gone, yet they witnessed the van suddenly veer sharply to the left and then back to the right, then dangerously jitter left and right. To their surprise, it then left the road completely and collided head-first into one of the trees that lined the road.

They looked at one another, shocked. "Well this wasn't in Jess' plan," said Meg. "What do we do now?"

"It's no good asking me," replied Zac, "I wasn't paying much attention."

"What do you mean, you weren't paying much attention? How could you not have been paying much attention?!"

"I got thinking about food - juicy cheese burgers to be exact. With gherkins and tomato and... kinda drifted off."

"UGH! You are such a massive loser, Zac. If we get through this alive, I swear I'm gonna kill you! Come on, we had better go take a look."

They ran up the road hurdling fallen antiquities and saw the van crumpled against the immovable Cedar; its bonnet forced upward revealing a steaming engine. They then heard the sound of a struggle and it seemed that Kaylock was thrashing around in the back, screaming hysterically.

"Do you suppose he's injured?" asked Meg, who was already prepared to offer assistance regardless of the man's despicable behaviour.

Zac didn't immediately reply, but instead looked at his sister and shared her concern that they may have caused someone a very serious injury, or worse. "Bloody hell, we might have killed him!"

Their minds were soon set at ease though, when the man in question suddenly sprang from the rear of the van with all of his limbs intact. His behaviour, however, was something far from normal, because on first glance it appeared he may have been covered in red ants or something, for he frenziedly wriggled, squirmed and itched like a man destined for crazy town. To their complete amazement he then proceeded to strip, right there beside the road. First he whipped off his coat and discarded it, then he pulled off his jumper and threw that aside revealing a tattooed pot belly and a pair of podgy man-boobs. And he wasn't stopping there either, because he then lay down on his back and frantically began wiggling out of his jeans.

The twins looked at one another totally speechless, as the man in front of them reduced himself to a pair of spotted boxer shorts accompanied only by socks and shoes. He stood and leapt away from his discarded apparel, looking at it in horror like he had seen a ghost. He then staggered for a moment, shook his head and turned toward the house. That's when he came face-to-face with the two painted warriors blocking his path.

Meg and Zac suddenly found themselves in a difficult and potentially dangerous situation, one they should never have entered into, and felt extremely vulnerable standing off against this angry, volatile and desperate adult. This grown man, wise and experienced in life, whom they had completely humiliated. He didn't move an inch and neither did they, but they knew that should he take so much as a step toward them, there was little they could do to stop him.

He looked them up and down, not sure what to make of them. Did he even know who it was behind the painted faces and filthy clothes? Did he know they were unarmed and frightened out of their minds? Well it transpired that perhaps he didn't, because *he* made the first surprising move - by stepping backward. He was retreating. The scale had tipped, giving the twins the instant edge of superiority. All it then took was a single step forward from them to send Kaylock fleeing into the trees. The twins had won the battle and heartily hugged one another while jumping around.

"What the hell just happened?!" asked Meg incredulously.

"I have no idea, but it was bloody good fun!"

"Did you see his face, Zac? He was totally terrified of us!"

"I know! We whooped his bad-guy butt. Seriously!"

"We totally did!"

"We are like, proper bad-asses!"

"Yeah we are! We… WHOA! WHAT'S THAT?!" Meg abruptly halted their celebrations in the robot-dance style and grabbed Zac's arm. She had heard a squeaking sound and, furthermore, noticed that the discarded pair of jeans belonging to Kaylock had begun twitching on the ground. "There… something is moving. See it?"

"Uh-huh," replied Zac, who had instantly turned pale.

"This isn't one of your stupid pranks is it, Zac?"

"Nuh-uh."

They both gulped before tentatively stepping closer to investigate. There then came a similar squeaking noise from inside the van followed by something falling over and smashing.

"What was that?" asked Zac, nearly jumping out of his skin.

"I don't know," whispered Meg. "Why don't you take a look?"

"Pardon me? I'm not going in there. You saw what happened to that man!"

"OK, OK - calm down, brave soldier. We'll look together."

Zac reluctantly agreed and they both approached the pair of grubby size XXL denims that were now clearly on the move. Meg picked up a stick and prepared to carry out an inspection, while Zac positioned himself behind her. "I thought we were going to do this *together?*" she reminded him, pulling him back around to her side. Once in range, she proceeded to stretch out both her arms and hook the jeans onto the stick. She then slowly raised them into the air and held her breath as she yanked the stick upward. Almost immediately, something dropped out onto the floor from one of the trouser legs. Something small and fluffy.

"Is that..." asked Zac hesitantly, "a ferret?"

The twins looked at one another with the exact same expression and couldn't help but smile, when they saw one of Charlie's pet ferrets looking innocently up at them. It was Marty, the black and brown one, who seemed entirely oblivious to the mayhem he had caused. A moment after, the white one and his partner-in-crime, Doc, appeared at the rear of the van.

"Can you believe it?" asked Meg.

"Well it certainly explains a lot," replied Zac.

Meg bent down holding out her hand toward Marty, offering him a lift. "Hey, boy."

"Careful, Meg. There's nothing worse than a friendly animal that isn't - you might get bit."

But the little fella didn't bite back at all, in fact, he happily scampered up Meg's arm and lay across her shoulders like a scarf. She then went over to the van and allowed Doc to run up her other arm where he joined his friend. "I guess they like me," she smiled.

"I hope you're right because if they don't, you'll be the next one to lose your trousers! Now, let's get back and check on the others."

34

With a single gesture from Mrs Blackwell's gun, Jess was instructed to join Charlie and the old folks. "Your aunt was trying to tell you, Master Midsummer, that *someone* was hiding in the kitchen. You really should listen to your elders."

Charlie suddenly felt thoroughly deflated and his desire to be a hero was melting faster than a bowl of rocky road in summertime.

"Bugger," said Jess, as she took her place with the others.

"Watch your language, young lady!" snapped Auntie. "A true lady never allows her manners to lapse whatever the circumstance."

"I'll give the instructions, grandma," ordered Mrs Blackwell. "Now shut your royal cake hole!"

"Bugger," replied Auntie.

Mrs Blackwell waddled into the room and all eyes followed her progress. "Now, children, my almost completely useless associate, Mr Kaylock, informs me that you somehow managed to overpower both him and his team, and that you took from him the fabled treasure known as the Sunrise Ruby. I don't know quite how you managed it, but it seems that one of his men has become lost in some underground dungeon, while the other has simply disappeared. I really must congratulate you on your bravery and ingenuity and I'm sorry they had to destroy your precious cell phones and what-not. However, business is business and so I must insist that you return what is rightfully mine. Right now, if you please."

"You mean… the ruby?" asked Charlie innocently.

"Of course the ruby, dummy! Now hand it over."

"Why, Mrs Blackwell," asked Jess. "What *has* happened to your accent?"

"Oh that - did you like it, dear? I thought it was simply spiffing, as you would say."

"Can't say I did to be honest. After all, there really is nothing more disturbing than an American trying to pull off a British accent. I know, I used to watch the Disney Channel - a lot. Still, it wasn't the worst I've ever heard - that honour goes to that guy in Mary Poppins, but credit where credit's due, you pulled it off pretty well and were it not for your little slip ups, I may have been fooled."

"Slip ups?"

"That's right. A moment ago you mentioned our cell phones, well we call them mobile phones this side of the pond; and earlier you upset our friend Zac by promising chips for lunch, but instead provided crisps - another translation faux-pas. Perhaps you meant to say potato chips?"

"Is that all, dear?"

"Hardly, because back at the fountain you said highway, when you should have said motorway, but perhaps the biggest give away of all was something you *didn't* say."

"Go on," said Mrs Blackwell, now intrigued to hear more.

"I failed to mention it at the time but it makes perfect sense now. In one of the letters I assume you wrote to Lady Midsummer, you said, and I quote *"You had better knock on wood that you find the ruby"* unquote. Well to knock on wood is unmistakably American, as we all know us Brits say *touch* wood. Isn't that right, Barker?"

"Quite right my dear!" he confirmed proudly. "Damn Yankie-Doodles coming over here, messing up our vocabulary with their alphabet soup..."

"Thank you, wrinkly person!" barked Mrs Blackwell silencing him. "Look, sister, so I don't speak the Queen's English, but neither does most of your silly little country from what I can tell. So what's your point exactly?"

"My point is this: Lady Midsummer, when you were telling us about the history of the Sunrise Ruby earlier, you mentioned that your father almost lost it in a game of cards, right?"

"That's right my dear," replied Auntie, "but..."

"And you also mentioned, that the man to whom he almost lost it was an American... and a cheating one so it sounded." Jess was merely testing the water at this point but she seemed to have struck a nerve, for if looks could kill, the one she received from Mrs Blackwell would have struck her down where she stood.

"MY GRANDFATHER WAS NO CHEAT!" Her sudden outburst was unsettling, as she was now both armed and irate.

"You were related to that man?" asked Auntie incredulously.

"That's right, your hoity-toity ladyship! My grandfather, Louis Francis Black, in case you didn't know. He won the ruby fair and square from your drunken excuse of a father, Thomas Bixby Junior. Only your family, it seemed, didn't want to part with the gem and denied the incident ever happened. My grandfather gambled everything he had that night, but instead of becoming a multi-millionaire he lost everything. His money, his home, even his reputation after he was branded a cheat and a liar. He was a proud man, my grandfather, and refused to admit that he tried to steal the ruby. For his pride - and to satisfy your family's lie - he received two years in prison."

"That's terrible," announced Charlie. "Tell me please, what become of your grandfather?"

"Why he served his sentence of course; not like he had a choice. After his release he was deported to the states and returned to his home town of Punxsutawney, Pennsylvania, far away from you bloody Brits..." Mrs Blackwell paused when she noticed a noise coming from the hall where footsteps could be heard approaching from the entrance. She held her finger up to her mouth making the *shush* sound before hiding behind the open door. A moment after, Meg appeared complete with ferrets, plus Zac, accompanied by Cookie. They saw their friends in the dining room and excitedly bounded in unleashing a wave of verbal diarrhoea.

"Jess! Charlie! You'll never guess what happened!"

"We were stoning Kaylock's van and he drove off!"

"And all these antiques fell out the back, it was carnage!"

"Then he trashed some flowerbeds..."

"Before totalling the van against a tree!"

"Then he stripped, like, proper stripped. Butt naked!"

"And... there was a stand-off... and we were like, grr, and he was like, whuurt! Then he ran off!"

"We even found your ferr…"

They stopped only when they noticed Jess, Charlie, Lady Midsummer and Barker, all staring solemnly back at them, shaking their heads from side to side. "What is it?" asked the twins as their smiles began to fade. They soon realised what, when Mrs Blackwell stepped from behind the door with gun in hand, at which point their happy expressions disappeared altogether. "Bugger," they said in unison. They were instructed to join their friends and did so without protest. Seeing their owner, the ferrets hopped onto Charlie's shoulders, while Cookie jumped up and sat on the table beside Meg.

"Now where was I?" uttered Mrs Blackwell. "Oh yes, once state-side, my grandfather spent the rest of his life in near poverty, but managed to find happiness when he married my grandmother, Harmony Wolfe. They met in an orphanage where they both worked caring for the children. In time they had a son who went on to have a daughter, and the story of deception and treachery was passed down through the generations. Down to me."

"What's she on about?" whispered Zac.

"Not now!" replied Jess.

"Hang on a minute," questioned Charlie. "So… are you saying… you're Louis Black's granddaughter?"

"That's right, master poopy-pants. So what?"

"So… aren't you a bit old then? You know, to be his granddaughter. Shouldn't you be around early twenties or something?"

While the others caught up, Mrs Blackwell sent Charlie a thin smile. "Excellent observation, lord posh-bottom. I guess those private math lessons have taught you something after all. But in order to answer your question, perhaps it will be easier to show you." With her free hand, she reached up and delicately pinched the hairy mole on her cheek between finger and thumb. Then, to the wonder of all those present, pulled it off.

"Eww," grimaced the girls.

"Does that help you understand?" she asked. "No? Well how about this…" Grasping her bulging chin and giving it a firm tug, it came away in her hand. She then tossed that away and the animals watched it fly through the air thinking it was a toy. As the others looked on in utter astonishment, she proceeded to remove her glasses and drop them to the floor, followed by a wig and lastly, a fleshy, rubbery mask, revealing the face of a pretty young lady. By this time, Barker had fainted and slumped down in his chair beside Auntie, while the others simply found themselves thunderstruck.

"Errm," said Zac, "can someone tell me what on earth is going on?"

"She's the granddaughter of Louis Black," whispered Jess.

"Oh right. Who's he?"

"*HE*..." replied the young lady, after spitting two oversize false teeth from her mouth, "...is the man whose life was ruined by the great and honourable, family Midsummer."

"And you are?" asked Meg.

"My name, is Claire Louise Black-Wolfe, and I am here to take my family's rightful possession of the Sunrise Ruby."

With that said she calmly strolled into the room opposite her audience who never took their eyes off her, or her pistol, for a moment. They watched as she unzipped a podgy body suit and let it fall to the floor as if it were a summer dress. Without the makeup and padding, she now appeared to be in her late teens and had a short crop of flame-red hair. She wore black leggings and black vest, and even removed a pair of coloured contact lenses revealing eyes of the lightest blue.

Charlie gazed at her dreamily, like he did the posters on his bedroom wall that Auntie didn't approve of. "She's so hot." For his comment, both Meg and Jess gave him a sharp, disapproving nudge in either side of his rib cage. "Sorry, did I say that out loud?"

Miss Black-Wolfe, now free of her cumbersome guise, stepped aside and ruffled her hair. "You know, my father - who' up there looking down or down there looking up - taught me how to steal treasures from some of the most secure buildings in the world. The Louvre - piece of cake; Berlin Neuse - afternoon tea; Tower of London - walk in the park. All nailed using a Kinect sensor and a Raspberry Pi. But your ruby, Lady Midsummer, proved surprisingly problematic and turned out to be secured in a very unique - and dare I say old-fashioned - way. I tried to reason with you. I sent you letters asking that you return it so we could avoid this whole dirty business, but you were as stubborn as an old goat. That's why I had to employ some heavies to come and turn the place upside down."

"And take the rap for stealing the ruby, no doubt," said Meg.

Miss Black-Wolfe winked back at her and smiled. "Don't tell them, will you." She then looked a little sickened and sniffed the air. "Can anyone smell manure?"

While the children looked at one another questioningly, there came another sound from the hall suggesting someone else was about to join them. Miss Black-Wolfe again instructed everyone to be silent and resumed her position behind the door. A moment later, Fräulein Bertrümn entered the room looking pleased. "Kinder!" she announced buoyantly. "I have opened gates, we can leave! It is wunderbar..." But as Meg and Zac had done before her, she stopped talking when she noticed the ever increasing number of grim faces looking back. Then, once again, Miss Black-Wolfe quietly revealed herself to the latecomer. "Das ist schlecht!"

"Join the others please, Fräulein. And get your hands up, ALL OF YOU!" At this point, Barker regained consciousness and noticed he was the only one with his hands down, but one gesture from Miss Black-Wolfe saw his arms shoot straight in the air. "That's better. Oh, and I love the makeup by the way, kids - very scary. Not so sure about yours though, Fräulein. Then again, you were always a little overzealous with the mascara if you ask me."

"I do not know this person, ja?" whispered Bertie to Charlie.

"It's kind of a long story."

"I think I know this person," said Zac rather unexpectedly. "You're him, err... I mean, her."

"Zac, what *are* you taking about you idiot?" hissed Meg.

"Meg," intervened Jess, "let me handle this. Zac you idiot! What on earth are you talking about?"

"The jewel thief," he continued.

"What jewel thief?" asked the others.

"*The* jewel thief. The one that's been in the news. I saw it on TV the other night. You're her aren't you? You're the famous Wolf."

The young lady curtsied as she replied. "The one and the same."

"Good work, Zac," said Charlie totally spellbound, and even the girls had to admit that was pretty impressive. So, while Zac stood looking pleased with himself and Charlie gazed dreamily at his captor, most of the others simply stood as the clock in the hall whirred into life and chimed midnight. When it had finished, Miss Black-Wolfe raised the gun and extended out her other hand.

"Now, seeing as we're bottom of the ninth and you're probably expecting the cops any minute, I'll take the ruby if you please."

Charlie lowered his hand to his pocket, but Jess grabbed his wrist and held it firmly in place. "If we give you the stone," she replied, "will you promise to let us go?"

"Sweetheart, if I had wanted you dead I would have let Kaylock and his goon take care of you at the fountain."

"I want to hear you say it. Say, I promise I will let you all go."

"Let us go *alive*, Jess," whispered Zac, just to clarify the proposal.

"Oh, yes, right. Let us go, *alive*."

Miss Black-Wolfe admired Jess' spirit and the concern she had for her friend's welfare. "I like you, young lady," she told her. "I like the cut of your jib - and your friends too."

"What's a Jib?" asked Zac, but instead of an answer he received a loud *shush* from the others.

"You've got guts with a side of sass," continued Miss Black-Wolfe. "Reminds me of me, when I was your age. So... with that in mind, you have a deal. I promise. I'll even pinkie-promise, fist-bump and lock it should you require."

Once satisfied she had guaranteed everyone's safety, Jess released Charlie's arm and he pulled the sparkling jewel from his pocket. With the others watching in revered silence, he then placed it onto the table and slid it across into Miss Black-Wolfe's open hand. The moment it made contact she fell hopelessly into dark devotion. Her blue eyes seemed to burn like fire. Nothing else mattered. No one else was around, just her and her treasure. Cradling it in her palms and without speaking or looking up, she backed toward the door.

The children and the others, believing their ordeal was nearly over, slowly lowered their hands when suddenly and completely unannounced, Kaylock appeared at the door. He collided with Miss Black-Wolfe with such force she was knocked to the ground. She landed on her front and watched as both the ruby and her gun went skidding away across the floor. "Kaylock, you idiot!"

"What the?!" he replied furiously. "And just who the hell are you?" He stood gasping for air wearing an outfit fashioned from a discarded potato sack above his now soiled Italian shoes. His hair was wild like he had been electrified and any exposed flesh was red with stings, scratches and bites received from the woods. Everyone, even Meg and Zac who had some prior exposure to his situation, had to double-take his bizarre appearance.

"What did you do to him?" uttered Jess.

Miss Black-Wolfe climbed to her feet and faced off against her employee. "Mr Kaylock, it's me, your boss - Mrs Blackwell!" He looked dubiously over her shoulder at the others who were all nodding back at him, but he remained unconvinced, for all he saw in front of him was just another meddling young upstart trying to pull the wool over his eyes.

"Do I look like an idiot, Miss?" There wasn't a person or animal in the room who thought he didn't and when the young lady in front of him persisted, he simply shoved her backward. She stumbled awkwardly, banging her head on the corner of the table where she slumped unconscious to the ground. Kaylock then rushed over and picked up both the gun and the ruby and immediately pointed the weapon toward the others, whose hands were again raised into the air.

"Bugger!" they all said together.

"Well this is a grand turn out," sneered Kaylock. "I'll be able to take care of you all in one go." He then saw the children in their war paint which seemed to disturb him. "Say, you look familiar. Which one of you jumped me earlier? You two I reckon." He focused in on Meg and Zac, who remained silent.

"Why don't you just leave us alone?" asked Charlie. "You've got the ruby."

"That's right," agreed Meg. "After all, the police will be here any minute and..."

"SILENCE IMPETUOUS INSECTS!" bellowed Kaylock. "Let me explain something to you lot and I appreciate you're all bursting with teenage angst and eager to get back to doing the things you deem important in life - like texting, tweeting and twerking. The thing is, in case you hadn't noticed, I don't listen to snotty-nosed, booger-eating, bed-wetting, spot-squeezing, soft-handed, long-haired, lazy, work-shy, hoity-blooming-toity, bank-of-mommy-and-daddy, snappy-chatty, facey-bookie, tablet-toting, pull-yer-friggin-jeans-up, SPOILT BRATS!"

"Then perhaps you'll listen to me!" replied Auntie, boldly stepping forward and taking down her hands.

"And just what gives you that idea, *grandma*?"

"That's Lady Midsummer to you, sir. And to answer your question, as it stands you are facing a charge of robbery, false imprisonment and possession of a firearm. You are morally reprehensible without doubt, yet with a good lawyer you might get away with eight-to-ten in the slammer. Don't make things worse for yourself by doing something silly with that gun. It is high time you bit the bullet and read the writing on the wall!"

"Pardon me, madam," said Barker tapping her on the shoulder, "but I'm afraid you just said a mixed metaphor and..."

"OH NOT NOW, BARKER!"

There followed a slight pause while Kaylock considered Auntie's warning, but a moment later he burst into loud laughter suggesting he wasn't going to be heeding her advice. "Why thank you, Your Ladyship, I really needed a good laugh. But tell me, how will they pin anything on me... if there are no witnesses around to talk?" His expression changed to reflect his terrible intent as he raised the gun and pointed it straight at Auntie. "And you're going to be the first to bite any bullet, my lady."

Everyone shared a sickening feeling when they realised what was about to happen. It had become a nightmare they desperately wanted to wake from. Out of instinct more than anything, Jess took hold of Charlie's and Meg's hand beside her and Meg held Zac's. Auntie then took hold of Charlie's and Barker's and they all closed their eyes tight. It appeared they were all out of miracles, but there was actually one more yet to come.

With their eyes closed they didn't see the large figure who was as wide as the door frame arrive behind Kaylock. And they also didn't see Kaylock be lifted clear off his feet. Cookie barked and everyone opened an eye to marvel at the site of their captor being carried away kicking and screaming.

"W-WHAT?!" yelled Kaylock. "WHO IS THERE? WHAT ARE YOU DOING? ANSWER ME!"

"RENARD!" shouted Meg joyously.

"Renard?" questioned the others.

"Bark!" yapped Cookie.

They all watched as the giant ducked under the door frame and carried Kaylock, kicking and screaming into the hall where he placed him down and disarmed him. Then, using just his bare hands, he bent the gun barrel ninety degrees before tossing it away.

"RENARD!" bellowed Kaylock, as he aggressively pushed and prodded the man towering above him. "HAVE YOU LOST YOUR MIND?! JUST WHAT DO YOU THINK YOU ARE DOING YOU OVERGROWN BIPED?! HAVE YOU FORGOTTEN THAT YOU WORK FOR ME? NOW, BEFORE I CUT YOU OUT OF THE PROFITS COMPLETELY, I SUGGEST YOU DO SOMETHING USEFUL. COMPRENDO?!"

The children accompanied by Bertie, arrived in the hall to watch events unfold. Renard said nothing, but glanced behind to where the faces of Meg and the others looked expectantly back at him. He returned his attention to Kaylock and grasped him firmly by his make-shift vest, pulling on some chest hair in the process. "YEOOOW!!!" screamed Kaylock, as he was once again raised off the ground. "WHAT ARE YOU DOING? PUT ME DOWN!"

"Sure thing, boss," replied the giant. "Oh, but just before I do there is something I need to tell you."

"WHAT?!"

"I quit!"

With his resignation tendered, he launched his ex-employer backward sending him several meters through the air until he crashed into the grandfather clock. In a daze, Kaylock slumped onto his knees while the clock's intricate workings rained on top of him in a chorus of destruction. He eyes rolled back and he fell forward.

The giant turned to face the children and shrugged his shoulders. He looked awkward, still unsure if he had done the right thing. Meg stepped forward ahead of the others and took hold of his hand while smiling up at him, only then did his face brake into a large smile and he began to laugh openly. He crouched and scooped Meg up as if she had no weight at all and spun her around. They shared a warm embrace before Jess and the boys realised this man was a friend and joined them. Renard affectionately held the children as gentle as a father with his new born babies, and Auntie and Barker marvelled at the site of him carrying four teenagers.

"Renard, you saved us!" said Meg. "I knew you had a good heart I just knew it."

"Well, I guess you were right, little one," he replied in his kind, deep voice. "I guess you were right."

He placed the children down at which point Meg introduced her fascinating friend to the others. "Guys, meet Renard. Renard, meet the guys. Oh, and may I present Her Ladyship, Lady Midsummer."

"Charmed I'm sure," announced Auntie, holding up her glasses and looking bewildered.

"Pleased to meet you all," said the giant. "Oh, and sorry about the clock, Madame."

"That's quite alright, Mr Renard," replied Auntie. "Given the present state of the house, I don't think anyone would notice anyway. Besides, Barker will have that glued back together in no time, won't you dear."

Everyone besides Barker shared a smile, up until Renard suddenly looked deadly serious. "And who is this beautiful creature?" he asked. Auntie, Barker and Bertie all glanced behind themselves to see who he was addressing, but it was only when he walked over to the maid and delicately took her hand did they know. He raised it to his mouth and gently kissed it, instantly sending her cheeks bright red. "This belle fleur standing in front of me, like an angel sent from the heavens."

"Adalwolfa Pickelhaube Bertrümn," she replied nervously. "At your service."

"Enchanté, Mademoiselle. Now, permit me to introduce myself: my name is Rénard Rèné Dupônt, and I can honestly say that I have never seen such beauty. Such natural, untainted exquisiteness."

"My saviour."

The others looked on and witnessed love doing its work. "Aww, how romantic," said Meg.

"Think I'm gonna throw up!" replied Zac, who received a nudge in the ribs from Jess.

"Love truly is an amazing thing," sniffed Auntie. "There is someone for everyone in this world and there is no greater gift than to love and be loved." She took Barker's arm and smiled at him, while beside them, Renard and Bertie remained mesmerized with one another.

"Well said, madam," replied Barker. "I couldn't have put it better myself."

"Well this is awkward," said Zac in the silence that followed. He promptly received another nudge in the ribs, this time from Meg. "OW! Will everyone stop doing that!"

"Speaking of love…" announced Charlie before returning to the dining room. The others followed and saw him crouching beside Miss Black-Wolfe, checking she was breathing and feeling for a pulse.

"Is she…" asked Meg.

"No, she's alive. Just out cold. Perhaps she needs mouth to mouth?" He had offered his services with enthusiasm, however, a telling off from his aunt dashed any hopes of that happening, by him at least. It seemed that Miss Black-Wolfe had received a nasty bump on the head which was also bleeding a little, so the others helped to lay her in the recovery position and Barker carefully wrapped her head with a bandage.

"She'll be fine now," said Jess, "until the police arrive."

"Then the Wolf will be caged forever," added Zac, somewhat regrettably.

35

Just as everyone's nerves began to settle there came a clattering of objects from the hall and they all rushed back to see what it was. They saw Kaylock, who had regained consciousness, exiting through the front door. They followed although not in pursuit, but rather to enjoy seeing him flee and be sure they were rid of him. On arrival at the entrance they found themselves near blinded by lights shining from outside, forcing them to shade their eyes.

It transpired that while they were tending to Miss Black-Wolfe, a number of vehicles had arrived in the courtyard and formed a semi-circle. There must have been fifteen, maybe twenty or even thirty of them, plus several motor-cycles, all with their lights on full beam power. And, standing between them and the house, was a podgy silhouette with hands behind his head, which they could just make out to be Kaylock. There was no talking or communication taking place, just dazzling lights.

"Is it the police?" asked Meg.

"Can't tell," replied Jess.

"If it is the law enforcement," enquired Charlie, "shouldn't they be arresting someone by now?"

"One would expect that to be the case, Master Charles," agreed Barker.

"Well, I guess there's only one way to find out," said Zac pushing past the others. "ARREST THAT MAN!"

There came no verbal reply, but a moment later footsteps could be heard on the gravel and a number of people encircled Kaylock. They instructed him to lie face down on the ground and not to speak, which he obeyed without resisting. They then proceeded to use packing tape to tie his hands and ankles, as well as placing a strip across his mouth. The moment he was secured, two persons appeared to sit on him for good measure.

"Is that how the authorities do things these days?" asked Auntie incredulously, although no one had an answer to give.

Someone then shouted out: "OK. It's OK," which was followed by the lights dimming to a more agreeable level. An army of silhouettes then advanced toward the house wielding a variety of make-shift weapons, ranging from gardening tools to paint guns and from broom handles to movie-replica swords.

"Perhaps it's the Feds," speculated Zac, "or the CIA. Those guys don't mess about."

The crowd congregated in front of the main entrance and came to a stop, where a handful of people stepped forward. "Jess?"

"Megan? Zachary?"

The voices sounded familiar. "Mum? Dad?" questioned Jess and the twins through narrowed eyes. They looked at each other for a moment struggling to believe it was true, until their parents stepped forward and they saw it with their own eyes. "MUM! DAD!"

The children lovingly embraced their parents and the parents lovingly embraced their children. Watching over them, Auntie proudly placed her arm around Charlie, while Renard held the hand of maid Bertie. It was the children's parents who had come to their rescue. Not the police. Not the FBI nor the CIA. Just their plain old boring parents. *And* they had brought back-up in the form of many of the people from the community: extended family members, neighbours, shop keepers, garage-workers, farmers and even complete strangers from passing canal boats. They also recognised the faces of several school peers including Matt the Bean, Irish Rich, Bed-Head Beth, Football Brandon, Lipstick Linda and Hairspray Phil.

It truly was a surreal spectacle, especially so with the sight of many people sporting random body protection fashioned from anything they had to hand: rugby and hockey padding, motorcross protective headgear and armour, ski goggles, and even a set of matching Viking helmets to name a few. The ramshackle mob's efficiency, however, was never in doubt because some younger children were already standing guard over the squirming Kaylock with some very serious looking foam-dart crossbows and water guns, just hoping he dare try and escape.

"Oh my poor dears," fretted Mrs Hewes inspecting Jess and the twins. "What have they done to you? Thank God you're all OK. When we heard the news, well we just, we just…"

"Freaked," added Mr Hewes.

"Mom, Dad," said Zac excitedly. "You wouldn't believe what's happened to us today! You see there were these jewel thieves…"

"JEWEL THIEVES!" exclaimed the parents.

"Yeah and giant rats…"

"GIANT RATS!"

"…and secret passages, and, and…"

While the twins clued their parents in, and added some questionable exaggerations, Jess received a barrage of hugs and kisses from her nearest and dearest. "Oh my precious, my sweet, sweet, precious. Just look at you my poor sweetie."

"Mum!"

"You're filthy, phew and a little stinky too! You need a good soak in the bath you do."

"Mum, you're embarrassing me!"

"I tried to ring you, then I tried to ring the twins, then I rang the police…"

"Mum, please!"

"Here, sweetie, let me clean you up." She took out some tissue, dampened it with her tongue and, to Jess' horror, attempted to apply it to her face.

"Mum! Honestly, I'm fine. But what are you all doing here? Where are the police?"

"Well…" began Mr Birchwood, before he was interrupted by a voice that sounded familiar.

"Well you see, it's kind of a long story."

"JAKE!" exclaimed the girls, who immediately ran over and hugged him.

"Whoa, easy! I have my reputation to maintain you know."

"I knew you would come through for us, Jake," said Meg. "Didn't I say, Jess?"

"Hey, it was no sweat," he replied modestly. "I'm just sorry it took so long. You see me and Basher had a little trouble persuading the fuzz to get off their butts and come down here. Then one of their cars crashed into a hedgerow on the way; apparently the driver swerved to avoid an inflatable crocodile. There were skid marks and everything - and not just on the road! Still, I see you took care of business here."

"Yeah," replied Meg casually, "like you said, it was no sweat."

"Thank you, Jake," said Charlie arriving behind the girls.

"No problem, rich boy. Any time."

"So you finally did something good for someone else," said Zac as he approached his archenemy. "Does this mean we're going to see a new Jake Jenkins around school?" He offered up his hand toward Jake, who accepted it.

"Guess we'll just have to wait and see."

"So, Jake," asked Meg, "where is Basher?"

"Oh, he's sat in his mum's car over there, but won't come out. He's worried you'll tease him over him peeing himself and crying earlier."

"He did what?!" exclaimed the others.

"Whoops, did I say that out loud!"

Jess and the twins went on to introduce Charlie, his family and remaining staff to their families, plus everyone else present and there were many *how-do-you-do's* all around. They had almost finished as the sound of sirens could be heard coming down the approach road and it wasn't long before the familiar flashing lights of the police force arrived behind the other vehicles. The villagers parted (and hastily hid from view any illegal weapons obtained from car boots) as uniformed officers rushed toward the main entrance to await their commanding officer, who was evidently not in the greatest of shape.

"Lady Midsummer, I presume?" he eventually puffed on arrival. The man, who was in his late forties but looked several years older, was woefully overweight. His shirt was not even tucked in at the back, not that he could see round that far. He reached the front entrance and inadvertently let out a cheeky, squeaky backfire. "Ahem, pardon me. I am Chief Superintendent Johnson-Thomson of the Northrumptonshire county police force and I have been informed by some local 'miscreants', that you are experiencing some sort of... incident?"

"You are indeed correct, Superintendent," confirmed Auntie.

"*Chief* Superintendent," he replied.

"Oh whatever. The point is, sir, that you and your tinpot police force have turned up several hours too late! These brave children, confounding expectations, have already dealt with the intruders *and* saved us all from a horrible ordeal."

"Madam, I can assure you we responded as quickly and efficiently as possible, given the situation."

"Well that's a load of bull!" objected Jake, causing a gasp from the onlookers. "I'd hardly call banging me and Basher up in a cell before having three helpings of cake, efficient!"

"*Ahem*, why that was just a misunderstanding," squirmed the Chief under the questioning glare of those around him. "I mean, how were we to know you were telling the truth?"

"Perhaps you should have done your job, sir," replied Auntie, "and followed up on their report."

"But, madam, I..."

"Oh don't madam me, young man!" The associated uniformed officers tried not to smirk as they watched their commanding officer being roasted by the old lady. "I have friends in high places, who will be hearing of your sloppy behaviour I can assure you!"

"Oh really," shrugged the Chief, hoisting up his trousers at the waist. "Like who?"

He had barely finished not caring when the sound of an approaching helicopter, no wait - helicopters, was heard, and everyone present looked to the skies. The noise grew louder until it seemed it couldn't get any louder, at which point two black objects appeared directly above, creating a downdraft strong enough to blow hats and wigs from anyone wearing them. Bright search lights then shone down onto the crowd and a moment later several ropes were lowered to the ground, followed by masked men who rappelled down them.

"WOW!" exclaimed Zac, holding up his camera to record the action. "IT'S THE FEDS!"

"I think you'll find, young Zachary," replied Auntie, "that it is the finest fighting force in the world: Her Majesty's own, Special Air Service."

Zac and Charlie looked at one another like they had received the gift they had always wanted. "The S-A-S!"

The soldiers were dressed in full black combat gear and wore balaclavas so that only their eyes were visible. They carried automatic firearms with laser-pointing scopes, which made even the police feel nervous, and quickly secured the immediate area while more soldiers rappelled down and entered the house. Some didn't even bother using doors and jumped straight through the windows, shattering the glass and tearing down drapes. "WHOA!" exclaimed Zac and Charlie in total awe.

Renard, who suddenly felt a compelling urge to make an exit, received a grasp of his arm from maid Bertie, who held him firmly in place. They were joined by two of the soldiers who positioned themselves beside Auntie and one of them spoke into his wrist watch. "This is team, *ahem...* *Strawberry Cheesecake* - the area is secured, over." He lowered his arm and stood waiting, before commenting to his fellow soldier. "We really have to stop letting her choose the team names!"

"Uh-huh," grunted the other man.

There was no reply to his watch communication and it wasn't clear as to exactly who he had spoken to, or that anyone had actually heard him. However, almost immediately the choppers hovering above departed, leaving Auntie's beehive hair-do drooping heavily to one side. One of the police officers then retrieved the Chiefs' hat which had been blown away (and peed on by an as yet unidentified dog) and returned it to him. Shortly after a third helicopter arrived at the scene, although this one was white, larger in size and had more lights on it; Meg likened it to a flying limousine complete with blackened windows.

Some of the soldiers had ignited flares and placed them in a clearing beyond the line of parked vehicles. They blazed a brilliant red and filled the area with smoke like a firework display, signalling a make-shift landing pad for the chopper which came to rest with precision in its centre. As the rotors slowed everyone present, including the police officers, gathered and watched with baited breath for the visitor to reveal themselves.

First, a door at the front opened and two people stepped out: one man and one woman. They were dressed in identical attire - black suits with black sunglasses, shiny black shoes, and both wore a white communication plug in one ear. They were met by four armed soldiers before they opened a side door and offered assistance to what looked like an old, but able, person. Once out, the VIP visitor immediately headed toward the house with the security persons and soldiers on either side. As the entourage parted the onlookers, people started bowing and kneeling like a Mexican wave in reverse. What followed was this: there has never been nor will there ever be again, a look of such astonishment on the faces of those people present, when Elizabeth II, Queen of England, arrived in front of them.

"Your Majesty!" said the children and their parents in absolute amazement. They bowed and curtseyed but not discreetly and with dignity, but rather awkwardly and excessively.

"Lizzy!" exclaimed Auntie.

"Josey!" replied her Royal Highness, before they hugged one another affectionately. To the surprise of those around they then executed a handshake and fist bump to envy any style developed in the playground. "Sic!"

"Totally," agreed Auntie.

"And Barker, my man. How the devil are you?"

"If I may be permitted to use the vernacular, ma'am, then I am truly buzzin."

Auntie then noticed those around them remained crouched. "Oh get up, children, and stop fussing. We're all friends here. Isn't that right, Lizzy?"

"Why of course," agreed her Royal Highness. "And may I say, I am relieved to see you all in one piece. From what I hear, you've all had a dreadful time here..." She paused and suddenly appeared repulsed. "Good heavens, what *is* that offensive smell?"

The children looked at one another mortified, desperately wanting to avoid identifying themselves as the pungent offenders. Meg thought fast, "It's, um... probably the country air, Your Majesty."

The Queen narrowed her eyes contemplating their appearance, then she smiled. "Why of course, dear. You're probably right. After all, I have been in stuffy old London for some weeks now. But then again, I should be used to such an unpleasant odour, what with all those politicians hanging around the place. Now, if you will excuse me for just a moment..." She turned to face the crowd and looked over the top of her glasses. "SUPERINTENDANT!"

The cumbersome officer of the police force appeared at her side looking very uncomfortable. "Um," he mumbled pathetically, "that's *Chief* Superintendent, Your Royalness."

"Not for much longer! I want to see you in my Windsor office first thing tomorrow morning. Is that perfectly clear?"

"Yes ma'am."

"And don't be late, I'm taking the family to Lego Land."

"Yes ma'am. I mean, no ma'am."

"And for goodness sake lay of the doughnuts!"

"Yes ma'am. Of course, ma'am. Thank you, ma'am."

With the chief taken care of, her Royal Highness turned back toward Auntie and noticed the colossal Renard standing in the background. His appearance startled her, causing the security officers by her side to place hands on guns holstered inside their jackets. "And who is this... err, gentleman?" Renard tried to remain calm while his beloved Fräulein squeezed his hand. He felt an overwhelming urge to be somewhere else, but would undoubtedly be taken down immediately if he dared run. He knew he must give himself up and face the consequences for the part he played in the robbery, yet the children saw him as their saviour and were prepared to defend him.

"He's the, um..." began Charlie.

"The err..." stuttered Jess.

"He's, he's..." mumbled the twins.

"He is my gamekeeper," announced Auntie with pride. "Recently appointed on a trial basis, but the job is his – if he wants it."

Renard looked overjoyed and broke into a large smile, but tried to act casual as not to raise too much attention. "It would be an honour, Lady Midsummer," he replied. "And thank you."

The Queen, who had been eyeballing him suspiciously, suddenly seemed quite happy with it all and a wave of her hand saw her security people stand at ease. "Jolly good," she announced. "Now then, get the kettle on, Barker, if you've still got one that is. I'm simply dying for a cuppa!" The old butler, who it seemed was putting in overtime, bowed and was about to head off to the kitchen, but before he did, the Queen announced one or two more orders. She turned and addressed the crowd in the courtyard. "Would anyone care for a hot chocolate... or a brandy?" A brief moment of silence followed, then there came an almighty cheer from the masses - and a look of sheer panic on Barker's face. "Oh don't worry," she assured him. "My team will help you. Now come on, Josey, one is catching a cold derriere out here!"

Her Majesty took Auntie by the arm and led her into the house with Barker fussing behind. They in turn were followed by the long line of security persons, the children's parents and extended families, the police, then the villagers and canal folk. It took a moment for Jess and the others to come to terms with what had just happened, but they were soon joking and celebrating the end of a day they will almost certainly never forget.

"That was quite an adventure," remarked Charlie as people filed between them. "Things just won't seem the same after this."

"You mean when news of our crime-solving prominence hits the news?" asked Meg.

"Yeah - and when people hear how we kicked ass!" added Zac.

Meg looked at him sourly, "That is what I just said, butt-breath."

"Whatever, like I was *going* to say... we could be famous. They might make a movie about us!"

"Four kids and a dog," replied Jess. "It'll never take off."

"Hey, Charlie," said Zac, "I just thought - we made a bet earlier, remember? That I could get you to gamble before the end of the day?"

"Oh yes, I forgot about that. I guess I owe you..."

"Well here's the pound. You win, Charlie - you didn't gamble."

Jess shook her head at them, "Blimey boys, it's a miracle we got through the day alive with you on the team."

"What do you mean?" they both enquired.

"Never mind."

"Well one thing's for sure," said Meg, taking Jake's hand and smiling up at him, "it's been one heck of a ride."

"It sure has," he replied smiling dreamily back.

Jess and Charlie looked at one another surprised, yet pleased at this hot new piece of gossip. Zac, on the other hand, didn't know what the hell was happening. "Wait, what is going on here? Are they..."

Jess quickly took him by the arm, "Why don't we go get something to eat, Zac? You must be famished."

"Well, I am quite hungry," he replied, looking over his shoulder as he was marched away.

"You coming with, Charlie? You know three's company, right?"

Charlie hastily caught up with them when something occurred to him. "OH MY GOSH!"

"Get over it, Charlie. They're just kissing is all."

"No, Jess, I mean - I just thought, what about Miss Black-Wolfe?"

"Out of your league, Charlie."

"Wait… what I mean is, we forgot about her. And the ruby!"

They returned to the hall which now resembled a party that had over spilled. People were talking and joking and there was even live music blaring from the sitting room, where some of the canal folk had struck up a band. Civilians were taking selfies with the police officers, police officers were taking selfies with the soldiers, and soldiers were taking selfies with suits of armour and ancient weaponry. Social media would have lit up with the news, if anyone could have gotten any signal.

"Pardon me," said Charlie, while they navigated both the crowd and the clutter. "Excuse us, coming through." On arrival to the dining room they found it equally jam-packed with no immediate sign of Miss Black-Wolfe. It was a hotbed of activity with hardened soldiers wearing flowery aprons distributing refreshments under the command of their interim, and incredibly strict, commander Barker. This was easier said than done given the state of the place, but they still managed to pull it off somehow. Jess and the boys surveyed the many faces in the room and looked under the table, but found nothing there besides Cookie chewing on a rubber mask. They checked with the police who assisted in the search, but failed to locate the young jewel thief - or the Sunrise Ruby, anywhere.

36

After his experience in the cabin, Donald the groundskeeper decided that life was too short to live alone and returned to his beloved Alba to rediscover his family. He opened a Punch and Judy show on Portobello beach, assuring thousands of children enjoyed their summer holidays just that little bit more. His departure, however, meant a vacancy needed to be filled in the Midsummer estate, a result of which saw two new groundskeepers appointed and offered long-term residence in the cabin: one fast-tracked British citizen - Monsieur Rénard Dupônt and his new wife, Fräulein Pickelhaube Dupônt.

They married on September 16th beneath a white marquee at the Midsummer estate, with Auntie covering the cost of the entire event, thanks to her near bazillion-pound pay out from the insurance companies to cover items damaged and stolen. The wedding included an all-you-can-eat buffet and, as neither bride nor groom had any family to invite, Jess, the twins, their families and everyone else who arrived at the house that night back in June attended. Between the bride, groom, adult guests and members of the Northrumptonshire police force, they managed to drink Auntie out of ninety-eight bottles of vintage champagne - more than half of her reserve, while the children polished off their combined body-weight in fizzy drinks and ice-cream. Auntie used the occasion to try out her new smart phone and selfie stick, but somehow managed to end up with twenty-three photos and a HD video of the marquee roof.

Of course, with an outstanding vacancy for a cook, plus the maid formally known as Bertrümn joining the gardening team, meant there were two openings in the house staff. Auntie then insisting that old man Barker hang up his shoes and retire also meant a replacement for him was needed. So, in addition to William - the new cook, and Jayne - the new maid, both of whom were employed from the local village, a new and considerably younger butler was taken on.

The old couple can be found pool side most sunny afternoons, receiving a pedicure whilst sipping tall Manhattans alongside their adopted rescue dog, Mycroft.

Thanks in part to the statement of facts given by the children, plus the comprehensive video evidence provided by Zac, (Gorgeous) George Kaylock was charged and convicted on multiple accounts. These included conspiring to commit a robbery, trespassing, nine counts of false imprisonment, possession of a firearm, attempted assault, attempted murder, dangerous driving, driving without a seatbelt, driving without insurance, driving without road tax, driving without an MOT, fifty counts of destruction of private property and one count of animal neglect. He received ninety-nine years imprisonment and passes the time hustling fellow inmates.

His colleague, Laurence (Burk) Birkenhead, who was trapped beneath the fountain, was overjoyed when the fire brigade finally came to rescue him, but less so when he realised the police were there too. He was convicted of conspiring to commit a robbery, trespassing, five counts of false imprisonment, possession of a dangerous weapon, attempted assault, eight-hundred counts of destruction of private property, one count of damaging an antique moose and multiple counts of upsetting swans. He received fifty-nine years imprisonment and passes the time assisting Kaylock in hustling fellow inmates.

The mysterious young jewel thief, Miss Claire Louise Black-Wolfe, was never seen again - and neither was the infamous Sunrise Ruby for that matter. She regained consciousness that night while Jess and the others were in the courtyard wondering what the bright lights were. She opened her eyes to see two small, furry animals running away with the priceless gem, and, after an ill-timed game of catch-me-if-you-can, she managed to reclaim the ruby and exit the house through the trapdoor in the sitting room. She used the tunnel to escape, not in the direction the children had taken, but along the narrow pathway that came from the east. It is unclear as to exactly where the tunnel let out, but there was a report from Dirty Den - the security guard in the Royal Ordnance Depot way back in Daventry - that stated an intruder 'distressing' his dog, Bess, in the early hours of Sunday morning.

There were no further reports of the mysterious Wolf in the news. There were, however, recorded donations of several million dollars to a number of children's charities across the world over the following months. All of which were from an anonymous, flame-haired young lady.

After their experience, Jake and Bashir retired from the bullying game to the relief of countless year seven and eight pupils. The rumours of Bashir's less than heroic behaviour eventually leaked (and snowballed with Chinese whispers) and spread throughout school like wildfire. After that, he wouldn't dare show his face in the playground for fear of being bullied himself - and his new seat on the school bus was right behind the driver, alongside that kid who was always feeling sick.

Jake, who has been dating Meg, for several months despite her brother's objection, knuckled down in the classroom and managed to pull up his grades from below-average to acceptable. They spend most weekends together at the Midsummer estate, helping to care for the wildlife. They also brought some fresh new ideas to the gardens in the form of topiary hedges shaped like giant chocca mocca lattes and video game characters.

Charles (Charlie) Midsummer became a confident young man and went on to become captain of the school cricket team, as well as chair of the math club. He even has a large fan base of nerds and geeks who seem to worship him. He recently started dating the spotty, brace-wearing, ginger-haired Veronica Applegate - the schools mathletics champion, with who he broke the record for the number of respective events won in a single year.

Zac took his love of gadgets and technology and decided to apply them in a practical way. After hacking into the school website and student database using various phishing, click-jacking and SQL injection techniques, he was given the job of redesigning the whole thing in the after-school supplementary IT class. It was either that or face criminal charges for his actions. He enjoyed being there too, as it meant he would miss dinner at home whenever Jake came around.

Jess' dad, Mr Birchwood, won his seventh consecutive Village Christmas Light Competition gold award, after festooning the family home with four giant inflatable reindeer: Bing, Danny, Rosemary and Vera. Those plus eighty-one thousand, programmable LED twinkle lights. He's already planning next year's display.

The events of that June day undeniably changed the lives of those involved, but its effect would also go on to touch the lives of countless others. You see, Lady Midsummer received so much money from the insurance pay out of the stolen Sunrise Ruby (which she was glad to see the back of anyway) she felt compelled to give something back to the community.

After planning was approved, diggers and construction crews arrived at the site of the old Daventry outdoor swimming pool on February 6th the following year. By the middle of June on a scorching hot day, Auntie, accompanied by Charlie, Jess, the twins, their families and pretty much everyone from school and the village, cut the tape and declared the new pool officially *open*. She then proceeded to do a perfect cannonball in the deep end followed by everyone else.

The entire site had been completely regenerated. The changing rooms and showers were demolished and rebuilt from the ground up, as was the reception and park area. There was even an exciting new addition of a flume and wet play area for the younger children. Refreshments were available from a tuck-shop stocked full of locally made sandwiches (plus the obligatory sweets, juices and fizzy drinks), all of which were provided by Stanton's convenience store. But the best part of all was that even though Auntie offered to fulfil the sites running costs for the foreseeable future, the community decided to come together and agreed to run it entirely as volunteers. Auntie did, however, insist on providing a modern wind turbine and solar-panels to help keep running cost down.

She had brought the site from the council, paying over the asking price in order to get things moving quickly. In fact, they were so grateful to finally have some spare funds they immediately went on a spending spree, purchasing several new air conditioned buses to serve the village and school runs, as well as building a new skate park in the field beside the shop.

With the pool up and running a number of clubs were quickly established that attracted people from all over the county. These included water polo, a SCUBA diving school, plus an aqua-aerobics club to name but a few. Auntie's generosity didn't stop there either, as she donated money to several good causes in and around the village including the church of St. James, the village hall, and the Canal and River Trust. The bowling green also underwent a generous renovation and gained two new honorary members – Auntie and Barker, and all the local sports clubs received new kits. Oh, and she even replaced Jess and the twins' beloved mobile phones.

And what of Jessica Birchwood I hear you ask? The unofficial leader of the successful crime-solving quartet. Well, Jess applied her love of water and volunteered part-time at the pool helping teach children to swim. In school, she became elected as the youngest head of the student union in its history and would be remembered as one of the most popular and well organised placements ever known. Despite flunking maths, she excelled in English language and literature, and would go on to write a successful novel based upon that unforgettable day at Midsummer Hall, under the pseudonym: L C Bygrave.

Answer to giant's riddle in chapter twenty-one: a hole

My lost Lido and Me: A short tribute

If one thing has influenced Midsummer's Secret the most, it perhaps has to be the iconic outdoor swimming pool, A.K.A. the Lido. But not just any outdoor swimming pool - the open air swimming pool of Daventry, Northants.

We are the lives we have lived. Our childhoods define who we are - for better or for worse - and I am perhaps living proof of this, because that place is so much more than just a memory to me. It is a lifestyle now hard-coded within me. It represents a time of joy and happiness spent with friends, family and best-mates. Freedom and fresh air. Fun and laughter. Endless summers fuelled on nothing more than cup-a-soups, ice-pops, 10p crisps and penny sweets.

It was the place everyone went to. The young and the old. The haves and the have-nots. Where rival school gangs relaxed as one. And who can forget those school swimming galas, with crowds of frenzied parents cheering their children on. As an adult, I can seldom pass so much as a stream in a field without feeling the desire to throw myself in and I find the sun reflecting on water simply hypnotic. Surfing, body-boarding, skim-boarding, snorkelling, scuba diving, kayaking and cliff jumping – I've tried them all and long to do them each and every day I sit glaring at a computer screen. How I wanted my daughters to experience the same wonderful thing in their childhood. In a digital age where the majority of under-tens have never played outdoors on their own, and when technology is all consuming. Alas, like many other Lidos around the country, Daventry open air swimming pool closed its doors in 2006 and is now nothing more than waste ground.

This is perhaps more of a melancholy tale than you would expect, considering the site was actually mostly 'crowd funded' long before the phrase was coined. You see, the Daventry community pulled together to raise funds after children drowned whilst swimming in the local reservoir, raising the majority of the £41,970 by early 1960 (to put that in perspective, my parents purchased a brand-new, two-bedroom house in Daventry for £3000 in 1963). The complex, opened in May 1962 by none other than Olympic gold medal swimmer, Judy Grinham, had two large pools plus a paddling area for toddlers and would see hundreds of people queuing to get in on some days. It was an oasis amongst a concrete jungle that reminded people, if only for a day, that they were human beings, not humans doing. Eventually though the running costs became too much for the council to bare and they finally made the controversial decision to close the site. The once social hub of the borough shut its doors for good in September 2006 after forty-four years in service.

You can find more information on Daventry Open Air Swimming Pool and many other lost (and remaining) lidos online - just search 'lost lidos', as well as the Daventry town library if you are local. The 'Daventry in History' Facebook page also has a number of nice photos (in colour) I would have included here in the book, but I was unable to track down the owners to obtain the required copyright. You can see these here:

https://www.facebook.com/media/set/?set=oa.551004945062627&type=1

Do you have a lost lido story? I would love to hear it.

Back in the beginning, May 1961. Best Monday morning ever.

Mayor Starts Swim-Pool

WITH A CHROMIUM-PLATED SPADE PRESENTED TO HIM BY DAVENTRY SWIMMING POOL ASSOCIATION MAYOR HENRY SMITH LIFTS A TURF TO START THE DIGGING OF DAVENTRY'S OPEN - AIR, £37,000 SWIMMING POOL.

When he had finished bulldozers started on the job.

The ceremony took place on Monday morning, and Coun. Smith, after being introduced by association president Ald. R. E. Fleming, said: "This is a proud moment in the history of Daventry.

"Never before have I known a project to take on so well with the public. We have people of all denominations coming to our meetings and working for nothing.

"Some of our councillors have expressed doubts about the future of this but I have enough faith in old Daventry—and new Daventry—to know that public support will continue.

"I want to see this paid for and the money turned into a building fund so that a top can be put on the pool.

"That is what is making the bottom so expensive, and people will redouble their efforts now to see that it doesn't become too great a burden on the rates."

The grand opening, Saturday 5th May 1962

Judy Grinham Opens Swim-pool

The local newspaper coverage of the opening began with the following:

"***No Goose - Pimples For Judy***. *Former Olympics gold medal swimmer Judy Grinham opened Daventry's £42,000 open-air, unheated swimming pool last Saturday – but she left the goose - pimples to the locals.*

Miss Grinham opened the pool by cutting a tape across the door. The water was opened by British Timken's Sub-Aqua Club, who gave a demonstration.

Welcoming the pool, Miss Grinham said that drowning was second only to road deaths in the toll of deaths from accidents. Two-thirds of the country's population were unable to swim – and it was heartening to see the interest, local organisations and councils were taking in the provision of swimming facilities."

She was welcomed by the Mayor, Coun. L. .E. Whitmee, who said *"the opening of the pool was probably the most outstanding event in the history of the borough."*

Pictured below is Britain's champion girl springboard diver, Linda Carawardine, showing the locals how it's done; in the big pool deep-end, August 1976. She worked as a lifeguard at the pool where she could practice regularly on the Olympic-standard board.

My brother, parents and I, in the shallow end of the middle pool. This was September 1979.

My Nan and I, in the baby pool, 1979. I was two years old then. I can still remember how that felt under foot.

The busy Abbey School Swim Galas 1985/1986. I am bottom middle.

The middle pool in the early 90s. The precarious spiral slide is just visible.

The same spot today.

The larger pool showing just how popular the site was. Year unknown.

The same spot today.

The larger pool shortly before being filled in. 2007.

The same spot, today.

Printed in Great Britain
by Amazon